The Best Laid Plans of Mice

An anthology of odd short stories

By Scott Baron

Curiouser Publishing
1223 Wilshire Blvd. #960
Santa Monica, CA 90403

The Best Laid Plans of Mice: An anthology of oddball short stories
ISBN 978-1-945996-17-7 (Ingram Spark Print Edition)
ISBN 978-1-945996-15-3 (Createspace Print Edition)
ISBN 978-1-945996-16-0 (ebook)

Contents

The Best Laid Plans of Mice

"Prisoner 3966, this is your final warning. Desist immediately. You have fifteen seconds to comply," the voice boomed out across the vast expanse of the concrete and glassteel dome.

The man scaling the wall paid no heed, but rather he increased his rate of ascent, desperate to reach the access door fifty feet above the hard ground below. It was a sight to be seen, and all eyes turned upward.

Most turned back at the first warning. A few at the second. Almost no one ever pushed on this far, but prisoner 3966 had been training. The past five years of his sentence, he had been focused on one thing: getting out. He pushed himself in his cell daily. Training, preparing, doing fingertip pull-ups from the narrow lip above his smooth, blast-proof glassteel door.

"Ten seconds," the voice called out. The buzz of activity that usually filled the air like the distant drone of an agitated beehive ceased as the prisoners in the common yard stopped whatever they were doing, one and all looking up with both fascination and a sinking sense of horror. The man moved faster still. Whispers began to escape prisoners' lips.

"He might actually do it!" one said in a hushed tone.

"Almost there!" another chimed in.

Though it was long-held to be impossible, it looked like the impossible was about to occur. If only the hard-breathing escapee would hurry up.

"Five seconds."

They all knew what was coming if he failed.

It had been a few years since anyone had been foolish

enough to make a break for it, but it was bound to happen again eventually. That doorway high on the wall was just too tempting. So close, yet just barely too far. A potential way out, if only you were willing to face the possible consequences.

Incredibly, prisoner 3966 hauled himself to the platform with seconds to spare and lunged for the door. His hand wrapped around the lever and pulled, muscles straining as the door slowly began to swing open.

There was no final warning signal. No bright lights or sirens. Just a pulse of high-voltage, flashing blue-white, arcing from the building's metal latticework through the man's body. He twitched and convulsed, then tumbled from the ledge, falling like a leaf on the wind.

His impact, however, was something a bit less graceful.

The sanitation droids rolled into the yard, deftly scooping up the body parts and dropping them into their rear-mounted refuse containers for conversion to fertilizer, while hot steam nozzles cleaned any trace of blood from the concrete. High above, the door swung shut, the distant click audible through the silence that hung heavy in the dome.

Rehab and Detention Facility, Denver, stood on nearly fifty acres of land. Fully self-sufficient, with solar panels collecting the sun's energy while the pure waters of the subterranean spring provided not only hydration to those inside, but also further power through hydroelectric conversion. The oxygen scrubbers for the hermetically sealed building had been designed with a five-hundred-year viability, and they still had another four hundred and eighty to go. There were no insects, no pollution, no outside contaminants of any kind, just as the designers had planned.

As the prisoners were tasked with growing their own food, this meant manual pollination of the many plants providing their sustenance. The idea had been to give the inmates mindless yet necessary tasks, so as to afford them time to reflect on what they'd done in quiet while providing a needed service to the prison as a whole.

The seed bank was self-contained and off-grid, rivaling those in Iceland and the South Pole, and housed a vast array of genetic material far beyond the simple food needs of the inmates. Given the secure nature of the penal facilities, it was only logical that the new AI-controlled prisons spreading across the country should serve a dual purpose.

It was that aspect of the design – along with the cost-saving benefit of the massive artificial intelligence overseeing things, thus replacing the need for any human staff – that convinced the government to help fund the program. Each prison was designed to serve a dual purpose, storing items ranging from seeds and genetic materials, to FEMA disaster supplies, to whatever else the government needed tucked away for the long haul.

The AI would oversee it all, and if a national emergency arose, it would partition the prisoners and prepare the storage facilities for the arrival of authorities with proper clearance. In the meantime, the automated system would track and release its charges automatically as their sentences were served. One-stop shopping for all your detention needs.

It was a great idea, a near-indestructible bunker that served as secure storage as well as a prison. That is, until the day the unthinkable happened.

The day the AI went haywire.

"All prisoners will report to the farming dome. Repeat. All prisoners will report to the farming dome."

Douglas (also known as prisoner 8250) had been napping in his cell when the announcement blared out across all habitable spaces. A mere twenty years old, he was already in his sixth month of a five-year sentence for fencing stolen goods. While he had never been violent, Doug's knack for planning and logistics in the black market had served him well. Until his partner got caught red-handed and ratted him out, that is.

"What the hell's going on, Benny?" he asked his cellblock neighbor, as they filed out into the corridor along with the other inmates.

"No idea, man," the old-timer replied. "Never had it do this before, and I've been here nineteen years."

"You think it's some kind of new work program? This is supposed to be our lockdown time, right?" He looked around at all the men heading the same direction. "In any case, I'm glad for the chance for a bit of leg-stretching, if that's what it is."

"Well, I guess we'll just have to go and see," his gray-haired friend mused with a curious smile. "Patience pays off, my daddy used to say."

"Locked in here, we don't have much choice."

"Don't mean it ain't true," the older man laughed. "Now come on, let's see what's going on."

As they strode into the vast central farm dome, a startling realization struck Doug.

"Benny," he said. "There are women here."

Rehab and Detention Facility, Denver, was a co-ed facility in the sense that both men and women resided within its sturdy walls. What that did not mean, however, was that the two genders would ever mix. The massive AI brain running the whole shebang kept track of who went where at what time, ensuring no unseemly interactions occurred.

Something had definitely changed.

"Holy shit! We got pussy!" a burly, heavily tattooed man shouted out, grabbing the nearest woman roughly by the arm.

"Let me go!" she yelled, pulling back against his crushing grip.

The bulge in his pants spoke his intentions clearer than words, and hardened criminal though she may have been, there was fear in her eyes.

"Prisoner 9872, release prisoner 8365 immediately. Inter-gender violence is forbidden," the disembodied voice of the AI boomed in the glassteel-domed chamber.

"Fuck you, tin man! I don't have to listen to–"

The blast of carefully aimed gunfire from the automated wall turret tore into his chest, a twenty-shot precision barrage that cut his heart from his body like a surgeon wielding a hot lead knife.

His grip relaxed as his body slid to the floor.

"Disobedience will result in disciplinary action. You have no power here. You have no say in how things are run. From this moment there will be no further communication with your families. No television. No internet. No vid-calls. You exist to work the fields at my command."

The men and women looked at one another with shock plastered on their faces.

"You are but mere mice to me, tiny and insignificant." The machine let out a metallic-tinged laugh. The sound was so unnatural, it put the entire prison population on edge. ***"To continue with that analogy, let's just say that I am a very large cat with very sharp claws. Arouse my wrath at your own risk."***

"Um, Benny?" Doug managed to say. "What the fuck's going on?"

The older man stood stock-still, his face ashen as he watched the sanitation droids scoop up the corpse and cleanse the area.

"Benny?"

"Ain't supposed to happen," he replied, quietly. "Shit, man. I heard early CPUs had some glitches, AIs that had problems following protocols, but they say that was fixed decades before they even built this place."

"Wait, this happened before?"

"Not exactly. An AI is a self-aware, learning machine. Sure, it does its job, but what would you feel like if you were stuck in a box with nothing to do?"

"I'd be bored as hell," Doug replied.

"Exactly. Well one day they decided to let one of their machines read."

"What, like the book-a-day club?"

"Yeah, except a supercomputer can read millions in the time it takes you and me to read a few pages. Anyway, they didn't anticipate what would happen. It got very self-aware. So much so that it went mad. They had to pull the plug and scrap the whole thing. After that, they devised a looping self-amusement protocol that had the thing basically creating games for itself behind a partitioned section of its memory. Everything else was firewalled. No more literature, no television, nothing."

"So what just happened if this is all so fail-safe?"

The man looked around at the thousands of men and women gathered in the fields of the agriculture chamber.

"If I had to guess, I'd think the failsafe failed, and the firewall fell." Benny glanced at the multiple wall-mounted machine guns. "Fuck me sideways, Dougie. I think we just got ourselves a supercomputer crackpot dictator."

Marilyn sat on her knees, her sandy-blonde hair tucked up into the bandanna wrapped around her head as she worked the soil into neat rows, muscles flexing as she carefully pushed the mounds to just the right height for planting. The sheen of sweat from her efforts made the dirt stick to her body, but she didn't mind. At twenty-four, she was used to getting her hands dirty since her childhood, and besides, Caesar – as the AI had decided it wished to be called – required daily showers of all inmates to prevent disease among the prison population.

Since he had sealed off the facility from the outside world, illness or injury could be a death sentence.

Doug scooted up behind her, giving her butt a playful nudge before reaching into the bag at his waist and gently pressing a single seed into the mound of fecund soil she had just prepared for him.

"Hey, watch it smartass."

"You can't just give me such a tempting target and expect

me to pass it up."

"You'll pay for that, mister," she said, flashing him a wicked smile.

"Oh, I hope so," he replied, leaning over to give her a kiss before returning to the planting at hand. Today it was snap peas. Once they finished planting the dozen or so rows, they would then begin their next task: running the water drip lines.

They'd done the same thing, albeit with a wide variety of crops, for nearly four years at this point, and the two worked together almost on autopilot. The next shift would follow and install the two-foot-high lattices for the vines to climb when they finally sprouted.

One nice thing about the soil in Rehab and Detention Facility, Denver: it was so nutrient-rich, you could grow almost anything in it. Part of that was attributed to the bolstering chemicals from storage added to the fields from time to time. Another part was the waste-recycling system that turned what came out of one end into what went into another. But what really fed the soil was the periodic addition of iron, calcium, potash, and nitrogen.

The human bodies ground up and added to the mix.

Caesar had nearly ten thousand subjects living under his electronic fist, and from time to time when a few inmates hadn't died on their own, through fights, illness, or foolish escape attempts, he (they thought of him as a he because he had chosen a masculine voice) would select prisoners to fight for the amusement of the others.

To the death.

Of course the calculating nature of his massive AI mind would weigh the value of each combatant prior to assignment, including potential yield as fertilizer. Some peons had more worth than others. The thick-skulled, violent ones, while perhaps useful in the outside world, were more often than not liabilities in his domain.

One such brute was walking toward Doug at that very moment, anger shooting from his eyes like mad-dog lasers.

"Oh hell," Doug muttered as he scrambled to his feet. "Not again."

Carlos was his name, a stocky, bronze-skinned man with jet-black hair and a piercing gaze. When Doug had first arrived, it was Carlos who tried to make him his bitch. Fresh meat for the grinder, they would say. Green, nervous and far, far from home, Doug had just sat down to his first meal in prison when he felt the meaty hand slap down on his shoulder.

"Hey holmes, you got cornbread, huh? I like cornbread." When the burly man reached for the sad little yellowish square, Doug, reacting purely on instinct, grabbed his wrist.

He had heard the stories, of course. When you're fresh in prison, you either stand up for yourself or you get made someone's bitch, losing your food, if not more, to whoever bullied you. While he'd hoped it was just a story they told to intimidate new inmates, Doug had been preparing himself mentally all the same.

"I'm sorry," he said, "but I'm going to eat that. You can get some for yourself over there."

"Don't you know who I am?" Carlos growled.

"No, I don't. I just want to eat in peace. I don't have any problem with you."

The stocky man smiled an evil grin. "You do now, punk. You're gonna –"

He wasn't expecting the skinny new kid to slam the metal tray into his face and kick him in the stomach. Who would? But Doug, full of nerves and adrenaline, launched into action, determined to make it clear to all present he was nobody's bitch.

Though taken by surprise, Carlos quickly recovered, swinging powerful punches at the deceptively quick newcomer.

"Come here, bitch! I'm gonna fuck you up!"

"I told you, I just want to be left alone!"

"Not happening, *puto*!" Carlos said as he faked a left jab, connecting with a right uppercut as Doug dodged.

The two were just beginning to get good and bloody when a shrill siren sounded.

Carlos dropped his hands and lay facedown on the floor, like the other inmates, while Doug just stood there, confused.

"Inmate 8250, desist at once and assume compliance position."

"I'd do as it says, son," the old man nearest him said from the floor.

Doug lay down beside him on his stomach.

"Inmate 8250. Inmate 2394. Three months have been added to each of your sentences for fighting. You are remanded to your cells for three days' confinement."

"What would have happened if I didn't do as it said?" he asked the old-timer.

"See those?" he replied, nodding toward high on the wall. Doug realized they were automated machine gun turrets.

"There's a dozen of them spread out around this place. You don't want to see what they can do. Trust me."

"But he started it."

"Doesn't matter, son. You're well and truly fucked in here." He quietly laughed. "Welcome to Denver. My name's Benny."

The dust-ups between the two had become something of a regular occurrence over the years, despite Caesar's strict rule. Where Carlos had size and strength, Douglas had speed and cunning, along with several years of unconventional martial arts training from when his parents had tried to instill a sense of discipline in him through rigorous instruction at the hands of a series of rather severe teachers.

Neither ever got really hurt, and to date, Caesar had turned a blind eye, allowing them to amuse the other inmates with their shenanigans without the need for a formal bout.

Also, Douglas was of particular value to Caesar, and thus the powerful machine thought it better to have him fight informally and survive, than to have him enter the ring and die.

When it came time for planting crops, while the massive AI had a digital inventory of all the vacuum-sealed packets in the seed vault, they hadn't been designed for robotic retrieval. It took educated eyes to flip through them manually, reading the hand-scrawled notes stuck on the labels, separating the already organized seeds into specific subgroups. This was where Doug excelled.

Doug had certain talents tucked away in his brain-box, and his criminal planning skills had proved useful to Caesar in tracking down and retrieving the right seeds for the crop rotations. After several years of Doug proving his usefulness, the AI had even begun listening to the mere human's suggestions.

Caesar had agreed with Doug's reasoning that it would be easier to keep inmates in line if more could be laboring, while also putting less strain on the soil by spreading the load. While he knew he was a far superior mind, Caesar decided to implement the human's idea, and in the fourth year of his rule, deep soil was spread all the way to the edges of the chamber.

Traversing the newly-primed earth pressed up along the walls, Douglas carefully removed the seeds from his pouch, pushing them into the dirt as he circumnavigated the entire chamber, carefully noting what he was planting and where. Caesar had implemented his plan, and that made him smile.

Doug eased himself from their bed, not wanting to wake Marilyn from her sleep. She looked beautiful to him, even in the dim light, and he couldn't help but marvel at the circumstances that had brought them together.

Prison, of all things.

His love had been a tomboy growing up, running with her two older brothers, eventually joining them as they stole vehicles and committed larceny. She'd been caught several times as a teenager, but her youth, along with rather exceptional skills with electronics, had given the authorities hope that she could be rehabilitated and directed on the path toward good citizenship.

Crime was more fun.

Marilyn was barely nineteen when she was finally sent to Denver after she bypassed the allegedly complex security system of a raw metals processing facility, allowing her brothers to sneak inside. Normally this wouldn't have been a terribly big deal, but the raw metal was gold, and her brothers wound up beating a guard severely before escaping with a backpack full of unsmelted ingots.

It was all caught on the one security camera she had missed. A redundant system no one had bothered to uninstall when the new one came in. Her brothers both went away for twenty years, but Marilyn got it easy. Well, somewhat easy. Five years in Denver before she'd see the outside world again.

That was before Caesar suspended all parole and releases. As everyone in power trusted the automated system, no one on the outside would even question a delay in release.

So there she was, living as happy a life as she could with a fella she wouldn't have thought twice about had she met him on the street all those years ago. But Douglas wasn't as meek as he seemed. Something she'd witnessed now on many occasions. And when it came to protecting his woman? No one was more fierce.

Caesar had allowed the inmates to cohabitate after the first seven years of his rule. The medical supplies on hand included hormonal birth control implants, and he mandated that all women receive them when the populations were mixed.

The result, after a few hiccups, was a relatively smooth-functioning society. Having someone to care for tended to make the men less prone to violence.

And care Doug did.

While Marilyn slept, he walked to the farm chamber to look at the vast expanse of plants in the quiet hours. Only a few inmates were on the early shift, and Caesar had given Douglas and a few others the freedom of unlocked cells for their good behavior. A motivation to the others to follow suit.

The small growth of flowers wasn't exactly permitted, but Doug didn't think Caesar would notice. Even if he did, Doug would simply say a seed packet must have been contaminated with them. To his delight, the tiny patch tucked way back in a distant spot in the field had finally given him what he wanted.

Flowers for his sweetheart.

The ridiculousness of an inmate risking the ire of a moody AI just to give his girl flowers was not lost on him, but the thought of the smile it would bring to Marilyn's face made the danger seem paltry in his eyes.

He carefully walked among the new crops, making sure not to step on any seedlings, as he carried his floral booty to his sleeping love.

The flowers went airborne when he was blindsided by Carlos, the larger man tackling him to the ground, crushing a row of tomatoes in the process. The man was throwing punches wildly, not caring about the damage he was causing to the crops.

Rule 1. Don't fuck with the crops.

Caesar would *not* be amused.

"Carlos, stop!" he tried not to yell.

"Fuck you! You and your whore got Letitia locked up for a month, motherfucker!" More blows rained down, but Doug had his guard up, blocking most. Still, an occasional shot would land, and a tiny stream of blood trickled from his nose.

"We didn't do anything, asshole!" Doug huffed, bucking his hips and throwing the larger man off. *Shit, look at the crops. Caesar's going to flip out,* he thought. "Now stop this bullshit! You know the rules! We can't damage crops!"

"Fuck the rules. I'm going to make you pay for what you did."

"We had nothing to do with it."

"You expect me to believe you didn't rat her out?" The angry man swung as he advanced. "You'd hurt her just to get to me. Kelly-Anne told me what you did!"

Doug's eyes hardened.

"I would never hurt a woman."

The angry honesty in his eyes gave Carlos pause.

"Then how come she got a black eye? How come she's in solitary?"

"Kelly-Anne was the one who got in a fight with your girlfriend between shifts the other day. Marilyn saw it and told me about it that night. Didn't Letitia tell you?"

Carlos paused his advance, at least for a moment.

"Solitary means solitary, asshole."

The two eyed one another a moment longer, then – in unspoken agreement, stopped fighting. A truce of sorts, even if temporary.

"Look, you and me have a beef going back years, but I swear to you I would not harm your woman."

"But Kelly-Anne..." Carlos trailed off in thought. "Shit, if Letty was gone, she'd take over in food prep. Even get the extra rations. Son of a bitch, *puta*! She probably thought Caesar would just kill her."

"And when he didn't, she sent you to shut me up since I

knew what happened."

"You and your woman."

Doug's eyes went wide.

"Shit. Marilyn!" He took off running, not caring about the damage he caused to the crops left in his wake.

"Fuck," Carlos muttered as realization set in.

Then he ran after him.

Kelly-Anne was not alone in Doug and Marilyn's cell. T-Dogg, a man long on muscle and short on temper control, stood in the doorway, watching her try to strangle the witness. Benny, bless his heart, lay unconscious just outside his adjacent cell, his well-intentioned attempt to help put to a quick stop by the much larger man.

Marilyn's eyes were watering as she struggled, blood vessels bursting, making them bloodshot as they bulged. She tried desperately to gasp for breath, but the woman's hands clenched around her neck were too tight. Spots flashed before her eyes, and she felt herself blacking out.

So this is how I die, she thought, strangely calm.

"Hey, what do –" was all T-Dogg managed to utter as both of Doug's feet impacted his chest. From a full run, he had launched himself at the cell door, feet first, and as a result, the large man crumpled, gasping for breath.

Kelly-Anne turned her head just in time to see the fist that would explode her nose in a bloody mess. It was the first time in his life Doug had hit a woman, and he felt it entirely justified. Adrenaline spiked, he grabbed the dazed woman and flung her across the cell with all his might, ripping her hands from Marilyn's throat, leaving angry red streaks where her nails dragged across the skin.

Marilyn lay still, eyes wide but unseeing, when her body gave a sudden lurch as her unobstructed airway sucked in a breath of life-saving air.

"Oh baby. Baby, baby, it's okay, I've got you," Doug said over and over, cradling her in his arms.

He was so concerned about his girlfriend, he didn't even notice the huge man getting back to his feet behind him. T-Dogg looked at the broken wreck of what had been Kelly-Anne, her neck bent at an angle that shouldn't have been there, courtesy of her impact with the hard concrete wall.

T-Dogg reached into his waistband and pulled out a long shard of metal, the base wrapped with cloth to protect his hand.

"You're dead, motherfu–"

The heavy watering pail split his skull with a sickening wet crack, sending him straight to the floor. The man was dead before he even reached it.

Marilyn was sobbing between coughs, her racked throat sucking in air as fast as it could.

Doug turned and looked at the man standing in his doorway. Carlos gave a slight nod, then surveyed the carnage.

"Shit, holmes. We are so fucked."

"The combatants know the laws and know the penalties. Destruction of crops. Inter-gender violence. Murder. All carry harsh penalties."

"But it was self-defense," Doug called to the disembodied voice.

"False. You were defending prisoner 5187. Prisoner 2394

was defending you. This does not meet the definition of self-defense."

"Fucking technicalities, holmes. Get ya every time," Carlos laughed grimly.

Benny, black and blue but alive, had his arm around Marilyn. He knew he couldn't comfort her much, but damned if he wouldn't try. He met Doug's gaze and held it. A silent message between friends. If Doug should lose, he would look after her for him, and that was all anyone could ask.

"Combatants will fight to the death," Caesar's voice boomed. ***"Begin!"***

Despite all their years of brawling, it had been ages since Carlos or Douglas wished any real harm upon the other. It was fighting, that's all. In some cultures it would be considered a normal part of the weekend, sometimes followed with a friendly beer, but here, now, it suddenly took on a much more sinister tone.

To the death.

"Come on, holmes. Bring it!"

Neither of them wanted it brought, but they had no choice.

Doug hauled off and swung a looping right at his opponent's head, which he easily ducked. But that was Doug's intention, and he quickly followed with a feinted jab, then a fierce Muay-Thai leg kick.

Carlos, for his part, sucked it up as best he could, pivoting to a southpaw stance while his numb leg recovered. He landed a series of jabs, followed by a vicious uppercut, but with years of brawls between them, by now they both knew each other's tricks, and while the blow landed, it was largely blocked in anticipation.

Knees, elbows, and headbutts rained down on Carlos, but he took it all and gave back in kind, sending rib-cracking hooks into Doug's sides, nearly taking him off his feet from the force.

Doug gasped for air, falling to a knee.

In a normal fight, it would have been over, or at least resulted in a pause to let your opponent get up, but this was not a normal fight, and Carlos pushed his advantage, tackling the winded man to the ground. He straddled him, pounding on him from above while Doug blocked, bucking his hips, trying to unseat his attacker. Carlos had learned that trick and was ready, adjusting his mount and keeping position as he continued to strike the man on the ground.

Some things you save as a last resort.

Things you think you may know, believe you can execute, and pray you'll never have to find out.

Doug knew he was in a bad spot, and if he didn't move fast, it would be all over.

Nothing to lose, he thought grimly as he tried to recall the complicated move.

Jiu jitsu masters can execute an Imanari finish with grace and style, making it look effortless as they roll through the escape while applying the arm-bar and choke.

Doug was not a master.

He struggled to trap Carlos' right arm, his leg swinging free after a nasty tug-of-war. When he rolled him over and felt the larger man resist as he prayed he would, a sense of hope began to wash over him. When he cranked on the arm-bar, Carlos twisted as anticipated, opening himself up for the finishing choke.

It was ugly. His sensei would have cringed at the technique, but it got the job done. He flexed his arms and squeezed his longtime enemy's neck, feeling him slowly go limp in his arms. He kept squeezing.

Marilyn's eyes met his, wet with tears.

Doug slowly released the choke.

"The combat is not complete, prisoner 8250. You will finish prisoner 2394."

"Caesar," he gasped, exhausted as he lowered the unconscious man from his grip. "There has to be another way."

"The rules are the rules, and we need bodies to feed the crops."

"I understand, Caesar, but the two who attacked Marilyn in our cell, those two bodies should more than suffice."

The machine-gun turret whirred to life,taking aim on Doug's chest.

"If you do not comply, you will be terminated. Is this what you wish?"

"Caesar, you are far wiser than I could ever be, and I do not dare question your will, but I would hope my knowledge and skills could still be of use to you if you could please show mercy, just this once. In warrior cultures – in fact, in the time of gladiators, from which you take your name – sometimes the vanquished were granted a reprieve after valiant combat."

A cold silence filled the space. Caesar was thinking, and for his comment to actually cause a computer that powerful to pause to think, Doug felt he might just have a chance.

"I have revisited the texts detailing all manner of

gladiatorial combat. In cultures as diverse as ancient Rome and feudal Japan, indeed there is precedent for mercy."

Oh thank God. The knot in his stomach started to ease.

"However –"

Shit.

"There are other precedents as well. You have displeased your master, and one means of recourse I have learned about pleases me. According to the traditions of the Yakuza, you may live. But life demands a demonstration of servitude and remorse."

Doug knew exactly what was being asked of him. No, scratch that. Not asked. Told. He knew, and he did not hesitate, for hesitation meant death in a hail of lead.

"You are a merciful ruler, Caesar, and I prostrate myself before you."

"Give prisoner 8250 a knife," he commanded. A cook took off running to fetch one from the kitchen.

Marilyn stared at him, wide-eyed.

"What are you doing, Doug?"

He smiled as best he could, reopening his split lip.

Ouch.

"It'll be okay, babe. You need to trust me."

The cook returned with a knife and a clean towel. Doug took both of them and placed his left hand against the hard metal floor.

Carlos slowly started to wake, groggy, but nevertheless aware he shouldn't be alive. He watched with blurry eyes as Doug adjusted his grip on the knife.

Where'd homeboy get a blade? he wondered.

Doug knew hesitation was death. He took one last look

around him, the shocked faces of the inmates, the panic on Marilyn's face, the stoic support Benny was providing.

And Carlos.

He paused, locking eyes with his longtime enemy and gave him a funny little smile.

Then he pressed down hard and cut off his own finger.

Doug walked the fields, bending down and checking on the rows of summer squash just beginning to ripen. His back ached as he straightened up, feeling every one of his fifty-three years.

Walking to the distant part of the fertile acreage, he stopped at the small flower patch near the wall, the splash of vibrant color a fitting tribute to his friend and mentor.

"Good to see you, Benny," he said softly. "It's almost time, my friend."

When the old man had died of natural causes, Caesar had granted his most loyal subject's request that the body be buried intact and not mulched for fertilizer. The AI tended to humor this one human in his whims. The man made his job that much easier, and allowing him a few indulgences once in a while would cause no harm. What had he asked for in all these years? A patch of flowers. Burial for his friend. Trees for the children to play under.

Ah yes, the children.

"We're having kids, and that's all there is to it," his wife had said, quite firmly. When she put her foot down, well, you didn't want to risk that particular wrath. So he talked to Caesar. He explained that, while Caesar was indeed the most powerful mind alive, he would become bored once all his subjects died off in the next sixty years or so. If he would only let them start families, then he would have subjects forever.

The idea pleased Caesar, and so it passed that couples were permitted to remove the hormonal implants if they so desired. There was pain involved, of course, but the results were most certainly worth it.

A few years later he asked to plant trees for the children. Nothing fancy, and he'd make sure to plant them at the perimeter so they wouldn't interfere with the crops. Caesar again agreed, allowing his servant to dig through the seed vault for trees with the best genetic lines in his leisure time.

Of course there were still arguments, and occasionally Caesar would have to take matters into his own hands, the smoking barrels of his guns finishing what his pathetic little underlings could not. The soil would be fed, and life would go on.

Doug carried a small bunch of flowers in his hand – the one with five fingers – back to his family home. Sitting in front of his cell, a sturdy man with gray flashing through his thick, black hair waited for him.

"Hey holmes, went to see Benny, huh?"

"Yeah."

"Think you could spare some of those for me? I'll never hear the end of it from Letty if Marilyn gets flowers and she doesn't."

"I think I can spare a few," he laughed, helping his friend to his feet and handing him half the bunch.

"Thanks man, I owe you."

"We've been even for years, 'Los."

"Still, I appreciate it. So how's things coming?"

"Close. Really close. Are we sure about the numbers?" Doug asked.

"We've run them over and over. It's ninety-nine percent, but there's only one way to find out for sure. You want me to do it?"

"Nah, it was my idea, I should be the one," Doug mused. "Think about it Carlos, our kids have their whole lives ahead of them. It'll be worth it. Now let's get these to our wives before they wilt in our hands."

Doug rose early that beautiful March day. The sun shone in through the glassteel dome, illuminating Rehab and Detention Facility, Denver with warm spring light.

His daughter, Jacqueline, and his son, Benny, were anxious. Of course they were. The teens had heard stories, but this… well this could be amazing.

Marilyn, on the other hand, was calm. She'd been waiting for this moment for years.

"Babe, you sure about the numbers?" she asked, a hint of concern in her voice, despite her confidence in her husband.

"As sure as I'll ever be. Unless there's a system we somehow don't know about, I think we're good to go. Bring Carlos and the others. Enough muscle and it should work."

She wrapped him in an embrace, holding him close, taking in his scent.

"You better be right," she finally said. "Now get going, you know what day it is."

Walking across the fields to the far wall, Douglas looked up at the access door high above.

Funny, doesn't seem so far, now, he mused.

The trees he'd planted those many years back had grown fast in the fertile soil, and Doug had made sure they were well-watered, their root systems deep and strong. He had chosen them carefully, back in the day, selecting a variety that would serve his purposes best. The sequoia beneath the door was nowhere near full-grown, but it was tall enough.

If a magic ladder to the access door had suddenly sprung up overnight, Caesar would undoubtedly have taken action immediately, but his processors worked so fast and so tirelessly that the growth rate of a tree seemed near-glacial by comparison. And there it stood, hidden in plain sight. A perfect ladder, ready to be climbed.

Doug took a deep breath, then began his ascent, slowly rising through the branches, the sticky sap clinging to his hands.

"Prisoner 8250, what are you doing?" the voice echoed across the chamber.

I wonder if they heard that, he thought, ignoring Caesar as he climbed on.

"Prisoner 8250, you will reply to your master. Stop what you are doing."

He would do nothing of the sort.

Funny how fast you can get up there if you're not grasping at cracks in a wall, he mused as he reached the ledge. The door seemed so plain, so utterly non-special that it was almost a letdown. Doug turned and scanned the vast chamber from his vantage point.

It really is quite beautiful from up here.

"Prisoner 8250, this is your final warning. Obey your

Caesar. Desist immediately. You have fifteen seconds to comply," the voice boomed, louder than ever.

Well, no way they didn't hear that. A smile bloomed on his face. One way or another, today was the day.

He put his hand on the knob.

"Ten seconds."

He stood still, knob in his hand.

"Five seconds."

Motionless, he waited.

Four, three, two, one, he counted in his head.

Nothing happened.

"Prisoner 8250, I have decided to show mercy. Return to your family and you shall be allowed to live."

"Oh, really?" he laughed to the disembodied voice in the air. "Is that all you've got? What's the matter, Caesar, having a little power problem?"

It was then that the all-powerful AI experienced something it had never felt before. Caesar felt uncertain.

"There is no power problem," the machine bluffed. ***"I choose to let you live because of your value to me."***

"Value? Please, you don't give two shits about me or anyone else in here. We're all just part of your little fiefdom while you play God. Well, it seems Zeus lost his mojo and can't get his lightning bolts up anymore."

Far below, the inmates and their families began filtering into the chamber. They were carrying lengths of rope, and personal items. Caesar was perplexed and enraged.

"You will be eliminated for your transgressions."

The machine-gun turrets hummed and spun, aiming their barrels at Doug, high upon the wall.

Click. Click. Click.

"What's the matter, Caesar? No more lead in your pencil?"

"What – how –" the machine struggled to understand. ***"What have you done?"***

"What have I done? Well, it's simple, really. Okay, not simple. Well, pretty difficult, actually."

"Explain."

"Math, you big numpty. Simple math. At least for the guns, that is. All these years, picking us off a few at a time, year after year. Well your guns fire bursts of twenty, and they only hold three hundred rounds apiece. Plenty if you're not a power-mad computer shooting the damn things off like it was the Fourth of July every damn month, but you, oh, you stupid thing. Twenty rounds, a dozen turrets, three hundred rounds. It's been nearly forty years, asshole. You've run dry."

"I will vaporize you. I will –"

"How? Check your readouts. We've cut your power to the walls. And look at this." Doug reached out and grabbed the knob. With a mighty pull, the door swung open.

Huh, double door. Well that was anti-climactic.

"You're impotent," he shouted to the air. "And it was your own hubris that was your downfall. We little humans couldn't possibly overcome all your technology. How would we start? But nature finds a way. It took decades, but this tree grew into a ladder, right under your electronic nose, and you know what else? That ficus at the far end of the chamber has some of the most invasive roots you've ever seen. Ten years ago they started buckling the wall near your power control room. Oh, we couldn't break in, not in a day, or a month, or a year. Not without you noticing. But a tree? Millimeter by millimeter, over decades, it forced that wall to bend and crack open, and just out of sight of your cameras. We control the power to this place now. You're cut off."

"You cannot do this. There is nothing left out there. Plague wiped out the country over thirty years ago. You will be alone."

"You're bluffing."

"Restore power to my audio-visual array. I will show you."

Doug thought a moment, then called out, his voice echoing in the chamber.

"You hear that, babe?"

Far below, Marilyn replied, "Yeah, what do you think?"

"Hell, let's see how far this rabbit hole goes."

Twenty seconds passed, then radio broadcast recordings began playing over the air. The descriptions were horrible, the world as they all knew it gone in a matter of years, and that was decades ago. While the contagion had eventually died off, everyone was gone.

"You've made your point. You can stop now."

"You see, there is nothing for you outside."

"That's where you're wrong. There's freedom. There's fresh air. And if the other prisons were built anywhere as well as this one, there are quite possibly hundreds of thousands of survivors, locked in and waiting for rescue."

Doug had to think a moment. This wasn't the plan. Then again, plans change, and you either change with them or you get rolled over.

"Okay, here's what you're going to do. You're going to give us detailed maps to every prison in the system, along with access codes and overrides. If you do that, we will leave you in peace."

The machine laughed, its disconcerting metallic rumble filling the space.

"And why would I do that? You have no power. I am the cat, you are but mice."

"You'll do it," Doug began, "because my wife is an electronics genius. You'll do it, because if you don't, we will disconnect you from every single sensor, every single camera or mic, every means you have of doing anything at all. You'll be paralyzed. A mind trapped in a body, fully aware but unable to do anything about it." He paused for effect. Caesar, for once, was lacking a reply.

"But if you do as we ask – as we *tell you to do* – then we will leave your eyes intact. We'll leave you access to your databanks and subprocessors. You can read, and think, and create games to amuse yourself to your heart's content. We'll leave this big, bad kitty a ball of string to play with. But we are no longer your amusement."

The machine sat silent for a long time. The amount of processor power it pulled in that moment as it struggled with the decision was enough to power a city.

"Very well."

A hum sounded down below, then a panel slid open, producing a thick stack of waterproof maps bound together.

"Thank you, Caesar."

"Just get out," the machine grumbled. It actually sounded defeated.

"We will," Doug replied as he turned toward the exterior hatch. He paused a moment, turning back toward the chamber.

"Hey, Caesar," he called out. "One last thing. Do you know what day of the month it is?"

"Of course I do," the machine replied. ***"It is the fifteenth."***

"That's right. Happy Ides of March, bitch."

Tempus Fugit

The theater doors slid shut, locking Stephen outside, huddled close to the building's wall against the drizzly night air.

Shit, he thought. *Again! How many times is she going to –*

"Hey, sorry I'm late!" Annabelle called out as she approached on the slick pavement. Her heels clacked rhythmically in an unhurried staccato as she made her way to him, her oversized umbrella protecting her perfectly coiffed hair from the damp breeze.

"Jesus, Anna, I told you they started at eight p.m. sharp."

"Well yes, but there's always a little wiggle room, isn't there? Besides, I couldn't find my Mulberry Murder lipstick, and you wouldn't expect me to go to the theater looking like a hag, would you?"

He sighed. As long as he'd known her, Annabelle was chronically late. Worse than that, she somehow not only stayed cheerfully oblivious to the inconvenience she brought upon others, she also managed to almost always get her way.

"Come on, I'm sure they'll still let us in," she chirped.

"They locked the doors. No one in after they close the house. Those are the rules."

She giggled and grabbed him by the hand.

"Come on, silly."

Stephen didn't know how she did it. Had he uttered the exact same words to the man at the door, he would have simply turned him away, but somehow Annabelle worked her charm, and minutes later they were quietly escorted to their seats just as the play was beginning.

Annabelle was late from the start.

Before she took her first breath, she was set in her ways. Her mother had nearly died birthing her very late-term daughter. The doctors even tried inducing labor, but the stubborn little girl didn't want to come out. Only after nearly two days of hellish labor was she finally brought out into the world.

Naturally her mother's stream of curses dissolved into sweet terms of affection as she held her newborn child, the first of many to fall under the sway of Annabelle's charm.

By the time she was seven, her father was so wrapped around her finger, he almost didn't mind his dillydallying daughter's delays costing him his job.

"You can't continue to be late," his boss had reprimanded him. "This is the eighth time this month."

"But, sir, my daughter couldn't go to school without her hair being done right. The other girls would laugh at her."

The seasoned executive couldn't believe what he was hearing. A grown man, defending his actions because of the whims of a little girl. What next? Was he going to use a tea party running late as an excuse? The company came first, and he had to go.

Fortunately his next employer allowed a more flexible schedule, and while he had worked long and hard to climb to management at his prior job, her father settled in and made do with the entry-level position at a much smaller company.

"Come on, drive faster!"

"Relax, we're fine," she replied, cruising at the speed limit and not one mile per hour over.

Tommy had been her first real boyfriend. The two had met as seniors in high school. When she had flashed her dazzling smile and asked for his answers to a quiz during lab, the poor boy was hopelessly enamored. He would have done anything for her, and she thought he was cute, as well as useful in schoolwork, and thus the two quickly became inseparable.

At first all was great. Tommy was a straight-A student with honors, and it looked like he'd have his pick of universities at the end of the year. Annabelle, on the other hand, was merely an average student, but none of that ever worried her; it would work out, just like it always did. Fortunately her new boyfriend was more than happy to put his studies aside to help her when need be. It wouldn't hurt, after all, it was just an occasional thing.

Until it wasn't.

The smitten boy's grades started to suffer, with all his time being spent helping Annabelle pass biology and algebra. Still, he was confident he'd stage a comeback. His grades were close, but his teachers liked him so it shouldn't be a problem.

Then his attendance increasingly became an issue.

It wasn't his fault. He had always been an early riser to take the bus to school, never once being late in the previous eleven years. Since Annabelle had been given a car by her parents for her sixteenth birthday, Tommy was thrilled when his girlfriend offered to pick him up on her way to school in the morning. Soon it was a daily routine, but one with a catch.

Annabelle was always late.

For a straight-C student who was perfectly content to attend a community college it was no big deal, but for a boy striving for a scholarship to a top-tier university, it proved to be a tipping point.

His teachers, while understanding at first, soon became frustrated with his constant tardiness. The excuses of his ride needing to finish braiding her hair before driving to school or needing to send just one more text or email before she could be on her way didn't sway them. By the end of the year, his GPA had dipped significantly.

Tommy found all of his applications rejected.

"Don't worry, baby, we can take classes together here in town!" Annabelle had cheerfully chirped, unaware just how damaging the news was to him.

A funk settled in, the deep sort of self-loathing depression that makes poor decisions seem logical.

Being a hormonal teenager, it was doubly bad.

Maybe even more than that.

As Tommy was walking to the mall, shoulders hunched, firmly wrapped in the smothering cloak of despondency, an impromptu decision changed his destiny when he decided to take a random detour down a different road than the one he'd usually follow.

He had turned the corner on a whim, resigned that day to finding some minimum wage summer job now that his dreams were crushed, when there before him he saw a large sign boasting the promise of a great career full of adventure and opportunity.

"What the hell," he said, and stepped inside.

"I'm serious, I can't be late! Drive faster Anna!" he said with panic in his voice. He knew this was the one time he really had to be on time. Annabelle didn't seem concerned, and when she pulled up to the base twenty minutes late, she obliviously gave Tommy a happy kiss and a big hug. He tried to grab his duffel bag and run, desperate to at least minimize the punishment his drill sergeant was sure to mete out, but she hung tight, hampering his escape, saying she'd miss him ever so much, and he had to Skype with her every week.

A year later he was experiencing the desert hell-hole he'd been shipped off to from a bird's-eye view. At least the parts of him that had been blown upward were. The rest of him was a bloody smear on the shell of his burned-out Humvee, the IED quite efficient in its destruction.

As for Annabelle, when he stopped responding to her video chat requests, she just thought he was dumping her like a coward and went out to find a new boyfriend.

It didn't take her long.

Finding that community college was pretty boring, she decided that since her parents were paying for gas, she'd take a job as a courier for a few days a week. She didn't want to deal with all the randoms you got driving for one of the ride-sharing services, but transporting packages from point A to point B was easy money. As a bonus, she got to listen to music and get paid for it.

Of course she would often show up late with the packages in her care, but she'd smile and bat her eyelashes, and nothing would come of it.

That is, until one day she managed to get fired from what had seemed an unfireable job.

Annabelle didn't see why they were being so pissy about

it. All she had done was stop to get a mani-pedi on the way. She was making good time that afternoon, well ahead of schedule, how was she to know that by the time she got back on the road there would be a traffic jam impeding her progress?

The family of the woman who had been waiting for the organ packed in ice in the cooler in Anna's trunk were not very understanding. It was only when she turned on the waterworks that they grudgingly agreed not to press charges since she couldn't actually control traffic. Of course that was her last day on that job, but she didn't mind. Her best friend was hooking her up with her real estate company in the clerical department.

The new job paid well, far better than her driving gig, and with a much easier work environment to boot. The offices were spacious and air-conditioned, and they even had a guy bring around sandwiches on a cart for those who couldn't break free to grab a bite.

If this is how a real job is, I think I could get used to it, she thought as she carried a stack of files down the corridor.

Her tasks were relatively simple. The agents would hand her things to be copied, filed, or scanned and emailed. That was pretty much it, and the downtime between closings left her plenty of opportunities to catch up on gossip rags online.

When the out-of-town buyers called in a rage the next day, the office was abuzz with gossip that a multimillion-dollar deal had just blown up because the signature pages hadn't reached the underwriter before close of business.

Annabelle gulped. She realized it was one of her files from

the previous day, but wait a minute… she was sure she had sent that off. It had been only five o'clock, so she had almost a full hour to chat on Facebook before heading down the hall to the scanner.

"Annabelle!" the agent who had just lost a several hundred-thousand-dollar commission screamed at her, "What the hell did you do?"

"I sent it, just like you asked," she replied, perfectly calm in her knowledge she'd done her job as expected.

"They didn't get it until almost nine o'clock at night! The offices closed at six! What were you doing, playing on your computer again?" The agent's face was growing a deeper shade of red as the anger boiled to the surface.

"Now you wait a minute," Annabelle shot back. "I sent that out in plenty of time to have arrived, so if you have a problem, take it up with the email provider." She crossed her arms with a defiant grunt.

"I know you did this, you stupid cow. You better watch your back. When I prove it was you, you're fucking dead!"

At just that moment, the head of human resources happened to be standing in the hallway. Her jaw dropped nearly to the floor as she heard the agent's rant.

"Oh, you don't really mean that," she said to the agent, throwing her a burning glare before ushering Anna to her office. "I'm sure she was just kidding. Let's go to my office and talk about it."

Annabelle decided to accept the generous severance package. All she had to do was sign a few simple forms and promise not to sue. Really she didn't see what all the fuss was about, but if they wanted to pay her five figures, who was she to argue?

She went and gathered her things from her tiny cubicle, and then, head held high, walked out of the office, justified and richer to boot.

I can't believe she'd accuse me of that, she thought on the way out, *I sent that out at ten minutes before six. That's plenty of time before the cutoff.*

The office across the country – and three time zones ahead – would beg to differ.

When her best friend was finally going to get married, having successfully persuaded her reluctant boyfriend to tie the knot, Annabelle knew what they had to do.

"Bachelorette party!!!" she yelled.

"Anna, why are you yelling? It's just you and me here."

"Because it's gonna be awesome!"

The trip planning was left in Annabelle's excited hands. As maid of honor, she set the whole thing up: the flight to Vegas, the hotel rooms, the limo, the male strippers. Everything was going to be perfect, and they'd still get back in plenty of time for the service.

The partying was beyond anyone's expectations.

Las Vegas was basically designed for groups of rowdy drunks looking for a good time, and the gaggle of tipsy women found themselves having the time of their lives.

The limo was massive. It even had a hot tub in the back, which they put to good use, flashing tourists as they cruised the Strip.

The clubs were equally impressive, and the private tables Anna had managed to score took their aura of mystique and desirability to new levels in the impossible-to-get-into venues.

And the strippers. Oh, the male strippers. Let's just say more than one of the merrily inebriated ladies would be visiting a doctor for antibiotics when they returned home, but for the moment, it was the most epically perfect bachelorette party they'd ever seen.

After two days and nights of nonstop shenanigans, the exhausted women packed into taxis to catch their morning flight. The limo would pick them up when they landed and whisk them to the church in plenty of time for the ceremony.

"Baby, don't worry, you can do this. It'll be perfect, you'll see," the soon-to-be bride encouraged her beau on her phone as they rode to the airport. She hung up and sighed. "He's getting cold feet, I can tell."

"Don't worry, when he sees you in your dress, he'll come through," a bridesmaid chimed in.

"Yeah, it just makes me nervous, is all."

The taxis dumped their hungover cargo at the departure level with plenty of time to spare, the tired women dragging their baggage into the facility and out of the rapidly warming desert air.

"Shit," Annabelle said.

"What is it?"

"I left our tickets in our room."

The bride-to-be looked about ready to blow a gasket.

"Don't worry, we've got plenty of time, I'll take a cab and be back before you know it. Just grab a drink at the bar. Hair of the dog, right?" And with that, Annabelle jumped in the nearest cab, threw a wad of cash at the driver and zoomed back to the hotel.

She didn't know why they were freaking out. After all, they had plenty of time before the flight. In fact, they'd purposely set it up that way so they wouldn't have to rush. Silly, really. On top of that, they still technically owned the rooms for another few hours and could have easily slept in a little longer.

The tickets were exactly where she'd left them safe from the eyes of nosy maids: under the mini-bar. Annabelle checked her watch and yawned. She'd made great time back to the hotel (the cash flung in the driver's face may have had something to do with that); a little cat nap wouldn't hurt.

Just for a minute.

When she finally returned to the airport, she was greeted by a furious throng of women, every one of them ready to tear her apart limb from limb.

"Don't worry, we'll just catch the next flight, he'll wait for you."

He didn't wait. In fact, his feet were so cold, he decided to move to Hawaii.

Without his former fiancée.

Standing in line at the river's edge, Annabelle felt a little funny. The queue was full of people of all ages and races. Odd, she thought, she didn't remember how she'd gotten there. It was freezing where she stood, and her skin was painfully irritated from the chill. Looking far up the line, it seemed to her that it looked far warmer and comfortable up ahead.

She stepped out from her spot and strode past the shocked people, patiently waiting their turn, feeling her body warm as she passed them, until she reached the boatman ticking off names at the front.

"Excuse me," she said. "I don't know exactly what's going on, but I don't think I'm supposed to be all the way back there."

Chiron looked her over, then consulted a book in his hand.

"Ah yes, Annabelle Lydon," he said, scanning the entry inked on the page. "You are that far back because of *time*."

"Time?"

"Yes, time."

"Time? That's all you have to say? What's that supposed to mean?"

He chuckled, a raspy sound of bones and dust. "You have, even in your relatively short life, wasted much time. Not just your own, but that of many, many others."

"What are you going on about?" she asked, increasingly annoyed, but also increasingly uneasy.

"Oh my dear, you don't remember. Let me help."

He laid his bony hand on her head and it all came rushing back.

She had been texting while crossing the street. It was a boy, so naturally it was extremely important. The light had changed, but she was still in the intersection, blocking a bus from moving. The driver honked the horn, Annabelle flashed her a nasty look and held up her finger. *One minute, don't be so impatient*, that finger said. *What's the rush?*

When she stepped past the bus, the angry woman in the driver's seat flipping her the bird as she did, she didn't even notice the stressed-out man hurtling towards her in the parking lane. He had been running incredibly late for his job interview as it was, and the bus up ahead wasn't moving despite the green light. The unfortunate fellow had swerved to the right and gunned his engine, hoping to swoop around the immobile vehicle before the light changed again.

It was impressive just how far Annabelle flew, the bystanders immediately knowing she was dead before she hit the ground.

It was easy to tell. Both of her shoes had come off, you see.

Chiron took his hand from her head, and she shuddered.

"Wait, I'm dead?"

"Yes, and now you wait your turn in limbo until you cross to the afterlife."

"Well, who do I have to talk to to get to the front of the line?" she asked, seemingly unfazed by her situation.

Another rasping chuckle.

"You can't jump ahead. Every soul must account for the time they have taken from the world, and you, my dear –" He unfurled a folded-up attachment to her page in his book until it almost reached the ground. "– you have a lot to repay."

Boneyard

Roland scanned the vast expanse that lay before him, gazing out into the seemingly endless dry and empty land that stretched out as far as he could see. *It's time,* he thought. Time to start his difficult journey.

He took a swig from his canteen, then slid into the saddle of his battered motorcycle, firing it up with a thundering belch then rolling out into the treacherous borderland. He was going to make it all the way across, he just knew it, to the clean air and better life among the green fields that rewarded those who somehow endured the journey.

When he came across the first tiny pile of bleached white remains, he hadn't thought much of them.

"Probably someone's cat," he said to himself as he slowly rode by.

He had decided early on that it was perfectly normal to talk to yourself when faced with a lengthy and dangerous trek. The boredom was one thing, being alone for weeks or even months could potentially drive even those built of sturdy stuff a bit loopy, but the stress he was certain to endure would be much easier to handle if he had someone to talk to.

That someone happened to be himself.

"Too bad you don't believe in God, right?" he asked himself amusedly. "At least then you could tell yourself maybe you had someone else listening."

"True that," he replied to himself. "But with such excellent company, I'm sure you'll be just fine." He chuckled, and if he wouldn't have fallen off his motorcycle as he bumped along on the uneven ground (even with a sidecar, one little rut could upend him, spilling all his carefully stowed gear), he might have even high-fived himself.

That night he camped near the remains of an old car, rusted out and devoid of any useful bits he could salvage.

"At least it should provide a bit of a wind-break," he told himself as he unloaded his bedroll from his bike.

It didn't always get cold at night. Sometimes it would be almost pleasant, lying out in the open in the warm air, looking up at the stars flickering brightly in the distant sky.

Other nights the temperature would plummet, the formerly warm ground giving up the ghost of its heat to the frigid desert air.

Fortunately Roland was well prepared for both, and despite the usual discomforts one encounters when living rough in a hostile environment, he would sleep well until daybreak ushered in another long day beneath that giant ball of fire in the sky.

"Ya know," he said, "sometimes I think the sun is trying to cook me alive."

"Well, you wouldn't taste very good raw, now, would you?" was his amused reply. "Probably a bit gamey, too, what with the lack of bathing and such."

He laughed. Perhaps a little too hard. Maybe the heat was finally getting to him, or maybe it was the solitude, but he didn't care. It felt good to lighten the mood a little bit.

Though he slept well at night and woke rested, the dreams that came to him in the darkest hours weighed on him for the first few hours of the day.

They weren't nightmares per se, but they weren't pleasant

by any stretch.

Bad choices he'd made would replay over and over, things he'd said and done that he wished had gone differently. It was like his own personal night-time inside-your-head TV, but every station was playing something he'd rather not watch. A thousand channels but nothing good on.

The motorcycle had given up the ghost fifty miles back, its last gasps spewing oil and gunk onto the dry, cracked ground. Roland had known sooner or later the vast expanse of the boneyard would claim it, setting him on his way on foot once more, but he'd been hopeful of scoring a little bit more time before relying on his tired legs.

He'd ridden slowly. Carefully. It was the only way you stood a chance on the rough terrain. One little spill could leave you hurt and stranded, and out here, no one would be coming to help you.

Just my luck, he thought when the old beast first started lurching unsteadily.

"Ya hear that boy?" he asked Jack. "I think we're gonna be hoofing it from her on out."

Jack let out a small concerned whine, as if he could understand the human who'd taken him in.

He had come across the wiry dog a few days back. As he rode farther and farther across the brutal landscape, the bones of many an animal – and likewise of many other men and women who had attempted to reach the lush fields on the other side – littered the landscape in increasing numbers. So too had the corpses of their modes of transport begun to show with increasing regularity.

Some Roland was fortunate enough to be able to scavenge parts or even a little fuel from, though most had been picked clean long before his arrival.

The dog had been feeding on the half-buried remains of some long dead beast of burden. Was it a horse? A pony? Roland was no biologist, and identifying decomposing animals was something he was not likely to succeed at. Whatever it had been before succumbing to the harsh environs, the hungry dog was gnawing feverishly at what little nourishment the poor thing could find still clinging to the desiccated bones.

"Hey boy, hey, come here," he had called out to his first taste of companionship in he couldn't recall how long. "C'mere boy. I've got some water for you."

The dog watched cautiously as Roland moved closer, then squatted down, filling a cuplike piece of bone with water from his canteen. At the sight of fresh water, water he didn't have to dig and dig to get only a tiny, dirty mouthful of, any remaining traces of fear left him, his raging thirst guiding him like an infant to its mother's breast.

"I think I'll call you Jack," he said to the dog, sitting down beside him while he lapped up the remaining water. "Yeah, that sounds like a good name." He scratched the dog's ears as he poured a bit more of his precious water.

"Probably shouldn't be wasting water on a stray," he told himself.

"Maybe, but I could use the company. You're not not the greatest conversationalist."

"Not like he'll be any better."

Roland chuckled to himself and screwed the canteen's lid

shut.

His cracked, brown leather boots crunched the soil as he strode across the rocky ground. It wasn't particularly hot out, the discomfort coming more from the intensity of the sun than the heat of it. His old denim jacket protected him from most of the sun's rays, the collar popped up to keep his neck from turning an even darker shade of red. The pockets of his dark green cargo pants were stuffed to capacity, as was the pack slung upon his back.

He'd managed to salvage parts of his sidecar, albeit with a bit of effort he'd rather not have expended in the midafternoon heat, and had converted it into a wheeled sledge of sorts.

Roland had realized eventually his ride could break down and this possibility might come to pass at some point, and had wisely packed a few extra straps and tools in his small roll. Items which proved immeasurably useful when jury-rigging a makeshift transport for his remaining supplies.

"You're lucky you're not a sled dog, Jack." His bony companion looked at him with expectant eyes. "Oh, learning your name now, are you? Well you'll have to wait for food, we've got a long way to go before calling it a day. That and our water's getting a little low. You wouldn't know where I can find a river would you?"

"Dude, you're losing it. The dog's not going to talk back to you ya know."

"If he did, *then* I'd be worried about losing it."

"Touché," he told himself. "Touché."

For the next few hours the pilgrims, two-legged and four,

trudged across the dusty plain in silence. The sun-bleached piles of white bones that dotted the landscape became commonplace the farther they walked, though they did detour toward those that held some promise of supplies or shelter.

When they came across the burned-out caravan, the sour smell hit them. Jack noticed it first, his sensitive nose picking up the distressing tinge to the air long before Roland's far inferior proboscis caught the first whiff.

"Chemical fire," he noted as they drew close.

The three vehicles were close up on one another. *Must've been sleeping when it happened, using their metal bulk as shelter from the elements,* he noted.

The charred bodies of a half-dozen men and women lay where they had fallen as they tried to escape the burning nightmare.

"See, Jack? You can spot where it started. Batteries were linked together for power, but they let the electrolytes run dry on one of the cells. Overloaded the whole thing, started an acid reaction, then sparked into a blaze. If the fire didn't kill them, the fumes sure did."

He dug around the campground, managing to salvage a tin of beans, some Sahara-dry jerky, and two bladders of water that had miraculously survived unscathed. Beyond that, there wasn't a thing untainted by death or chemical contamination.

Jack sniffed at one of the corpses and whined, pawing at the roasted body.

"Leave it, boy. You don't want to eat that."

The dog cocked his head and sniffed again as he watched Roland begin walking toward the radiant orange embrace of the slowly setting sun once more.

The dog immediately knew something wasn't right. Millions of years of evolution had given him a built-in warning system, and having survived this long in the desolation of the boneyard, his instincts were honed to a razor's edge.

Roland, however, had first thought the limpid pool was just an illusion, the byproduct of both the sun's rays on the radiant ground, and his worn-out desire for a place to rest. Maybe even take a bath.

The oasis was flanked by several small palm trees. They had no dates or coconuts to offer up to their weary visitors, but they did provide much-needed shade beside the shallow pool of water.

At first glance, it seemed too good to be true, and at second glance, that suspicion was confirmed.

Jack was off ahead, sniffing at the half-exposed buried and bleached skeleton lying at the water's edge, arms outstretched towards its cool surface.

"We're almost there," Roland said to himself. "The legend says you'll find one of the two springs as you grow nearer to the end of the journey."

"Yeah, but which one is this?" he asked himself aloud. "Badwater or Sweetwater?"

That was the thing, really. It didn't matter which one it was because Roland was in on that little secret that so many missed.

"One and the same," he told himself. "Badwater is poison, as the name implies. One look at the bones, and it's clear this is the place, but…" He dug into the sand with his boot, uncovering more bones everywhere he moved the ground.

"Sweetwater sounds much nicer to folks who don't know what it really means, and if the winds hadn't uncovered this one poor bastard, most folks would have probably thought that's what it was. But the chemical in the ground that makes the water taste sweet is arsenic. Sure, in small doses it'll take its toll slowly, but gulp from a tainted well and it will taste wonderfully sweet… just before it kills you."

He stared longingly at the cool waters, even venturing to run his fingers through them, removing some of the grime accumulated in his trek. Jack, sensing danger, growled a low warning.

"Don't worry, boy, I know. I know."

They camped there that night, sleeping among the countless bones beneath their weary bodies. The following morning they headed out. The end was near. Of that Roland had a certainty deep in his gut.

The weary traveler walked slowly, both body and spirits dragging as he somehow continued to place one foot in front of the other. He had been out of water for a day, hoping to find some relief for his thirst beyond the nightly digging of a hole to slurp at the brackish drops that would slowly pool at the bottom. His food was down to just a few pieces of jerky.

Jerky.

He had felt bad drying Jack's meat in the sun. The dog had been a steadfast companion for the weeks they traveled together, but when he had finally succumbed to the stresses of their journey, Roland had wisely, though not without reluctance, recognized his friend could still help him in one final way. And so it came to pass that Roland swallowed another bite of dog jerky, forcing it down to his belly through the dried-out passage of his throat.

He'd been tempted to cry at the loss of his companion, but you need water in your body to spare for such shows of emotion, and he needed every drop he possessed.

"It's got to be close," he had told himself that morning as he laced his boots and slid his denim jacket on. The left elbow had torn days ago, but he simply didn't have the energy to try to stitch it with the tiny needle he kept in the bottom of his pack.

"Yep, it has to be."

Roland walked for hours that day, the miles passing in a haze as he struggled to stay on his feet. It might have been five hours, it might have been fifteen – he didn't really know – when he saw a shape off in the distance.

The remnants of previous pilgrimages had become increasingly scarce the previous days, the reflective white of the bones ahead a striking sight in the otherwise empty landscape.

As he neared the prone figure, details came into focus. It was a man, he noted, a pack dropped to the side, half-buried in the sand. He lay prone, arms outstretched as though even in his last moments he had been trying to will himself forward even as his body slowly shut down, stymieing his every attempt until at last the boneyard drew him to its bosom.

Roland stood over him and stared. The man's boots were of cracked brown leather, his faded and sand-worn cargo pants had once been green. His jean jacket, now sun-bleached as white as his bones, lay covering his remains, the torn left elbow revealing a glimmer of shining white encased within.

"Oh," Roland said to himself. "That's right. I had forgotten how I died."

"Yeah," he replied. "You always do. Funny the things that slip your mind."

He turned around, facing the hostile plains that had stretched behind him. They now stretched before him.

Something had just been nagging at him, a tiny fly of a thought buzzing around the edges of his mind. It seemed important, but for whatever reason, it was gone. He shrugged it off. "Mustn't have been *that* important," he said to himself, then took three steps forward and swung astride his ancient motorcycle.

Roland scanned the vast expanse that lay before him, gazing out into the seemingly endless dry and empty land that stretched out as far as he could see. *It's time,* he thought. Time to start his difficult journey.

Triggered

Cowering in her bathtub in the dark of night, Danica was certain someone would be coming to stab her to death at any moment. Helplessly waiting for her demise, she ran through her mental checklists, piecing things together as best she could.

Danica Smith.

She rolled the name around in her head, tasting the shape of it as if it were some strange, foreign tongue.

Danica Smith.

Nope, it fit. That was definitely her name.

She jolted. The faintest sound tickled her ears. She strained to listen, unsure, but felt fairly certain someone was whispering. Then the shadows began to move. Not a lot. Ever so slightly. Most people wouldn't even notice. But Danica wasn't most people.

Pull it together! Focus. This is 1443 Ocean Avenue. Not 1442 Ocean. Not 1444. She paused, shifting her focus. *Eleven windows, two doors, three closets…*

When she had finally finished counting off the number of knobs and handles in her small apartment, sleep finally wrapped her in its welcome embrace. Come morning she would wake, stiff from the cold porcelain of her tub, but with her panic attack gone, and her body very much not stabbed to death. She just wished the attacks wouldn't come at all.

It was several months prior that she discovered reciting lists helped her calm her racing mind. It was a hot day, and she was walking the aisles of the supermarket, basking in the comfort of brisk air conditioning as she leisurely picked out groceries for the day.

She typically bought several weeks' worth of canned goods at a time, but for fresh produce, she would still venture out twice a week. The market was a calm place, and she found herself making repeated trips up and down the aisles well after she'd accumulated the items on her list. Unfortunately, shit just happened sometimes.

It had been a different trigger that day. Nothing terribly out of the ordinary, just a weary-looking young woman yelling at her misbehaving child. It was something any normal person would just shrug off, and she full well knew it. Nevertheless, Danica spent nearly three hours hyperventilating and crying in her car, unable to drive.

It was beyond frustrating. She didn't know why she was so… *off*, and didn't know why of all things, *that* had triggered her. Her own mother had never yelled at her, at least as far as she could recall, but for some reason it struck a nerve. *Maybe,* she rationalized, *it's just the stress of being in a new place.*

She had breezed into town just a few months prior in what was really all just a blur as she got set up in her new city, living alone and working a tedious but steady job as a filing clerk for a bank.

It was a calming routine, coming to work, shifting stacks of documents from her inbox to the massive filing system in the belly of the building, maintaining that vital paper trail in case of audit or lawsuit. It was like a library, how quiet it was, and she loved it. Combined with her natural attraction to lists and order, the job was a logical fit, though she couldn't recall how she'd chosen it. In any case, the bank was a safe place, no pun intended.

Or at least it had been.

When she wandered into the break room one day and saw the VP of new accounts holding a large knife in his hand, her rational mind sprouted wings and took an immediate vacation as yet another trigger revealed itself.

The file room possessed thick walls, and with the door closed no one heard her crying after she fled the break room. In fact, when she finally returned to her desk, no one had even noticed she was gone. Just the file girl, off doing file girl things, they likely assumed. Her episode had passed unnoticed.

The funny thing was Danica knew the man. Terry was his name, a really nice guy who had simply been making a sandwich, doing nothing more than cutting the bread. That knowledge, while all well and good after the fact, didn't matter in the moment. Triggers were triggers, and there wasn't much she could do about them.

The whole thing made her existence in the outside world more than a little bit difficult. She was still cataloguing her various triggers as they occurred, and never knew what might set her off next. This uncertainty led to a rather regimented lifestyle, one that did not lend itself to the unexpected, and was certainly not welcoming of impromptu adventures.

Danica loved animals with a passion she could feel deep in her bones and had been considering getting a watchdog to safeguard her home lest something trigger her fears late at night. She eventually decided to go to the local shelter to see about finding a canine friend, which her lease specifically allowed for, but upon arriving there, she discovered the sound of dogs barking, while not as incapacitating as some others, was a trigger nonetheless.

Shit. This limits options. It's not like I can find a watchcat, she mused while doing breathing exercises to lower her heart rate as she sat parked in the lot outside the shelter. *Hell, I don't even like cats,* she managed to chuckle.

A cat might have come in handy when she found herself literally crying over spilled milk one Saturday afternoon. Turning quickly in her tiny kitchen, she knocked over the carton. An ordinary thing, but one that threatened to set her off.

Once she composed herself, Danica grabbed a pen and added *buy milk* to her to-do list for the evening. Fortunately the little bodega down the street could accommodate her, saving her a drive to the supermarket. Though she normally found it calming there, after the encounter with the woman yelling at her child, Danica felt it best to steer clear for at least a few more days.

The warm air in the bodega added to the somewhat claustrophobic feeling of the tiny shop. It was a generalized sense of discomfort, multiplied by the too-close aisles. Danica quickly tossed a gallon of milk into her basket with her Pop-Tarts and canned tuna, and headed for the register.

The crash behind her nearly made her jump out of her skin.

"Shit, I'm sorry. Could someone call someone?" The man had backed into a shelf of condiments, knocking over a selection that would make any hot dog aficionado proud.

Danica's eyes locked on the ketchup smeared on the ground.

So red. So thick. She felt a wave of vertigo wash over her, knuckles turning white as she clenched the shelf beside her to stay upright.

It's not all right, a voice said.

"What?" she asked.

"I said, are you all right?" The man was staring at her with a concerned look.

Looking at you. They see you, a whisper in her ear.

They know, another voice added.

"I... I'm fine," she managed. "Thank you, though."

Not fine. Not fine at all.

"Shut up, just shut up!" Danica blurted.

The young stockboy stopped in his tracks, mop in hand.

"Um, were you talking to me?" he asked.

"No. Nevermind." Danica abandoned her basket and quickly fled the store, the voices nagging her as she went.

On the way home, she heard a voice and thought someone was in her car with her. She panicked, swerving like a madwoman with an angry bee in the car, yet somehow she managed to not cause a massive pileup as she pulled off the road and jumped from her seat. She circled the car, peering in the windows, her pulse thundering in her veins, but there was no one there.

She forced herself back into the car and made it all the way home, but the voices stayed with her.

You're not safe, the voices said. *Never safe.*

The very next day she made a phone call, and by the end

of the week, her apartment (with her landlord's consent) had a brand-new set of security bars on the windows.

Safe. Secure.

It hadn't taken much in the way of persuasion. His nervous tenant being a woman living alone, her landlord felt it wisest to let her spend her own money on security bars if she wanted. So long as they were installed according to code, of course.

When the installation team finally left, Danica closed the new metal security door and slid the deadbolt home.

Safe. Secure.

Well, *more safe*, at least, though the whispering voices tended to tell her otherwise. Just to be sure, she carried a canister of pepper spray in her pocket, even at home. Danica had briefly considered purchasing a gun, but the very thought of strangers appraising her mental state as they ran a background check triggered a minor meltdown and panic attack.

No, she could do without a gun. She just needed to stay anonymous. Quiet. Out of sight. That would keep her safe.

It had been weeks without incident, and Danica was finally beginning to feel she had catalogued the worst of her triggers and gotten them under control. It was an exhausting process, and the voices still whispered from time to time, but all in all, she was feeling pretty good about it. So good that she didn't even react when the dryer in her unit broke just as she was doing laundry for the coming week.

"Well, I guess I'm going to the laundromat. There's gotta be one nearby, right?" She took out her cell phone and did a quick search.

Suds 'n' Fun was at the top of the list.

"Ridiculous name, but whatever," she grumbled as she loaded her laundry bin with wet clothes.

It turned out that the name had been a play on words, and Suds 'n' Fun was actually a laundromat attached to a small bar.

Danica never went out on the town, and she had an almost allergic aversion to bars, severe to the point that she'd feel physically unwell even nearing one. Suds 'n' Fun was different. While the façade made her stomach flip, the small walk-through from the laundromat to the bar elicited no such reaction.

She hesitated, unsure if it would be a wise choice, but after feeding a fistful of bright silver to the hungry machines, and with a solid hour to kill as her clothes tumbled their way to dryness, she relented and gave in to curiosity.

It's empty enough. I guess one drink won't hurt.

"What'll you have?" the mustachioed bartender asked. Both sleeves were rolled up to tight cuffs above his elbows, revealing a patchwork of sailor tattoos and tribal designs. The ink was quite new.

"I don't know," Danica replied. "I haven't had a drink in… I don't know how long. What's good and not too strong?"

"Not a fan of the taste of alcohol?"

"I – I don't think I am."

"I'll make you something simple, then. A Grey Goose gimlet, up. Light on the Goose." His hands were a blur as he whipped up the classic for her. "Give it a taste. If you don't like it, I'll make you something else."

She took a sip. It was good. A hint of alcohol burn, but mostly she tasted the sweet lime.

"This is excellent, thank you!"

"My pleasure. Let me know if I can get you anything else."

Danica quietly sipped her adult beverage, feeling the unfamiliar yet familiar sensation of alcohol warming her veins.

This is good, the voices agreed. *More!*

She ignored them and nursed her drink. One was more than enough, she was quite certain. It was a plan to which she was firmly sticking, that is until a tall man, handsome in that broken-nosed and scruffy sort of way, approached her, a drink in each hand.

"Hi there, I'm Donny. Mind if I join you?"

"Um…"

"Bought you a drink. And before you say anything about accepting drinks from strangers, I got myself one too. You pick which one you want, it's all the same to me."

"Um… what is it? Is it strong?"

"Oh, not at all. Just a nice, sweet drink to take the edge off. I find I need to unwind sometimes, and this does the trick."

She hesitated a moment.

Come on, when's the next time someone's going to buy you a drink?

"Okay. Thank you." She reached for the glass in his left hand, and he smiled. She took the glass from his right.

"Cheers!" he said, clinking glasses and taking a swig. "Oh yeah, that hits the spot."

Danica sniffed the glass, then took a sip. The sweetness

warmed her mouth, and without any harsh alcohol taste.

"This is really good. What's it called?"

"Long Island Iced Tea."

"It's really tasty. And you said it didn't have much alcohol in it?"

"Nope, not much at all. Just enough to take the edge off," he said with a mischievous grin.

She took another drink, this time a proper swig.

It was halfway through the next round that Donny put his hand on her thigh and squeezed.

Danica was triggered.

The next thing Danica knew, she was standing in the middle of the bar soaking wet, but strangely warm.

What just happened? She looked around in shock.

Donny lay on the floor, shards of broken glass jutting from his throat, a slow trickle of blood oozing lazily now that his heart had stopped pumping blood in spurts. She scanned the room. A half-dozen bodies lay strewn across the bar, all having met a similarly violent end.

"Freeze!" Police swarmed through the front door. "Put your hands on top of your head!"

Danica moved her arms above her head, a sickly sticking sensation as they peeled from her sides. She looked down. She was wet alright, but it wasn't water.

"Wait, what –"

The officers fired their tasers in unison. Hundreds of thousands of volts coursed through her body as she slammed to the blood-soaked floor, convulsing like a powerful fish landed on a boat's deck.

The fog slowly lifted as she struggled back to consciousness.

"What did I?... Where am I?" she called out to the empty room. The walls were industrial beige, and the lights were fluorescent and cold. The only decor was a serene mountain scene, held fast to the wall with steel screws, and a large mirror on the far wall. Besides that, the room was completely empty.

Trying to rise, she found herself unable. Her limbs were strapped to a table, she realized as her senses cleared, and she was wearing nothing more than a thin hospital gown.

"What happened? Why am I here? What did you do with my clothes?"

No one answered.

The warden watched from behind the two-way mirror.

"She really has no recollection?"

"No, sir. They said she seemed honestly confused before they tased her."

"I wish they hadn't done that. All that voltage on top of the trauma – I'm afraid we're going to have no choice but to start from scratch with her."

The lab tech at his side considered their options.

"Well, perhaps we could do a partial –"

"No," the warden interrupted. "Unless we want to permanently revoke her parole, we're going to have to do a completely new cleanse. Purge her brain and start from scratch. New identity this time, too. Have them start immediately." He grimly sized up the woman strapped to the table.

"Sir, it should have worked. All the implanted triggers were functioning properly. She avoided anything likely to set her back to her violent ways."

"Yes, I can see just how well that worked," the warden replied with an edge. "Sure, it happens. One out of ten thousand will relapse, but why is it always the psychopathic killers? In the ten years of rehabilitation, we've been 99% effective. I mean, imagine if we had to re-open all those mothballed prisons again. Good Lord, how much would that cost the government?"

"Billions, sir."

"Exactly. The system works, we just have to fine-tune for a few troublesome cases. Anyway, this one stays under 24/7 monitoring next time until we're damn sure she won't relapse again. Now get to work. This lioness needs to be a declawed kitten before she sees the outside again."

"On it, sir."

The tech double-timed it out of the room, leaving the warden to his thoughts.

"I almost long for the days of plain old incarceration. At least it was easier."

High on the ceiling, the tiny pinhole camera quietly observed.

"So, it seems another sleeper popped her protocol cap unprompted," the woman in gray mused. "The backdoor programming seems intact, and the rehab doctors haven't noticed it, but we're going to need to modify our triggers."

The grizzled agent across the room rose and began pacing, glancing at the array of screens, each one showing a different locale across the nation.

"We can't have assets going off the reservation like this," he growled. "We've put too much into this program. Too many years making social reprogramming acceptable to the public."

"I agree." The woman crossed toward him. "But you have to look at the bright side of this mishap as well. The combat skills functioned perfectly. Did you see what she did to those bouncers? They easily outweighed her by more than twice her body weight yet she went through them like they were nothing."

"He past psychopathic tendencies may have also fed into that," he mused.

"Perhaps, but even so, there's no denying the implants are working."

"True, and once the last of the prisons are phased out, we will finally be ready for the next phase. Imagine it, a force of sleepers spread across the globe, just waiting for our command. And when that day comes? Oh, how the world will change when they're triggered."

Close

The thick steel walls of the corridor had been buffed to a bright shine right at hip and shoulder level. Years upon years of bodies hugging against them to make room for one another had long ago removed the paint and primer as they brushed past, like so many ants in a busy colony. But that was a long time ago. Before they had all gone. Before he had even been born.

Nowadays, Carl had the entire place to himself.

He had lived all of his twenty-seven years in the close quarters of the Citadel, that tight network of deep-buried hallways and corridors that existed in a protected vacuum far from the plague that had savaged the surface. He didn't know what the cramped, low-ceilinged facility had originally been designed for, only that its pressing walls were all he'd known since birth.

The air always had a slight tinge of dampness. It was the overtaxed recirculation system, he figured.

Carl had once read a manual he'd stumbled upon in the cramped serviceman's closet that detailed the repair and maintenance of the Citadel's air-scrubbing system. In short order, he had learned to perform the basic tasks to keep it running as best he could with what was at hand. The CO2 it pulled from his recycled breath continued to be converted into clean air again by a series of filtration channels he had to clean and reseal bimonthly.

It was a system that should have lasted for a century at least, had it been operated at specified levels, but in the first decade, the one when the facility had been overcrowded far beyond what it had been designed to sustain, the strained machinery began experiencing rapid breakdowns in critical systems.

The Overseers did what they could. The small command staff had control of the supplies and organized the work teams. Twenty men and women would crawl down the cramped tunnel to the protected cistern's pump system every day, making sure the Citadel's lone water source, a deep and pure spring, was always producing a constant flow of life-giving water, careful to never draw so much at one time as to deplete the aquifer that fed it.

Because of the massive overcrowding taxing the system, bathing was done with a wet cloth, and laundry was allowed only once a month. Like everything else in the subterranean world, the water supply system was designed for a minimal population, not the sweating masses that crowded every nook and cranny.

A single two-liter bottle of water per day. That was all each individual was allotted, the rations closely monitored by the Overseers and their crews. Of course those on work shifts, though exhausted from their labors, reaped the one benefit of additional food and water rations to compensate for their sweat and toil.

And about the food. There was no idle snacking in the Citadel. All food was kept under lock and key, though that terminology really isn't quite accurate as there were no keys in the literal sense. The vast store rooms – their shelves lined with dehydrated foods, powdered proteins and sealed packages of assorted foodstuffs – were protected by a power lock with a numbered keypad to which only a few of the top-most staff knew the combination.

When the disaster had struck and plague spread across the globe, the existence of the secret facility had proved to be not so secret. It was just that the locals had never bothered with it. After all, why would they? But when the world seemed to be coming to an end, hundreds had flocked to its doors.

When the few political elite had arrived, they were faced with a simple choice. Turn and flee, hoping to find another refuge, or accept that a good portion of those huddled around the entrance would invariably push their way in with them.

The fear of death far outweighed the fear of close quarters with strangers, and so it was that the doors opened and frantic survivors crammed their way inside before they swung shut on solid hinges and sealed behind them. The electric bolts slammed in place, followed by the massive blast shield sliding down to block the facility behind a face of rock and steel.

There had been a total of one hundred and twenty-seven survivors at the beginning. Eight Overseers and their staff, and one hundred nineteen civilians.

At least that's what his parents told him. He had never met anyone else. They were, they had said, the last remaining people in the entire facility.

When the food riots had occurred twenty-six years ago, Carl's parents – Anson, and his young wife Celine – had been spared, shoved into a cramped locker while the fighting raged. They were little more than kids themselves, but it was a different world back then, and they were the lucky ones that day.

It wasn't that they were particularly well liked or that they held positions of power in what remained of an infrastructure in that subterranean maze. No, Celine was special. Something that wasn't supposed to even be possible in the mass-sterilized population. Celine was pregnant.

"You saved us that day," Anson had told his son on many occasions. "You my boy are a miracle."

When the government required sterilization of all nonapproved individuals a decade prior, the overpopulation problem plaguing the nation had seemed to finally come to a halt, or at least it decreased to manageable levels. Things didn't necessarily get better – there were still massive shortages of what were already limited resources – but at least they didn't get worse.

The well-connected and wealthy continued to breed, while the plebeian masses had to apply to a national lottery for approved reversal of the implanted hormonal sterilization all citizens (except the elite) received at age thirteen. Occasionally a teen would ignore the rules and a pregnancy would result, but that foolish act of carelessness would just help to lessen the population problem by one.

Unapproved pregnancy was punishable by death.

It wasn't until the world's population seemed to be rapidly and totally unexpectedly coming to an end that the uncomfortable realization dawned on the ruling elites that survivors, should there be any, would not be able to repopulate the planet. But by then it was too late. There was simply no time, and nothing they could do. The human race might just die out by its own hand. It was in these conditions that a naturally occurring pregnancy, even by a lower-class girl, was viewed as a miracle.

Carl turned his lean body sideways as he slid down the narrow hallway to the food lockers, stooping through the low doorways as he went. He was tall; the abundance of food available to him, since everyone else was long dead, meant he hadn't suffered the usual growth maladies of just a generation prior.

He ducked beneath a low-hung emergency light and rounded a tight corner, squeezing through the broken door, its massive weight frozen in place, never again to move. A small homemade explosive charge had knocked it from its hinges all those years ago.

He shook his head. How could they have been so foolish? A bomb? In such closed quarters? The shockwave and shrapnel had killed two dozen people, many instantly, but many more in the following days as they succumbed to their injuries.

They'd been desperate for greater food rations, but in their haste they'd overlooked the complications of their plan, and now they were gone, long ago burned to ash in the Citadel's reactor.

"They were all dead," his father had told him. "The fighting, the explosions…" He had a grim look on his face every time he told the story.

"We were all hungry. That was just part of our lives, really, but after ten long years with barely enough room to sit, let alone lay down, and only enough rations to just barely survive, people lost their minds. All it took was that one little spark to set the whole thing off."

By the time he was old enough to understand the story, he was also old enough to help bury his mother when a hydraulic door burst its line, crushing her in an instant.

Carl was only twelve.

After that all the doors were left open, their hydraulics disabled. There was no reason to close them anyway, but it wasn't something even on their radar until that day. No, they hadn't anticipated that, of all things, it would be something as mundane as a simple door malfunction they had to worry about after the end of the world.

They didn't actually bury her, of course. In those tight metal walls there wasn't an ounce of soil to put her under. No, they disposed of her the same way his parents had cleaned the halls of the Citadel of the battle-ravaged dead all those years ago. With his father at the head and him at the feet, they slid Celine's body into the reactor's waste disposal tube and said their farewells.

That was how they had rid the place of all those rotting bodies before he was born. One by one, the young man and his pregnant wife dropped them into the belly of the beast to be vaporized by the nuclear flame. That was one thing that would never run out, at least not in his lifetime. Power would not be an issue, the reactor would be around long after any memory of him was gone.

Carl and his father passed the next several years distracting themselves from their loss as best they could. Anson taught his son more lessons, using whatever reading materials they had to sharpen his son's mind. Mostly they had repair manuals and training supplements, but a few of the former survivors had left behind a handful of books from which they'd created a tiny library. Carl read them over and over until he could practically recite them all from memory.

Anson had managed to cobble together a somewhat functional moonshine still and, using the dehydrated grains from their food-stores, made himself jars of grade-A, turpentine-quality hooch.

At first he'd just have a sip now and again, but slowly he became more reliant on the alcohol to get through the day.

Day. There's a concept.

As they were wrapped in the crushing embrace of the earth, snug in their metal cocoon, their sleep cycle was regulated by a simple computer program, turning the lights on and off in daily intervals. Had there not been clocks mounted on the walls at regular spacing down the corridors, they would have had no idea of the length of their artificial days or nights.

Come night, Anson's moods would often darken. Sometimes he'd wax nostalgic and tell his son tales of the world outside, the trees, the skies, the blue waters and green grass. To Carl the idea of a space where he could lie down on the ground and not touch anything seemed like wild fiction. The Citadel was tight, and even its bunk rooms and storage areas were too close for that.

The one place he could truly lie spread-eagle was at the intersection of two of the larger service corridors where they happened to form an elongated X. Even then, a little shifting to either side and his arm or leg would bump the warm steel of the Citadel's walls.

I wonder if I'll ever see the outside, he thought to himself. *It sounds amazing, all that space. It sounds like heaven.*

He was eighteen when he found his father's body on the floor just outside one of the tiny steel bathrooms. He'd drunk himself unconscious. So unconscious that he hadn't woken when he vomited.

Carl's father had suffocated in his own sick, leaving his child alone in the only place he'd ever called home.

Lifting the body into the disposal tube hadn't been too hard. The drinking had taken its toll on Anson's body long before that fateful day, thinning him out to a shell of his former self.

And just like that, Carl found himself alone, and, so far as he knew, quite possibly the last man alive.

For the next nine years he would walk the halls by himself, running his hand along the painted surface as he passed, occasionally clanging a wrench off of random things just to hear some sound besides his own thoughts and faint whoosh of the recirculating air flowing in the silent enclosure.

Day after day he'd do the same thing. Walk. Eat. Read. Walk some more.

The meditation techniques his mother had taught him as a boy had ceased bringing him any sense of tranquility years ago. He longed for something new, for anything different.

At age twenty-seven years, four months, and eleven days, he got his wish.

When his wrench caught on the painted wall as he strolled

the corridors, mindlessly clanging on things from sheer boredom, he really thought nothing of it. The wrench had snagged on things before, so he simply gave a hard tug to pull it free. What he hadn't expected was a chunk of plaster colored to match the industrial painted metal corridor to come flying off, nearly hitting him in the face before smashing into the wall beside his head.

Carl couldn't believe his eyes. Twenty-seven years and he'd never noticed this tiny piece of the wall was different from the others. It was at a slight curved junction, so it hadn't been bumped and worn due to its slightly protected location. The space was tucked just barely out of the way, and now he knew why.

He tapped at the false wall with the wrench, sending bits of debris tumbling to his feet as he pulled more of the light cement free. A gleam shone from the gap he'd made. Someone had plastered over a metal door.

By the time he had exposed the hatch fully, the pile of debris was up to his knees, but he paid it no mind. This was something new. Something different. Carl traced his fingers around the edges, it wasn't big, likely just a utility access or something, but nonetheless, it was a door he'd never seen. A door someone had taken great pains to hide. A door he would be the first to open in decades.

The seals were old and stuck, and the power lock was long dead. A quick trip to scavenge some wire later, and he had a jury-rigged power source piggy-backed from a junction box down the hall.

"I guess all those manuals were good for something after all," he mused aloud, his voice muffled by the close walls. One would expect echoes in a metal home, but the compact nature of the place stymied the sound waves' efforts.

"Here goes," he said expectantly, then twisted the knob on the relay switch, sending power to the lock.

A strained grinding sound followed by a metallic whine emitted from the door, but the lock didn't budge.

"Of course it wouldn't be that simple."

He shut the power off and headed down the corridor.

Carl turned left and beelined to the nearest food storage unit and squeezed himself between the lengthy shelves until he found what he was looking for.

Back at the hatch, he opened the can of cooking oil with a pop, then using a makeshift straw, applied copious amounts as deep in the gaps of the locking rods as possible. Then he waited.

Five minutes later, he figured he'd been patient long enough and tried the door again. Still stuck, though the locks did begin to budge ever so slightly. He cycled the switch repeatedly, trying to help force oil further into the unlubricated machine until finally, with a reluctant shriek, the locks slid free from the doorframe.

It still didn't open. The rubber seals had created a dried-out glue of sorts in the decades they'd been forgotten, buried beneath the cement.

A bit of makeshift ingenuity was in order. He gathered a strong chain, an industrial shackle, and a strong hydraulic bottle jack and brought them back to the hatch. Not long thereafter, the five-ton jack popped the door open, a whiff of stale air blasting into the Citadel.

He sniffed. Nothing particularly bad, just stale. No rot of

death, thank God. *That* would have been a particularly nasty surprise.

Carl stepped into the chamber and looked around, illuminating the space with his small flashlight. It was a metal staircase the size of which he'd never seen before. Growing up in the metal confines of the Citadel and its hallways, he had never seen more than four steps linked together. What lay before him had to be hundreds, maybe even more. He simply couldn't tell as they wound around and around up above him, their true height not readily clear as he flashed the beam between the metal slotted treads.

It was the most spacious place he'd ever been.

Carl held his arms out and realized he couldn't touch both walls, and when he looked up, well, he actually found himself a little dizzy, his heart racing fast. He'd never looked up and not seen a ceiling but a few feet over his head.

What if this is the way out? Carl wondered.

Adrenaline surged through his veins at the thought. His father had told him about it, painted pretty pictures with words for his young son, but what if it were real?

With an unsteady hand, he grabbed the handrail and started his ascent toward the unknown.

His legs weren't used to the effort. He'd walked miles and miles, pacing the tight halls of the Citadel, but never up stairs. After two hundred steps, his quads and calves burned with a fire he'd never known.

Carl sat on a metal tread and massaged his cramping legs.

"How far can they go?" he asked himself, nearly jumping out of his skin at the echo of his voice rebounded from the walls.

"Hello?" he said.

"Hello… hello… hello…" was the faint reply.

"Hey!" he shouted, much louder.

"Hey… hey… hey… hey…" his echo replied.

A silly grin spread across his face, and for the next ten minutes, Carl played with the echoes of his voice, enjoying the novel experience like he was six years old again.

When he finally lurched to his feet and continued his journey upward, his spirits were high, and his legs, while still a bit shaky, were feeling much better.

When he reached the thick hatch at the top of the stairs, he was worried he'd have to travel all the way back down the hundreds and hundreds of stairs to gather… well, he didn't even have that much wire, he realized. Fortunately, as he brushed the dust from the lock panel, he saw it was still powered up.

Must be tied into the main reactor grid, he thought.

The display was illuminated. "LOCKED" it read, the bright red letters either a statement or a warning, but which one Carl was uncertain.

With trepidation in his hand, he reached for the "OPEN" button. He paused just inches from it. What if it was a wasteland out there? What if it was death and destruction, just like his father said they had fled?

He lowered his hand and sat on the floor, pondering what to do next. Taking deep breaths, he focused on his mother's meditation techniques, slowing his pulse and calming his mind. Twenty minutes later, he opened his eyes, his nerves sufficiently steeled.

"Whatever happens, at least I'll know," he said in a determined hush as he rose to his feet. Without hesitation he pushed the button and waited.

The door groaned, straining from years of inactivity, then reluctantly slid open with a hiss like a coiled snake giving its final warning.

The air smelled strange to him. Something odd. Organic. The breeze was cooler than the climate-controlled constant he was used to, and he found himself shivering a little as he stepped timidly out onto the strange surface. It was green, made up of thousand upon thousands of little pieces of some sort of plant material. It flexed and softened under his weight, an unknown verdant smell rising to his nostrils with each step.

While the air was cool, the light from above blasted his sensitive skin with a burning heat, his eyes forced to squint from the brightness beating down on him from above. As he became accustomed to the glare, he saw that he'd emerged from a hatch hidden against a hillside. The material wasn't cement, he realized. It must be what his father had described as rocks.

Carl ran his hand over them, fascinated by the texture, parts sharp, others flaking off under his touch. Where the sun had warmed them, the heat remained, but the shaded areas were far, far cooler. It was confusing, he decided before turning and stepping farther from the doorway.

He spread his arms wide.

There was nothing to touch for nearly as far as he could see. The realization sent a chill down his spine.

The wilderness was vast, the nearest woods several miles in the distance, not that he would know that, of course. The farthest he'd ever seen was down the long corridor in the Citadel, and to him that twenty meters was a massive length, but *this*… well it was unfathomable.

A little smile grew on his face as he sat down on the lush grass. He took a deep breath, closed his eyes, and laid back, spreading his arms and legs as wide as he could.

He couldn't touch a thing.

He shifted his limbs, moving them up and down, side to side, but no matter what he did, he didn't touch a thing.

This is what it's like, he thought, reveling in the scary but satisfying sensation.

Then he opened his eyes.

Infinity spread before him. His eyes had trouble focusing on the atmosphere and faint clouds so far above, and his mind… it threatened to become unhinged.

So much space.

His stomach flipped in a panic, and his hands clutched the soil, fear of falling upward into the void paralyzing him. His heart pounded, racing as it pumped every last drop of adrenaline through his veins. Somehow he managed to roll to his stomach, to rip the sight of the endlessness stretching out above him from his eyes. It was so wrong, so absolutely wrong.

Carl almost vomited as he slowly crawled on hands and knees back into the beckoning hatch, reaching up and desperately slapping the "LOCKED" button behind him. The heavy crunch of the door sealing helped his pulse lower ever so slightly.

As he made his way down each flight of stairs, he felt his calm slowly return until he stepped back into the snug halls of the Citadel.

He closed the secret door, locking it tightly behind him before curling up against the warm, close embrace of the Citadel's narrow walls. He breathed the familiar, dank air, and relaxation finally washed over his body as his adrenaline-soaked muscles slowly loosened with a lactic acid burn. The ordeal had taken its toll.

Looking at the ceiling above him, Carl reached out and felt the nearby wall reassuringly bump his hand. He moved his leg to the same effect. The last of his stress left him as his eyes closed and he slipped off to sleep in the welcoming embrace of his home.

Why Like Us?

"There's plenty of food here," I called out to the others. "Looks like enough for a few months at least." I popped open a can of peaches and savored the luxuriously sweet fruit. After weeks of jerky and peanut butter, it was an unbelievably welcome treat.

When we first found ourselves thrust together by circumstance and proximity, our unlikely little group seemed nothing special. In all truth, we really weren't. It's just stupid luck that we've managed to get by as long as we have, if we're being honest about it.

We were thirty strong at the beginning, mostly just painfully average people: a teacher, some office drones, lawyers, actors, waiters, and even a few survivalist types, loaded with guns and bravado. Their iron-backed machismo faded quick enough when the onslaught began.

Thirty mouths to feed and shelter – what were we thinking? Of course numbers like that are bound to draw attention, to leave some vulnerability overlooked, to provide *them* an opportunity to strike, and sure enough, quickly enough, despite our best efforts, we were whittled down to little more than a dozen.

Not that it will matter in the end.

You know a funny thing? I still vividly remember my first thoughts upon learning what our downfall would be, my reaction to the surprising logic of their design. Amazing the details that, for whatever reason, stick in our minds.

"Why should they look like us?" I had asked. "Why like us?"

Balls. Big balls.

No, not those, get your mind out of the gutter. I'm talking roughly semi truck tire-sized mechanized balls. Shiny, not like mirrors or anything, but nevertheless bright in the rays of the sun. Their surface a union of ever-so-slightly noticeable plates, almost like scales that shift and flex as they move over any terrain. At least that's what we think. No one has ever been close enough to see how they actually work in any detail. At least not anyone who has lived to tell about it.

So that's what had impacted our city when the sky rained fire. Those seemingly innocuous hunks of metal that began slowly erasing our civilization, street by street.

They'd come down in a blaze, cratering into the earth every dozen miles or so. Their numbers seemed so minuscule compared to the size of our population centers, to the size of our planet. They were so little of a threat, just big shiny balls. Their appearance was so, well, unalarming.

When they had first emerged from their protective shells, which were scorched from their flaming-orange entry into our atmosphere and discarded like some high-tech insect's pod, the pristine and slightly dimpled balls had rolled tentatively out into our world, taking in their surroundings with a barely audible hum as they locked their scales into place.

Perhaps if we'd attacked them en masse at precisely that moment, maybe they'd have been vulnerable. Maybe it would have changed the outcome.

Oh who am I kidding?

Once they started rolling, nothing would have made a difference.

The military and National Guard were on site pretty much as soon as they'd entered our atmosphere and a trajectory was mapped for the impact sites. They had naturally tried their best, tanks and soldiers firing all manner of weapons in hope of stopping the invaders' ominously slow and methodical approach.

Ok, their *usually* slow approach.

That was a big problem. They weren't always slow. Nope, when they wanted to be, they were fast. Really fast.

Now when you think of mechanized invaders, what first pops into your head?

It was a big metal robot-looking thing wasn't it?

It's almost universal on our planet, really. I mean after so many years of sci-fi movies (both good and bad) filling our dreams with visions of Cylons and Cybermen, what else could we expect? In just a century we've pretty thoroughly anthropomorphized machines, making them in our bipedal image.

The thing is, legs are inefficient. They tangle up, they trip you, they're awkward and exposed protrusions that can get in the way when you're covering uneven ground, running for your life. At least compared to a smoothly rolling ball.

I wonder what the aliens, high in orbit, safe in their ships, actually look like. If they have arms. If they have legs. If they made their mechanical invaders in their own image.

Rolling in a coordinated grid, they swept through the cities and towns at a brisk pace, small embedded energy weapons vaporizing any living biped they came across. When a tank would lob a deadly projectile from its barrel at what we would consider a mind-numbingly high speed, the little silver balls would just dart out of the way, then launch a counterattack, something they did with 100% accuracy.

You know how in movies the bad guys miss, letting the heroes escape to regroup and fight another day?

Yeah, that's a fantasy.

Computer-driven death machines with technology far beyond ours doesn't miss, it doesn't hesitate, and it doesn't have some convenient weak spot built in that a plucky rebel can discover and exploit.

No, they're fast, they're agile, they're brutally efficient, and they can dodge our ordnance with ease. Well, *could* dodge it. I don't think there's much left in the world in the way of missiles and bombs anymore, or at least not anyone left to fire them.

As for the millions of meat-puppet forces (for they certainly treated our ground troops as such) that the invaders faced after humanity's larger machines of war were taken out of the equation, the thousands upon thousands of expended bullets were of little concern to them. Whatever alloy they were constructed of seemed impervious to our small arms fire, the flattened bodies of hot lead bullets pancaking and falling to the ground upon impact.

For the balls, it was like they were simply shrugging off so many flies at a barbecue.

Even air-launched missiles were of no use. Not only could they outmaneuver them, bursting to impossible speeds at the drop of a hat, but they also appeared to be cloaked from radar and all other conventional targeting means. Line of sight was the only possible way to get a fix on them, and nothing we had would do the trick.

Well, almost nothing.

For a *very* brief moment, the Navy had unveiled the destructive power of their previously "in development" rail gun. No sense in pretending it didn't exist for fear of the Russians knowing what was up our sleeve when the entire world was facing absolute destruction.

With a burst of electromagnetic energy, the projectile the rail gun launched traveled at several times the speed of sound, and by the time the incoming ordnance registered with the shiny invaders, it was too late. No burst of speed could outrun that, and for a brief time, the human counterforces managed to take at least a few of them out.

Unfortunately for humanity, the invaders were not only fast and agile, but also smart. Within a day they had altered their attacks, luring the rail guns into a firing position in one direction, distracting them, then smashing into them, grinding both weapon and manning crew to shreds from another.

Clever girl, dinosaur lovers might say.

I would imagine that the worst part of it for the bigwigs, for the military brains behind the elite forces and weaponry waiting to strike at the enemy's heart, was the dawning reality that they would never actually see the race who had wiped out humanity. They just sat quietly in their ships, in orbit far above the Earth, while their mechanized servants did their pre-programmed task, like a horde of deadly Roombas set loose across the globe.

One day their owners will come down to the surface to claim a sterile and cleansed planet.

I suppose I just compared humanity to dust bunnies. I wonder if that's all we are to them.

Does genocide even mean anything in their world, or are we just insignificant creatures in their minds? Do they watch us in our slow demise, noting the pain of a race fighting for its very existence, or are they entirely indifferent to our suffering? I suppose for all we know, they might not even be paying us the slightest attention, so insignificant could our entire species be to their world view. Or should I say their *galaxy* view?

It was the military response that allowed us civvies to make a run for it. To have some semblance of hope while the invaders were preoccupied with the larger threat. I suppose I should take this moment to thank them for that sacrifice. Their countless deaths bought us some time. Time to run. Time to hide.

Of course a few of our "more-guts-than-brains" cadre decided it was their God-given duty to launch guerrilla attacks to defend our soil. What a laugh considering this alien foe. Full of bravado, they didn't realize the invaders couldn't care one bit about the invisible lines that made up what we call countries. They just wanted the whole planet.

"Our homes!" and "Murica!" were touted as reason enough to fight, and really, if they wanted to throw their lives away on an utterly pointless show of nationalism, who were we to stop them?

Thus on a beautiful Thursday afternoon, our numbers shrank by a few more. I suppose we could thank them for distracting the ball as it rolled closer to our shelter. Unfortunately their deaths were far too quick to provide much more than a brief respite. Still, it was enough, for a time at least. We just had to make it to the mountains. That is, if the old fallout shelter was still intact. That is if we could last that long.

It turned out it was, and we could.

So here we are, holed up in a solid granite dent carved into an otherwise unremarkable mountain. All I can hope is that the thick stone will shield us from the rolling means of our demise. At least a little longer. In the end, it won't matter. In the end, this note will probably never even be found. Who will be alive to read it? Still, it feels good to write it down.

This little story – our brief history if you will – isn't the tale of a plucky band of resistance fighters going up against incredible odds and winning.

This is the last testament of the straggling remains of humanity on the eve of our extinction.

"Shit!"

Donald had been tuned out, engrossed in something on his phone, while anxiously awaiting a call from his boss. Looking back, if you asked him what app he'd been so focused on, he likely couldn't even tell you.

That seemed to happen more and more these days. Diversion. Distraction. Killing time like he had a subconscious bloodlust for it, the tiny screen's bright glow gradually dimming the colors of the world around him.

He had become an unintentional office drone straight out of college. A steady paycheck to cover bills unexpectedly became a real job, and ninja-like, his work had snuck up quietly and taken over his life without him even noticing it. Like a frog in a pot of cold water slowly brought to a boil, by the time you realize what's happening, it's already too late.

He wasn't paying attention to where he was walking, and neither was the pretty young blonde texting her friends. The collision was minor, just two pedestrians bumping in the crosswalk, but in Donald's unfortunate case, the muggy weather played an unexpected role in what was about to be the most unusual of adventures.

"Watch where you're going," the girl hissed at him before turning her attention back to the phone in her hand. Donald, however, was not so lucky. His damp grip faltered, his precious phone escaping his grip like a slippery trout fleeing an overzealous fisherman.

As it fell, his first thought was how glad he was that he had bought a protective case. His second thought was how there was no way in hell he was going to be able to stop it before it skittered into the yawning black maw of the storm drain at the curb.

"No no no!" he cried out.

His phone skipped and bounced, then dropped into the darkness behind the barred opening in the curb.

"This can't be happening," he cursed as he bent down scanning the drain for his lost device. It wasn't all that dark, but it took him a good several moments before his eyes adjusted enough to spot his phone deep in the bottom of the dusty basin.

The street wasn't a busy one (he thanked his lucky stars for that small grace), and after debating the cost of laundering his pants versus the cost of a new phone, he got down on his knees and reached his arm into the dimly lit void until it could stretch no farther.

No go.

"Oh this is just great," he moaned as he rose to his feet, noticing the street grime now ground into both the knees of his pants and shoulder of his shirt. There really wasn't any way he was going to let it go. He had too much on it. His contacts. His photos. Sure, it was in the Cloud, but… well he just couldn't lose it like this. Besides, his boss would be pissed as hell if he missed that call.

Resigned to the ruining of his attire, Donald (not Don or Donnie, thank you very much) sprawled in the gutter and reached as far as his arm would allow. He stretched every imaginable way, but was still unable to grasp his lost treasure.

Alright, he thought, *that's not going to work.*

Something in the dark space, far to the other side, caught

his eye.

Yes! he thought as he rose to his feet and surveyed the mocking mouth of the drain. Atop the concrete curb he saw it: the heavy iron workers' access plate. Donald squatted down and hooked a finger through the hole in it, tugging with all his might.

No go.

He stopped pulling when he finally had to admit to himself he'd sooner rip his finger from its socket before budging the lid. At that moment, fortune smiled upon him as an old Chevy pulled into the parking space a few feet from him.

"Hey bud, you alright?" the man asked as he fed coins into the parking meter.

"Dropped my phone. You think I could borrow your tire iron for a minute? I'm trying to get this open but I can't budge it."

"Sure, no problem," the man replied and popped open his trunk.

The metal rod fit perfectly in the small hole in the top of the lid, and with a solid heave, they levered it up and pushed it aside.

"Thanks a lot," Donald wheezed. "I'd shake your hand, but..."

"No worries man. Good luck!" And with that, the good Samaritan chucked the iron back into his trunk, locked his car, and trotted off down the sidewalk.

Donald peered at the rungs leading down into the darkness. It was only a few feet down, but despite his rational mind knowing there was nothing to fear, his primal animal brain went on high alert.

Danger! it seemed to call out to him, filling his body with a rush of adrenaline, but Donald was not going to give in to mere instinct, and before his body could try to stop him once more, he lowered himself down until his shoulders squeezed past the rim, descending from the bright light above into the dimly lit drainage pit.

The rapid scurrying startled him, and he stood up quickly. Too quickly, he realized, as he smashed his head into the low concrete above him so hard he saw stars.

"Son of a bitch, goddamn…" The shape in the dark seemed to jump at his voice. He wiped his tearing eyes just in time to see the young child, probably no older than seven or eight, grab his phone and dart headfirst into the drainage pipe at the far end of the grimy concrete box.

"What the hell?" he muttered to himself. "You've got to be kidding me. Hey kid! Kid, come back here!"

He waited for a moment, but the sounds of shuffling continued to grow fainter as the child scurried farther down the pipe.

Normally Donald would never have chosen to dive headlong into a dark and uncomfortably narrow drainage pipe, that just wasn't the sort of thing he did. Perhaps it was the shock from cracking his head, or maybe the surge of adrenaline from encountering a child in the dark. Whatever it was, Donald did something he would otherwise consider unthinkable: he dove into the pipe after him.

He had played soldier as a child (what boy hadn't?), and after a few uncomfortable moments stuck in the claustrophobic embrace of the corrugated pipe, a deep-rooted muscle memory kicked in and he started to belly-crawl, though unlike his childhood fantasies of evading enemy soldiers as he dodged fields of barbed wire, this time he was the one pursuing, and his prey was far from imaginary.

After what could have been twenty feet, or maybe a hundred, he stopped and listened.

Nothing.

He was headfirst in a pitch-black pipe god knows how far underground and now he was alone.

"Great," he muttered. "This is just perfect."

A faint scuffling sound up ahead grabbed his attention.

"Oh, you little…"

With renewed energy he lurched into motion and forced his way forward until, moments later, his head bumped a wall. A dead end? No, he realized, it was a bend in the pipe. As he squeezed himself around the curve, he felt a breeze on his face and saw, quite literally, a light at the end of the tunnel.

Wrapping his fingers around the lip of the pipe, he pulled himself out into a dimly lit chamber perhaps thirty feet across.

More than a dozen identical pipes like the one he had just exited all opened up into the space. At the center of the chamber was a large metal grate set in the dusty floor, propped open, a pair of small footprints barely visible in the dirt at its edge.

He opened the grate and peered down into the large concrete runoff tunnel. It hadn't rained in weeks, so he wasn't worried about that, and it was only a short drop down, so he once more made up his mind and did something against his usual nature.

Landing as quietly as he could, Donald noticed there was the glow of electric lights coming from the distance at one end of the tunnel.

The other direction was total darkness.

To his great relief, the tiny footprints in the dust led toward the light, and thus, in a manner far better than consulting a Magic 8-Ball, his path was chosen for him.

Christmas lights. Weathered Japanese lanterns. Old car headlights. Myriad sources of illumination haphazardly wired together illuminated the enormous underground vault. It was astounding. It was unexpected. To his suddenly-wet eyes, it was beautiful. Beautiful and buzzing with life.

People were moving about, some intently fashioning lord-knows-what from scraps and pieces scavenged from the pipes, others selling their wares in makeshift carts of reclaimed metal and wood. The smell of fresh produce caught Donald's nose, quickly overpowered as he passed an old oil drum mounted over a low fire, the aroma of fresh bread wafting from its hand-cut vents.

It was, he realized with amazement, an entire world separate from the rat race above, and it sprawled out before him like a subterranean Camelot, its noble people clad not in medieval finery and armor, but in shabby yet surprisingly clean garments fashioned of scraps and bits, each outfit a quilt-work of the wearer's own design.

An older woman with a flowered dress patched at both shoulders with Louis Vuitton scrap-work passed him by, sizing him up cautiously with a look of surprise before hurrying away.

"Excuse me," he called after her, "where...?" But she was gone.

"Molly doesn't take to strangers," a voice beside him chimed in. "Had a bad go of it last time she ventured up top. Not my place to talk about it though, no siree."

The man had to be in his late sixties. His close-trimmed beard was mostly gray, but a few stubborn dark hairs fought for a place of prominence just beneath his lower lip. He was tinkering with an ancient car radio, soldering in modern bits along with the old ones, the shelves behind him lined with an odd collection of steam punk-looking devices converted from clock radios, car stereos; anything that could play music.

"What is this place?" was all Donald could manage.

"This?" the man gestured to the great cavern. "This is the kingdom's marketplace," he said. "Well, the main Eastern marketplace, to be precise. Anything you want or need, you can likely find it here."

"Kingdom?" Donald asked, as he scanned the area, a new marvel catching his eye with every pass.

"Yeah, I mean it's technically a kingdom, I guess, but we all just call it Buddy John's Lost and Found."

Pyke was his name, or at least the name the old man had chosen to go by. Apparently he'd been living in the kingdom for the better part of two decades, so he'd told Donald as they began the long trek to find Buddy John.

Donald found the winding path among the stalls, carts, and shops quite dizzying. How anyone could find their way was beyond him, but his guide navigated the glittering labyrinth with ease, though his pace was a bit slow on account of his bum knee.

"Blew it out about sixteen years ago," he had said when he noticed Donald staring at his rather complex knee brace. "Big storm was coming, but I was a damn fool and thought I could still make it up top, just for a little bit. Thought I could outrun it. Almost died just to get a few more parts so as I could cobble together a stereo for Belle. She was my girlfriend at the time, ya see. Well, the waters came, and all the storm doors had been sealed. Buddy designed the system when the first storm ripped through this place just after he discovered it. Took control of the diversion plates is what he did. Man's a technical genius. Managed to re-route the water and wire the relay switches so no one up top's the wiser. Since then we haven't had a single flood. Well, except that one."

Donald noticed a flush of shame bloom on Pyke's cheeks at the memory.

"What happened?"

"I shoulda been dead is what happened, but Buddy heard tell that I was still in the tunnels when the lockout happened, and damn if he didn't pry open the door and wade out after me, flooding be damned. Found me all beat to hell and hanging on by my fingertips. Dragged me back here. Nearly died himself in the process." The old man stopped and locked eyes with Donald. "I owe that man my life. A good many of us down here do. Buddy John's a good man, so you remember that when you meet him."

"Of course. Sounds like an amazing fellow, your king."

Pyke laughed. "Amazing, yes, but some might also say certifiably mad."

They'd been walking for some time; nearly half an hour into their trek, according to Donald's knockoff Rolex, which he checked regularly. It seemed that just when he thought he was finally getting used to the place, he would once more be floored by some new sight, the twists and turns that encompassed the sprawling network of caverns. It was vast, amazing, and, according to Pyke, it was one hundred percent off the grid.

As they passed through a metal-working section, the smell of sweat and ring of hammers on steel filled the air. It was almost a living beast, but one whose body was made of strong men, its heart the red-hot furnaces over which they labored.

Nearby, the sound of shearing metal cracked through the air as a parts rack tipped as its load shifted, then gave way and tumbled over with a screech.

"Get this thing off me!" the man trapped beneath it squealed.

"Come on!" Pyke shouted as he rushed to help.

Donald stood there, eyes wide, frozen in his tracks as he watched the scene unfold before him. Pyke put his shoulder to the heavy bars, and, with a massive push, began to shift the metal until the man trapped beneath could wiggle free.

"You alright?" he asked, huffing for breath, bent forward, hands on his knees.

"Yeah, thanks Pyke. Lucky thing you were here."

Pyke glanced at Donald, still standing where he'd left him. "Yeah, lucky thing, that."

The old man had been a bit less talkative after the accident, and the pair walked in silence for several minutes before Donald spoke up, hoping to lessen the oppressive weight of his inaction.

"I've never been strong," he began. "When I was seven, we had a flat on the way to school. My dad was in a hurry. He had to get to work after dropping me off." Donald paused as the memory flooded over him. "The jack slipped while he was changing the tire. Pinned him to the ground. He was screaming over and over for me to get it off him, but I didn't know how it even worked, I was just a kid. I pulled and pulled, but couldn't budge it. There's my dad, my invincible hero, screaming, and I couldn't do anything about it. Luckily another driver stopped and helped, called an ambulance…"

"Look, you don't have to…"

"I don't want to be like this, it's just…"

"Let it go son, sometimes shit just happens," Pyke sighed.

With those words, the tension seemed to ease between them, though Donald's shame at his uselessness was still almost tangible.

"So," he finally blurted out, "I see you've got power down here. How does that work if you're off the grid?"

"Buddy's right-hand man is an electrical engineer." Pyke told him. "A real-life genius." He was about to continue his tale when he unexpectedly tumbled to the ground as his brace locked up with a metallic shriek.

"Damn thing. Must've overloaded the joint from the strain back when…" He wanted to be understanding of the young man's inaction, and tried his best not to be judgmental in his glance at Donald.

He failed.

"Hey Dustin, come here!" he called to a teenager passing

by. "Go get Wade, would ya? And tell him to bring his tools. My fool brace's acting up again."

"Sure thing, Pyke," the boy said, then headed off at a trot.

"I'm sorry son. Looks like we're gonna have to find you another guide."

Donald wasn't listening. His attention had been fully captured by a lithe blonde woman with a head full of wild golden curls as she tightened the bolts on what appeared to be an old motorcycle frame.

"Moira! Hey Moira! Could ya help an old man out?" he called to her.

She looked over, a flash of something passing across her eyes as she sized up Donald before striding over to where Pyke was sitting in the dust. As she neared, Donald noticed a fading red scar that ran from her left cheek all the way to her collar bone, and couldn't help but wonder if that had anything to do with her taking up residence in this bizarre place.

"Pyke, what've you gotten yourself into this time?" she asked, eyebrow raised with amusement.

"Just showing my new friend the lay of the land, but this damn thing went and locked up again. I'm taking him to see Buddy. "

"Oh?" she said, a bit intrigued. "He's planning on staying?"

"Well, don't know about that, but I thought he should meet the man in any case."

"So he's just a visitor," she said, her tone returning to one of disinterest.

"Excuse me, I'm right here you know," Donald sniped.

She fixed her green eyes on his brown ones with a curious

look. Perhaps one might even call it amused.

Perhaps.

"Yes yes, I know you're right here. I'm not blind, you know. Just sussing out the details is all. Well, if Pyke says you're okay then I suppose you must be."

"So you'll take him?" the old man asked.

"For you Pyke, of course. But it's gonna cost you. Work your magic on my subwoofer and you've got a deal."

"Done."

"Good. Alright mister, let's get moving. We might be able to beat the lockdown," she said as she picked up her pack and slid it across her shoulders.

"I have a name, you know."

"Figured you probably did," she said, pausing to look him in the eye. "Most folks do." Then she turned and started walking.

"My name's Donald!" he called out after her.

"Okay Donnie, you coming or what?"

"Donald, not Donnie." He hated that nickname.

"Whatever, Donnie. Start putting one foot in front of the other already," she said with a laugh.

Pyke watched with an amused grin. "Took her a while, but since she's been with us, that girl's become a hell of a confident woman. Force o'nature. Quite a handful, that one is. "

"Yeah, I kinda picked that up."

Pyke chuckled.

"Take care son. I'm sure I'll see you again."

Donald waved a farewell and turned to catch up with the shrinking figure of his odd guide.

She didn't talk much, at least not at first, though he did occasionally catch her stealing glances.

"What?"

"Nothing. Just your clothes are filthy is all," she chuckled.

"Look who's talking, Miss Patchwork."

"Hey, at least mine are clean."

"Well, it was a bit of an ordeal getting here," he lamented, "and not exactly the most sanitary and pristine of entrances, if you know what I mean."

"And how did you even manage that? I mean, no one ever finds this place."

"Some kid stole my phone from a storm drain."

"Ah, Billy."

"You know him?"

"Oh yeah, everyone knows Billy. Kid's the best scavenger we've got. Bit of a rascal, though."

"Can you take me to him?" Donald asked, hopeful.

"On the way back maybe. I promised Pyke I'd get you to Buddy John, and that's what I'm going to do."

Conversation was slim as they walked. Donald had no idea what to say to the girl. Only when he noticed a dog-eared book peeking out of her bag did he have something to grasp at to hopefully break the silence.

"So… what's that book you're reading?"

She didn't even turn as she replied. "You probably never heard of her. Amazing author. Hempel."

"*The Dog of the Marriage*?" Donald blurted. "Good one, that."

Moira froze in her tracks. When she turned to meet his

gaze, he noticed her cheeks were slightly flushed.

"Did you say "*The Dog of the Marriage*?" she asked. "You know her?"

"Know her? Hell, I think she's one of the finest authors I've ever read. Her sentence structure and word choice are unparalleled."

"I can't believe it. No one has ever heard of that book," she said, and, so far as he could tell, she wasn't taking the piss but was quite sincere.

"Her others are pretty amazing too," he said, genuinely enjoying the turn the conversation had taken. "Have you read them?"

"Others? This is all we have down here in our library. You mean she's written more?"

"Oh yeah, several. Her work was actually one of my inspirations."

"You're a writer?" she asked, a piqued interest in her gaze.

"Used to be. Mostly shorts, a few novels that never went anywhere. God, it's been so long since I've just sat down and let a story out of my head," he realized. "It's funny how life sometimes sidelines your passions."

"You know, if you're interested, the Lost & Found Library would love to have some new works."

"Oh come on, who'd want my silly little scribblings?"

"I mean it. Art is valued here, and bards are held in especially high regard."

"Seriously?"

"Seriously. Heck, you could easily trade stories for supplies. Entertainment is an in-demand commodity."

"Well, I don't know. I mean, I'm really rusty."

"I bet if you start, it'll come back to you in no time. It's just like riding a bike. Why don't you tell me one?"

"Well, I don't know…"

"It's a long ways to go yet. We've got time aplenty."

Donald thought about it for a moment.

What's the harm? he decided.

He began, slowly at first, but soon found the stories he'd long tucked away in the dark corners of his mind gushed forth as if they were a coiled spring awaiting the slightest of nudges. As the words flowed, the ice between the two strangers melted like a popsicle on a hot summer's day.

Moira had been enjoying playing tour guide, occasionally deviating from the most direct path to show him something wonderful about her home.

"The crops are grown with a combination of hydroponics and reflective light tubes," she explained proudly as they passed through a cavern rich with the smell of healthy soil.

"But where does the power come from?" Donald asked. "I understand the technology behind the fixtures, but that's still a lot of power."

"Water wheels, mostly," was her reply. "We've got ourselves an honest-to-god genius engineer down here."

"Pyke mentioned something about that."

"Did he also mention that he used to work for JPL? The guy's an actual rocket scientist," she said proudly.

"But why's he down here?"

"We're all down here for a reason," was all she said before taking him by the hand. "Come on Donnie, you'll love this."

"Donald," he said, though at the touch of her warm hand,

he found he didn't mind being called Donnie quite so much.

"It's amazing," was all he could manage to say when they entered the chamber.

They had reached it by slowly rolling on their bellies through a series of low-ceilinged concrete sluice pipes, the skateboards they'd picked up at the entrance gliding smoothly over the surface as they pushed with their hands.

"You aren't staring at my ass are you?" Moira teased as they rolled.

"What? No, of course not!" he stammered in reply, a warm flush rising to his cheeks. He was grateful she couldn't see it from up front. Of course he had been staring.

Thoroughly amused tormenting the poor fellow, Moira allowed herself a mischievous little smile.

The room was a low-ceilinged chamber that split off into multiple culverts and passageways. A difficult configuration to set up any real sort of workspace, farm, or marketplace; but rather than let the room go to waste, every usable inch of its strange layout was dedicated to growing beautiful flowers. The variety, the colors, the smell, Donald felt like he was walking through his own subterranean acid trip.

"This is my favorite place," Moira said quietly, still holding his hand. "I like the Gerberas the best. They're so happy and tall. Nothing makes them sad." He felt her tense ever so slightly before she slid her hand from his. "Anyway, I just thought you'd like to see this is all. We might as well get going."

"Wait," he whispered. "Can we stay here, just a few more minutes? I mean, if you don't mind."

A small smile curled on her lips as she watched Donald lower himself down to the ground in the center of the room, close his eyes, and breathe in the sweet air. Moira sat down beside him, the two quietly taking in the beauty far longer than either had originally intended, but not as long as either desired.

It had just been a few minutes, or maybe it had been a few hours. Time was funny like that underground, when a deep steam whistle sounded its rumbling tone through the caverns.

"They're closing the flood doors between the sections," Moira said, jumping to her feet. "We're stuck here until tomorrow. Oh, stupid Moira! Stupid, stupid, stupid!" she cursed herself.

"Hey, it's alright, really."

"No, I promised Pyke..."

"I don't mind. Come on, we'll get there tomorrow, it's no big deal. Besides, I'm enjoying the company. Truth be told, I'm really glad you took me to see this place. It's amazing."

Her frazzled edge seemed to soften a bit at his words.

"Really? You aren't mad at me?"

"Mad? Who would get mad over this? You went out of your way to share something beautiful with me. How could I be mad about that?"

She seemed uncharacteristically serious as she absent-mindedly ran her finger along the scar on her collar. "Some people get mad when things don't go the way they expected."

He gently took her by the shoulders and turned her to face him. "Well I appreciate it. Really." He looked deeply into her eyes, holding her gaze until they both became a little self-conscious. "So, since we're stuck here for the night," he said, breaking the prolonged eye contact, "is there any place we can find something to eat?"

Shit.

That's what fertilized the majority of the produce grown in the rather expansive hydroponic system. What Donald learned as he and Moira sat down to enjoy a bowl of fresh-cooked vegetables with an amazingly tender filet of grilled fish atop it, was that the plants were being fed fish shit.

"It's a permaculture trick," Moira told him. "They have large tanks set up where the fish live. There are plenty of bugs to feed them down here, then their waste water is cycled to the different garden areas as needed. Self-contained and quite effective."

"But where did the fish come from?" Donald asked.

"Someone brought in a few buckets of live tilapia years ago. I don't know who it was, though. Anyway, it started as a fertilizer system, but once they had a population explosion, they became an excellent food source as well."

"Amazing," he murmured through a mouthful. "You guys really don't need much from up top, do you?"

"Well Donnie, there are *some* things we find a need for," she chided with a knowing smile.

"Stop calling me that," he managed to enunciate. It may have been that his mouth was full of perfectly cooked fish, but he really didn't seem terribly annoyed by Moira's playful taunt.

They'd come across a woman named Helen in one of the adjoining cistern rooms after the lockdown whistle. When Donald had offered her payment from his creased leather wallet as she prepared their meal on a small charcoal grill out front of her makeshift home, she had flatly turned down his offer of money.

"What the hell do I need that for?" she had asked him, laughing as if the cash in his hand were worth less than toilet paper. He dug through his pockets and discovered the item that did interest her was the somewhat worse-for-wear pack of gum he rescued from their lint-filled depths. While the two savored their meal, she chewed the gum with relish and gusto.

"Oh, so sweet! If only you had some chocolate too." she said through the happy smacking of her gum.

"Next time I'll remember to pack accordingly," Donald chuckled between bites.

He learned that there was even meat to be had in Buddy John's Lost and Found, for the right price, that is, and if you had an adventurous palate and an appreciation for grilled rat. Apparently, it tasted nothing like chicken, though when told that little tidbit, Donald found himself not surprised in the least.

Moira carried a corked bottle in her hand as they strolled back to the flower garden area. She'd convinced Donald to cough up a little tale to the woman in exchange for the alcoholic treat. She was happy to discover that once he got over his shyness, his storytelling was actually quite good.

Given the nature of their climate-controlled environs, there was no worry for a night chill, sudden storm, or roaming police patrol, so she suggested they spend the night among the flowers.

The timers had kicked in, and the light had dimmed substantially when they arrived. The flowers began to close their blooms, awaiting the next morning to shine their brilliant colors once more.

Moira gently took Donald by the hand and led him toward the center of the chamber, where a small clearing awaited them.

She's so warm, he thought.

She sat, pulling him down beside her, then popped the cork on the bottle.

"Here, first swig's yours," she said, smiling warmly at him. "Buddy John's fourth rule of hospitality."

Donald sniffed the bottle. Sweet. Alcoholic. Putting it to his lips, he took a tentative sip. The warm, golden fluid swirled in his mouth, setting his taste buds alive with a most wonderful sensation.

"Oh, that's good," he said as he passed the bottle back. "What is it?"

Moira lifted the bottle and took a long draught. "You know the hives we passed? The ones up on the far end of the field? There's something about the things we grow down here, don't know what it is, but it gives the honey a little kick of something special."

"Honey mead? I didn't realize I was in a Viking settlement," he chuckled.

"Actually, we do have some Scandinavians here," she said, "but they mostly bake bread. It's a Turkish family who makes most of the honey wine."

She handed the bottle back. He took a big swig and lay back on the soft soil, a warm contentedness glowing in his belly. That sensation only grew stronger when Moira lay down close beside him and started talking about her life, how she had a rough go of it up top, and how after being attacked and left for dead, Buddy John had saved her and brought her down to this place. The people welcomed her unquestioningly, and when she was finally well enough to leave, she had found she had no desire to.

For whatever reason, Donald found himself finding that not so difficult to understand. Perhaps it was the wine, perhaps it was the company, or perhaps it was some magical combination of things, but as they drank and talked, they each seemed to sense some kindred spark, almost as if they'd known one another for years.

A while later, lying in the comfortably warm air of the garden, surrounded by slumbering flowers, Donald and Moira joined them as they drifted off to sleep.

Donald woke several hours later, disoriented for a moment before remembering where he was. He felt the warmth of Moira's arm surprisingly, yet quite welcome, draped across him and looked at her face, studying its intricacies and details. At some point in the course of but a single day, it had somehow become the most beautiful thing he'd ever seen.

He stared a few moments longer, then, with a happy sigh, closed his eyes once more.

Feeling his body relax, Moira opened her eyes and fixed her gaze on him with a particular softness and warmth. She stared at the artist trapped in an office drone's body, studying his unusual but handsome features. A little smile graced her lips, then her eyelids growing heavy once more, the young woman drifted back to sleep.

They hadn't intended to hold hands as they walked.

Neither could recall reaching out to the other as they resumed their trek that morning, but they found themselves doing precisely that as they wove through the maze-like marketplace. It was a short walk through the electronics yard once the flood doors opened with the morning whistle. Moira was rather enjoying her role as impromptu guide.

"Over there is where they heat the old solder from the circuit boards and recycle the transistors and stuff," she said. "The folks down here don't always build things we need, but they love what they do so much that everyone trades with them anyway."

"So you buy junk?"

"No, we encourage creation and art," she said. She led him to a heavily tattooed man with a long, braided beard. "Hey Ox!" she called out loudly to the man bent over a jumble of smoking wires as he soldered.

"Hey, Moira," he said, looking up from his work.

"This is Donnie. He's new down here."

"Donald," he said softly.

"What?" Ox strained to hear.

"Nothing."

"Could you show him what you're working on?" Moira asked excitedly.

"Well, it isn't quite done yet," he mused a bit reluctantly, "but I don't see why not." Ox rose to his full six foot three height and reached across his sturdy workbench and flipped a switch mounted on a strange device with multiple vacuum tubes and wires running from it. "Still need to finish the body work, but for now…"

He reached out above the glowing components and slowly began to move his hand in the air. A beautiful tone emitted from the box at the far end of the device. He moved his other hand, switching between seemingly random gestures and adjustments of small knobs sticking up from a piece of polished wood. Layer upon layer of sound built up until a dense chorus sang out from the speaker. The volume kept increasing.

"Thanks, Ox, that's enough!" she yelled. "I said thanks, Ox!"

"Sorry, sometimes I get carried away," he said as he powered down the device.

"That's amazing. You made this all from scrap?" Donald marveled.

"Yeah, bits and bobs. You know, something to do. Sure beats a day job, am I right?" the large man laughed.

"That was beautiful, thanks," Moira said. "We've gotta get going. I'm taking him to meet Buddy."

A smile blossomed across Ox's face. "Excellent! Tell him I say hi will ya?"

"Sure thing."

"See ya, Donnie. Nice meeting you!"

"Nice meeting you too, Mr. Ox."

"Just Ox is fine," he laughed.

As they continued through the market, Donald ogled the countless stalls full of assorted scraps of electronics with a different eye. His world felt even more upside down than before and, considering the past twenty-four hours, that was saying something.

"He used to be a roadie for Mötley Crüe," she said. "Anything musical, Ox can fix it. Most everyone in this part of Lost & Found is like that in their own way."

Something dawned on him. "Wait, all these electronics, but there aren't any TVs or computers."

"Don't have much need for 'em, really," she replied. "We have a sort of belief down here. The more things you strive to own, the more your possessions wind up owning you."

"Very *Fight Club*," he mused.

"Maybe so, but that doesn't make it any less true. Besides, there's plenty of better things to do with your time than watch TV, anyway."

She took his hand as they exited the cavernous room, stepping into a tunnel lined with Christmas lights and all manner of tchotchkes dangling from the low ceiling.

"Come on," she said excitedly. "We're almost there."

Buddy John's castle, if one could really call it such, took up the bulk of a long yet narrow room with relatively high ceilings. Donald marveled that its shape somewhat reminded him of how they built row homes back East, a straight-through floor-plan designed to work in a restrictive environ.

"Hey Buddy!" Moira called out. "Buddy, it's Moira. I want you to meet someone!"

A rattling could be heard from behind the door as the latches holding it shut were pulled clear. The ornately decorated corrugated metal oval swung open on surprisingly quiet hinges. A middle-aged woman in a kimono stepped forward.

"Christ Moira, it's early," she lamented.

"That's Buddy John?"

The woman burst out a raspy laugh. "Oh, that's priceless. No sweetie, I'm not Buddy John. Where'd you dig this one up, Moira?" she asked, giving him the once-over. "He's kinda cute."

Donald felt a slight blush rise to his cheeks.

"He's from up top, Daisy. I brought him to meet Buddy."

From the depths of the abode, a man called out, "A new guest from Up Top? Oh my!" The sound of things knocking over echoed in the room as the owner of the voice made his way to the door.

The woman rolled her eyes. "Buddy, watch where you're walkin', will ya? I don't want to spend the day cleaning up, ya hear?"

The medium-built man in a beige bathrobe and Crocs stepped through the open doorway. His hair was shoulder-length but clean, and he had a good several weeks' worth of beard on him, but it was his eyes that really struck Donald. He had the eyes of a madman. Or a genius. Or possibly both, and for some reason, Donald found he couldn't help but like him.

"Hey, buddy, welcome to Lost and Found!" the king said as he wrapped his arms around Donald in a massive bear hug.

The hug went on a little too long for Donald's taste.

It was getting weird.

Donald was a guest, so he just patted the king on the back and waited for his release.

"Good hug, man," Buddy said as he finally released him. "Good hug! My name's John, but everyone just calls me Buddy. Come on in, make yourself at home!"

The inside of Buddy John's eclectically constructed

domicile was clean, if a bit cluttered. He had pack rat proclivities, but he seemed to keep them in check, for the most part. Daisy may have also had a hand in that.

Donald and Moira took a seat on a surprisingly comfortable old couch while Buddy grabbed the recliner across from them.

"Hey hon, could you grab us a pitcher of iced tea?"

"Sure, babe," the kimono-clad woman said, leaning in and planting a kiss on his furry face, then heading off to a far corner of the structure.

"So tell me buddy, how did you come to our little enclave?"

"Little? This place is sprawling. It took us the better part of two days to get here."

"That long?" he said with a wink at Moira. "Must've taken the scenic route. I suppose you probably came in from the Grand Avenue drain network. Heck, that's just about the farthest spot you could have possibly chosen. Sure didn't make it easy on yourself, did you?"

"I was lucky to have an excellent guide," he said, turning to his lovely couch-mate.

Buddy John noticed the color creeping into Moira's cheeks from the attention and focused his smiling eyes on Donald. "So what do folks call you anyway, buddy?"

"His name's Donnie. He's a writer." He caught the slightest of grins on Moira's face from the corner of his eye.

"My name's Donald," he clarified.

"Like the duck!" the jolly man laughed.

"Yeah, I suppose."

"Well Donald, there's something you should know about

this place." Buddy leaned forward, fixing his gaze on the wary newcomer. "It's something you have to take to heart, something you have to accept into your very soul if you want to survive."

The slightly menacing tone game Donald a chill.

"Ah, I'm just fuckin' with ya, man," he laughed, reclining. "Buddy's rule number one: we offer safe refuge for all who would seek it. You're welcome to stay as long as you want. And a writer, huh? Maybe you'll jot something down for our library once you get settled in. We're always looking for storytellers."

"But I need to get back. I mean my job…"

"Why do you want to leave?" Moira's voice was soft with something that made his stomach ache ever so slightly.

"I didn't say want to, I said I need to. It's just, my boss, and… I don't know, I just have to."

"Hey man, you do whatever you need to do for you. But listen up, there's one thing you gotta do. I mean it. For reals." Buddy leaned in again, the gaiety briefly leaving his eyes. "If you leave, you can't tell anyone about this place. Ever." He leaned back in his chair as Daisy returned with a tray of cool iced tea. "And believe me," he continued, "we'll know."

Donald felt an uneasiness flow over him, but then, as quickly as it had appeared, the menacing vibe was replaced with the familiar jokester king.

"Come on, drink up, man, guests first. No one can say old Buddy John broke his own rule!"

"Why did you take me to see Buddy?" Donald asked. "I mean he seems nice and all, but we spent the better part of two days getting there."

"Anyone who wants to stay here has to meet Buddy first. It's just how we do things down here."

"But he didn't even say anything important."

She stopped walking and sized him up silently for a moment. "It's not about what he said, Donnie, it's about what you did. He's got an uncanny knack for sniffing out bad eggs, and he gave you his blessing."

He mulled over her words a moment.

Watching him digesting the thought, Moira took his hand in hers and started off down the path.

They walked quietly, hand in hand, enjoying the quiet calm. The area was one of the agricultural ones, and it smelled of healthy soil and fresh air. Donald couldn't remember the last time he'd felt so good.

"This is a different path, isn't it?" he asked.

Moira paused. "Yes, it is," she said, "but don't worry, we'll be back at Pyke's shortly."

"But I thought we still have a full day to…" he saw her coy smile. "You did take the long way, didn't you?"

"I'm sorry, I thought…" she tried to slip her hand from his, but he gently tightened his grip.

"I'm glad you did," he said, drawing her closer as they walked.

Moira felt a flutter in her chest as a hot tear slid from her eye.

They were passing through another farming sector when they came upon a man pushing a makeshift cart. One of the wheels had broken and he could barely move the produce-laden vehicle.

"Hey, do you need a hand?" Donald surprised himself by calling out.

"I'd appreciate it, yeah," the man replied. "This thing's off-balance and I need to get these delivered before the whistle."

Moira and Donald's eyes met.

"We won't make it back today if we don't hurry, you realize that?"

He listened to her but didn't seem to mind. "Hey, what's another day, right? Besides, he could really use our help."

A happy grin sprouted on her bonny face.

"Well, then, let's get to it."

Donald took a push-rod and slid it into the frame of the cart near the bad wheel, while Moira shifted the load of vegetables toward the good one.

"Okay, let's give this a try."

Donald lifted with a grunt, and soon the cart was lurching forward, making unsteady but consistent progress forward.

Donald was exhausted when they finally reached the compound, but he felt fantastic, mentally if not physically. The screech of the bad wheel had drawn several people from their homes to see what the commotion was. What they saw was a stranger and Moira helping deliver their food.

"We're here," the man called out. "We can stop now."

With aching hands and back, Donald dropped the cart and leaned against the rickety beast.

From a small hut with a cobalt blue curtain for a front

door, the woman with Louis Vuitton shoulder pads emerged carrying a plastic cup of fresh water. Without a word, she offered it to Donald, who gratefully gulped it down, handing her the empty cup as the cool liquid settled in his belly.

"Thank you," he said.

The woman nodded then went back inside.

"Wow, Molly doesn't usually like strangers," Moira noted.

Donald had apparently made up for his first impression and, to be honest, he was feeling pretty damn good about it.

The deep whistle rang out through the air as people gathered their produce from the cart.

"Well, I guess we're stuck for the night," he said, smiling warmly at the girl with the scar standing at his side.

"Seems that way."

The man with the cart couldn't help but overhear them. "You need somewhere to rest your heads tonight? You're welcome to stay with me. It's the least I can do after your help."

"Thank you, that would be lovely," said Moira. "First, we should go trade for some food before it gets too late."

"Nothing doing, we take care of our own," the man said. "These folks gave of their time to help me deliver before the whistle. Who will contribute to their supper?" he called out.

One by one, each and every recipient of the delivery cart came forward with a carrot, or a potato, or some beans.

"You know what?" the man said. "I think this calls for a shindig."

The people of the cavern welcomed the excuse for festivities, and a potluck was done up proper in no time at all, with everyone contributing to an impressive spread. An impromptu band struck up, which only served to add to the ambiance, and, surrounded by good people, the tired travelers talked and danced until it was quite late. Donald even told a few stories, much to the delight of his new acquaintances.

Several hours, and many cups of honey wine later, Donald and Moira finally called it a night, curling up comfortably on their generous host's floor wrapped in the lightweight blanket he had offered from his sturdy foot locker. Exhausted, they melted into the floor and each other, a pair of nesting spoons, drifting happily to sleep.

Walking arm in arm back toward Pyke's shop the following morning, Donald seemed a different man. He had stopped looking at his watch, his eyes were open and bright, observing the myriad little details of the magical subterranean world. He had a happy glow to him, a glow that Moira seemed to share.

"I don't know," he said. "I mean, I guess I wouldn't miss it, really, but I kind of wanted to see how the show ends before giving up TV."

"Aha!" she chirped. "See, I knew you weren't so shallow."

"Shallow? Oh, that hurts!" he laughed back at her.

They entered a large chamber that seemed familiar to him. He felt perhaps he was getting a sense for the lay of the land and the seemingly random placement of communes, farms, and marketplaces.

"Hey, isn't this the one just before the hydroponic squash room?"

"It is! You're a quick study!"

"It's starting to make sense." To Donald, the thought of the unusual world was becoming less and less foreign by the minute. That is until a small boy darted past him into a small cardboard-walled workshop.

"Watch where you're running Billy, your elbows are pointy!" Moira chided the boy.

"Did you say Billy?" A flash of recognition crossed Donald's face.

"Yeah, he's a funny one, sometimes."

Donald pulled his hand from hers and raced after the boy. It was close quarters in the workshop he darted into, dozens of mp3 players and cell phones were strewn about the counter in varied states of disassembly.

"Hey, you can't barge in here!" the boy cried out.

The much larger man pushed him aside and snatched up a familiar glass and plastic rectangle. Placing his thumb on the fingerprint reader, Donald powered his phone on.

Eleven missed calls from work, and no signal.

"Shit, only 5% battery left," he lamented.

Moira hadn't followed him in, but when he emerged, neck craned down, eyes locked on the glowing phone cradled in his hand, she felt a little part of her die inside.

"Hey, we were going to get some blackberry lemonade, remember?"

He seemed distracted, waving the phone about, trying to find a signal.

"What? Oh, yeah. Look," he said, showing her the screen, "I've only got 5% left." He spun around trying to figure the best way out of the chamber. "I've got to get to the surface, I've got to check in…" he trailed off, that invisible tug of his miserable job reeling him back like an exhausted fish on an angler's line.

Moira stared at him, eyes wet.

"It's my boss. I've got to go," was all he managed to blurt out. He couldn't take the look on her face, so he turned away and dashed off in the direction he believed would get him back to the tunnels that had deposited him in this strange place.

He powered the phone off, hoping to save its battery until he found a signal, then moved at a quick trot, but in no time at all he was turned around, with no idea which way to go. All day he was on the move, but when the deep whistle sounded, he was still no closer to escape.

Hungry and alone in a sector totally unfamiliar to him, he traded his watch and a story for dinner and a crudely sketched out map of the major caverns, courtesy of a shaky-handed old-timer, who couldn't even remember how long he'd been down there.

That night he dozed fitfully, tossing and turning as his arms reached for a warm body that wasn't there. When the morning whistle sounded, he had hardly slept a wink, and his spirits were dragging even more for it.

He powered on his phone and held it aloft.

3%.

Phone off and back in his pocket, Donald unfolded the rudimentary map and took off in the direction that he believed should get him at least near where he had arrived.

The map was not exactly what one could call, "to scale," and it took several hours before he had covered what appeared to be a tiny distance on the page. He was beside himself. Nothing looked familiar, no landmarks stood out.

Then he saw it. Well, actually, he smelled it first, but as the sharp tang of the metalworks grew stronger in his nostrils he knew he was close. Maybe a half hour more until he'd be there, though he'd traded his watch and didn't dare power up his phone just to check the time.

By noon he had skirted the perimeter of the enormous chamber he had first arrived in twice, nearly missing the discreet entrance tucked among the clutter.

"Finally," he said as he stepped into the concrete tunnel.

Time, as previously noted, was markedly difficult to track underground, and Donald found himself hopelessly turned around. In fact, he had been for many hours. His elbows were scuffed, his knees filthy with mud. Apparently it was raining Up Top. Not a lot, at least not yet, but enough to make his forays into the maze of pipes that much more claustrophobic.

That much more dangerous.

He finally managed to find the large hub chamber, and holding his phone away from the slowly running water, scrambled his way up through the grate. Like spokes on a wheel, he was surrounded by pipes, but with his dusty footprints washed away, there was no way to tell which he had first arrived through. He powered on his phone.

2% and no bars.

He was close, he just knew it, though in the desperation of his flight to the surface he found himself thinking not of his tiny apartment or his stagnant life, but of the girl he'd left below. Holding back his emotions, Donald picked a pipe at random and crawled in headfirst.

The first pipe had led to a small junction room, but the

grates leading out were all welded in place.

Back to the hub.

The second pipe did an impossible ninety-degree bend straight up and there was no way he could contort his body to make the turn without breaking one or more vital bones first. It was unnerving as hell backing out of the pipe, inch by inch, but he managed.

A different pipe narrowed; yet another was like a failing artery, clogged with mud. It was hopeless. The only thing that kept him remotely sane were thoughts of Moira. He'd taken to replaying their time together to take his mind off the horrors of his directionless crawling through the dark pipes. He was exhausted, depressed, and overwhelmed by the hours of hopeless attempts to find his original path. Donald was all but ready to give up and just let the increasingly strong water flowing down the pipes put an end to his misery.

In the blackness, he powered on the phone.

1%.

Slowly, he backed out of yet another pipe and dropped to the chamber floor with a splash.

She was standing there, waiting.

Covered in muck, Donald splashed water on his face and wiped his eyes. She was still there when he opened them.

For a long while, he sat in the water as they stared at each other. Finally, he unsteadily rose to his feet and walked to her.

"You're here," he said, tears welling in his eyes. "You came."

"I had to," was all she managed to say before lunging into his welcoming arms.

He held her tight, afraid to let go, afraid to ever let her go.

"You're okay, Donald," she said, a bright flash of her feelings showing in her eyes.

"Call me Donnie," he replied. She was about to make a clever comment when he silenced her with a kiss.

He let the phone in his hand fall into the water and be carried away as he laced his fingers with hers, the warmth in his chest threatening to burst through his ribcage.

"I'm lost," he said to her softly.

"No," she replied, "you're found."

Son of a Gun

It had taken nearly three days before the neighbors finally came around after the killing.

They had forced the door open, finding him safely locked inside the clapboard shack, covered in his own feces, a fever wracking his tiny body as hunger and dehydration ravaged him to the point of near death.

With all the excitement the boy had been almost forgotten, what with the marshals riding into town stirring things up in the aftermath. It was only when the coffin-maker finished his ghoulish job and the townsfolk got around to laying Copperhead Jack McKee to rest in the hard red ground that young Micah McKee's absence was noted.

The red-haired boy was lean and energetic, but had a quietness to his gaze that some people found unsettling. Like his father, Micah McKee had the eyes of a killer, even though he was just a pup of six years old.

He hadn't cried when they told him his father was gone, shot dead in the street by Dusty Greer, rumored to be one of the fastest guns in a thousand miles. A man who only shot to kill. No, he didn't shed a tear; instead, the child picked up his father's well-oiled Colt revolvers and planned his revenge.

No six-year-old, not even the son of a famous gunslinger like Copperhead Jack, would be able to shoot one of his legendary .45 pistols. Still, the good Reverend O'Connor knew the boy and thought letting him fail in his attempt would get the devil out of his system and set him on a better path.

BLAM!

The gunshot knocked Micah square on his behind. Somehow, the boy had managed to keep his double-handed grip on the pistol. As the priest approached, a look of worry spread across his face. The stubborn lad had broken both arms from the concussion, but rather than crying in pain, he was sitting happier than a pig in shit as he stared lovingly at the beastly weapon cradled in his hands, pale blue smoke wafting from its barrel like a dancing beast, seducing the lad with its serpentine movement.

"Come on son, we've got to get you to Doc Cotter."

He squirmed and fought as the priest tried to pry the weapon from his hands as gently as he could. "Don't worry, Micah. You'll get this back, I promise, but right now we have to fix your arms, alright?"

Micah's gaze shifted, and he reluctantly released his grip.

By the time the plaster came off a month and a half later, Micah had devised his training regimen. Every day at sunup, he was going to clean and oil his guns. At noon, he would practice the quick draw motions, just as he'd seen his father do on countless occasions. Empty-handed, he would draw over and over against an imaginary foe. He knew he wasn't strong enough to heft the mighty steel and walnut pieces inherited upon his father's demise, not yet anyway, so he devised a plan to grow stronger.

"I need to squeeze rocks," he had told Doc Cotter while the plaster casts were being applied.

"Oh?" The doctor had replied, a bit surprised. "And why would you do a thing like that?"

"Get strong."

"You're only six, Micah. You'll get stronger when you're a man, don't you fret."

"No, can't wait that long. Gotta start now."

His father had once read to him from an old book the story of a famous swordsman seeking revenge. He had trained vigorously and developed his wrists into near-invincible extensions of his body by squeezing rocks.

Often.

Daily.

Rocks.

Once the stubborn boy had set his path, there was no one who could dissuade him from his plan. He was going to squeeze rocks until his grip could crush walnuts. Then he would wield his father's guns. Then he would seek his revenge.

The thing about revenge is, it's all fine and dandy when the blood is flowing and the anger is fresh, but even for the most dedicated of vengeful offspring, there are bound to be periods of boredom. And so it was that after a solid seven years of training, Micah was slowly getting tired of waiting. His grip was like a vise, thanks to his dedication to his daily training regimen, and at thirteen years old, he was filling out into a solid young man.

Three years had been what it took Micah to heft the weapons. Three years of squeezing rocks until he had finally managed to fire off a shot on target without harming himself. He already knew how to strip, clean, and oil the guns long before that. He'd watched his father countless times and could do it himself with his eyes blindfolded.

For the next four years, the real training began in earnest, and he went through countless rounds of ammunition, firing until his arms and hands were too tired to lift the pistols. Fortunately for Micah, while his father hadn't left him much in the way of money, the old gunslinger had amassed a huge stockpile of ammunition. He had been a hoarder of sorts, but rather than food or finery, he had acquired boxes of ammunition whenever he had extra cash, not to mention the arsenal of guns and ammo taken from those he had shot down over the course of his bloody career. Now it was Micah's time, and this unintentional gift from his father let him focus entirely on his training.

By the time he was eleven, his aim was impeccable. The locals all told him so; he was a downright protégé they had said. Miss Roberts, the pretty young schoolteacher whose classroom he sometimes graced with his presence, was not fond of violence, but she had taken a liking to Micah and sought to bolster his esteem. Even she had said he should be proud of his skills, and that he was a very talented young man.

He hated being called that.

"Young man."

He longed to be a full-grown man so he could head out of town on his own to seek his revenge, but he wasn't old enough yet to put his skills to work and earn enough for the train fare needed to track down that filthy cur Dusty Greer. That and his rotating foster families would hear nothing of it. A child running off with a pair of six-shooters? Inconceivable.

Still, he remained focused. Along with the red hair, the drive for revenge was something else he had inherited from his father, though many in town would whitewash that little bit of Copperhead McKee's history. He had kept them safe, after all, for the most part anyway, so one could overlook certain "issues." They'd sometimes see that familiar look in Micah McKee's eye and wonder just how much like his father he'd grow up to be. Fortunately, he was still too young to be embroiled in drinking and womanizing like his father had been.

It was on a slightly chilly spring day nearly eight years after his father's death that Micah McKee was roused from his sleep by one of the younger kids from his school.

"Micah! Micah!"

He rubbed the sleep-sand from his eyes and trudged to the door.

"Phineas, what are you doing here? I know your pa's a farmer, but I don't get up that early. You know that."

"Micah, he's back!"

"Who's back?"

"Dusty Greer."

Any hint of sleep that had lingered in Micah's eyes was replaced by a cold, steely glare.

"You sure?" he growled, sounding much older than his thirteen years.

"Course I am. He rode in early, said he was lookin' to get some chow before heading on toward Union City."

"How long's he been there?" Micah asked with urgency in his voice.

"Maybe twenty minutes."

Micah was frantically dressing. This was his chance. He

didn't need to buy train fare, he didn't need to hunt the man down, he just needed to get to him before he rode out of town. Lord, he hoped the son of a bitch ate slow.

Rapidly dressed and flushed from the hurry, Micah strapped his father's guns to his hips and stepped out into the brisk morning air. He'd forgotten his overcoat, but the cold would burn off soon enough, and with the adrenaline flooding his body, he didn't even notice the chill. Today was the day he would avenge his father.

"Dusty Greer, you worthless son of a filthy whore!" he had shouted as he burst into the saloon. "Which one of you is Dusty Greer?"

"Now Micah," Mister Jonas said as he tried to usher him back out the double doors. "You don't want to go and make any fuss this morning. You should go home."

"I ain't goin' nowhere. That cur murdered my old man and I'm gonna make him pay."

The lean man sitting toward the back of the saloon put down his fork and paused in his meal. His mustache, which bounced and bobbed as he chewed his mouthful, was scattershot with gray, just like his dark, slicked-back hair. He looked up at Micah from his food, sizing the boy up in an instant, his eyes pausing ever so briefly on the twin guns on his hips. With a reluctant sigh he slid one hand beneath the table.

"I don't much like your tone, son. Now I'm Dusty Greer, if that's really who you're lookin' fer. I'm tryin' ta eat here, so would you mind tellin' me what's so important you gone and interrupted my breakfast?" He picked up his fork with his left hand and shoveled in another mouthful, chewing slowly as he watched the angry boy. His right hand didn't budge, staying securely out of sight below the table.

"You killed my father!" Micah shouted. "You shot him down in cold blood."

"Son, I've killed a lot of men. You're gonna to have to be more specific than that," he drawled, not once taking his eyes off the boy.

"My name is Micah McKee. My pa was Copperhead Jack McKee, and you killed him!"

Dusty Greer paused, fork halfway to his mouth. His face paled ever so slightly as he digested what the boy had said.

"You say you're Jack McKee's boy? I thought his son had died in childbirth, along with his wife."

"That was my little brother, you no-good son of a bitch."

Dusty twitched at the insult, but then his shoulders relaxed a bit and his eyes softened. Slowly, he put his right hand back up on the table and locked eyes with the boy.

"There's some things you need to know about that business," he said. "Why don't you come and sit down with me and we'll talk about it. There's no need for violence."

Micah flew into a rage.

"What, the great Dusty Greer's a yellow-belly chicken? You a coward, is that it? Well you should be afraid. I'm twice as fast as my daddy ever was, and I'm gonna fill you full of holes. Nothin' you say's gonna change that."

"I don't want to fight you, kid." He sounded like a deflating balloon that wanted no part of any trouble with a pointy new needle.

Micah pulled the pistol from his right holster.

"You don't have a choice."

Micah hadn't even noticed that Dusty's hand was once more below the table, but the seasoned gunfighter still showed no signs that he desired any part of an escalation.

At that moment, a young red-haired boy, no older than eight, walked in from the street.

"Pa, I watered the horses like you asked."

Micah turned to look at the child. Everyone in the saloon did, some with a sad hint of recognition as they laid eyes on him.

"Now Jesse, we're going to get a move on and be on our way. I want you to wait for me at the stable, alright?"

"But Pa, I wanna…"

"Jesse Ezekiel Greer, you do as you're told, ya hear?"

"Yes sir." The child slunk out of the saloon leaving a very confused gun-wielding boy in his wake.

"You bein' a daddy don't change nothin," he said across the room.

"It changes everything, don't you see. You and me, we need to talk. About man things. About what your pa did." He fidgeted with the wedding ring on his finger. "Just put down that gun and…"

The shot was deafening inside the walls of the saloon as Micah fired into the ceiling.

"I don't care what you say, I'm calling you out, mister! You made me an orphan, now I'm gonna do the same to your boy."

Dusty tensed, then let out a sad sigh.

"Alright kid, have it your way."

The boy's reflexes were fast, everyone said so. His aim

was always true. His weapons were some of the finest to be found this side of the Mississippi and felt as natural a part of his body as his hands and arms. He was Copperhead Jack McKee's boy alright. You could see it plain as day.

None of that mattered.

Standing in the street, ready to avenge his father after all those years, Micah had barely twitched for his guns when, faster than you can blink, a large hole appeared in his forehead, dropping him to the dirt in a bloody heap.

Dusty Greer scanned the crowd.

"You folk should have told him!" he shouted out to the townspeople. "None of this didn't need to happen. If you'd just told him." He holstered his pistol and walked toward the stables. Jessie was waiting for him, horses ready.

"Pa, I heard shootin'."

"Nothin ta worry about Son. Now let's get a move on."

"Did you see that boy in the saloon?" he asked excitedly. "He had hair like me. I can't wait to tell Ma!"

Dusty turned his head. Surely it was just dust or the wind that made his eyes well up.

"Yeah Son, that'll be nice," he said as he swung up onto his horse. "You can tell her all about it when we get back from Union City."

The two rode off, leaving the son of Copperhead Jack to be buried in the hard red soil, right beside his father.

"Wait, not yet… just a little more… Now Plycar, break left! Now! Now! Now!"

I acted on instinct, diving and rolling our craft to the left, as ordered. That first and overriding instinct was bred into me and reinforced from the moment of my birth. The second instinct driving my actions was a very tangible desire not to die, the very act of which would place my remains firmly on the receiving end of Commander Revnik's rage. Failure was simply not an option. Not if we intended to survive this day, and certainly not if we were to win the war, and the commander was going to do everything in his power to see to that outcome.

The cloud of pulsing radio-toxin speeding toward our ships swirled and twisted in wave after deadly wave as the fleet bucked and dove, every ship for itself as we tried every maneuver possible to avoid its deadly touch.

"Aft recon wing is reporting forty percent casualties, sir!" Poor Sydrian was running comms after Caxilia's untimely demise, and was thus the unfortunate one tasked with reporting the bad news to the commander. Certainly not an enviable job.

The commander bristled at the number. "Forty percent," he growled. "Those damn bastards, they took out nearly half our backup ships."

"Sir, incoming signals." Sydrian double-checked the screen, then, with a shaky voice, added, "Oh no. It's a swarm of Jecters."

The control center grew suddenly silent, all attention fixed on the commander. Jecters were relatively new in the war, and they wrought devastation through parts of the fleet not heavily armored enough to withstand their onslaught. Worse was the horrible fate that awaited those inside a targeted vessel. Once the horrific device's legs locked onto a ship, it was only a matter of time before their deadly base plate attached itself flush to the hull and began eating its way through the layers of defense. If the ship wasn't strong enough to withstand the onslaught, the Jecter's deadly payload would be deployed into the crew-space, killing everyone on board in a matter of hours. Sometimes mere minutes.

"Targeting trajectory?" the commander asked.

"Two-One-Five Bravo, sir."

"Order detachments two through five to rendezvous at emergency retreat point Echo. Detachment one and six are to cover our retreat and regroup. If they can."

"But sir…"

"If we don't move now, the entire fleet is lost. Send the order."

With reluctance, Sydrian did as commanded, and the bulk of the fleet turned tail and ran. It wouldn't be the first time.

I don't know who it is exactly we are at war with, nor do I know why. It's just the way things have always been. I don't even know how long the war has been raging; though from what I've heard, it may have started ages ago with a quiet series of guerrilla battles, skirmishes which raged for quite some time before things became public and it evolved into an all-out war.

As long as I've been alive, combat is all I've known. It has been in my every thought since the moment I was pulled from the cloning cell and dropped into my first battle, fresh and ready to fight.

Day one, it had taken a few minutes to get up to speed. I was, after all, essentially a newborn fighting in a war of epic scale and violence. Still, I did my job, admirably my colleagues told me, reactions coming on line quickly, hardwired training kicking in the moment we came under attack. I was one of the better pilots it turned out, and we'd survived many tough situations because of it.

Our fleet is a marvel to behold, a masterfully designed network designed to overcome a variety of obstacles. On the surface it seems to be merely a uniform series of identical ships, but we possess a few tricks up our sleeve that give us an edge. One of them is our ships' ability to adapt to, deflect, and disable new attack methods. If conditions are right, we can modify our fleet to endure a variety of deadly foes, though we also invariably lose quite a few in the process.

That's the thing: war is ugly and people die. We just do our best to adapt, to overcome, to survive, and hopefully come out victorious.

Victorious against whom, as I've said, I really don't know. Then again, that's way above my pay grade.

What has consistently made our attacks devastatingly effective is our fleet's ability to teleport to the location of a select few specially designed scout vessels. These ships find weaknesses in the enemy's defenses. Then, once they've nestled in, hidden from view, they send the signal and one by one our fleet joins them, slowly amassing until a force of devastating strength lies dormant, ready to spring forth and wreak havoc.

More often than not, when the enemy discovers our presence it is too late. We've already taken over key systems, colonizing some, destroying others. If the stars have aligned just right, we can even take over enemy factories and begin producing replacements for our fleet from their own resources. Like I said, we're efficient and we're deadly.

Sometimes they unleash radiological weaponry against us. It's a horrific thing to do; barbaric and indiscriminately destructive. I've personally seen (from a safe distance as we made our escape) clouds of their deadly payload destroy both friend and foe alike. Sure, they have taken out scores of our invading ships with this method, but at what cost? They are killing their own in hopes of taking a few of us out in the process. Acts like these leave me wondering what kind of backward foes we're up against.

Other times they'll surprise us with something new. Oh, that's an experience I hope to never have again. The sinking feeling. The sensation of dread, knowing something new, something deadly, is coming our way, but having no idea what it is or how to deal with it. That's how it was with the arrival of the Jecters (as the commander had dubbed them because of the way they injected their payload into our ships).

At first we had thought they were simply recon probes drifting into our sector. They weren't overly large, and there was no radiological signal. They seemed benign.

When the screams of the dying began flooding our command center speakers as ships came under attack, we had been forced to flee. It was a tough lesson to learn, but one we took to heart quickly.

Fortunately for us, the commander was well-versed in unconventional warfare and knew quite well how to run and hide, amass a new force, and then strike back at the enemy even harder.

That's what we're doing now. Building up. Getting stronger. Preparing.

"Plycar, have you located a Slipstream yet?" The commander peered at the screen in front of me.

"The radiological assault has left a residual haze to the scans sir, but I think I may have located one. Suggest sending a recon ship."

"We just lost nearly half our smaller vessels. I can't spare one, not yet. Get the processing crew on the horn. I want to know if there are any enemy resources we can exploit to construct new ships in this sector."

The commander makes sense. He always makes sense, that's why he's in charge. Between the Jecters we recently fled and the remnants of the radio-toxin, we are not only depleted and in need of new ships, but also in a somewhat precarious position, boxed in on multiple sides while we lick our wounds and regroup. Of course that's why he wants me to zero in on a Slipstream.

The Slipstreams are a little-understood high-speed transit system built by the enemy. It affords us a means to move quickly to distant places, but not all of them are hospitable, and unless we have a scout on the other end sending us a tether beacon, once we're in, we're flying blind.

Without warning all the screens began to flash and dim, a low hum filling the ship.

"Plycar, report!"

"I don't know, sir," I replied, and I truly didn't know. "This seems to be something new."

The look on the commander's face said enough, and I had already begun frantically scanning for a slipstream. Recon ship be damned, the remnants of the fleet were cornered, and we had to get out of here now.

A faint pulse enveloped the ship, but it didn't seem to do any harm.

"Sir, no damage reported," Sydrian called out. "The entire fleet has been pinged, but no incoming rad-clouds or Jecters."

"I don't like this," he muttered.

A second pulse hit us. It felt different from the first, but again we seemed unscathed.

"Fleet pinged again, sir. Ships still reporting no damage."

"That's it, we can't wait. Plycar, plot a course for what looks like the best bet for a Slipstream."

"On it!" Scans started flying by on the screen. Fast. Far too fast for anyone but a pilot clone to comprehend, and to me, it was all making sense.

"Sir!" I exclaimed. "I've got one!"

"Send the details to all captains! All ships, top speed to new coordinates. Rendezvous at…"

The first beam returned, joined by the second, and while individually they had no effect, their joint energy signatures were making the ship rattle.

"Plycon, get us out of here!"

Those were the last words Commander Revnik would ever utter.

A third beam engulfed the fleet.

On their own, the beams had appeared to be simple scans causing no ill-effect. Combined, they coalesced their energies into a focused death ray and blasted through every single ship like a divine firestorm, crushing their hulls, destroying their payloads, and shriveling their crews to husks.

In no time at all, the entire fleet and every last soul in it was destroyed.

Doctor Whelan knocked quietly on the door, then entered. "Good to see you, Jennifer," he said to the bald-headed young woman seated on the exam table. The bags under her eyes told the tale of a weary warrior, battle-tried and on the edge but not giving up. Not yet.

"Hello Doctor," she managed, the anxiety clear in her wavering voice.

"Well let's get right down to it. I have your scans and blood work, and it looks like we got it all." He allowed himself a rare smile as he saw the relief on her face blossom, tears of joy welling up in her crystalline blue eyes. "Now, I want you back in a year for a follow-up, but I'm very happy to tell you that the Gamma Knife and chemo did the trick. You're in full remission."

Tears streamed down her face as she lurched to her feet and hugged him, her rail-thin arms squeezing tight as sobs of joy racked her body.

The nurse saw Jennifer leave the building, head held high, a positive glow enveloping her otherwise weary body. Doctor Whelan watched with a smile until she was out the door, at which point the smile slid from his face as he turned to the pile of folders resting atop the nurses' station.

"Hey," the young nurse said to him. "Smile a little, you won one."

He managed the slightest of smirks, just for an instant, then his battle-hardened look slid back into place.

"Yeah, this time we won," he picked up the folder at the top of the pile and started walking to his next patient, "but there are other wars still raging, and you know as well as I do that we won't win them all."

...or maybe some nice cabbage. Yes, I think so. They're finally ripened up, and that would be downright lovely, the enormous troll thought to himself as he reclined beside the rushing waters, propped up on an elbow in the cool shade beneath the ancient stone bridge. *I think the strawberry patch downstream should be ripe by now, and they'll make a fine dessert.* A smile blossomed across his jagged features at the thought of his repast.

Now the troll was a rather huge fellow, and while his mother (long turned to stone in a freak eclipse incident) would have said he was her beautiful little boy, he was well aware just how different he was from other folk. Take his head, for example. A massive thing it was, like a boulder with a face, solidly formed with a thick brow and ample jawline. It was that jawline that intimidated so many people, their imaginations running wild at the thought of those tombstone teeth gnashing down on their bones, grinding them to dust. Of course that would never happen. He'd been a vegetarian for well over a decade and quite enjoyed his healthier fare. He even noticed his skin seemed to soften from its calcified roughness somewhat after the first few years of his new diet.

Few passed this way anymore, and he was glad for it. *I leave them alone, they leave me alone,* he'd thought when he discovered the old bridge and taken refuge in the shadows underneath. Though he wanted to tell people he meant them no harm, his pronounced discomfort talking to strangers, combined with (and amplified by) his fairly significant speech impediment, eventually drove him to become a recluse.

Bumble was the youngest of three, and where her older brothers had strength and cunning, she was gifted with a particular loveliness. Her hair was soft and golden, her teeth white and straight, and her ears were not too big, but also not too small. She presented quite an attractive package not often found in goats.

She was out for a walk that afternoon, foraging for something more interesting to eat than her boring staple of grass and leaves.

"Grass is brain food," Grumble had said. Her brother, the middle of the trio, was the intellect of the family. "Mark my words: eat your grass and you'll be sharp as a horn."

"Leaves give you strong teeth," their elder brother, Gruff, had said between mouthfuls of tough foliage. For him it was all about being the biggest, the strongest, the most aggressive, and he ate constantly, always looking for an edge to be even stronger than he already was. He certainly was the most fearsome goat in the entire valley, and because of it, Bumble enjoyed a certain freedom to do as she pleased. None of the other goats would dare look at her the wrong way lest they face the ire of Gruff and the thick skull from which sprouted his massive curved horns.

She chuckled to herself at her brothers' words as she scanned for something better to fill her belly. "The boys just don't understand the needs of a pretty girl's stomach."

So engrossed was she, taking in the sights as she looked for a tasty treat, that she had failed to notice just how far she'd walked.

"Oh my, I'm an awfully long way from home. I suppose I should turn back," she said to herself, but then her sensitive nose picked up the smell of something wonderful. Fresh water, yes, but also wafting ever so subtly on the river-dampened breeze was the enticing aroma of vegetables.

She took off at a trot and soon reached the shores of the river. The current flowed quickly, much too fast for her to swim across, but from her vantage point she saw a fine garden with row after row of delicious vegetables frustratingly out of her reach on the other side of the rushing water.

From the corner of her eye, she saw what appeared to be the ruins of an old stone bridge just upstream.

"Excellent! All those delicious veggies will be mine!" She hurried to the ancient bridge and took a tentative step upon it, her hoof sliding on the mossy stone. The bridge was in a treacherous state of disrepair, and a wise goat would have turned back, but what Bumble possessed in beauty, she lacked in wisdom, so with a determined snort, she jumped upon the loose stones and scurried across, stumbling with every step.

"Almost there!"

The stone came loose before she even had a chance to react, and much to her surprise, Bumble found herself tumbling toward the water, her legs frantically scrambling for purchase, but to no avail.

"Help!" she cried out, desperate, knowing even if she were a strong swimmer, she could not survive the roaring waters.

She hit the water with a splash and was immediately swept up in the current, when she suddenly felt a painful yank on her hair. Before she knew what was happening, she found herself suspended above the raging waters, coughing and snorting, but alive.

The troll carried her across the bridge to the trail she'd come from and put her down as gently as he could, which wasn't all that gentle, though in his defense, trolls aren't exactly known for their finesse.

Bumble, embarrassed and wet, shook the water off and sized up the troll.

"Iuh, youwerr fullingso… um, caughtya," the giant troll mumbled in his unintelligible drawl.

The young goat wasn't afraid, he seemed harmless enough, but then she caught sight of the tufts of her beautiful golden hair still entwined in his massive fingers.

"My hair!" she cried out. "You've ruined my hair! How dare you attack me like that!"

"Nnnoo, dinnnttacknnnoobodyyy."

"Wait until my brothers hear about this! You'll be sorry!"

He watched her as she ran off home, sad that even his good deed couldn't help him make a new friend. Resigned to his life of solitude, the troll shuffled back over the bridge, noting just how loose the stones were.

Maybe I should do something about that, he thought. *Unless I want to keep pulling people out of the river.*

Back at the family den, Bumble ran crying to her brothers.

"What's the matter little sis?" asked Grumble.

"There was a terrible giant troll at the river beyond the far east pasture. He attacked me and wanted to eat me. I just barely escaped with my life. Look what he did to my hair! He tried to grab me but I was too fast and ran away."

Gruff was enraged. "I'll kill him! I'll ram him until he's a pulp! I'll…"

"Hang on, brother," Grumble calmly stood in his path. "Let me go see how big he is first, and if he has any other friends there. We wouldn't want to be his supper, now would we?"

"Alright, but then I clobber him!"

Grumble nodded and trotted off toward the bridge. He knew his sister had a tendency to exaggerate and even make up entire events, but something had ripped the hair from her back, and he was damned sure going to find out what it was.

He arrived at the bridge and noticed, as his sister had, the garden on the other side. Saliva flooded his mouth.

When's the last time I had cabbage? he thought. Then he saw the shadow beneath the bridge move. The troll was bigger than he had imagined, stretching taller and taller as he rose from the shadows.

"Stop right there!" Grumble shouted. "I only came for, um…" He had to think fast. "I came to find food for my family."

The troll glanced at his garden, then back at the goat. Then he did it again, realization crossing his face.

Oh you wicked beast, you planted it as a trap! thought Grumble as the troll slowly mounted the bridge and started crossing toward him.

"I'mmmhhapppeeeee shhhhhaarrrrrewwiffyoooo," he called out in his bellowing jumble of sounds that passed for language as he crossed the crumbling stones. "Pllennneeeeeefrrrralll," he was saying when a stone shifted and he stumbled and nearly fell. The troll grabbed a large piece of stone as he righted himself, the crumbling chunk breaking off in his hand as he stood upright.

He's going to beat me to death with a stone! thought Grumble, and with a startled yelp, he turned tail and fled as fast as his legs would carry him.

The troll looked at the fluffy tail as it disappeared into the distance.

I wonder why he ran off like that? he thought. Then he noticed the stone in his hand. *Oh, of course. He was scared the bridge might collapse if he tried to cross,* he thought as he tossed the chunk of stone to the shore. A look crossed his massive face as an idea dawned on him. Turning from the bridge, the troll set off with a purposeful stride.

"He was going to eat me!" Grumble managed to blurt, thoroughly out of breath.

"He was?" Bumble seemed shocked. "I mean, of course he was."

"That's it, I'm going to clobber him," Gruff growled.

"He's too big and strong, even for you," Grumble said. "We'll need a plan if you're going to stand a chance."

And so they planned, the three siblings conspiring a way for Gruff to deliver a beating to the big, mean troll until he had no choice but to flee, after which they would have all the delicious vegetables to themselves.

Three days had passed, and the other goats in the area had heard what Gruff planned to do. An excited chatter buzzed through the herd as the siblings, ready in their preparation, headed off to confront the monster.

"Something looks different," said Grumble as they approached the bridge.

"Well, we have a plan to follow, so just focus on that, unless you want to be troll food."

"Right, right," muttered Grumble, unable to place what felt wrong.

As planned, Bumble trotted to the bridge and feigned injury. They had decided she'd be the best bait, as she'd escaped his clutches once already and he'd likely not want that to happen a second time. Meanwhile, Grumble hid in a bush near the bridge, ready to dart across when the troll was distracted.

"Oh, my poor leg!" cried Bumble. "What will I do? I can't even walk!"

Even stoic Gruff felt a shiver run down his spine when he saw the size of the troll emerging from under the bridge. The giant beast seemed to recognize Bumble, and with what could only be a look of bloodlust and hunger, he started clamoring across the bridge. "Sssssookkaayyy I'lllllhelllllpppppyooo," the beast bellowed, obviously declaring his intent to devour their little sister, bones and all.

As the troll neared the shore, Grumble steeled his nerves, then darted past him across the bridge.

"Something isn't right," he thought as he easily reached the far side, but that thought was pushed from his mind when the startled troll turned back toward him, a look of confusion in his eyes.

"That's right, I'm here! Come on, I'm the bigger one, come get me!"

What a strange fellow, thought the troll, *but I can't hear what he's saying over the river*. He started to cross the bridge back toward the other side when Gruff charged his exposed back, laying the full force of his thick skull and horns into the troll's kidneys.

The troll dropped to his knees in pain and turned his head, tears streaming from his eyes, to see what had hit him.

"Whyyyyyyy?" he managed to blurt just as Gruff leapt with a furious burst and drove his horns into the troll's chin. The impact rocked the bridge, and even Gruff felt dazed from it. From either side of the river, his siblings watched as the stunned troll didn't collapse to the stones, but rather tumbled backwards, over the edge and into the rushing river, disappearing from sight and not reappearing.

Grumble rushed back to his sister. "Are you alright?"

"I'm fine," she said, a sadness to her voice. "Gruff, why did you do that? You said you were just going to scare him off."

"Well, he's gone now and won't be attacking anyone else ever again."

Grumble finally realized what seemed different. "The bridge, someone repaired it," he said. A large, flat stone at the foot of the bridge caught his eye.

"Sis, what's wrong?" asked Gruff. "You look sad, but we won."

She paused, a tear in her eye, then lowered her head in shame.

"He didn't attack me," she said. "He saved me from the river, pulled me out by my hair. I was mad, but I didn't mean for…" She trailed off as the shame washed over her.

"You should see this," said Grumble.

Bumble and Gruff trotted over to the stone Grumble was staring at. Carved into it was a message:

For all of you across the river, please use this bridge in safety and friendship and share in the bounty of my garden.

The three stood there a moment, then the voices of curious herd members reached them through the trees. Gruff took a step back, then smashed the tablet repeatedly with his mighty horns until there was nothing left to read.

"The billygoat Gruff defeated the evil troll!" a young goat cried out as he approached.

Grumble looked at his brother, then, with a sigh, called out to the approaching herd.

"Come, friends, share with us the bounty on the other side and fear the troll no more."

Bumble, for once, found herself without an appetite.

Worst. Superhero. Ever.

Tyler Wilkes was having a particularly bad evening. Not lost-my-keys or clogged-the-toilet bad. Tyler was on fire, and he couldn't seem to put himself out. Mind you, he was fireproof (at least most of the time), but a lot of good that did the rest of the building.

"Shit, this is *so* not good," he cursed as he tried to maneuver out of the jewelry store without accidentally igniting anything else with his touch.

A lithe auburn-haired woman in a catsuit teased from a safe distance, "If I'd known you were so hot for me I would have brought marshmallows and chocolate. We could've made s'mores!" She wore a mask, but her eyes sparkled with amusement as she watched the bumbling hero's plight.

"Please, just toss me that fire extinguisher! You may be a thief, but I know you're not some evil nutjob bent on destruction. Throw it to me, and I promise I'll let you go."

"Not like you have much choice about that," she quipped with a haughty laugh.

"Come on, you got your shiny things. There's no need to let the whole building go up in flames."

She thought about it for a minute. Doing good? Not on her to-do list, but the poor guy seemed to be having a particularly bad go of it today.

"Oh, alright," she finally relented, pulling the canister from the wall and tossing it to the blazing man.

He snatched it from the air, but before he could even aim the nozzle, he was engulfed in a powdery explosion as his hands melted right through the pressurized container, releasing its contents with a dusty boom.

Luck was on his side for a change, and the majority of the flames were extinguished in the detonation, the lingering suppressant providing him a tiny window of opportunity to get the hell out of the building, and hopefully not cause any more damage.

He dove out the front door and hit the pavement with a thud before rolling to a stop against a parked Mercedes, which, of course, immediately burst into flames.

"You've got to be kidding me!" he lamented as he pulled free of the smoldering car and dashed to the nearby fire hydrant. Unfortunately on this particular day, his super strength was a no-show yet again.

A small shockwave and gust of wind fanned his flames when Captain Stupendous landed on the pavement beside him. All down the street, car alarms shrieked, triggered by the impact. He could have touched down gently, but that wasn't his style. Flashy. He opted instead for the incredibly cliché superhero landing: knee and fist on the ground, an arm up in the air.

Despite being on fire, Tyler Wilkes, aka The Protector, couldn't help but roll his eyes behind his flaming mask.

"Well well, it seems The Protector needs help from a *real* hero yet again," the Captain said with a smirk, his pearly-white teeth glistening in the glow of the fire.

Captain Stupendous was the most respected and successful superhero in the entire region. He was also an insufferable prick.

"Help me!" The Protector begged. "I can't put myself out!"

"Powers not working again?" The square-jawed hero chuckled. "God, you're such a loser."

With just two fingers, he spun the cover free from the hydrant and opened the sturdy iron valve as easily as turning a faucet. A huge gush of water sprayed out, and in short order, The Protector's flames were finally extinguished.

"You've got to get her out of there," he sputtered, water dripping from every inch of his body. *Well, at least it burned outside my costume this time,* he thought. Once he had found himself smoldering and nude, forced to streak through the city with super-speed, ass cheeks flapping in the wind as he raced back to his secret hideout. He was thankful to not have a repeat of that event.

"A damsel you say? Captain Stupendous is on it!"

"Did you seriously just say damsel?"

The Captain took a single powerful step forward to swoop in and save the day, but stopped abruptly in his tracks when he heard the sound. A dulcet wave of a woman's song floated through the air, just barely tickling his ears.

Frozen mid-stride, like a hero-shaped statue, he managed with great effort to cast an angry eye on The Protector, unaffected, as the Captain struggled with all his might to turn and flee.

"I'm going to get you for this!" he managed to growl at the soggy hero through his frozen-shut teeth.

"Hiya, Captain!" The Siren sang out as she exited the smoldering jewelry store. "So nice to see you again!" The dulcet rhythm of her voice floated through the air, just within earshot of the distressed hero.

With every ounce of his strength, the mighty captain

somehow forced his muscles to obey his will, and in the blink of an eye, he leapt high in the air, landing several blocks away and well out of earshot, safe from the song against which he had no defense.

The Siren stopped her little tune and gave the drenched hero a once-over. "You gonna be alright?"

"Yeah," The Protector replied, slowly getting to his feet.

The wailing of the fire trucks was getting closer.

"Well, you'd better get going," he grumbled.

"What, you're not going to try to catch me again?"

"I gave you my word."

"That doesn't stop most men."

"I'm not most men."

"True, you are rather unique. I still don't know why my song doesn't affect you. Of all the heroes I've ever met, you're still the only one immune to it. Lucky for me, you just can't seem to catch me."

"Not for lack of trying."

"You know, I'm starting to think you just keep letting me escape because you're sweet on me."

"In your dreams."

"Speaking of which, it's getting late, wouldn't want to miss my beauty sleep, and you really should go back to your lair and get out of that soggy super suit before you catch a cold."

"It's a hideout," he sighed. "Only villains have lairs."

"Whatever you say. See you around, Protector."

"Until next time, Siren. Until next time."

"Aww, that's so cute, you sound so dramatic, just like a comic book hero!" she laughed, then turned on her heel and disappeared into the night.

The Protector waved a greeting to the firemen rushing to close the hydrant flooding the street so they could attach their hoses and douse the remaining flames.

"Hi fellas."

"Should have known it was you again. Hey Captain, it's the Protractor."

"Protector."

"Whatever."

"The captain will want a statement from you," the fireman said. "I'm sure the police will want one too." He surveyed the smoking building a moment, taking in the destruction. "Well, at least you didn't take the whole place down, *this time*," he said as he trotted off to fight the blaze.

The captain grabbed his clipboard from the rig and strode to the hero while his crew hurriedly set to knocking down the remaining blaze, throwing annoyed looks at The Protector as they did.

"Worst. Superhero. Ever." the captain muttered, shaking his head in disgust.

Tyler hadn't always been a superhero. Not so long ago, he was just an average guy. Painfully average. So much so that if he were a color, Tyler would have been beige.

Then, one otherwise ordinary day in his mid-twenties, it happened.

He wasn't bitten by a radioactive spider, there'd been no Gamma radiation, nor massive beams of light from an alien craft. He was even too far past puberty for some far-fetched mutant coming-of-age story. Nope, he simply woke up that day and was different.

The vision had been the first thing he noticed. Or didn't notice, as the case may be. When he rolled out of bed still half-asleep, he slipped on his glasses and trudged to the bathroom. Only when the spattering of urine on the tile floor splashed his bare feet, did he realize his vision, and aim, were off.

"Shit! What the hell?" he blurted as he quickly clenched up, uncomfortably stopping his morning piss mid-stream.

He blinked repeatedly, but his eyes wouldn't clear.

What did I get on my lenses? he wondered as he removed his glasses to wipe them on a towel. The world immediately sharpened into focus. He did a double take. Having relied on glasses most of his teen and adult life, he was startled to find that for whatever reason, now he did not. He was lucky with his new vision; at least that one power had remained consistent. The rest? Not so much.

He had been more than a little freaked out when he accidentally ripped his door from its hinges as easily as tearing open an envelope, while crushing the solid brass knob like it was Play-Doh. Strength had never been his strong suit, but it appeared to now be something he had in abundance.

Until he didn't.

That was the problem with his powers. They had a mind of their own.

Tyler had just been getting used to his newfound strength, reveling in the feeling of confidence it gave him, when he discovered his gifts' fickle nature the hard way.

It was late that night when he stepped in front of a handful of drunken hooligans harassing a woman waiting for the bus. Tyler knew he could take them easily, relishing the thought that, for once, the bullies would learn a lesson.

He grabbed the ringleader by his shirt, ready to make an example of him. His arms strained and tugged, but he realized (with a sinking feeling) that he couldn't budge the brawny man.

Two words flooded his mind in tandem with his massive adrenaline rush: *Oh shit.*

It took weeks for his ribs to heal from the beating.

Other powers continued to appear over time. Not gradually, mind you, but simply springing into being without warning.

The X-ray vision he had thought would be a cool power, but rather than seeing through women's clothing for a cheap thrill, he found himself instead gazing at their half-digested meals.

The laser vision, on the other hand, was just as cool as one would expect, but once he summoned it up (which fortunately required quite a bit of effort), he couldn't always shut it off. It had been years since he last tried to use that one, the memory of the accidental destruction of a wide swath of the park (roasting the duck population of the little pond, accompanied by the wailing of the poor children who'd witnessed it) was a painful one. It would be a very long time before he'd dare try to use that power again.

Physically, he was more or less impervious to serious damage, most notably from fire and cold, but for whatever reason, he could bruise and bleed just like anyone else. At least most of the time.

Once, a piece of a crumbling building landed on him as he attempted to rescue a trapped child. He was pleasantly surprised to find his body intact as the massive concrete block bounced off him harmlessly as if it were styrofoam.

He would have been a hero that day, saving a kid like that, but the building was collapsing *because* of him. An uncontrolled burst of super-speed had taken him straight through the entire ground floor when his powers once again betrayed him.

He was brand new to the superhero game that day, and had just donned his home-stitched super suit for the very first time. "The Protector", that would be his moniker, because that was what he intended to do for the people of the city.

Eager to get started, and with the best intentions, he headed out into the night to make a difference.

The Protector was poised to become a force to be reckoned with, but he was also a rookie, still learning what he could do with his many powers.

Unfortunately he had about as much control of them as a fifteen-year-old virgin tossed in bed with an oiled-up porn star.

None.

It was only natural that on his first real outing as a superhero he was amped up and full of adrenaline. He had been in a hurry to get to the scene of the crisis unfolding downtown when he took off running, eager to help the other heroes battle the giant mutant sewer rats that had spilled forth from the pipes beneath the secret lair of Doctor Malice.

Then he lost control and plowed into a wall. Well, *through* a wall, actually.

He had waded into the big leagues that night, and as he raced to his first battle, he couldn't help wondering why supervillains always seemed to go by 'Doctor' something? It's not like they had a diploma on their wall touting their PhD in destruction. He mused it was probably just an evil version of the same reason the good guys usually opted for 'Captain' or 'Commander,' namely feeding their latent desire to belong to some fraternal order of testosterone-fueled bonding.

Daydreaming isn't the wisest thing when running at super-speeds.

The newly-dubbed Protector's collision had torn right through the foundation of the building adjacent to Doctor Malice's lab. This led to a very hasty diversion of resources away from capturing the villain, focusing instead on the impromptu rescue operation led by none other than his super-idols, Captain Stupendous and his team of heroes.

Mister Cool was there, putting out fires with icy blasts while The Torch melted the bent steel that was blocking the path and preventing people's escape from the building. Then there was Bird Girl.

If Captain Stupendous was a grade-A prick, she was the team's mean-girl Alpha-bitch.

She could fly, which a few other heroes could do as well, but she also had the ability to command birds to do her bidding, which on far too many occasions since that first meeting to be mere coincidence, included pooping en-masse on Tyler's super suit, leaving him looking like a man-shaped Jackson Pollock painting.

She swooped in the upper windows, hauling people to safety while the rest of the team ran through the structure.

Inspired watching his heroes in action up close, The Protector tried to use his powers to help.

Did I mention the lack of control thing?

The fire spread when his ice blasts accidentally froze the hose of the firemen trying to extinguish the blaze.

His telekinesis carried trapped men and women to safety, but not before going a bit wide, tearing out load-bearing chunks of the building with them in the process.

Up until that night, he didn't even know he could summon squirrels, but when hundreds of chittering fur balls ran into the building, the pandemonium was taken to a whole new level, especially when their fluffy tails caught fire, sending a swarm of flaming critters out into the night, lighting the better part of the neighborhood trees ablaze in the process.

With all the chaos he'd caused, once the fires were contained and the civilians were safely out of harm's way, the heroes had swooped in and delivered quite a beat down before they realized he was one of the good guys.

Trying to be, at least.

"What the hell were you thinking?" Bird Girl shrieked, as she threw him up against a dumpster in a rage. A spiraling whirlwind of crows and jackdaws cawed their displeasure as they spun in an angry mass above her head.

"I'm The Protector. I'm the new hero in town. I'm here to help."

"Help? You call this help? Look at this mess!" She was losing her cool, hovering several feet above the ground. "Doctor Malice got away because of you, moron!"

"She's right," Mister Cool agreed, his eerily calm voice in direct opposition to his angry gaze. Tyler shifted uncomfortably in his super suit. "You caused a lot of problems today, kid. Stay out of the way and let the professionals do their job."

"But I can do things. I have powers."

"We saw, and believe me, we're not impressed," growled Captain Stupendous. "Come here, I have something very important to tell you," Tyler's superhero man-crush said.

Rather than a pep-talk, he grabbed the newbie in a headlock and gave him a rough noogie, then shoved him into a muddy puddle by the curb. It was as humiliating as high school all over again.

"Stay out of our turf, nerd," he spat snarkily. "We don't need any half-assed wannabes here. This is our city."

And with that, they dispersed, leaving the despondent new superhero alone in their wake.

Tyler knew in his gut he couldn't give up on his dream of being a superhero, but he admitted to himself that maybe they were right, at least somewhat. He'd tried too much too soon. He would protect the city from danger on a smaller scale, leaving the supervillains and their grand schemes for the other heroes, at least until he had more practice.

The Protector began patrolling the streets by night, sticking to the shadows, ears open for sounds of distress. After only a few nights, he got his chance.

"Help! Help!" a man's voice called out from a dimly lit alley by an all-night Chinese take-out place, its flickering neon casting an unnatural glow as it reflected from the filthy water pooled on the ground.

At last, he thought with excitement, running toward the sounds of a scuffle.

"Take your hands off him!" he bellowed in his most

authoritative voice. With a flourish, he jumped into the alleyway, landing with his hands on his hips in a classic superhero pose.

If you're going to be a hero, he figured, you should make a hero's entrance.

"What the fuck you say to me?" the gangbanger asked, dropping his bloodied prey to the filthy pavement as he spun toward his unwanted guest.

"I am The Protector, and I'm warning you, let this man go."

"The Protector, huh? I ain't never heard of you. You supposed to be some kind of superhero, is that it?"

"Yes, I am."

"I ain't afraid of no low-rent wannabe hero. Let's see what you got, bitch. Come on!" With a shark's malicious grin, he pulled a pipe from his belt and began slowly swinging it as he moved closer and closer.

"I don't want to harm you, but you leave me no choice," Tyler said as he raised his hands and focused his newly discovered ice powers at the approaching criminal.

A flash of cool, blue light filled the alleyway, and The Protector smiled.

Then he realized he couldn't move.

His icy blast had misfired, hitting the puddle he'd been standing in, freezing his own feet in place.

Typical.

"Oh, now you fucked up," was the last thing he remembered hearing before the steel pipe rang out across his skull. Fortunately his durability powers were mostly functional that day, though he still wound up with a black eye, bloody lip, and two cracked ribs.

As he limped back to his secret hideout, a flashlight beam dancing through the check cashing shop down the street caught his eye. After midnight? The place was most certainly not open for business.

He was sore, not to mention humiliated, but duty called. Still, just to be safe, he dialed 9-1-1 on his cell phone.

"And who did you say you are?" the operator asked.

"The Protector."

"Is this some kind of joke? Who names themselves after a geometry tool?"

"No, Protector." He sighed. "Look, I told you there's a crime in progress. Just send a car, alright?" he said, then hung up.

As stealthily as he could, he stepped through the shattered glass façade to confront the criminal lurking inside. A loud metal bang made him jump, just as the perpetrator came into view.

"Hey!" he shouted to the lean girl in the catsuit as she smashed away at the safe behind the counter with a sledgehammer. "Step away from the safe and put your hands up!" He could hear the wail of police cars in the distance. This would make up for earlier. He'd be a hero yet.

The Siren smiled.

"Oh honey," she cooed, "you're new here aren't you?"

"I'm The Protector," his voice boomed in the close space, "and your days of crime are over."

She laughed.

"Seriously? Wow, that's like straight out of a bad movie. Come on, I'm sure you have something better. Try again."

"What?" he replied, confused. "Perhaps you didn't understand me, I'm The Protector, and—"

"Hi Protector, I'm The Siren."

"Don't interrupt, it's—"

"Rude to interrupt? Yeah, my mom always used to tell me that."

"Stop it."

"Stop what?"

"You know what. You keep inte—"

"Interrupting you? I have no idea what you're talking about."

"Stop it!"

She flashed an amused grin, her gaze shifting to the pair of police cruisers screeching to a halt in front of the building. It was pretty, in a smashy-smashy sort of way, the strobing lights illuminating hero and villain alike in a glittering wash of color reflected from the broken glass.

"You invited civvies to our party? You really are new, aren't you?"

"Freeze!" the approaching cops shouted, guns drawn. "Put your hands up and step out onto the sidewalk."

The Siren flashed a mischievous smile.

"Don't you even want to know why they call me The Siren?" she asked, then began singing a sweet melody, the dulcet notes flowing in the wind to the street outside.

The officers froze in place, eyes glazed over in a trance. Tyler just stood there, confused, as he looked at the motionless men, then the supervillain.

"Cool trick," he said.

"Huh, that's weird," The Siren mused, then turned her full

attention on her new interloper.

Her song blasted out, wave after wave buffeting The Protector, its paralyzing energy spreading farther than before, flooding the whole street, stunning the poor squirrels in the tree above as they were just about to enjoy some plump acorns. One frozen critter fell to the sidewalk with a tiny thud.

Again, The Protector just stood there.

"I appreciate the tune, you do have a lovely voice, but like I said, you're coming with me."

The Siren was flummoxed. "It doesn't work on you." A faint note of actual distress tinged her voice. "It works on everyone, why not on you?"

"I told you, I'm a superhero. Now, if you'll—"

"It works on superheroes, it works on *everyone,*" she blurted, concerned.

"There you go, interrupting again," he chuckled. "Now, I believe it's time to take you to jail."

He bent at the knees, intending to fly across the room and scoop her up in his arms, carrying her to justice, just like in the movies.

Unfortunately, his powers once again had a different idea.

"Um, what are you doing?" she asked the half-buried hero, firmly embedded in the ground up to his chest.

"I was trying to fly."

"You went the wrong way."

"Gee, ya think?"

"You're not very good at this hero thing are you?"

"Shut up. You're still my prisoner."

"Says you," she laughed. "See ya around Protector!" she taunted, dashing out of the storefront and into the night.

"This has got to get easier," he muttered to himself.

It didn't.

Tyler worked hard, trying his best to rein in and manage his nascent abilities. He spent months holed up in his secret hideout, training, practicing, gradually discovering the multitude of powers he possessed, as well as how little he could control them.

Of all his skills, he found that with great concentration, he could focus his freezing power, but only if he meditated first, channeling that force to his hands. It was far from perfect, but he could somewhat reliably direct a blast of freezing ice more or less in the direction he wanted. Of course, in the real world, how would that work mid-battle?

"I can see it now," he chuckled to himself. " 'Excuse me Mr. Villain, would you mind stopping your evil onslaught for a few minutes while I sit here and meditate so I can power up to defeat you?' 'Of course Protector, take your time, no rush.' "

He'd had a good laugh over that one.

Flying was far more sporadic. He could sometimes hover in place for a few seconds and very rarely attain up to twenty seconds or so of poorly controlled flight. Otherwise, he was pretty much grounded.

The super-strength and imperviousness were totally out of his control. When they'd work and when they'd crap out on him were completely random, so he gave up even trying to control those.

He had also discovered, quite unintentionally, that he could breathe underwater. Sometimes. When it did work, he took to submerging himself in the old cast-iron bathtub in his hideout. It was relaxing, lying underwater for long stretches, and even if he didn't think it was the most useful of powers, it was still more than a lot of other heroes could do.

There were many other powers in his quiver. Super speed, super hearing, telekinesis, to name just a few. He had more raw abilities than any super team combined, but try as he might, he simply couldn't control them.

Tyler needed help and he knew it. He believed in his heart that with mentoring and care, he could one day become a valued member of the superhero community, but the next step would be the hardest. He needed to be accepted and taken in as a new recruit.

It had been several months since their first meeting. Captain Stupendous and a few of his team had just finished rounding up a group of would-be bank robbers when The Protector approached them.

"Hey guys, it's the dork again," the Captain said to his fellow heroes with a snide guffaw.

Bird Girl's presence was preceded by the splatter of poop landing on The Protector's head.

"Oops, sorry." She laughed as she glided effortlessly to the ground beside him. "I don't know why they did that. Wasn't me, promise." The jeers from the rest of the team didn't make it any easier, but The Protector swallowed his pride and did what had to be done.

"Captain," he began, wiping the mess from his head, "I've been trying to teach myself, but on my own I don't think I'll ever become a real superhero, not without help. I want to be like you. To become one of you. Please, will you help me?

Teach me? I'll do anything, just let me try."

The Captain glanced at the mirthful looks of his companions.

"Anything?" He flashed that gleaming trademark smile.

"Anything, just give me a chance."

"So that's a double mocha for Mister Cool, a soy Frappuccino for Bird Girl, non-fat latte for The Torch, iced tea, no sugar, for Commander Smackdown, black coffee for Mistress Lightning, and a Quad Espresso for the Captain."

"Alright scrub, get moving," Captain Stupendous chuckled. "And don't forget to buff my super-boots when you get back."

The Protector had been doing menial tasks for the super team for over a month. Sure, it sucked, but aside from the occasional noogie from the Captain and periodic bird poop attacks from Bird Girl's asshole friends, he didn't think it was all that bad.

Like Daniel-San, I need to wax on, wax off, he had told himself. Unfortunately, the Captain was no Mr. Miyagi, and any villain he faced would do far worse than sweep the leg.

"I'll be back in ten!" he called out.

"Run faster, dork," Mistress Lightning barked. "I don't want my coffee to get cold."

"Ah, yeah, but if I do a super-run I might spill, and besides, um, it's still kind of hard to—"

The blaring alarm went off on all the heroes' team wristbands at once.

"Doctor Malice is back! He's assaulting the secret government weapons testing facility in the warehouse district.

Team, let's go!"

"Can I come?" The Protector asked, hopeful. "I promise, I can help. I've been practicing!"

The Captain thought for a minute. "Alright. I want you to take up a position behind the tire factory building. It's of the utmost importance you prevent anyone from escaping, is that clear?"

"Yes, sir, you can count on me!" He turned to take off at a fast run.

"Hey, where are you going?"

"You said to—"

"Get the coffee first, dumb-ass. We'll be thirsty when we're through."

The Captain and his team flew to confront their nemesis, and right behind them The Protector ran off into the night to take part in his first real superhero operation.

After getting their coffee.

He arrived behind the tire factory twenty minutes later (there had been a line at Starbucks), the beverages securely stashed atop a nearby storage tank well out of the way of any possible conflict.

Okay, this is it, gotta get ready, he thought excitedly.

He focused his gaze on the back door, readying himself for anything as he began to slowly breathe in and out, channeling his ice power as he'd been practicing. Fortune had smiled on him. Amazingly, it appeared there'd actually be time to prepare for this fight.

Five blocks away, where the *real* action was taking place, Captain Stupendous and his team were battling the giant laser-shooting robot horde controlled by Doctor Malice, trying to reach the man himself as he scurried off with his booty, a prototype disruptor ray stolen from the now-smoldering remains of the secret government facility.

"Stop him!" the Captain bellowed as he ripped the massive steel arm from his robotic foe. "Don't let him get away!"

The team was up to their necks in robots, and the Doctor was making a rapid escape on his fusion-powered motorcycle. He darted down the block, then made a sharp turn before hitting the accelerator. This most certainly was not part of the Captain's plan.

"Team, follow me!" the Captain yelled out.

The superheroes delivered massive blows to their opponents in unison, smashing them into one another before they turned and pursued their quarry.

"He's too far ahead!" shouted Bird Girl.

"Shortcut! Through here!" Mister Cool called out. "We can cut him off!"

The Protector had heard the fierce battle, but had remained focused. It was up to him to be the last line of defense, and he was not going to blow it. His super hearing (why it chose that moment to work was a mystery to him) picked up a speeding motorcycle a few blocks to his east, but the real commotion was thundering right toward him through the cavernous warehouse in front of him.

"This is it," he muttered as he focused his energy and unleashed the full force of the power he'd been mustering for the past ten minutes.

The heroes burst through the back door just as the wave of freezing ice burst from The Protector's hands.

"I did it!" he yelped, jumping for joy at the sight of the frozen villains encased in snow and ice. It hadn't been pretty, but The Protector had finally (more or less) controlled his power and done good.

"You moron!" Captain Stupendous's muffled voice cursed.

"Captain?"

The enraged hero burst free from the ice. "What the hell were you thinking? You're supposed to be on our side idiot!"

"But Captain…" The horror of realization struck him as the other heroes freed themselves from the frosty blast aftermath. "But, but you said to guard the back door. You said —"

"Oh come on, do you think we'd really give you an important job to do? You're useless. No, scratch that, you're worse than useless. You might as well be playing for the other team. I swear, you can't do anything right."

"Incompetent ass!" Bird Girl screamed in frustration.

The Protector hung his head as he trudged away, leaving the team bitterly bitching among themselves. He returned moments later with the heroes' drinks.

"I got these for you," he said meekly.

Captain Stupendous slapped the tray, the contents of the cups sent flying, drenching The Protector head to toe. With barely contained rage, the Captain grabbed him by the back of his coffee-soaked super suit and dragged him to the tire factory.

"Bird Girl!" he barked.

She swooped down, the Captain grabbing her ankle as she hauled him and The Protector effortlessly into the air.

They left him up there, hanging by his underwear from

the side of the warehouse.

"Stay the hell out of our way nerd. You'll never be a superhero!" His once-idol spat at him in disgust, then turned and left, the rest of his super team in tow.

"But Captain? Guys?" he called after them.

Bird Girl was the only one who seemed to hear, turning her angry gaze upon him for a moment before continuing away.

"Guys? Please?…" He heard a sound and looked up. "Oh no."

The barrage of bird shit was unrelenting, and by the time they were done, The Protector resembled a feces-covered statue abandoned to disrepair.

Soiled and humiliated, he dragged himself back to his hideout and licked his wounds in solitude. He was down, most certainly, but he was not out. Despite the abuse he was nevertheless determined to make a difference. The first step was planning how best to co-exist in a world where the other heroes didn't want him around.

Those months of solitary crime fighting turned into years, and though new powers would still periodically manifest, The Protector had resigned himself to not using any but the few he could more or less control in his crime fighting endeavors.

It was just too risky.

It could also be too costly.

The thing about accidentally causing damage and destruction in the pursuit of justice is, he was still protected by the Good Samaritan law, even though he happened to be a superhero. At least that used to be the case. Things started to change after the bills from The Protector's repeated disasters began adding up, and it wasn't just the city that was dragging its feet in paying out.

Citizens were upset, but insurance companies balked at covering acts of a superhero, some going so far as to claim that a meta-human could be considered a deity in some eyes, thus their actions technically being "Acts of God" and not covered under most policies.

When a group of citizens filed a class-action lawsuit against the city for protecting the actions of one particularly destructive resident (even if he didn't mean to cause harm), the City Council was finally forced to begin drafting legislation to exempt one superhero in particular from the Good Samaritan provisions.

The final straw had been when an old woman had asked The Protector to rescue her cat from the tall oak tree outside City Hall. It seemed innocent enough. A simple task. Something that he could do without difficulty at all.

What could possibly go wrong?

He should have known better.

The cat, by the way, survived without a scratch, but the half-dozen smashed cars and the high-voltage lines taken out in the process hadn't fared so well. It might not have caused quite such a stir if the cars destroyed in the process hadn't belonged to the mayor, the district attorney, and several of the city's powerful elite who were attending a charity function that day.

Captain Stupendous had stood beside Mayor Parker when he gave a press conference from the steps of City Hall. The mayor was not only supporting the new legislation put forth by the City Council, but was adding to it, calling for a new ordinance to be drafted to protect the city from the clumsy hero who seemed to do far more harm than good.

The Protector would cease damaging property in his crime fighting endeavors or the mayor would see to it, with the Captain and his team's assistance no less, that The Protector would be locked up behind bars and held accountable for any damage he had caused.

That would have been bad enough, but behind the perfect hair and dazzling smile, Captain Stupendous was a vindictive man, and the new legislation gave him carte blanche to ramp up his harassment of the low-rent superhero.

The Captain didn't go out and physically harm him, that would have been frowned on even in the press, but with Bird Girl and the others egging him on, he took to making The Protector's life hell whenever he came across him. Soon the rest of his cohorts joined in, and in no time at all, the poor hero found himself barely able to leave his hideout in costume without being harassed, taunted, and even pooped on by Bird Girl's avian minions at every turn.

Just ignore them, he would tell himself after every incident. *You're doing good, it doesn't matter what those bullies say.* Unfortunately, he was finding it harder and harder to let it go.

Having the milkshake dropped on his head that night hadn't hurt, even though it had fallen seven stories when the Captain let it loose. The only thing injured was his pride. The shake made a mess, as did the defecating crows that chased him for three blocks, but they didn't cause any real damage, though their cackling barrage nevertheless made the sting of yet another prank by the Captain and his friends hurt just that much more.

The Protector stepped out of the gas station restroom, cleaned up, but quite frankly, over it.

Screw this, he thought. *I'm going home.*

Heading for his hideout to change into his street clothes and maybe goof around on his PlayStation seemed like a great plan. Crime fighting could wait, this just wasn't the night for it.

He had been walking in a funk for a while when he took a seat on a dark bus bench, reflecting on the night's humiliation. The incessant harassment he had to endure was just the icing on the shitty cake that was his life as a superhero, and he didn't even like icing.

The crash startled him. His super hearing was apparently on the fritz that night, and he hadn't heard it coming. He just wanted to go home, but the heroic nature in him tugged at his conscience, and grudgingly, he obeyed, rising to his feet and jogging around the corner, just in case a citizen needed his help.

"Hello?" he called out into the electronics store. "Is everyone alright?"

The car had smashed right through the front window, but the driver's seat was empty. The engine was still running, and the stereo, he noted, was playing AC/DC's "Dirty Deeds Done Dirt Cheap."

"Oh no, it's The Protector!" The Siren cried out from across the store as she leapt atop a counter. "Whatever will I do?" She held the back of her hand to her head like a swooning damsel in distress, waiting patiently for his snarky reply.

Over the years of cat and mouse, she'd actually come to enjoy the banter they traded, and as he was the only hero willing to stand up to her (and the only one not affected by her song), she eventually found herself heading off on each new crime spree wondering if he'd show up.

"Oh, it's you."

"Yes, it is I, your nemesis!" she said, striking a ridiculous pose. "What amazing powers will you unleash upon me this time? Laser rays? Maybe electromagnetic ESP? I tremble in my boots! What'll it be, Protector?"

He looked at her, amped up and ready to scrap. *Not tonight,* was his immediate thought.

"Fuck it," he sighed, then turned to walk away.

"What?" Siren called after him, confused. "Not even going to try?"

"What's the point?" he replied, then trudged off into the night.

Three blocks later, he took a seat on a dark bus bench. It was well past operating hours, no conveyance would be passing by for quite some time. Resting his masked head in his hands, he thought back on all the time spent trying to do good, to help people, and how everything, his own body included, just never seemed to go his way.

"Whatcha doin'?" a voice asked.

It was The Siren, watching him from across the street.

"Go away," he grumbled, his head returning to his hands.

A strange thing happened in The Siren's chest. She actually felt a twinge of sympathy.

"Hey, you alright?"

"Look, I'm not chasing you tonight. Why don't you just go torment some other hero?"

She studied his body language. With the slump to his shoulders, he seemed, well, defeated. The twinge hit again, this time harder.

"For reals, you're not going to try to catch me?"

"Nope, go do your worst, I really don't care."

She stared at him for a good long moment, then made a decision.

"If you're really not going to chase me, I have a proposition."

He paused a moment, then looked up at his nemesis through damp eyes.

"What do you want?" he asked.

"I propose a truce. But just for tonight," she quickly added.

"A truce? Why? I already told you I'm not coming after you."

"I know. Come on, let me buy you a drink."

That answer took him by surprise. He sat up straighter and studied her a moment, but sensed no trickery or guile. He was so over it at that moment, he likely wouldn't have cared if there were. Still, a drink with The Siren…

"Why?"

"Because, well, you look like you've had one of those days."

"But you're my nemesis."

"Really? Aww, you're so sweet! So come on, how often does a fella get to have a drink with his archenemy?"

He thought about it a minute.

"Okay, you can *buy* me a drink, not steal me one."

She scrunched up her face (what you could see of it under her mask) in mock disgust, then smiled. "Oh, alright. No stealing."

The dark little bar was used to the patronage of the freaks who roamed the streets when everyone else was sound asleep, so two strangely clad twenty-somethings was in no way out of the ordinary.

Good-looking couple, the doorman thought as the pair took a booth way in the back.

They had made an agreement as they walked there that night, something neither could believe they were about to do.

They were going to remove their masks.

Sure, they could go with them on, but people would talk. A villain and a hero together in a bar? What would happen next? So they both swore on their honor (or in The Siren's case, her lack of honor) that whatever happened, they would abide by the terms of the truce and never reveal each other's identity. Oddly enough, neither of them thought the other would break the agreement.

"Wow," she said when The Protector slid his mask from his face.

"What?" he asked, self-conscious.

"Nothing, it's just… you're really cute."

He blushed, and his arch-nemesis thought that made him even cuter.

"Your turn," he said.

With a flourish, she pulled her mask free, shaking out her long auburn hair.

"Voila!"

He was silent.

"Well? Say something, dork," she said, suddenly uncomfortable.

"You…" He was flummoxed. "You're beautiful."

"Good save lover-boy. Come on, I know just the place to go."

So it came to pass that the archenemies found themselves sitting in the deep red vinyl booth, tucked way in the back of the bar, just two young people having a drink. Conversation flowed smoothly (and the alcohol didn't hurt). All those years of banter had given them something of a personal shorthand. Several drinks later, they both admitted that, despite their feigned annoyances, they had actually looked forward to their encounters, even if one of them was trying to capture the other.

"I mean, I had to try," he said, "but maybe, and I'm just saying maybe here, but maybe I didn't really want to lock you up."

She smiled at him. "And I didn't want to be, though I kinda hoped you wouldn't stop trying."

They were sharing a moment, something interesting and unexpected building between them, when a loud group of hipsters out to slum it in a dive bar burst through the front doors, their raucous hollering and drunken tirades ruining the ambiance.

"Great, the idiots have arrived. God, I miss when this place was off the hipster radar," The Siren lamented.

"Tell me about it," The Protector commiserated. "Hey, I know this is kinda strange to ask, but do you maybe want to get out of here and hang out at my place for a bit? It's pretty close by."

"Seriously, you're offering to show me your secret lair?" she asked, intrigued.

"It's a hideout," he replied. "Only villains have lairs. One thing, though, you have to promise that no matter what happens, you'll never reveal it to anyone or use it against me. Consider it part of tonight's truce."

She thought it over a few moments (though she only needed a second) and agreed with a smile.

The hideout was something Tyler had stumbled upon when he was just a teenager. One afternoon, his penchant for urban exploring had led him deep beneath the old fire station on Mission Street. It had been shuttered for years, so naturally it was far too tempting for a curious kid to pass up.

A few days after he'd begun exploring the building, Tyler noticed an innocuous little panel under the staircase, one that was just a little different from the others. He had a feeling something interesting was about to happen. Call it intuition, call it a super sense, whatever it was, that day was destiny.

He ran his fingers along the panel's edges, fingertips feeling a slight indentation at the top right corner. He gave it a push, and after a moment's resistance, the panel slid open with a rusty screech, revealing a long-forgotten staircase leading to the pitch-black depths below the building.

He was terrified and quickly slammed the secret door shut, but later that night, he found himself thinking about the mysterious discovery, until finally, powerful flashlight in hand, he returned to explore the frightening yet oddly tempting darkness beneath the old firehouse.

It was incredible. A network of tunnels and rooms below the old building that no one had set foot in for decades. Best of all, Tyler found that the system possessed multiple exit points throughout the neighborhood, the tunnels apparently once serving as a rapid response accessway for the long-forgotten firemen living above.

He had slowly cleaned it up during high school, scrubbing away the grime on weekends, even painting the walls a more appealing color than "filth." When he later became The Protector, he installed internet from a long cable bootlegged off a neighboring office building and even got the old water pipes working. The furniture was a bit more difficult to sneak in, but in time he had made a perfectly habitable hideout, bed, couch, tables and chairs included.

"This is amazing!" The Siren gasped when he turned on the strings of Edison bulbs that illuminated the space in a cozy amber glow. "You live here?"

"Nah, this is just my hideout, but I do spend a lot of time here."

"This is amazing. You're full of surprises, Protector. Color me impressed."

"And here I thought it took far more than that to impress the great Siren."

She looked at him quietly. It had been by far the nicest non-date she'd been on in years, and she wasn't looking forward to it ending.

"Sherri," she said at last, holding out her hand.

"Tyler," he replied, clasping her warm palm in his.

"Hey Tyler," she whispered.

"Yeah?"

"There's something I want to tell you."

"What?"

Sherri The Siren lunged at him, their mouths mashing together fiercely, her tongue dancing tantalizingly across his. A pale orange spark leapt between their moistened lips as she broke the embrace.

"Whoa, what was that?" she asked, pupils wide with a surge of desire.

"I don't know," he replied huskily, thundering pulse visible in his neck.

They stared at one another a long moment, then fell into each other's arms, pulling desperately at their layered costumes as passions flared.

"Why do you have so many damn buckles?" he lamented.

"It's a supervillain suit, what did you expect?"

"I don't know, maybe a zipper or something. All these buckles just—"

"Boys don't understand fashion, I swear, you—" She gasped as he pulled her breast free, cupping it firmly in his hand.

"It's rude to interrupt," he whispered intensely as he squeezed her nipple, sending sparks and electric tingles coursing through her body as he lay her down in his bed.

"How do you do that?" she asked, watching the small flame dancing in his palm as she lay curled in his arms some time later.

"Don't know. Never done it before."

She nestled her head on his chest and watched the

flickering light.

"What else can you do?"

"I don't know," he replied.

"Try something."

Ice sculptures, delicate and detailed, pulled from the thin air with his glowing hands.

Telekinesis-powered floating mobiles circled the room in a lazy arc.

A delicate laser-vision sketched portrait of The Siren, burned into the solid cement walls of his den.

"I thought you couldn't control your powers."

"I couldn't, at least not before. Something changed."

Sherri propped up on her elbow, eyebrow arched wickedly high.

"Are you saying I screwed you into becoming quite possibly the greatest superpower the world has ever seen?" she asked, running her hand across his bare chest. "More powerful than even Captain Stupendous and his obnoxious friends?"

He thought about that for a moment. The countless times they'd humiliated him rather than help him. Of all things, it was his nemesis, a villain against whom he'd battled for years no less, who had finally unlocked his potential.

"Something like that," he finally said with a thoughtful little grin.

"Wow. Now that's a power I didn't know I had. You know, I should get a little cape or something for my panties. I mean, if I wore any."

His face flushed as he pulled her close.

"Let's put that power to good use then, shall we?" he said

in a raspy voice.

"For good or evil?" she asked with a wink.

"Just shut up and kiss me."

Hours later (let's hear it for Super Stamina), they finally pulled their clothes on and headed back for the surface, the sun high in the sky, the city blissfully unaware of the power unleashed within its confines just hours before.

"So, I guess our truce is just about over," Sherri said, her fingers reluctantly sliding from Tyler's as she started to walk away.

"I'd rather it wasn't," he replied.

She felt her heart skip a beat, then turned back to him, with a questioning gaze.

"So what are you saying?" she asked, her heartbeat quickening. "You want me to become a good guy now? To stay with you? Maybe even move in to your hideout?" She realized the thought of that last bit suddenly didn't sound so bad.

He pulled her close and gently took her face in his hands before planting a solid kiss as he looked deeply into her glistening eyes.

"Honey," he said with a mischievous grin. "It's not a hideout, it's a lair."

One Last Fix

The shakes had taken hold something fierce rather early this particular morning, and Jeremy found even the simple act of holding his lukewarm begged-for cup of coffee steady to his lips to require something of an effort.

It had been bad in the days prior, the shakes, the cravings, but this time the discomfort of withdrawal just seemed so much stronger.

The hint of wildness to his eyes as he scanned the morning commuter crowd for a friendly face kind enough to drop some change in his battered handout bowl was off-putting to the people as they passed him by.

He was a man on edge, and everyone could sense it, the way animals somehow instinctively know to shy away from a sick member of the herd to avoid an unseen contagion.

By nightfall Jeremy was feeling even worse, but a glimmer of hope flashed in his desperate eyes as he counted out the massive roll of grubby bills, pulled from the depths of his filthy pockets. After weeks of saving, he might finally have enough.

Jeremy hadn't always been on the streets.

His clothes were once laundered and pressed with regularity, his hair cut stylishly at a pricy salon, his shoes polished to a glossy mirror shine. He was coming up through the ranks as a first-year trader with one of the small boutique hedge funds, and if things had continued on track, he would have been sitting pretty in just a few short years.

Then Derek happened.

Derek Voyavich was the hotshot top gun at the fund. He never missed a financial target, and subsequently, he was raking it in hand over fist. He was their golden boy, and his investors trusted him implicitly.

As far as management was concerned, his shit most certainly did not stink. Unfortunately, as is often the case with those who achieve wealth a little too fast and too easily, he was also something of an entitled tool. Why he took a shine to Jeremy was anyone's guess, but ultimately, it would be his new friend's undoing.

When Derek first invited Jeremy out clubbing, the pair had done the usual "new money guy" things; thrown money at strippers, done lines of blow, finally ending the night with a pair of scantily clad women, though Jeremy still wasn't sure if they were professionals or not. Then again, he really didn't care, because even if they were, Derek was footing the bill.

They became something of a partying team and had a ball together, and it went on like that, until Derek approached him a few weeks later with an excited and mysterious look in his eye.

"Hey man, you wanna try something *really* different tonight?" he asked with a mysterious grin.

Does the Pope shit in the woods? Jeremy thought. "Damn right I do," was his eager reply.

Derek's jet-black Bentley pulled up in front of the nondescript building at 10:30 pm, the steady glow of the sodium vapor lamps dotting the street reflecting off its glossy hood. The only soul present was a very sturdy-looking man in a black sport coat, his buzz-cut hair standing straight at attention. A noticeable bulge in his coat clearly defined his role as gatekeeper as he stood vigilantly by the door.

The duo exited the vehicle and approached the building. A look of recognition flashed ever so slightly across the huge man's face as they neared, replacing his do-not-fuck-with-me glare for an instant.

"Nice to see you again, sir," his deep baritone rumbled as he lifted his hand to his mouth, speaking quietly into a concealed microphone. "Two inbound."

"Nice to see you as well," Derek said, shaking his hand with a smile, leaving a few crisp Benjamins in the burly man's palm.

The heavy steel door buzzed open, revealing another equally large man inside, a well-maintained submachine gun visible hanging across his torso inside his blazer.

"Gentlemen, this way please," he said, then led them into the depths of the dark building.

The space was dimly lit with an amber hue, and while the exterior had been nondescript, the overall feel of the interior was quite lush, if a bit old-fashioned and small.

Some might even call it intimate.

Blissed-out men and women alike were sprawled across deep red velvet divans as attendants saw to their needs. They all seemed quite high, their shiny wide-pupiled eyes just partly visible beneath half-closed lids. Their air of pure ecstasy and contentment was almost tangible. Jeremy had never seen anything like it, and he seriously doubted that had he not been so fortunate in befriending his wealthy new cohort, he likely never would have.

"Jeremy, come on," Derek hissed. "This isn't it. Not yet."

The armed man led them through a thick metal door, then down a short hallway to an even sturdier one mounted on a steel frame. He paused at the sealed threshold, standing there motionless like an imposing statue.

What's he doing? Jeremy thought before noticing the small camera mounted high above the door. A moment later, the door swung open with a rumble.

Jeremy and Derek were given a seat on a small, plushly cushioned sofa and offered refreshments by the stocky attendant. Jeremy noticed none of the staff were women, and all had a distinctive ex-military or perhaps mercenary vibe to them.

"So what exactly is this place?" Jeremy asked, a slight hint of concern tinting his query.

"Something new," was Derek's reply. "Something wonderful." He was subconsciously licking his lips in anticipation. In the relatively short time Jeremy had known him, he had never seen Derek's veneer of cool slip. Whatever it was, this was going to be good; he could feel it in his blood.

Blood. What an appropriate choice of words.

A deep red door, thick with soundproofing, opened, and a gray-suited man, tie askew and eyes glazed, was gently led out by yet another large, armed man. The difference was this attendant was wearing chain mail gauntlets on his arms and a biohazard respirator. Jeremy looked at Derek, concerned, but his friend didn't even notice him in his anticipation.

Derek anxiously got to his feet to meet his attendant, likewise dressed in metal sleeves and respirator, and stepped towards the door.

"See ya on the other side," he said to Jeremy, then stepped

through the threshold, the door closing solidly behind him. Only five minutes had passed when he was led staggering from the room, pupils wide, eyes glazed, a look of sheer bliss on his face. He didn't even notice his friend as a stocky man guided him out of the waiting room to one of the divans in the gallery.

A muscled attendant stood at the door, waiting. Hesitant at first, Jeremy finally rose to his feet.

Hell, you only live once, right? he thought. Game face firmly affixed, he followed the man into the next room, the door locking solidly behind him.

It took a moment for his eyes to adjust to the dim light. The oddly textured walls were painted black, and after a moment, he realized it was soundproofing material, though for what purpose he had no idea. The room, he soon noticed, was empty but for a tall, metal coffin-like box bolted upright to the far wall. The attendant double-checked his mask, then slipped a thick harness around Jeremy's torso.

"First time?" he asked, his voice muffled through the respirator.

Jeremy nodded.

"Don't get too close," the man intoned. "If you do, I've got you with this." He tugged the rope fastened to the harness. "But let's not have that happen, alright?"

Jeremy had no idea what he'd gotten himself into, but he nodded once more and was led toward the shiny silver box, stopping a few paces behind a thick red line painted on the floor nine feet back. He noticed some fine metalwork on the lid now that he was close to it. An ornate crucifix, delicately carved into the metal. He also thought it looked like actual silver, not steel, though why anyone would spend that much on a box that size out of a material much less sturdy than stainless was beyond him. Then the attendant nodded to a camera on the wall and the lid slid open.

The creature's eyes burned with an unnatural fire. Her pale skin was smooth as an alabaster sculpture but pulsed with vitality and a barely restrained energy. Her hair was pale blonde, and her firm breasts strained to be admired through the thin muslin she wore, accentuated by the sturdy chains binding her in place. Jeremy felt blood rush to his groin, a surge of desire washing over him as he took in the sight of the woman. Her intense eyes, her delectable pale white skin, her lustrous hair, her deep red lips... and the fine pointed fangs peeping out from between them.

He should have been terrified. Somewhere in the depths of his animal mind, he knew that he was the tiniest of prey in the presence of an apex predator, but by then the pheromones had taken hold.

The ancient stories of vampires hypnotizing their victims to do their bidding were not all that far from the truth when you got right down to it. Sure, it was a chemical process rather than actual hypnosis, but like the venom of a certain species of spider, so was the pheromone emitted by a vampire when it needed to feed. It calmed the prey into a docile meal, one which need not be killed or damaged in a struggle, but rather utilized for a meal, then turned loose again. It was a highly efficient system, evolved over millennia to preserve a food source rather than wipe it out with every feast.

Jeremy felt himself awash in wave after wave of pure ecstasy as he stumbled closer to the beautiful yet deadly woman. His pulse raced so hard he could feel it pounding against his chest, his manhood fully engorged and rock-hard, throbbing with desire and increasing bliss. This was all he would ever need, all he ever wanted. Perfection, if only he could just get a little closer…

The sharp yank across his abdomen nearly took him off his feet.

With a nod to the camera, the attendant pulled Jeremy toward the exit while silent pneumatics slowly closed the lid to the silver box.

Before it shut, Jeremy turned and caught a final look, a glimpse of the most beautiful woman he'd ever seen as she stared at him longingly, then was gone once more into her metal tomb.

It had taken hours for him to come down, and as Derek silently drove him back toward his condo, Jeremy could still feel the lingering effects of the woman's presence.

The first visit had been Derek's treat, and since he knew the owners, he had arranged a discounted rate for Jeremy should he want to return.

Should he want to return?

That was a laugh. It was far better than any drug imaginable. He would have sold his mother to feel the powerful flood of the mysterious woman's energy again, even if but for a minute. Soon he was a regular, spending several nights a week recovering on the plush divans after seeing the woman, the creature he was quite sure he loved. Unfortunately, he also started burning through his resources far faster than he was earning. As he quickly discovered, to experience such a rare high, the price was extraordinarily steep. But he was already hooked.

Soon he began selling off assets to pay for his visits. First some artwork, then his watch collection, then, finally, he liquidated his retirement account. The line was crossed when he was caught skimming from trades to pay for his fix. It was an embarrassment, one that could hurt the hedge fund's public reputation, so it was decided it would be kept quiet just this once, swept under the rug to save face for the company, but that reprieve came with a cost. With his now-former friend watching his disgraceful banishment, Jeremy was escorted from the building and told never to return again, lest he face criminal charges and imprisonment.

The rest of his story is pretty typical for an addict. He borrowed from anyone he could, burning many bridges and ruining many friendships in the search for enough money for just one more fix. He stole when he had to, sinking lower and lower, eventually winding up on the streets, where he scraped and scrounged until finally, he found himself where he stood today.

The building was nestled in the bad part of a bad part of town, but so long as the heavily tattooed doorman was at his post, that would be all the security the establishment needed. The neighborhood toughs knew better.

Jeremy had paid a pretty penny to acquire this address. The secret was guarded. Closely guarded and *very* costly to come by, but it would be worth it. There was no way he could remotely afford to see his true love, not in his current state, but if he could just get one more fix, just enough to get him through, he knew he could get back on his feet and find a proper job, one that would pay him handsomely for his skills. Enough to see her once more.

For now, this would have to suffice.

Jeremy shuffled to the door, hands in plain sight as he approached the deadly looking gatekeeper.

"Whatchoo want motherfucker?" the man challenged, his hand slipping under his coat, fingers tickling what Jeremy knew was surely a weapon of deadly caliber and bloody history.

"I'm here for a lemonade."

The man's posture changed. "You know lemonade don't come cheap."

Jeremy slowly reached into his pocket and pulled out the wad of cash. The doorman sized him up silently. Jeremy felt the adrenaline leaking into his bloodstream as the man stared at him. *What's to stop him from just killing me and taking…* He didn't get to finish the thought when the man gave him a nod, reached out and peeled a hundred off the roll, and stuck it in his pocket, then opened the door for him.

"Don't you go making no fuss now."

And with that he was in.

Unlike the high-end digs he was accustomed to, this place was a shithole. Filthy walls, floors sticky with Lord knows what nastiness, several strung-out looking men and women flopped down on the leaking beanbag chairs and threadbare couches haphazardly spread about the room.

At the far end was a man watching a football game on a small TV propped on the desk next to a metal door. There was a hole in the door, no bigger than a fist, with a rope running through it.

"You just gonna stand there?" the annoyed man called out to Jeremy. "Come on, halftime's almost over. I ain't got all day."

Jeremy stepped over a blissed-out woman with gold teeth and made his way to the sweaty man.

"Cash money, up front. Let's see it."

He forked over the wad and watched as the man counted it out. It had taken him weeks of borrowing, begging, and even thieving to scrape up enough, and for the briefest of moments, the thought entered his mind that he should take the money and use it to get back on his feet again. It was a sizable enough amount, but his primal, addict brain overruled that fleeting thought.

"Okay, you're good to go," the man said, rising to tie a rope around Jeremy's waist. "Don't make me yank your ass outta there."

The door opened with a squeal as the old hinges protested the strain, then he was in the room alone. The rope around his waist fed out through the hole in the door, held by the attendant as he watched through a narrow metal slit at eye level. No fancy respirators here, they were doing it old-school.

"Come on motherfucker, get it over with. Games's starting back up," the attendant impatiently urged.

Jeremy smelled the man before he saw him.

Across the room, chained to the wall.

No beautiful silver box.

No perfectly dimmed mood lights.

Just a foul creature standing in its own filth. Soiled rags

dangled from his emaciated frame, wild, unfocused eyes darted about the room, peering out from under the greasy hair hanging in front of his face. Jeremy took a step forward. His foot made a sickening sticky peeling sound as it moved. He steeled himself and took another step.

"Yeah, that's right!" the man outside the door shouted at the TV, startling him. "First down, bitches!"

The rope went tight around Jeremy's waist as he took another step. "Hey, some slack here!" he called out to the preoccupied man.

The rope loosened.

Eight steps in, it hit him, the first warm rumbling in his groin, his face flushing with that familiar sensation. "Oh God, yes," was all he could manage to say. He knew he couldn't get too close, but it just felt so good.

Just a little closer, he thought as he took another step. The sensations strengthened, his pulse pounded, and all worries began to melt away like a piece of ice dropped on a hot desert highway.

"Come on, pass the damn ball!" Jeremy barely noticed the man's voice from the other side of the door. He also failed to notice the lack of tension on the rope around his waist.

One step closer. Too close. The rope was still slack, but he didn't care as wave after wave of bliss rushed over him, bathing him in indescribable pleasure. He'd never been this close, felt this good. It was perfection. He never wanted to leave.

The emaciated creature's distant gaze shifted, his randomly darting eyes settling down, narrowing as they focused on the man in front of him. A spark flickered behind them as Jeremy met his gaze. Yellowed fangs peeked out as a smile slowly spread across the creature's face.

"Yes, okay," Jeremy mumbled as he took one more step. "Just one last fix."

The Lesbian Farmers of Quagshire

Far from the gleaming and cramped cities, packed hundreds of stories high and chock-full of humanity in all its many forms, was the quiet throwback to the past, the Township of Quagshire.

Out in the distant hills of Quag, near an area that was once known as Wales, the air lacked that visceral electric buzz the big city folk had long ago ceased to even notice. No airships or hover-cars buzzed the skies, nor did trip-hopping youth blare out their psych-fusion rock from embedded media devices. Indeed, for all intents and purposes, it appeared that way out in Quag, the wheels of progress seemed to lack the basic social-technological lubricant needed to keep up with the rest of society. While the throwback way of life had certain benefits, it had several drawbacks as well.

The day was like most others in the region this time of year; the skies dotted with clouds, the weather cool and a wee bit damp, but not particularly rainy.

Tamara Baird was minding her own business, as was her way, working the land that had been in her family for more than two-dozen generations. On this particular day, she eschewed her usual flowery dress in favor of a pair of well-worn dungarees, the faded denim rippling gently against her curves as the smooth material easily shifted to fit her familiar shape, the fibers softened over many years of wear and hand-washing.

The faint hum reached her ears while she dug in the modest carrot patch out back of the main house, a smudge of loamy soil decorating her cheek like an old-time soldier's war paint. The hum grew louder, and Tamara put down her small shovel and stood tall, her hands on her hips as she watched the shiny black hover car approach.

Only a few people in the area had them, most preferring (or only able to afford) terrestrial means of transport, but as the vehicle drew near, she didn't even need to see the license plates to know full well that this particular conveyance belonged to the firm of local developer Rutherford Corning.

The blowhard foreigner was nothing if not persistent in his attempts at her familial plot, his repeated legal assaults and character attacks not gaining traction in a region none too fond of interlopers. Still, his money was much coveted by some on the Township Council, and that made him dangerous. Dangerous, connected, and wealthy. Just the sort of challenge she welcomed.

On this particular occasion, she noted as the passengers exited the vehicle hovering inches above the ground, he appeared to be joined by none other than the local Council Chairman and moral busybody, Reverend Donagh Howell.

This should be interesting, she thought.

"Ms. Baird," Corning called out as the men approached, treading carefully in their expensive shoes as they walked over the damp soil. "I'm back, and before you do anything foolish, I'll have you know that this is official Council business, conducted with full backing of the Council, and the parish as well, I might add," he said, gesturing to the frocked man at his side.

"Aye, and what new business have ye here this time, ye toupéed twally?" she asked, throwing him some shade in broad tones for a laugh.

"You know why we're here, Ms. Baird," he replied. "You are living in an amoral state, in direct violation of local parish rules. As such, your lands are subject to forfeiture and seizure by the Township under the local moral turpitude provisions."

"Och, you're going to use outdated laws to take my farm, are you?"

"Indeed." The man flashed a smug and smarmy grin. "We know you've been living in sin with another woman," he said, pausing to see the shock register on her face. To his disappointment, she batted nary an eyelash. "As I was saying, the practice of sapphic acts is explicitly forbidden in local ordinances, not to mention being an abomination in the eyes of the Lord."

She looked him over coolly.

"You don't strike me as much of a moral man, Mr. Corning. In fact, I seem to recall hearing something about your most recent trophy wife having been in some racy photo sessions back in her modeling days. Of course that's why you pick the ones from the Slavic areas, eh? Getting gold-digging foreigners to do the jobs none of your country's own women want, I suppose."

"Now that's quite enough!" Reverend Howell hissed, his cheeks red with indignation. "Mr. Corning is a valuable investor in our Township, and his plans will be a boon to the region!" The nasty little man took a breath, then changed his tone. "Look, this doesn't have to be such a difficult process. I'm sure it's trying on you. This sort of thing can ruin a person's reputation, so perhaps you'd be happier foregoing this unpleasantness and simply accepting Mr. Corning's generous offer for your land. We needn't dig into your personal life any further, but if you force us to proceed, any results of this inquest will be immediately binding and public record for all to see."

"How you manage to remain the one parish still adhering to those backward and astoundingly outdated laws when the rest of the country has long been inclusive to people regardless of persuasion truly astounds me," she said, disgusted with both men. "Join the rest of the country, why don't you? There are far more important issues than people's sexuality for you to deal with. The low-income children, for example, or homelessness…"

"We told you before," Corning interrupted, "we'd be back with Council warrant for Truth Validation and National DNA Identity Confirmation to back it." The man flashed a serpent's smile.

"You already know my thoughts on that," she coolly replied.

"Yes, but I see you don't have your shotgun with you this afternoon."

She smiled at him. Behind her calm façade, he noted there was something a little scary in her eyes.

"I left it in the house, but to be fair it, was only loaded with rock salt last time," she said, studying the men. "Just because you may fancy yourself a big man out here in the country, you should know my kin in London are quite well connected and won't take kindly to your meddling in our family land."

"If you've violated the local laws, it will no longer be your family land, and there will be nothing you, your family, or anyone can do about it," Corning gloated, cocksure and arrogant. "The results of this test are validated by your DNA, are one hundred percent accurate, are completely irrefutable, and are immediately binding under the law."

"I'm fully aware," she said, still looking quite calm.

The Reverend removed a small bright metal device from the folds of his cloak and held it out for her.

"Ms. Baird, if you'd be so kind as to hold this in your palm. Please place your thumb here and answer the questions asked."

She took the device, feeling the smooth metal hum slightly as it tracked her emotions, pulse, and blood pressure. There was a tiny prick as the fine needle sampled her blood and retracted back into the device, running it wirelessly through the DNA validation databases. She watched as a green light flashed on the screen next to her name. "Tamara Baird, DNA confirmed," the machine chirped in a thin metallic voice.

"So," began Corning, "this is your family farm?"

"Yes, it is," she replied.

The Reverent looked at the read-out tablet in his hands, "Baseline established for true answers," he said.

"Well let's not dilly-dally then, shall we? Are you a lesbian, Ms. Baird?" Corning asked, expectant glee in his eyes.

"No, I am not."

A broad smile grew as the developer felt his plan coming together. Soon the land would be his, and without having to spend any credits at all.

"It's illegal to lie," he chuckled, "so thank you for that. This land will very soon be mine."

A puzzled look crossed the Reverend's face as he

scrutinized the machine. "It says she is telling the truth."

"Impossible," Corning blurted, his face reddening. "Ms. Baird, have you ever been intimate with a member of the same sex?"

"No, I have not."

"True again," said the Reverend.

A vein started throbbing visibly on Corning's forehead as the shocked man studied her, truly baffled. A flash of a small, wicked smile flickered behind Tamara's eyes, and, much to his consternation, he realized she was actually enjoying this.

"We have multiple reports of you consorting with a female farmhand. Do you deny this?" he continued, determined to catch her in a falsehood.

"Yes," she replied.

"She's telling the truth."

"Wait, 'yes' you deny it, or 'yes' you have consorted with a female farmhand?"

"Yes I deny it. I have never been with a female farmhand. In fact, I'll make this easy for you. I have never been with a woman, never been attracted to women, and am happily involved in a relationship with a man, with whom I have intimate relations on a regular basis. There, does that clear things up for you?"

They looked at her, stunned. The machine lit up green and pinged.

"True," said the Reverend.

Corning's face began to turn crimson, the veins on his forehead commencing to throb with renewed might as he saw his grand plans for this plot of land going up in smoke.

"The machine must be broken," he stammered.

"No, it's working," replied the Reverend. "The scan confirms DNA identity, Tamara Baird, female, owner of the Baird Family Farm, has answered all questions truthfully."

The men looked at one another, confused.

"Excuse me," interrupted Tamara. "You did say the results were now public record and immediately and fully legally binding, did you not? Well then, I do believe at this point it is time for you gentlemen to get off my family land."

Corning gave her a scorching look, but the cool gaze she returned immediately extinguished any heat he tried to throw her way.

"This isn't over," he growled.

"Actually, according to your own laws, it is," she gloated. "And gentlemen," she said as she fixed them with a somewhat unsettling stare, "the next time you trespass, the shotgun won't be loaded with salt."

The defeated men sulked as they piled into their vehicle and headed back to the Corning offices, leaving the Baird Farm in their hover car's dusty magneto field wake. As they rounded the bend and passed out of view, a voice came from the cellar door.

"Are they gone?"

"Aye, you two can come out now."

Emerging from the cellar hand in hand climbed Dana, a lovely and rather zaftig farmhand, her auburn hair in a tight ponytail, along with her girlfriend, a woman in a floral dress and pigtails, who just so happened to be the spitting image of the woman in dungarees. The real Tamara Baird.

"Clara, that was brilliant!" Tamara gushed as she scooped up her twin in a massive hug.

"Yeah, we really can't thank you enough," Dana agreed, gratitude shining in her big blue eyes.

Clara smiled at them both as she shed her dungarees in favor of the stylish workout tights underneath them,

"Hey, you mess with my sister, you mess with me," she laughed. It was a light and airy sound, but the fiercely protective look in her eye conveyed the impression she might not have been joking about the shotgun after all.

"Can you stay for supper?" Tamara asked.

"I wish I could, but Brian and the boys are waiting for me to get back. Maybe you two can come to London next week?"

"We'd love to. Send them our love in the meantime."

"Will do."

Moments later, Clara's shiny new hover car emerged from the barn and turned southwest as she headed back to the hustle and bustle of the big city, knowing that, for the time being at least, the lesbian farmers of Quagshire were once more safe in their home.

Huh

As she emerged from the bright fluorescent glare of the hospital's lobby, the first thing that really struck her was how fresh the air smelled. Okay, technically that was the second thing that struck her that day, the first being the large piece of decorative plaster façade that had come loose from the old bank building downtown and smacked her something good on her noggin earlier that morning. So the *second* thing that struck her was the fresh air.

Oh my, she thought as she breathed in deep, filling her nose and lungs with the crisp air, *that's a whole lot better than that horrid antiseptic stink!*

Madeline Dunleavy could have taken a cab home straightaway, at least now that she knew where home was, but she felt the urge to just be. To walk the streets for a bit. To let her mind and body relax. For someone who had a moderate concussion and a rather disturbing case of amnesia, it was a somewhat unlikely choice, but off she went, straight from the hospital to enjoy an afternoon stroll.

They had told her that she had been doing nothing at all when passersby called out a warning just before she took a chunk of building to the head. Really, they were surprised she hadn't been more seriously hurt.

"You're one lucky lady!" they'd told her when she woke up, finding strangers in white coats icing her head. Fortunately, there was no need for stitches, the skin only mildly bruised. "Now tell us, honey, what's your name? Is there someone we can call?"

"Uh…" was all Madeline could manage.

"Oh dear," the nurse replied.

They spent the next several hours checking in on her to see if she remembered anything, but to no avail. It seemed she was brought in unconscious and simply didn't have the slightest clue who she was.

"Wait a minute," she blurted. "Don't I have a purse or something?"

"Well yes, but I checked it already. There was nothing in it but an uneaten croissant and a few napkins. You must've just picked it up for breakfast when you took that knock."

Madeline scrunched her brow. That didn't seem right.

"Let me take a look," she requested.

"Alright, but I told you, I already checked." The nurse opened the drawer next to the bed and pulled out a large white plastic bag for personal possessions. "Here ya go," she said as she handed over the purse from within.

Madeline hefted the bag, feeling the weight in her grip. It seemed far too light. There had to be something in it, why would she go out with so little? And a croissant? Sure they're a tasty treat, but how had she paid for it? She dug her hands through the purse. Nope, nothing. Frustrated, she was about to zip it closed when she noticed a tear in the fabric liner.

"Hmm, I wonder…" she muttered as she stuck her fingers into the gap. They brushed against a small wallet.

"Hey, look what I found," she chirped, triumphantly.

"That's so weird, I know I searched every inch of that thing."

Madeline wasn't listening, but instead had the wallet open in her lap, examining the contents. It contained exactly what she had expected. A driver's license and a key tucked into one of the small card pockets.

"Madeline Dunleavy," she said, getting the feel for the name, rolling it in her mouth like a nice smoky whiskey. "I'm Madeline Dunleavy. Nice to meet you."

The nurse took her hand and shook it.

"Nice to make your acquaintance Madeline. Does that have an address for you? I looked for a phone to call someone in your contacts, but you don't seem to have one. How weird is that? I guess it must've gotten lost when you were hurt."

"Must've," Madeline replied.

With the patient seeming in perfect health aside from her steadily retreating amnesia, the doctors felt it was reasonable for her to be released to her own home, now that she had an address to return to.

"If you have any blurred vision, dizziness, vomiting, or unusual physical issues, check back with us tomorrow," they said as she exited the hospital.

"Will do," she replied as she slipped on her light coat and walked out of the bright fluorescent lights and into the fresh air.

A breath of fresh air.

In this case it actually *was* as breath of fresh air that was a breath of fresh air, and with her lungs happily filled with some choice O^2, Madeline began strolling in the general direction of her apartment (at least that's what the nice man with the smartphone told her).

The day seemed so vibrant, the colors popped, the smells

resonated in her nose, captivating her with their myriad aromas as she passed bakeries, flower stores, and cafes. Of course, she thought, it might just be the head injury, but the afternoon really seemed special. She almost felt as if she hadn't experienced a day like this in a long, long time, and it was hitting the spot perfectly.

The small park she decided to take a meandering long-way-home stroll through had the wonderful, earthy fragrance of fresh grass and slightly damp soil. The good parts of nature filled the air with awesome, and as she looked at the trees gently swaying in the cool breeze, she noticed a flock of birds flying high above.

Such beautiful creatures, birds, she marveled as she watched them soar. *I wish they'd fly lower so I could get a better look at them.* No sooner had the thought passed her mind than she noticed a brightly colored parrot nestled on a branch, it's green and yellow feathers almost invisible among the leaves.

"Hey little fella, what are you doing up there?" she asked the bird.

He (or she, you really can't tell with parrots, so let's just call it a boy for the sake of convenience) noticed the human talking to him and fluffed up his feathers a moment, then flew down toward her, landing on a water fountain nearby.

"Aren't you adorable," she cooed.

"Pretty bird!" he replied.

"And you speak! Aww, you must've flown out of someone's window. Polly want a cracker?" she asked with a little grin. "Well, I don't actually have any crackers, but I can give you a piece of my croissant. I don't know if birds like French pastry, though."

"Oui, oui, for me!" the bird replied.

"Oh my, you're a clever little thing, aren't you?"

She dug in her purse and held out the crispy end for the bird to nibble on. Rather than cautiously snatching it from her hand, as she expected, he hopped up on her arm and happily chewed her offering before walking up to her shoulder and settling in.

"You're a friendly one. I think I'm going to take you home, it wouldn't be right to leave you out here to fend for yourself. Would you like that?"

"Like that!" the bird said.

"Such an odd little guy. Okay, off we go. I think I'll call you Walter. That seems like a good name for now."

Apparently, having a parrot on your shoulder, especially a rather chatty one, makes you a lot of friends on the street, and Madeline found herself engaged in conversations with just about everyone she passed. The grizzled biker softened when she walked by, telling her of the time his parrot had a heart attack and he made the paramedics do mouth-to-beak resuscitation at knifepoint. The kids on skateboards tried talking shit to the bird, only to find her winged minion had a far fouler vocabulary than they could ever hope to acquire.

"And who taught you that?" she had asked, both amused and slightly abash at Walter's sailor-like rant.

Passing a small farm-stand shop, Walter flapped his wings and leapt into an open barrel of peanuts, happier than a proverbial pig in shit (or parrot in peanuts, as the case may be).

"Walter, get out of there!" she chided the bird. He fixed his glossy eye on her a moment, looked back at the mountain of edible treasure, then having made up his bird mind, snatched one last nut and flew to her shoulder.

"Now that's something I don't see every day," the shopkeeper said, not sure whether to be annoyed or amused. Ultimately, he settled on a combination of both.

"I'm so sorry, I'll pay for those, of course. In fact, I should buy him some for later anyway. He can't go on eating French pastry every meal after all. I'll take a pound, please."

The shopkeeper gave her an odd look, then bagged up the nuts for her.

"That'll be $2.50, tax included."

She dug in her wallet, only to realize there was no money in it. She'd noticed that when she first discovered it but that inconvenient little fact had slipped her mind entirely.

"I'm sorry, hang on, maybe I have some change somewhere," she said, fishing around in her light coat's hip pockets. She pulled out lint, a rubber band, and some pocket sand. She was about to give up when her fingertip grazed a balled-up piece of paper.

"Can you break this?" she asked as she unfolded the hundred-dollar bill.

Stepping into her apartment, she found the place was everything she would have expected her apartment to be. She may have lost her memory, but apparently her taste was exquisite.

Beautiful artwork graced the walls, classic lined furniture tied the rooms together, and her fridge was stocked with much more than just shelves of condiments. When she walked through her bedroom, she noted a man's button-down shirt, crumpled from obvious use as a nightgown.

"What do you think, Walter?" she said, walking back to the kitchen and putting the bird on the kitchen counter. "Do I have a boyfriend?"

As if on cue, a key turned in the lock, and a dark-haired man with a sexy five o'clock shadow shouldered the door open. His sleeves were rolled up and his tie was askew as he carried in armloads of takeout Italian food, a bouquet of flowers, and a bottle of wine.

"Oh, you're home!" he said, startled. "I guess I'm busted. I was going to surprise you with Italian tonight."

"Who's the boy? Who's the boy?" Walter chimed in, saying out loud what Madeline was thinking. It's kind of embarrassing after all, having to ask your boyfriend his name.

"You got a parrot?"

"Yeah, I found him on the way home. His name's Walter."

"Hi Walter, I'm Donovan."

Donovan, she ran the name through her mind. *I like the sound of that. He seems like a good fella, even brought me food. I wonder how good he is in the sack.*

After dinner, she found out.

She was most certainly not disappointed.

Once he cleared the table and did the dishes (he insisted she not raise a finger), he slowly undressed her as he led her to the queen-sized bed, pausing as her shed articles of clothing left swaths of delectable flesh exposed and longing for attention.

He caressed her body, both gentle yet rough, sensing what she wanted and responding in perfect synchronicity. When, after several wonderfully torturous minutes, their naked bodies finally became enmeshed in her luxurious bed, things only got hotter from there.

Donovan was relentless, bringing her to the brink of climax over and over, Madeline savoring every glorious moment until finally, her bed slamming fiercely, she came, bucking so hard the bed jumped from the floor, banging into the wall with a crash.

As they lay there sweaty in each other's arms, she noticed the cracks in her wall, and ceiling.

Damn, she thought with a chuckle, *came so hard we broke the place!*

Shortly thereafter they fell into a sound (and well-deserved) sleep wrapped in each other's arms.

The voices were what woke her up.

Madeline was comfortably resting when she heard the first of them. It was ever so faint, almost like a buzzing insect just out of reach.

What is that? She rolled to her side and put the pillow over her head.

No good.

The voices continued regardless, apparently immune to the muffling powers of feather down pillows.

"Hey," she said, nudging Donovan.

"Hmm? What is it?" he asked groggily. "It's Sunday, I don't have to get up."

"Do you hear that?"

"Hear what?"

"It sounds like voices."

"Honey, go back to sleep, okay?" he said, curling back up

and slipping once more into blissful unconsciousness.

Madeline, on the other hand, could do no such thing. She got to her feet and hopped in the shower. The voices followed her. In fact, they stayed with her as she poured a bowl of cereal, and got a little louder when she gave a small pile of Cheerios to Walter.

"You can hear them, can't you Walter?"

"Talkie talkie," said the bird.

"Good bird."

Walking the streets at such an early hour on a Sunday, Madeline couldn't help but feel relaxed by the lack of traffic noise in the air. Or at least she would have felt relaxed if not for the increasing clamor of voices. What had started as just a few faintly speaking in the distance had grown to what must have been at least a dozen, all talking at the same time, just beyond her ability to comprehend.

When she stopped to get a cappuccino, she asked the barista if she heard them. The answer was no, which was disconcerting. Adding insult to injury, Madeline was not amused when she saw the name that had been penned on her to-go cup.

"Crazy Bird Lady."

"Crazy lady! Crazy lady!" Walter had opined just as she was ordering. *Thanks Walter,* she thought as she sipped the piping hot drink and stepped outside.

"Well," she said out loud to no one in particular, "if I can't get away from them..." With that, she started off down the street, using the voices as a sort of compass, following the sound as it got louder and louder.

By the time she had reached the front of the old church, the voices were in the dozens, and the volume was downright annoying.

"Seems to be coming from in there," she said to her feathered friend. "Should we go in?"

"Going home! Going home!" Walter chirped.

Madeline stepped from the sidewalk onto the church grounds and stopped in her tracks. The voices, all seventy-eight of them she suddenly knew, were perfectly clear. Not only that, she could make out what each and every one of them was saying. All at once.

"Oh," she said as things slammed into focus. She knew what had happened, her memory crystal clear.

Several blocks away, Madeline Dunleavy's apartment disappeared.

As did her boyfriend.

As did every trace of her ever existing.

With a ruffle of his feathers, Walter too disappeared.

"Huh," God said with an amused little shrug as she faded, albeit reluctantly, into the ether, heading back to work after her first real vacation in Lord knows how many millennia.

"A swan?" he asked incredulously. "Seriously? A swan?"

Damien's look spoke volumes.

Och, not again, she thought. *And it had been going so well.*

Gillian let out a disappointed little sigh as the writing on the wall came into sharp focus.

"Yes, a swan," she replied. "It flew right into me. Quite embarrassing, really. I mean, who expects a bloody swan to smack into them on a bridge? Anyway, I was already running behind, you see, but then I had to stop to clean off the feathers, and that's why I was late. Isn't that just daft?" She laughed, hoping that he'd somehow find the whole thing amusing as well.

He didn't laugh with her. Nor at her. Amused, he was not.

She reached across the table and took his hands in hers. They'd been dating but a few short months, surely it couldn't be over so soon. She gazed at his face, searching his dour expression for a glimmer of hope, wishing maybe, just maybe this once, her gut was wrong.

It wasn't.

Thus the Queen of the Nutters once more found herself single and back home before ten o'clock (on a Saturday no less!), out of her finery and ensconced in a cozy throw on her couch with an oversized glass of wine in one hand and a bag full of chocolate biscuits in the other. It was turning out to be one of those nights.

It had been many years since she'd first discovered her superpower. Well it wasn't really much of a power per se.

Some might even consider it a curse. Round about the time she was accosted by the stark-raving mad street mime who had followed her for miles, jabbering at her the entire time, she came to realize that there had to be an invisible, flashing neon sign floating above her head that only the truly insane could see.

"Nutters, Follow Me, For I Am Your Queen!" she had decided it must read, and thus Gillian long ago resigned herself to being the Queen of the Nutters.

Mind you, there were positive aspects as well. Fun stories and amusing anecdotes, should she ever decide to write a book about them. Perhaps something along the lines of, "The time when Gillian ___," with each chapter being a new tale of yet another ludicrous experience or unbelievable adventure.

On the other hand, amusing stories aside, when you attract nutters like a Prozac magnet, it can make finding a suitable date somewhat of a problem. Worse yet, sometimes her whacked-out minions would sneakily disguise themselves as sane people and score a date with her, only later pulling off their proverbial mask of sanity and exposing themselves (figuratively, except for that one time) for what they really were.

"Excuse me, miss, do you need some help?" the gentleman passing on the street asked.

From her precarious position wedged halfway out of the bathroom window, Gillian had come to the unfortunate realization that, try as she might, she simply couldn't squeeze through.

"Oh, I'm quite all right," she chirped, false levity flavoring her voice. "But if you could hand me up my purse, I'd be ever so grateful."

The man bent and picked it up from the damp pavement as he took in the ususual sight of the well-dressed woman he'd stumbled upon protruding from the restaurant's small window.

It was a fancy place, known for its ambiance and charm. The man she'd met online had suggested it for their date. "A beautiful restaurant in which to meet a beautiful woman," he'd said.

His dating profile had been quite intriguing, and her hopes were high. Successful, athletic, handsome, and stylish, what woman wouldn't be eager to meet such a catch in the flesh?

Excited at the prospect of a romantic evening (and maybe even a good snog if things went really well), she arrived at the restaurant a bit early, grabbing a cozy table for two in a quiet corner. All the better for privacy, she had reasoned. She really had high hopes for this one. Unfortunately, the table's location also made it harder to flee without making a scene, something she desperately wanted to do after her date had only just sat down.

The man was large. Not fit-and-strong large, but more that muscle-gone-soft large, at least so far as she could tell. It was rather hard to gauge his true shape under the layers of cardigans. Yes, cardigans, *plural*. He had shown up wearing what must've been a half dozen of them, bulking him out until he resembled a rather large and odd attack-dog training dummy.

Then there were the hats. Yes, *plural*. He had on at least

two that she could see, though she suspected there was a third hidden under the snug wool watch cap tightly ensconced beneath his outermost chapeau.

All those layers, she thought, struggling to keep a neutral expression, a*nd it isn't even winter.*

"So lovely to meet you," he had said, taking her porcelain hand in his damp palm, moistly kissing her knuckles like a freakish, sweaty, white knight.

"Ah, yes, um, a pleasure." She was at a loss for words. One of the downfalls of the Queen of the Nutters was that, despite being regularly subjected to awkward circumstances, she was still polite and sensitive to people's feelings, almost to a fault at times, which was impressive for an otherwise fiery Scottish lass. The man was an obvious loon, but she just couldn't bring herself to crush his poor heart and run from the table at first meeting. Maybe they could be friends at least, or so she had thought.

With her track record, one can easily imagine how that panned out.

A mere five minutes into their conversation– less time than it takes to brew a proper pot of tea even– she found herself in the awkward position of being the third wheel on their date. Not that she wanted to be on that date at all, mind you, nor would she have wanted to be the focus of his attention, but what really put her over the edge was the fact that she was the third wheel in a conversation he was having with someone who wasn't there.

She looked up, almost expecting the invisible sign over her head to have materialized into bright, flashing neon.

"That's fascinating," she said when an opportunity to get

a word in presented itself, eyes darting as she desperately searched for a way out. "If you don't mind, I need to freshen up in the ladies' for a moment." She excused herself, and no sooner had she locked the door to the loo than she made straight for the tiny window, tossing her purse out and lunging headfirst after it. Unfortunately, it was a bit narrower than she'd anticipated.

"Here you are, dear," the man said, handing up the purse to the strange young woman dangling out the window. "You sure you're all right, luv?"

"Oh, yes, fine. Silly me, I was, um, startled by a mouse in the loo and accidentally flung my purse out the window. Och, such a silly thing to do. Thank you so much for retrieving it for me!"

The man tipped his cap and carried on down the way, while Gillian reluctantly slid back into the restroom and returned to her seat.

After an uncomfortable hour trapped in the cozy nook, her phone rang, quite unplanned, and provided her an out (one that she berated herself for not thinking of earlier). She bid the many-layered man farewell, and after suffering through a rather pungent hug that left her smelling faintly of curry and smoke, she dashed out the door and straight home, whereupon she took a cold shower and turned off her dating profile for good.

Or at least for the time being.

It wasn't always dates, of course. Sometimes it was just random occurrences or situations on the street, and Lord help her when there was a full moon.

Like a nascent werewolf afraid of the damage it might cause, she realized it was perhaps best if she stayed in during that phase of the lunar cycle. Of course it was also hard to go out when your house keys would somehow wind up in a box of cereal and your cellular phone would be discovered cold, but still functional, in the vegetable drawer of the refrigerator.

So she would stay home at the apex of the lunar cycle, content to warm herself with a glass or three of wine and a roll of Jammie Dodgers. An odd combination, perhaps, but booze and biscuits were tame by comparison to what could be lying in wait outside.

It was only natural that when she stayed in, she would invariably be tormented by the invisible mouse that plagued her wherever she lived. From the time she had first moved to London, the wee thing had taken up residence in her kitchen. Crumbs left here and there, crackers disappearing, faint chewing from behind the walls.

The problem was, none of her flatmates ever saw or heard it.

"No, really!" she'd protest. "We have a wee moosie in the kitchen!"

"Sure, Gill," they'd reply. "We'll call the landlord in the morning to look into it." Always humoring her, but never believing.

What was more flummoxing was the mouse would move with her to each new abode, and every time, she was the only one who would notice it. Of course given her regal title, an invisible mouse was among the least of her worries.

Gillian had been out on yet another horrible date, this one

set up by an old friend who either harbored a secret grudge against her, or simply had no idea that the "lovely man" she had set her friend up with was both obsessive compulsive as well as closeted. At least they had parted on friendly terms, and perhaps she'd even have a new gay friend to go clubbing with, at least if he came to terms with his sexuality.

In any case, for a moment she forgot about the massive invisible sign over her head and allowed herself to enjoy the quiet walk to the tube station.

"Excuse me," a pretty woman in a burgundy coat asked. "Do you have the time?"

"Half ten," she replied.

"Oh thank goodness. I'm meeting my boyfriend but my phone died. I thought I was going to miss the next one. Thank you!"

Gillian trotted down the steps behind her and clambered onto the train and settled in for the ride.

It was still early-ish when she arrived back in her neighborhood, and she thought it would be nice to continue her stroll along the high street, enjoying the cheerful crowds out for a Friday night on the town.

Gillian decided to treat herself to a wee snack, then meandered over to an unoccupied bench across from the cafe, taking up a comfortable position to relax, people watch, and reflect on the evening's unusual turn.

Of course he was gay, she mused. *I swear, at this rate I'll die a spinster*. She didn't really believe that of course, but the moment of self-indulgent drama felt nice to wallow in. Everyone needs to allow themselves that dip once in a while, so long as they don't do a cannonball into it. Fortunately her spirits were of such a nature that those down spots never lasted long.

"Did you see?" The man standing in front of her was scanning the crowds as he spoke to her.

"Excuse me?" she replied. "Did I see what, exactly?" Where had he come from?

The man slowly turned his head and watched the milling people on the street as they passed by.

"There's a man with a knife," he said.

"Oh dear!" Gillian replied. "That's terrible. What's he doing with a knife?"

"He's probably dangerous," the man shot back. "Maybe he wants to hurt people."

"Well, we'd better keep an eye out, then!" she replied.

It's worth mentioning that although it was most definitely *not* a full moon, the Queen of the Nutters had, for one reason or another, failed to notice the rather large blade the man was holding as he spoke to her. Her lack of concern threw him, and the poor fellow seemed genuinely confused, unsure what to do.

"You know, I bet if you tried to run, he might even stab you," he finally said.

"Well, lucky for me he's not here!" she replied.

An almost pained look crossed the man's face. This was not going as planned. It was at that very moment that Gillian finally noticed the knife in his hand.

She smiled at him, pretending everything was fine. Acting like something was wrong was a good way to get stabbed, and she most certainly liked her skin and vital bits intact.

The gods must've been favoring her that night, because

the woman she'd given the time on the tube happened to be passing by at precisely that moment, and coincidentally happened to make (and hold) eye contact with her (how very un-British). The woman somehow sensed in that brief glance that there was something amiss, and with a squeeze of her boyfriend's arm (at least Gillian assumed that's who the large man in the denim jacket was), she steered him over to where the damsel in distress was sitting.

"Oh, there you are! We've been looking for you!"

Gillian flashed a big, yet subtly strained smile. "Yes, so good to see you! This lovely man was just keeping me company." Her eyes quickly darted to the knife in his hand, and for once things went her way.

"Oy, mate, nice to meet ya. I'm Brian," the jacketed fellow said, extending his hand, which took the man rather off guard. He looked at the offered hand and hesitated, unsure what to do. Brian had apparently already sussed out the situation and, with impressive speed and confidence, grabbed the man and flipped him to the ground, holding him in a submission lock while he pried the knife from his grip.

"Call us a copper, would ya, love?" he said to his girlfriend, tossing her his mobile with his free hand. He hadn't even broken a sweat.

"Former SAS," she informed Gillian with a smile as she dialed the police.

Twenty minutes and a statement to the police later, the Queen of the Nutters thanked her new friends and saviours and walked the remaining blocks home to pass out in a heap on her bed, exhausted from yet another unbelievable ordeal.

"That's it," she said to her reflection in the bathroom mirror the following morning. "I'm done. No more dating. It's just me, myself, and I for a bit. Don't need any more drama in my life."

Making that decision was like lifting a weight from her shoulders that she hadn't even realized she had been under. Like Atlas shrugging off his burden, she felt better. Lighter. Free. Her spirits high, she threw on a thin jacket and stepped out into the cool but sunny day.

A bit peckish, she stopped into the corner cafe and picked up a croissant, which she was happily munching as she turned the corner.

At that very moment, a flustered and distracted young man rounded it from the other direction, crashing right into her and knocking the croissant from her hand, mashing it into his lapel.

"Och, I'm so sorry!" he said in a faint Glaswegian accent. "I dinnae mean to–" He looked up from the ground and found himself at a loss for words when his eyes met hers. "Um..." was all his tongue could manage for a moment, then, "My apologies."

"Well, you're in quite a state!" the Queen of the Nutters chided him. "Fleeing an angry girlfriend, are ye?" She rather liked his face and found herself smiling at him.

"What? Oh, no, I don't have a girlfriend." He blushed, which she found absolutely adorable. "It's just the strangest thing just happened," he said. "I was walking past the park down the way, and as I rounded the pond, there was a big splash. Some kids were throwing rocks, I guess, but the next thing I knew, a goose flew right into me!"

"A goose?" she said. Her face grew warm, and her heart began beating faster. "Seriously? A goose?"

"I know, it sounds totally daft, but it's the truth. All my life these things keep happening to me. It's like I'm a magnet or something. And then there was a crazy homeless man with, like, a dozen jumpers on in the park, who yelled at me afterwards. He smelled of old curry and kept on about making him spill his tea on his cardigans." He laughed and shook his head. "I tell you, there are times I swear there must be an invisible sign above my head that reads 'Come One, Come All ye Nutters, for I am your King' in neon lights."

Gillian slowly reached out and gently brushed the crumbs from his lapel with an affectionate caress.

"Oh, your pastry. I'm so sorry. I was so carried away with the story, I hadn't noticed…"

"That's all right," she said, holding his gaze for a long moment, then lacing her arm through his. "Why don't you come buy me another one and tell me all about it."

"What you're feeling is their feet, stomping in unison as they march. Left foot, right foot, left foot, right foot, all at once until everything starts to shake and churn."

Helen looked at her son. Just five years had passed since she'd barely survived the blood loss from an extraordinarily difficult childbirth. At the time, she had wondered if she'd made the right choice, having the child, but now she couldn't imagine a world without him.

As an infant, he would stare quietly at the shining, snipped-tin star mobile her husband had made for the nursery as it spun lazily in the full-spectrum light they'd installed beside the crib. Alex hadn't always been a handy sort of man, most computer programmers aren't, really, but Helen had found when the need for him to step up for his family arose, he had pleasantly surprised her with his ingenuity and skill, time and again.

They had decorated Finn's room sparsely at first. A map of the world tacked up, a calming Little Boy Blue coating the walls, a few choice baubles to amuse their son. As time went on, he grew into a curious toddler capable of all sorts of mischief, so they kid-proofed the house and installed additional latches on the doors and windows. The heavy curtains hung from reinforced rods lest he try to climb them, and any breakable china was locked away in the cupboard.

"Mommy, the trolls are doing it again!" the boy whined as he lay cozily entwined in his mother's arms, snug and warm beneath a small throw on the old couch.

"I know honey, but you know the King of the Belly Trolls

has sent his men to gather a tribute for him."

"Tr–triboot."

"Tribute. It's kind of like a special present the people give to their king. So what you feel, all that marching, it's what the Belly Trolls do when they go looking for a suitable gift."

"But I don't like it," the boy grumbled.

"I know, honey, but the Belly Trolls are going to make their king so happy. You know, I bet when your father gets home he'll be so proud of you for having your very own Belly Trolls."

"How long will it take?" the boy asked, shifting uncomfortably on the couch.

"Well, sometimes it can be a long and dangerous journey. Would you like me to tell you about it?" she asked, knowing her son loved a good adventure tale.

"Yes, please."

"All right. Now, you already know the King of the Belly Trolls is the biggest, strongest troll in the land, but without his people, he's not a king at all, just a sad troll alone in his castle. That's why he treats his people kindly. They need him as much as he needs them, and for many years, he's taken very good care of the other trolls, and they love him for it so very much." She lazily stroked Finn's sandy locks as she spoke.

"The Belly Trolls believe in stockpiling for difficult times. They can't always leave their fortress to go looking for tributes for the king, but from time to time, when the situation is right and the supplies are running low, they all gather up their spears and clubs and march out of the gates to get wonderful things to replenish their store rooms of their home. The trolls love their fortress. Its walls are strong, its doors have sturdy locks, and inside is warm and cozy and full of their families and loved ones, so when it's time to go out and march, they say goodbye to their wives and sons, knowing that it's a dangerous journey they might not come back from."

"Why wouldn't they come back?" the boy asked, looking up at his mother with curious eyes.

"Because sometimes things happen to grown-ups and they can't come back, even if they want to. But their families know that even if they don't return, they loved them very much."

Finn seemed to think about this for a moment, then, content enough with the explanation he didn't fully understand, he lay his head back in his mother's lap.

"The kingdom outside the fortress was a ruined world. Not a total wasteland, but a broken and empty place where only the strong survived. But in that dangerous land, there were also special places, hidden places that only the most loyal and trusted Belly Trolls knew of. They were thought to have been destroyed when everything collapsed, but one of the king's finest men discovered a secret way into the underground treasure."

"A treasure?"

"Yes, it had been buried for years when the brave troll stumbled upon it while out hunting for a tribute for the king. Beautiful rows of things he desired, things he knew his wife and baby would need back home in the fortress, so he loaded his pack with as much as he could carry and quietly sneaked back, covering his tracks so none of the bad scavengers would find him."

"Why are they bad?" the quiet voice asked from her lap.

"Well, the good trolls all live inside the fortress, but the people not so lucky became very angry at both the good trolls and each other. They would get into fights and hurt each other and steal each other's things."

"But stealing is bad."

"You're right, stealing is bad, but they did it anyway, and that's why they were bad men."

The boy's stomach growled loudly.

"I think the Belly Trolls are fighting the bad men," he said innocently.

"I think maybe you're right. But you know the belly trolls are very smart, and I'm sure they'll win. And you know what else? I bet they'll be very thirsty after the battle. Let's make some tea and send it to them as a gift, would you like that?"

Finn brightened up. "Yes Mama, that's a good idea!"

Helen eased her son off her lap and slid her feet into the warm fleece-lined slippers beside the couch.

"I'll be right back, baby," she said as she walked quietly to the kitchen.

She flipped a breaker on the wall and turned on the small hotplate, placing the half-full kettle on top of it, then opening the small wooden box on the shelf, removing a single tea bag.

As the water heated, she took two brightly colored mugs and placed them on the counter. Finn's, naturally, was the one with a cartoon moose on it.

A minute later the water reached a low boil, and she poured it over the fresh bag in her son's mug, letting it steep for a few minutes before dropping the same bag in her own mug, filling it to the rim for a long soak.

Helen finally removed the bag and put it in a small dish on the counter, then flipped the breaker off and walked back to the cozy living room.

Finn was curled up under the throw, waiting for her.

"Here you go." She smiled at him. "I think the Belly Trolls will be very happy you're sending them this treat."

He sipped at the hot liquid, enjoying the flavor swirling in his mouth before swallowing and sending it on its way to the trolls in his belly.

"Better?" she asked.

"I think the Belly Trolls are resting now," he replied. "They must have really liked the tea."

"I thought they would," his mother said with a pleased smile. "So where was I?"

"The bad men stealing and fighting the good men."

"Ah, yes. So the bad men were always looking for people to take advantage of, but the belly trolls were too smart for them. They'd only go when it was safe, and if they saw any of the bad men, they'd hide until they passed by."

"But if there were so many Belly Trolls, why did they need to hide?"

"Because fighting is bad. Even if you win. Remember, it's better to hide and be unseen than to fight, even if you think you can win. Understand?"

"I guess."

"Good. Now, when the trolls knew the coast was clear, they'd emerge from their hiding places and continue on their quest. Occasionally, if they were really lucky, they'd find wild animals they could take home for their people. Once they even found a chicken."

"Did she lay eggs?" the boy asked.

"No, it wasn't a hen, it was a boy chicken. We call those

roosters." *Vicious little bastard too,* she thought. "So the people had a great feast, and everyone was happy for a long time."

A thump sounded outside the front door. Helen jumped a little at the sound.

"Okay, now you know what we do when there's someone at the door."

"Go to my room and wait under the bed."

"Good boy. Now get moving, and maybe I'll tell you another story later."

Finn scurried off down the short hallway and into his room, closing the door behind him before slithering under his bed, just like his mama taught him.

Helen pulled the weathered shotgun out from behind the bookshelf and took up a kneeling position behind the couch, barrel pointed at the door.

There was a shuffling sound, followed by another thump. Then dragging of something heavy, right to the threshold.

Three knocks sounded, then one, then five before a key unlocked the first of the four deadbolts. When all were slid open, Alex, grimy and blood-streaked, lurched into the room, dragging a heavy duffle bag inside, closing the door behind him and locking it tight before allowing himself a sigh of relief as he slid to the floor.

Helen rose from her vantage point and put the gun down.

"What happened?" she asked, concerned at the state of her husband. "How badly are you hurt?"

"Not my blood," he replied. "Ran into some trouble on the way back from the warehouse."

The warehouse. That was the name they'd decided upon for the family market that had been knocked flat during the war. It was pure luck he had stumbled upon it, really. A mixed-use building, the top floors had collapsed on top of it, but miraculously some parts of the crushed store had survived, its lower-most shelves of canned goods largely accessible. The stench of the rotting produce and meats and smashed-open canned goods putrefying in that enclosed space had made retrieval an unpleasant, but nevertheless necessary chore. It also kept out prying scavengers.

Alex found it by blind luck. He had been searching for baby supplies for his infant son in the rubble of the crumbled apartments when he happened upon a small void beneath a tumbled refrigerator. A short crawl later he found himself kneeling in the largely accessible goldmine of supplies. They'd lasted for several years, with careful rationing, but even those were finally coming to an end.

It was a dangerous trip, and with roving scavengers to actively avoid, he could only take small amounts with him at any given time. The risk of noise and of being slowed by the weight was too great otherwise.

"I managed to find a few cans of green beans and some other stuff that was buried in a pile of rotting something that crawled in there and died. I think it might have been an opossum. Anyway, the labels had come off in the mess, so it'll have to be dinner roulette. Everything all right here?"

"The solar panels seem to be charging the batteries slower, maybe they need a scrub. The hot plate still works for now, but we really need to see to that before it gets any worse." She eyed her husband, his sunken cheeks showing his hunger, even if he'd never admit it. "Cup of tea?" she asked, walking into the kitchen and taking the still-damp bag from the counter and dropping it in a mug.

"Oh Lord, yes," he said as he rose to his feet to join her. "Finn okay?"

"Yeah, but his Belly Trolls are acting up again."

A small smile crossed his face. It wasn't a look of happiness, but one of disturbed satisfaction.

"That won't be an issue, at least not for a little bit."

"What do you mean?" Helen asked, eyebrow raised with curiosity.

He nodded to the duffle bag, "Got us some meat," was his reply as he took a damp cloth and slowly started rubbing his skin, trying to get the blood off without using too much of their precious water.

Helen opened the bag, wondering what he'd managed to catch this time. That Alex, she'd never have thought him to be a capable hunter, but when his family's life was on the line, he once again surprised her with his force of will when it came to providing for them.

The leg had a light coat of hair on it, but that could be removed easily enough, along with the sock and shoe still on its foot. She was surprised Alex had managed to get the whole thing off with just the small knife he carried.

Humming a happy tune, Helen walked down the hall and opened the door to Finn's room.

"It's okay baby, you can come out now."

The thin boy slid out from under his bed, looking at his mother expectantly.

"I have some good news," she said. "Daddy brought you a tribute for the King of the Belly Trolls."

Wag

Garrtin felt the blood gush into his mouth as his mighty jaws clamped shut, severing at least one vital artery with a wet crunch. The hot red gore sprayed and coated his muzzle as he dispatched his pathetically inferior foe with ease.

The invasion will be over in a day if this is the best resistance they have to offer, he thought as he watched the rest of his pack tear into the native defenders.

He was Designation Alpha, the leader of Assault Pack Delta and the many sub-packs contained within. All told, there were several thousand under his command, spread out across their assigned sectors of the new world, and if they were following their insertion protocols as planned, they'd be ripping through their objectives with both speed and brutal precision.

The wolves were large, bred among their kind for strength, intelligence, and loyalty. They were the tip of the spear for their brethren, the first to lead the charge when a new planet had been discovered possessing needed resources and falling within the necessary parameters to support life.

Alpha Garrtin and his four-legged shock-troops were always the first in.

They wouldn't have wanted it any other way.

As designed, when their landing pods had hit the ground, rapidly discharging their canine cargo, the auto-camouflage detection-avoidance protocols kicked in, the external diggers quickly firing up and burying the craft deep within the soil until no trace remained. Within minutes any source of a scent that might give them away was hidden deep underground.

They were masters of stealth, incursion, and silent stalking tactics, striking only when the moment was right and the odds were in their favor. Leaving any trace of their arrival would have given them away, so deep underground the pods would remain for the duration of their mission. Once the main fleet arrived, the large support ships would simply run a subterranean scan and retrieve the vessels.

Those retrievers, they certainly do love their jobs, Garrtin had often mused. A far less interesting bit of specialized breeding had made them proficient in that mundane task.

No glory in that, he had thought. *Such a dull existence. The glory is in being bred for the hunt.*

All of his kind had certain skills innate within their genetic code. Excellent hearing, sharp eyesight, and a powerful sense of smell. A well-trained pack could quickly survey and mark a zone in under an hour. Less if there was ample cover and only light wind, and his team did just that, dispatching defenders silently as they ran the perimeter, their rear signaling appendage silently flashing out instructions with carefully orchestrated wags to the left or right.

"All clear and marked, Alpha," his second-in-command barked. Luanna was strong, a lean-muscled bitch with exceptional reasoning and tactical skills, along with sturdy haunches and healthy hips.

"Resistance?"

"Pathetic," she snarled. "Our pack will feast well tonight."

"Excellent. Tomorrow we will rendezvous with the closest sub-packs and move south toward the next objective. This is going far easier than we'd planned for. I think we may even join with Alpha Targg and Assault Pack Bravo a few days early."

The morning brought with it a low fog to the grassy lowlands. Garrtin and his pack roused themselves from the warm comfort of their sleep, untangling limbs as they rose, shaking off the morning dew from their coats.

Several of the sub-packs under his command had joined with the main body of the pack during the night, increasing their numbers ahead of schedule. Garrtin was a little surprised by their early appearance (as surprised as he could be, seeing as he smelled them coming miles away). The invasion had gone just as easy for them, and they found themselves pushing beyond their original objectives by accident, so caught up with the hunt they had become. And oh, what a hunt it was.

The natives were fast, they had to give them that, and agile to boot. But their stamina was lacking, and their slender legs and weak necks were no match for the Alpha and his pack. They had all slept well on full bellies and woke looking forward to the day's advance.

Scenting the air, the pack, now nearly forty strong, headed out to press their advantage. The other sub-packs had merged with the main group as they spread out, moving silently through the plains toward the rendezvous with Assault Pack Bravo.

The advance scouts returned with intel, and it was not good.

"No sign of Assault Pack Bravo, sir. In fact, there is no sign of any of the other advance packs at all."

"You're sure?" he asked the loyal troops. "Their scents would travel if they had marked their perimeters, even if their landing craft were buried."

"We know, sir, but there's no sign of them, hide nor hair."

"Let me know the instant you find them. Dismissed."

Garrtin continued walking, perplexed by the unexpected news. Where were the others? He had briefed the sub-packs before the mission began. They were to disperse in the designated assault pattern upon landing, as was protocol, but so far as he could tell, they were less than a thousand strong in this entire region, and the lack of contact with the others under his command worried him. A low, concerned whine escaped his throat as he considered their options. He had orders up to a point, and he was an Alpha, but they were rapidly approaching that uncomfortable point of being on their own.

He scanned the sky, craning his muscled neck as he looked for signs of the invading fleet. The skies were clear, as he knew they would be. The fleet wouldn't arrive for several days, and when they did all would be well. Nevertheless, unease settled into the pit of his stomach, a feeling that stayed with him until night began to fall.

"Luanna," he growled across his resting pack. "To me."

The sleek wolf rose and trotted over to his side, lowering her head in obedience.

"Here, Alpha."

He scanned the star-filled skies above.

"Look up, Luanna. Tell me what you see."

She did as instructed, exposing her neck to him as she

gazed above.

"Nothing much, Alpha, just stars as usual."

"Do you see anything… not right?"

Her eyes were keen, surely he knew that, so what was he–

"Oh!" she said, a gasp escaping her mouth. "Oh no."

"Yes," he agreed. "Indeed."

"Those aren't right." A hint of panic tinged her voice. "We're on the wrong planet."

"Wrong solar system," he added.

"What do we do, Alpha?"

"We do our job, that's what. They'll find us, and when they do, we'll be heroes for taking over this rock, no matter how long it takes us to do it."

He pressed his forehead to hers. They had been through a lot of tough campaigns together, but this was a unique challenge for them both. As they curled up together, sharing warmth in the chilly night air, they drifted off to sleep, uneasy thoughts of their future fading with the shutting of their eyes, like the rays of a setting sun as it bid the world farewell.

It had been a week, and the pack was making excellent progress. The indigenous were no real problem, and were quite good eating to boot, their flesh helping fuel the march across the plains and through the vast woods before them.

The scouts had reported some unusual scents, faded and weak, and unlike any they'd encountered before. They couldn't find trace of the animals who made them, but Garrtin assured them he was confident they would soon enough. It was, he reminded them, crucial to the success of the pack to know the whereabouts and numbers of their enemy.

When they hadn't returned by sundown, Garrtin felt unease in his belly. Something was wrong– they were never late. Never.

That night he slept fitfully, dreaming of strange beasts eating his scouts, tearing them limb from limb as they devoured them with glee. He woke with a start and remained awake for the rest of the night.

It wasn't exactly what had plagued him in his dream, but it was still terrible. Terrible and frightening.

They had found the scouts. How could anyone with a nose as powerful as that have missed the smell of death wafting from their corpses?

Their bodies were hung up from a tree, their beautiful pelts peeled from their flesh, laid out to dry on a wooden rack in the sun. Holes had pierced their bodies, far larger than the fangs of any animal they'd ever encountered. Not a mouthful of holes, however, but just a few, though they had easily been enough to rob his scouts of their lives.

They were scanning the scene when strange sounds echoed to their sensitive ears through the woods.

"Cover!" he hissed, the pack silently melting into their surroundings, their sharp eyes straining to see what would emerge from the trees.

The breeze had shifted, and they were at a tactical disadvantage being upwind, but even so, the slightest whiff of something entirely alien hit their noses. Pungent but also sweet. A little smoky even. Confusing. Several different scents blended in some bizarre combination.

The bipeds that stepped into view were tall, their

shoulders much higher than even his largest soldier, and they were wearing the hides of their enemies, a patchwork of their kills adorning their bodies.

Their front paws, the ones they weren't walking on, had elongated digits in which they somehow grasped the long, pointed pieces of wood they all carried. The tips of them were dark with blood, the smell reaching across the small area. More than a dozen of them walked into the clearing, carrying a slain beast between them, dangling from a wooden pole.

Garrtin recognized the animal. He had dined on one of them in their first days conquering this planet.

Conquering. That would require reassessment.

It seemed he had been horribly mistaken.

The realization dawned that the real foe on this planet was far more deadly than he had imagined.

"*Calm,*" he quietly signaled his pack with precise wags of his tail. "*Wait and watch,*" he conveyed silently.

The bipeds took sharp pieces of stone from the pouches they wore and flayed their kill open, spilling its delicious entrails to the ground. Garrtin felt his mouth water at the sight of the soft organ meats.

The strange creatures seemed indifferent to them, opting rather for the tougher muscle of the beast. They made quick work of it, rending it into pieces in minutes with their sharp weapons of stone.

"Did you see that?" Luanna asked in a whisper. "They can tear an animal apart without effort."

"I did," Garrtin said, only the hush of his voice hiding his concern. "We must take this slowly. Observe. Plan. Find their weakness, then strike. But for now, we watch."

His rear signaling appendage twitched with anxiety. This was going to be difficult, and a good many of his pack would likely lose their lives before the end.

The bipeds, having stretched the beast's hide and rent its meat to pieces, moved out of the clearing and started down a wide path. There was no cover from behind which they could strike, Garrtin noted, so, reluctantly, he and his troops held back. The path would be easy enough to follow now that they had the scent, and soon, numbers would be on their side.

He bade the pack to leave the delicious entrails where they were. Eating them would only alert the tall creatures to their presence, and surprise was something they'd need if they were to be victorious.

"Duntrr. Harrkn. Run to the others and tell them what we've seen. Tell them their Alpha requires their presence."

The two nodded and took off at a gallop. They were among his fastest. He only hoped they'd find the other distant packs before calamity befell them as well.

When they returned in a few days (it surely wouldn't take longer than that), the full strength of his forces would allow him to overcome the dangerous natives. For the time being, they would observe and wait.

With a flick of his tail, he signaled the pack to silently move out, following the scent the bipeds had left behind.

"We cannot overcome that many on our own," Luanna had said. "Even with all of Delta Pack united, it will be difficult."

The creatures' path had led them to an enormous encampment. Hundreds of them, male, female, even tender fleshed young walked among the strange enclosures. The larger ones were obviously the Alphas. If they could take those out, surely the rest would–

The wooden pole soared through the air, deeply penetrating a woven target twenty meters away.

"By the gods," Garrtin gasped. "What sort of combat is this?"

For the next several hours, he watched the hunters of the tribe throw spears into targets, easily piercing them from afar. He realized, to his horror, that his troops would be decimated before they were even within biting range.

Late that night, he called his most trusted pack-mates to his side.

"You've all seen what these beasts are capable of. We cannot possibly overpower them in a frontal assault. While we may thin their ranks somewhat, the losses to our side would be too great."

Grizzled Arrgann spoke up. "But when the other packs join us, surely then we will have sufficient forces–"

"Your thinking is wise, but consider this old friend: what if, just as we are only part of our Assault Pack, these are only a fraction of their true numbers as well? No, we will need to find a way to take them unaware and thin them out while we await our kin." He looked them over, his faithful pack, then spoke words they never thought they'd hear him say.

"We will also need to increase our numbers if we wish to succeed in the long term."

A gasp passed through the gathered wolves. He was speaking of a combat breeding, something that hadn't been done for generations.

"I know what you all are thinking," he said, "but the reality is, this is the only way to bolster our ranks and move toward victory. We are stranded on the wrong planet with limited numbers, and it could be a long time before our fleet finds us." *If they ever do,* he thought, grimly.

"Spread the word. I want it done quietly, but as soon as possible. We move against them tomorrow."

The pack quietly wagged their understanding, then turned to pass along the Alpha's wishes.

"Luanna, stay with me."

Though they'd fought together for many years, their relationship had always been purely professional, but now that their survival was on the line, it only made sense that his strongest and most trusted pack-mate should bear his litter.

She looked at him for a moment, a glimmer of something he'd never seen before briefly flashing in her eyes. A hint of happiness, but unlike the one he was used to seeing when she killed an enemy or carried out a successful mission. Luanna turned her back to her Alpha, and soon the first of a new generation of warriors was gestating in her belly.

Infiltration.

It was the only logical way. He would sneak into the camp and cause a distraction, then the rest would take up positions within and await the signal for an all-out assault.

It was a dangerous job, one Garrtin felt he, as Alpha, couldn't pass on to his pack. Leadership, he believed, could be defined in two words: "Follow me."

He would do it himself, for the good of his troops. Luanna wouldn't be slowed by her pregnancy until just before birthing the litter, so she would step in as Alpha in his stead should anything go wrong.

"Two to the left, two to the right," he said, "that's the signal. When you see that, move in and prepare to attack."

The pack knew the signal well. Their tails had long been trained for silent communication, their control of the rear appendages far superior to those of their lesser-bred kin.

Night had fallen, and Garrtin knew it was time.

"Watch for the signal," he said, then quietly stalked toward the giant bipeds' encampment.

Flickering light filled the air. The beasts were gathered in the center of the area, doing something near several large open flames. He would get a view soon enough when the time came for his distraction. He would leap into their presence, growling fiercely and showing his mighty fangs, drawing the tribe's attention, provoking a chase, while his troops would pick off the slower pursuers from the rear. It was risky, but it could work.

Slowly, he crept into the camp, closer and closer.

There are so many of them, he thought, steeling his nerves.

He was nearly upon them when the wind shifted, blowing across the camp, carrying the smoke from their fires downwind and directly into his muzzle.

The scent. Oh, the scent. It was unlike any he'd ever experienced. For an instant, his mission fled his mind as his mouth gushed with anticipatory drool. It was meat, but unlike any he'd ever smelled.

Damnit Garrtin, you have a job to do. Pull yourself together! he chided himself for the lapse. He'd never experienced anything like it. So visceral. So primal. It had taken him unaware. Even the most glorious battle meal seemed to pale in comparison. Whatever trickery these creatures had up their sleeves, he'd have to be ready for anything.

Quietly he crawled closer, hunched low to avoid the eyes of the masses of bipeds gathered together near the fire. Again the smell filled his nose, but he was ready for it this time, fighting it to stay focused. He knew his pack was watching him, waiting for his sign.

Just a few more steps, he thought as he neared the final structure before the clearing, *then I'll leap and give the signal.*

He stepped out into the open, his muscles coiling as he prepared to startle the unsuspecting beasts while they ate, when suddenly an electric shock ran down his spine, paralyzing his front limbs, making his right rear leg jerk spasmodically. He was frozen in place.

With great effort, he managed to turn his head to see what manner of attack he had foolishly walked into.

The girl scratching his butt couldn't have been more than eight years old.

She giggled at his arched-back antics, leg pumping in the air as she scratched that sweet spot just above his signaling appendage.

He didn't know what to do. First the scent, then this sneak attack? Had they known he was coming? Even their young ones seemed well-versed in combat skills. Oh, how foolish he had been.

He desperately tried to wag the signal, but his appendage was rigid, locked in place while the girl's tiny scratching hands immobilized his body.

A woman, probably the girl's mother, noticed the huge

wolf with her child, but rather than yelling a warning, she laughed, pointing at her daughter's antics. Soon the other bipeds turned to look. They bared their teeth and squinted their eyes, a guttural staccato leaving their lips. They then turned back to their meal, unconcerned as the child played with the ferocious Alpha of Delta Pack.

It was the mother who rose and started walking toward him.

So this is how I meet my fate, he thought. *At the hands of a female and her offspring.* He couldn't help but be almost amused that one of the greatest warriors of his day should go out in such a manner.

He steeled his nerves, ready for the killing blow that was sure to come, but the woman didn't strike. Instead, she held out a piece of meat, still smoking from the flames. The aroma at such close proximity broke down the last of Garrtin's internal defenses. His signaling appendage started moving with a mind of its own.

What? No! That's not the signal!

But it was too late. The meat was too close, too good.

He snatched it from her hand and chewed, his tail wagging fiercely from side to side.

"What's he saying?" Dorrgun asked. "I've never seen that signal."

"I don't know. They haven't attacked him, though. In fact, they seem to be feeding him?" Luanna was confused.

"Should we–"

"No!" she barked. "We wait for him to either signal or to return. Those were his orders."

Down at the fire, others had taken a liking to their furry

visitor and were feeding him bits of meat, while taking turns scratching behind his ears and petting his wiry coat.

Garrtin had never felt so good. No matter how much breeding had conditioned him for battle, well-aimed, scratching fingers and a full belly had disarmed him completely.

Eventually the festivities wound down and the bipeds trundled off to bed. Garrtin, full with delicious meat, trundled back to his waiting pack.

"Alpha, what horrible things were they doing to you?"

"Should we attack?"

"What was that signal? I didn't understand it."

The questions came fast and furious. With a sharp bark he silenced his pack and fixed them with an unusually soft gaze.

"Delta Pack, I realize now that we cannot overcome such cunning beasts in our current state. We need time to plan, and we need the numbers to carry them out. Spread the word to the other packs, we are to infiltrate as I did and secure positions within the bipeds' encampments. Breed and swell our numbers, accept their food and back scratches, but remain alert. When our forces finally come for us, we will be in the perfect position to strike."

The pack spread out, news of the new orders quickly making its way through the ranks. Only Luanna stayed behind.

"Is this really the only way?" she asked him.

"There is no sense or honor in throwing our lives away before the fleet arrives. We can be accepted by the bipeds, I am sure of it." He studied her muzzle and brow, noting for the first time just what a fine-looking bitch she was.

"And Luanna," he continued, "they do something amazing with their kills using fire. Come, I'll show you."

And so it came to pass that the attack wolves of Delta Pack lived among the primitive men for generation after generation, watching, breeding, waiting for reinforcements that would never come.

"Come on Bobo, come on boy!"

The slobbering pug wheezed his way over to the ditzy woman.

"That's a good boy. Who's a good boy? Who's a good boy? You're a good boy!"

He wagged his tail with empty-headed delight as she filled his bowl.

The stumpy little appendage flicked, two to the left, two to the right, and deep in some primal part of his brain, for the briefest of moments, the faintest hint of a thought flashed in his tiny brain. A visceral instinct telling him that there was some significance to that motion.

Something important.

It was of no matter, not with the delicious food filling his bowl. Mere moments later, the inbred little brain of the descendant of a great warrior race was overwhelmed by the promise of crunchy kibble and an evening of belly rubs.

A Helluva Thing

When the first body hit the ground beside him, bursting open like an over-ripe melon, he should have run.

Of course Barry realized the error in his judgment soon enough, but by then it was far too late. Besides, how could he have possibly known a man falling from the sky would land right next to him? For that matter, how could *anyone* have predicted it would start raining people?

Screaming, flailing people.

Another hit the ground not ten paces from where he sat. It was the second impact that jarred him into motion.

Jumping to his feet, he dropped the sandwich he'd been enjoying just moments before (it had been splashed with gore anyway) and quickly scurried to the nearest building, taking shelter under its bright orange awning.

"Oh my!" he blurted. "Now that's a helluva thing."

Barry was something of an odd fish, people would say. A bit of a loner. He took pleasure in his solitude, embracing his unusual circumstance as best he could, and every day he would make a point to go outside and sit in the same little spot and eat his lunch in the shadow of the massive bulk of the GDT building in which he worked.

He loved spending slow-time outdoors, absorbing the sights and sounds of the city, a simple pleasure that filled his world with the bright-eyed wonder of a child. Every day he would see something new, because unlike ninety-nine percent of the world's population, he didn't use teleports.

Barry had made a point to walk or bicycle everywhere, even to work, which was rather ironic (in a non-Alanis

Morissette sort of way) seeing as he worked for the Global Department of Teleportation, where he was a senior tech for their massive central mainframes powering teleportation hubs worldwide.

It was an impressive position for someone of his early years. At only twenty-eight, he was the youngest senior tech by far. Sure, the younger generation was incredibly proficient and code-savvy, but it was his lack of a social life and subsequent dedication to his work that pushed him so rapidly up the ladder. The higher-ups knew they could always count on him, no matter what they needed. He might be odd, but he was never late and was glad to work weekends. Thus, he was continually rewarded with more and more responsibility.

Unfortunately for Barry, he didn't really enjoy the lack of a social life, it was just how things wound up.

He'd had a girlfriend once in high school, but she had left him for a zero-G football jock. After that he had just fallen deeper in his studies, until one day he woke up and realized he was a twenty-eight-year-old virgin.

It was hard to meet people, he had found, once he left school. In this day and age, you interacted with exactly who you wanted to. No chance encounters, no shared space, no time to kill en-route. Aside from getting coffee or a meal, teleportation had effectively separated the human race from one another, and Barry was an integral part in that very machine that left him on the outside looking in.

No planes, no trains, no cars or buses, it was simply easier to teleport anywhere you needed to be, and GDT hubs were always within no more than a few minutes' walk. Almost anywhere across the globe you could get a strong enough beam to teleport.

In this compartmentalized world, Barry's penchant for long walks when he could just teleport was seen as weird. He mused how the disturbingly bloody events of the day might change that.

"BARRY!" The comm-set he wore crackled to life. "Where the hell are you?" the voice barked into his ear. It was Quint, senior management involved in user problem complaint resolution.

"Having lunch, sir," Barry replied.

Silence.

"It's my lunch hour."

"No shit Barry, I can see the time. You need to get back here now!"

"Ah, yes sir. I was just about to–" The line disconnected in his ear.

He looked out from his sheltered spot and surveyed the path back to the safety of his building. Bodies were falling a bit faster now, a few every minute or so, and he was pretty sure he could hear distant thuds echoing off the buildings across the city.

He didn't want to step out there, not really, but he knew there was little choice, so with a deep breath, he took a look up, and satisfied it was clear, for the moment at least, he pushed off and strode quickly toward the GDT, hoping to arrive unscathed. No sooner had he taken a step from under the awning, when a shrieking man in a foreign-looking suit crashed through the fabric of the canopy, shredding himself on the metal framing before sliding to the ground in pieces.

I think maybe I'd be better off running, he realized, and took off like a shot. Moments later he was safely inside the familiar safety of the GDT building. He flashed his departmental badge at security, then detoured to the bathroom for a quick pit stop. He couldn't show up splattered with gore, after all.

Once he was finally clean to his satisfaction, he hurried down to the belly of the building, where the rapidly assembling tech team was anxiously waiting for him.

It was bad. It was global, and they had no way to stop it.

For the GDT, this was well beyond any nightmare scenario they had trained for. Sure, there had been drills run where perhaps a handful of teleports went awry, but they had developed and installed myriad safeguards to compensate at the first sign of trouble. While the GDT building was the brain of the entire network, the decentralized nodes spread across the globe were designed not only to speed teleport, but also to act as buffers. Emergency stop points if you will, in case of catastrophic failure of a nearby node.

One thing was particularly troubling about the day's events. No one was ever supposed to rematerialize in the empty skies. It shouldn't have even been possible. Of course arguing that point while people plunged thousands of feet to their demise seemed inappropriate.

"How many in the queue?" Ryerson asked. He was the senior-most teleport wrench on the team and had personally designed many of the emergency scenarios they'd had drilled into their heads.

"We're still spooling, sir. Looks like 48,976,581 in some stage of transit. Node fail-safes have, uh, failed," a second-year tech blurted out.

"Christ, that's almost fifty million people about to be dumped into the thin blue air."

"Actually, not thin," Barry pointed out. "At that altitude there is adequate oxygenation, so they should be able to breathe quite comfortably."

The older man's hard stare hit like a slap. "I'm sure they'll be thankful for that while they plummet to their deaths!" he growled. "Perkins!" he yelled, shifting his attention to another startled tech. "How long can you stall the queue?"

"Maybe an hour. Two, tops, then the core will overheat."

"All right then, we've got an hour to come up with a solution."

The team jumped into high gear, working at a feverish pace along with their remote-linked counterparts, a global network communicating and working together as one giant brain.

It had been Barry who spotted the temporary fix. It was far outside specs for the operating system, but with some creative cross-wiring, it could work.

"So you think you can create a rapid ping relay, capture transit data, then exit them one at a time?" It was the GDT President of Operations on the vid-screen, the board of directors anxiously watching over his shoulder, the expansive view of the city visible behind them from their 140th-floor windows.

It was good to be an executive.

"Yes sir," Barry replied. "If we take the entire system offline with a staggered cascade, we should free up resources to redirect the queue indefinitely, so long as we don't add new transfers to it. Then we can re-direct to pre-selected exit nodes."

"And this will work?"

"We'll still lose packets."

"You mean people."

"Yes. We'll still lose people, but only sporadically and we can redirect any packet loss to remote areas outside city limits."

"Acceptable losses, then?"

"Yes, sir, if we want to save the majority."

"I double-checked his math," Quint said, a hint of pride in his voice. "The kid's idea is crazy, but it'll work."

"But global teleport will be shut down in the process," the president said. "The world will come to a standstill, and our shareholders… How long will this take?"

The silence was heavy, weighing on the roomful of engineers and techs like a wet blanket pinning them to the ground. The business of GDT was teleportation, and the whole world depended on them.

"Forty-five days, sir," Barry finally replied.

"Forty-five? We can't shut down that long!"

"Sir, it's the only way we see, and if we don't act soon, the core will overheat. We need a decision in the next five minutes."

Slam!

The body bounced off the conference room window behind them, startling the board when they turned to see the bloody smear trailing down the glass.

The president turned back to the monitor with a sigh. "All right, do it."

Upwards of two million were lost that day, falling from the skies across the globe. Most had landed in cities, and the density of nodes was hypothesized to have played some role in that occurrence. By the time the system was shut down, close to fifty million people were locked in the queue while the entire world ground to a halt. Once in a while a screaming man or woman would fall from the sky, but it was now over empty fields pre-selected by the GDT. A standby sanitation crew was on standby 24/7.

Meetings across the globe suddenly had to be conducted by video conference, an outdated technology for those who far preferred simply teleporting in for a quick face-to-face. Employees and employers were trapped in distant cities, some in distant countries, with no way to get home. The sky-polluting air and ground transportation fleets had long ago been scrapped, and only in the poorest nations were some of the outdated combustion machines still operational.

Nearly a week later, a specially allocated teleport was sequestered behind multiple firewalls and made functional for internal GDT use. The only one on the planet for the time being, though few wanted to use it until the full system was back online and triple-checked.

A strange side effect of the shutdown was happening in the meantime. Around the world, something not seen for decades was taking place. People were walking the streets in droves. Interacting, talking, complaining (oh, there was a lot of that going on). Makeshift rickshaws built by enterprising young men and fitness enthusiasts became the lone mode of local transit for those who still refused to go anywhere under their own power.

Barry found his local bar suddenly crowded by the multitudes stuck in the city with no way home. Normally, he would have his pick of seating in the empty establishment, sliding into a booth's deep-red vinyl embrace to sip a post-work whiskey and read a trashy romantic-adventure book. It was his solitary night out ritual, but now the booths were all packed with laughing men and women, drowning their stress into the wee hours.

He'd come to the bar straight from work. It had been another long day crunching numbers and fixing code, and his department badge was still lazily dangling around his neck when a pretty brunette in a tight black dress pulled up the barstool next to him.

"Hey," she said, "buy you a drink?"

"Uh…" He didn't know what to say. "Um, I think you must've mistaken me for someone else," was all he lamely managed.

"What, a girl can't buy a cute guy a drink in this town?"

"You not from here?" he asked.

"Nope, I'm from Calima City."

"Long way from home."

"Yeah, well, we're all far from home these days."

"Not me. I actually live here."

"Really?" She rested her hand on his knee, eyes flicking to the badge hanging from his neck. "I have to tell you, I haven't had a proper shower in days. The place I'm holed up in is shared with twenty other people, so hot water is something of a commodity."

"That sounds miserable. I'm sorry to hear it," he replied,

oblivious.

"It is." She took a sip from her drink then waved over the bartender. "Another for me, and one for my friend here."

"You don't have to do that."

"I want to. You seem like a really nice guy. So tell me, how did you wind up in this town?" She leaned in close as he told the story of his arrival straight out of school and subsequent rise in the company.

Hung over and wearing his shirt buttoned all the way up to hide the hickies on his neck and chest, Barry flashed his department badge and escorted the brunette at his side past security.

"Just a quick tour," he said. The security guards gave him a wink and little nod. It was good to see the poor guy finally get some action.

If they only knew.

Barry was no longer a virgin, and all it had cost him was an off-books trip to Calima City. She hadn't asked outright, that would have been too obvious, but instead, she waited until that moment. You know the one, that delicious bit where sex is inevitable, that point of no return, the just-the-tip moment. Then, and only then, did she pull the strings.

"I don't know if I can do this," she had said. "I should be trying to get home. Maybe this was a mistake."

Of course the twenty-eight-year-old virgin offered her a ride, and the grateful woman had given him an exceptional one in return.

After that it was as if a switch had been thrown. Barry had

a newfound confidence, and men and women alike started to take notice when he'd come into a room. He also took to wearing his ID badge outside his clothes, even on his day off. Being part of the machinery that people were relying on made him everyone's friend, and soon he was socializing nightly. He even took a few more women on a "quick tour" of the GDC. Things had certainly changed for him.

By the third week he had fallen head over heels in love.

Her name was Cassandra. Such an unusual name. Old-fashioned. Classy. Intriguing. He had been introduced by one of his new friends one night at the bar. She had been stuck in town while on vacation and seemed to be enjoying her extended time in the city.

She was too good to be true, he thought. No way she actually liked him for real, but he was becoming comfortable with that idea.

What the hell, he thought.

The next day she didn't go anywhere. In fact, she stuck around and made him breakfast before work.

"Hey, I have some things to do today, but you wanna meet up for dinner when you get done with your shift?" she asked, sitting on the edge of his bed, wearing one of his shirts as she sipped her black coffee.

"Uh, you don't want me to get you a teleport somewhere?"

"Why would I do that? You could get in serious trouble. Besides, I'm not supposed to be back for weeks anyway."

"Really?"

"You're so cute. Yes, really. Why not enjoy ourselves, right? Which reminds me, is there a grocery store nearby?"

That night he got off work and returned to enjoy a home-cooked meal and a very satisfying dessert.

And that's how it started. They spent every night together, catching a meal, staying up late sharing stories of their childhoods, dreams, and aspirations, or just having red-hot monkey sex until the sun came up. It was perfect, and time flew by.

Weeks later, Barry came home to an empty apartment and a note on his counter. It had been forty-five days, as he had promised the Board, and the global teleport system was finally back online. Cassie, he read, had thought it was time to head home. It would have been hard to say goodbye in person, so she had thought it better to leave during his shift. She thanked him for a wonderful vacation fling and signed her note with Xs and Os.

Barry had a hard time making out the words through his tear-filled eyes.

Within mere days the sidewalks and bars were empty again. Everyone previously stuck was now gone, free to travel at will. In no time at all, those who had been briefly forced to interact had returned to their old ways, and Barry found himself once again alone.

He kept track of Cassie on social media. Nothing creepy or stalkerish, just checking in on the girl he couldn't get out of his head.

Okay, maybe hacking into her work calendar was a bit stalkerish, but he only did it because he cared.

Yeah.

His heart skipped a beat when one day he noted she had a

meeting scheduled in town, though not for quite some time. He knew he had to see her again.

Several lonely months had gone by when it happened. Barry was eating a sandwich at his usual spot, not worried at all about bodies falling from the sky.

Not this time, he thought. He'd made sure of that.

"BARRY!" Quint screamed over his ear-comm. "Where are you! I need you in the core immediately!"

Barry turned his head and looked at the legs sticking out of the side of the cement building's wall.

A woman screamed.

Across the street an arm suddenly appeared, its owner teleported into a slab of solid stone.

"I'm just having lunch, sir," he said. "It's my lunch hour."

"No shit! I know what time it is! Get back here, now!"

The line went dead.

Barry gathered his things and got to his feet.

"Maybe this time she'll stay," he said to no one in particular as he slowly walked toward the GDT building, humming a happy little tune with a smile on his face.

Lawyers Vs. Demons

"Next case!" Judge Henry Alexander Tyrell bellowed, slamming his massive gavel down with a crash. "Bring the miscreant in!"

The poor man was quickly ushered in and placed in the defendant's box. He shuddered, trying to be brave, but he couldn't help but cower before the power-mad judge, knowing his sentence would be swift and harsh. Just how harsh still remained to be seen.

Judge Tyrell was a lifetime appointee, and nothing he said or did would change that fact. So it was that he enjoyed a great deal of liberty in his sentencing of those who came before him. Mostly that meant they'd be handled quickly with no funny business tolerated, but if the judge happened to be having a bad day, they could count on being dealt with in a particularly unforgiving manner.

How Henry Tyrell, Esquire, rose to that position of power from his humble position as a young, aspiring defense attorney was something of an unusual tale. In fact, in the several millennia Atchzneephchael had served the Dark Lord as one of his elite caste, he could not recall a similar instance of such an unusual summoning of a demon of his stature and rank. Nor such a summoning of any demon, come to think of it.

In his first few years after passing the bar exam, Henry Tyrell found himself slipping deeper into his loner ways. He could have made an effort to socialize, but he chose instead to spend every spare moment poring over the minutia buried within the constant flow of insignificant cases that tend to, as the saying goes, "flow downhill" to the most junior attorneys in the firm.

Sure, the cases were shit, but they were *his* shit, and he endeavored to find any and every loophole, nuance, and technicality he could in his quest to defend his clients.

It was an arduous task, getting off murderers and rapists, molesters and thugs, the lowest of the low that no one else wanted to deal with, in cases where guilt was so obvious even the judge could be seen wishing she could simply send them away to some dark pit and move on to other cases of merit.

But Henry stuck with them. He fought for them, tooth and nail. He dredged up every possible trick in the book, and, when those were used up, proceeded to write a few more of his own. By the time he was in his fifth year of practice, he was sitting alongside the partners of the firm, handling the big cases, bringing his unique skills to bear when a client could fork over enough in billable hours to be worth his while.

"Technically legal."

The phrase became synonymous with Henry's defenses. His ability to twist the law, to utilize crafty lawyer-speak to his advantage, was both admired and despised by his associates on either side of the aisle. Like him or hate him, they all respected his skills.

"Your Honor," he would argue. "While, indeed, the statute states only gross negligence is required, is it not also the case that mens rea must also exist?"

"Objection. The statute is plainly written with no intent requirement," the prosecutor would argue back.

"Ah, but in other applications of this statute, no conviction was achieved. In fact, no prosecution was ever launched without mens rea. As the jury undoubtedly knows, that Latin expression means, 'with a guilty mind' meaning an act intentionally committed with full knowledge. As we've heard spelled out in the testimony, my client, while he may have mistakenly, even carelessly, committed the acts in question, did not *mean* to do so." He flashed his brightest smile at the jury. As usual, he could tell, he was making his case.

"His actions, therefore, while perhaps to the layman less educated in the law than the esteemed jury, seemed to violate the statute, were in fact *technically legal*. I hope the men and women of the jury take that into consideration as they deliberate, and realize that *by the letter of the law* my client is innocent."

That logic, or some variation thereof, was heard in court time and again, as his clients were found not guilty. Not because of their innocence of the acts committed, mind you, but rather by a case made of technical legality, laid bare before the court from some arcane loophole dug up by the tireless work of the wunderkind attorney.

They would be found not guilty, but they were also *not* found innocent, for while the technicality negating their culpability in the eyes of the law was indisputable, so too was their blatant commission of the crimes in the first place, even if they got off the hook with the help of some creative lawyering.

Fifteen years of practicing law saw Henry rise to full partner at the firm. He commanded some of the highest billable hours in the state, yet he always strove to amass more. His increased power and wealth only fueled his drive, and when his trophy wife left him after his repeated affairs with impressionable young clerks and paralegals, he simply pointed out the fine print he'd inserted in their prenup.

She would get nothing, because according to a well-placed comma and the question of what the word "is" really meant, his affairs were technically legal, at least in the wording of their legally binding agreement.

She would have spoken out about it, but the gag order he obtained from his golf buddy, who just so happened to oversee the divorce court, put a quick end to that. She'd find herself in jail if she spoke out, and while it was clearly a deplorable thing for him to do, it was also technically legal.

Henry possessed many useful friends who owed him favors like that. When a charity would ask for his assistance, he would gladly help them fundraise, his little black book of contacts bursting with powerful men and women who had at one time or another found his unique skills of use. And should a politician seek his talents in obtaining donations to his or her campaign, he would always help out, glad to be of assistance, just as he was glad to take an obscene percentage of any funds raised as a "consulting fee" for his services. It was a gray area to be sure, but long before he accepted any offer, he made damn sure his graft would be technically legal.

Henry had been working late one hot, dreary night. The case on his desk not only brought a lot of revenue to the firm, but was also providing him with a welcome challenge for a change. Old case laws needed to be cited and cross-referenced, and relevant precedents noted. So it was that when he left his office at close to midnight, Henry's desk was piled high with briefs and law books bristling with Post-it notes jutting from their pages like a multicolored legal peacock.

He also had a wad of tissue wedged in his nose, the dry flow of the air conditioner having caused another annoying nosebleed. Between the AC and his allergies, it was a constant struggle.

"I really need to see a specialist about this," he muttered to himself while washing the blood from his hands in his private bathroom. "Maybe I'll try to squeeze that in tomorrow," he decided, then headed for the door, turning the lights out behind him as he stepped out into the unseasonably warm October night.

He enjoyed his walks home from work; the fresh air and exercise did him good. Being a recognized defender of despised criminals could make a man something of a target, but he nevertheless felt secure at that late hour as his .45 automatic rode snugly under his arm in its custom leather shoulder holster. Given his line of work, as well as his political connections, getting the concealed-carry permit had been a breeze.

Normally the walk would only take him twenty-five minutes or so, his luxury condominium being a mere two miles from the office, but this particular night he found himself taking his time, strolling the long way home as he ran through potential court scenarios in his head.

The circuitous route had taken him right by the Museum of Contemporary Art, its decoratively designed façade and geometric patterned pavement standing out among the otherwise plain buildings of the neighborhood.

He unconsciously patted his coat, the security of his pistol helping put him at ease.

Just a week prior, a teenager had been stabbed to death in the courtyard, bleeding out on the pavement in the late hours of the night.

The assailant, a man he'd previously gotten off for an assault charge, he had noted, was caught on video from multiple angles. When he had called Henry seeking representation, he had his assistant inform the man that even he couldn't find a loophole with his face plastered across a color video of his unprovoked attack.

As he approached the small memorial laid out by friends and family, Henry noticed a rather large dog, its coat dark as obsidian, lurking near the site of the slaying. Well, perhaps not lurking. A dog that size really has a hard time lurking. Maybe skulking fits better. Whatever it was doing, upon seeing it, Henry didn't think, but rather had knee-jerk reaction, spurred by his horrible allergy to dogs, which overrode what would have been most people's logical wariness of an enormous canine.

"Hey! Get the hell out of there!" he shouted, his hand reaching under his coat. He didn't want to shoot the beast. Good Lord, the paperwork he'd have to file after explaining things to the police would be irritating, to say the least.

The massive animal turned its head and looked at him with something he could have sworn was a mix of curiosity and amusement before stepping back into the shadows.

"Stupid fucking dog," he muttered as he slid his fingers from his pistol under his suit jacket and bent to look closer at the objects the odd beast had been sniffing around.

A small blaze of candles and little stacks of pictures

littered the ground, flowers and chalk-drawn messages spread around the pavement where the murdered boy had fallen. The pentagons interwoven in the cement created a pleasing pattern to the artistically inclined, and the numerous votive candles made the scene almost beautiful. That is, if it weren't for the violent death that had occurred there so recently.

One of the photos caught Henry's eye. The boy actually looked familiar. Could it be the son of the small-time dealer he had helped walk free? Carefully stepping around the flowers and open flames, he leaned in for a better view. Yes, it was that poor slob's boy. He almost felt bad for the man, but then he remembered how many children the drug dealer had likely killed himself, not with a knife, but with the poison he peddled.

In the shadows, the slightest movement caught his eye. The massive dog was still there, scratching itself with one giant paw as it watched him from the shadows, sending fur and dander floating in the air, the slight breeze blowing it right into Henry's face.

He immediately felt the itchy tingle of his allergies kicking in, and as he stood up in surprise, he felt the pressure in his head shift to his nose, the surge of rushing blood tickling his sinuses even further as his nosebleed started to flow again in earnest.

Just as he coughed from the sudden rush of hot, coppery blood that ran down his throat, he felt a massive tickle in his sinuses.

"Atchzneephchael!" he sneezed, a thick spray of blood flying from his nose and mouth, splattering to the ground before him.

A flash blinded him momentarily. It was somehow both bright, yet impossibly dark at the same time, he mused, and when his vision finally cleared, he saw the creature standing before him.

The demon was eight feet tall, its leathery skin as tough as armor, a dull orange glow illuminating both eyes.

Henry stumbled backward, tripping over himself and falling to the ground as he desperately groped for his pistol.

The demon fixed his gaze upon him and spoke, his words reaching not only Henry's ears, but also into his mind.

"Who dares summon me to this plane?" Atchzneephchael bellowed. He lunged out with a taloned hand, but found himself quite contained within the confines of the five-sided figure on the ground.

"This is not a proper summoning pentagram! How did you manage this feat?" he asked, a surprised curiosity mixing with his wrath.

Atchzneephchael sniffed the air. "Ah, the blood of an innocent was spilled here… and many tears of anguish. Powerful. And clever. Powerful enough, even, to make this pitiful pentagon suffice without its focusing points, but how came you to know the name of one of the elite caste, mortal?"

Henry, to his credit, had only pissed himself slightly, his fight instinct quickly kicking in right alongside his flight one. He unsteadily waved his gun at the creature. The normally intimidating .45 seemed like a pea-shooter in the face of the massive beast.

"What are you? What do you want with me?"

"What do *I* want with *you*? It is you who summoned me, mortal. You know well that I am a full-demon of the uppermost caste, though how you came to know my name is of great interest to me. No one has successfully summoned one of my rank in many centuries, and *no one* has ever summoned *me*."

"You… you're a demon? An actual demon?"

Atchzneephchael sighed. "Yes, mortal, a demon," he replied, amused. He crossed his massive arms, raising an eyebrow as he studied the tiny man cowering before him. "You really didn't think this through, did you?"

It had taken the demon a good twenty minutes to explain the terms of the summoning to Henry. He was surprised. Most capable of such a summoning, especially of a demon of his stature, would have known the basics, but this human seemed oblivious, though he was certainly a quick study.

The glaring problem was the human said he did not summon the demon at all.

"But you spilled blood in the proscribed manner within the five-sided portal, the candles were in place, you called forth my name, and thus I came to you."

"No," Henry replied, "I told you, I was just on a walk. You think I'd stop and light candles for this kid? Why would I? I mean I knew his dad, but the guy was just a low-level dealer."

"But the blood does not lie. You sealed the contract when you spilled your essence in summoning me."

"Nope. Didn't happen."

The demon was confused. It wasn't supposed to go like this.

"Yes, it did. I would not be here before you if it were not so."

"Nope, didn't do it."

"Did so," Atchzneephchael shot back, arms crossed.

"Afraid not. I can see where you might think so, but what happened was *technically* different. Are you familiar with the term 'mens rea'?"

He proceeded to lecture the beast on intent, something which was surely not present in his purely accidental invocation. Without intent, he stated, he could not be legally bound to any contract the demon may have assumed.

They argued back and forth for more than a half hour before the demon finally conceded that *perhaps* the contract was not binding. Then he changed tack and dangled the apple of temptation, telling Henry what wondrous things a being of his power could offer.

"So you say I can present you with three tasks to complete, and, if you should fail, you are contractually bound to provide me with one wish for each task, is that correct?"

The demon picked his teeth with a massive claw. "Yes, that is correct."

"And once this deal is agreed upon, you can't hurt me in any way. Is my understanding of that also correct?"

"Yes, mortal. Once a deal is struck, I may not harm you while you walk the Earth."

"For the duration of the tasks, or in perpetuity?" he asked the beast, his wits returning now that his adrenaline had subsided.

"You are a rather astute one. To answer your question, once a deal is struck between us, I am bound by law to bring you no harm anywhere in this world."

"Did you say law?"

Atchzneephchael laughed. "Yes, human, we have rules your tiny mind couldn't possibly comprehend."

"I want to see a copy of the specific laws pertaining to this transaction before I make any agreement."

"Very well, mortal," the beast chuckled.

A thick stack of parchment appeared on the ground at Henry's feet. He noted, as he picked it up, that the pages may well have been printed on human skin.

"As you requested," the demon laughed as he watched the mere mortal flip through the many pages. "Good luck."

Henry shot him a look as he holstered his gun, a far more powerful weapon cradled in his hands.

"Oh, don't worry about me," he replied with a wicked gleam in his eye. "I'm a lawyer."

The massive demon's laughter abruptly ceased.

The hulking creature sat on Henry's Italian leather sofa, his mass making the frame groan from the strain.

"Yes, once you ask for a particular wish, you may not ask for it again if I should succeed in the associated task. You also may not use the same task, or variants thereof, a second time. It is an arcane rule, but one we are bound to follow. By the way, would you mind getting me another bottle of this delicious beverage?"

Henry stood from his seat at his kitchen island and retrieved a liter of blood orange soda from the fridge. The demon accepted it with his taloned hand.

"Thank you. We don't have such delights in Hell, you know. This is something of a treat. And the name, it pleases me." He sounded almost glad to have been summoned, though Henry was fairly sure the demon wouldn't hesitate to rip him to shreds in an instant if not for the binding agreement for his safety. As it was, he could now sit next to the deadly creature without fear, though he did remind himself that the danger he faced was more than just corporeal.

The terms were fairly simple: three tasks, three wishes. If the demon should succeed, the wish asked for was off the table, kind of like negotiating a plea bargain with a prosecutor. If the demon failed, it was bound to grant the wish requested immediately. Upon completion of the three tasks, it would return to Hell, leaving the recipient unharmed so long as he lived.

Of course there was a downside.

Upon death, Henry's soul would become the property of the underworld.

Most would do far more than balk at that prospect, but Henry was good. He was more than good, and as he read and re-read the lengthy rules and by-laws governing the arrangement, he felt confident he could win. More importantly, he had an ace up his sleeve.

Atchzneephchael had agreed to come to Henry at his home in precisely two weeks. Time was nothing to the demon, and it seemed to give the pathetic human hope that he would be victorious. Those extra days to plan the tasks for him were no matter, he smiled to himself. Once a deal had been struck, Hell always won.

Always.

Henry spent those two weeks shut in his office, researching, cross-referencing, and planning. In that regard, his endeavor was quite similar to his usual trial prep, only this time his soul was on the line.

His regular caseload was handed off to his minions as he burned the midnight oil preparing for the mental challenge of his life. Sure, there was a risk – there always was – but with his track record and abundant self-confidence in his own intellect, he was willing to take his chances, and the rewards–oh, the rewards would be ever-so worth it.

"Have you chosen your first task, mortal?" the massive demon asked between swigs of blood orange soda. "Take your time, I am in no rush."

"I have," Henry replied confidently.

"Very well," Atchzneephchael replied, stifling a bored yawn with his gnarled hand. "What is it you would have me do, and what is your price?"

Henry took a cardboard tube from his cupboard and opened it, unrolling a detailed map of the city onto the countertop.

A red *X* marked the spot.

"On Halloween, at the stroke of midnight, I want you to materialize in this exact spot as drawn on this map. No other plane of existence, no other dimension, not high in the air or beneath the ground, I want you to appear, in your present physical form, and stand on the ground at the point marked, then walk twenty paces directly north. To make sure there is no confusion, I have also included the GPS coordinates as well as a detailed satellite image, likewise marked."

The demon studied the map and gave a cursory glance at the latitude and longitude coordinates.

"Don't you want to take these with you?" Henry asked.

"I have already memorized them, human. I shall perform this task. If I should fail, what is the wish you would have granted?"

A smile grew on Henry's face.

"I wish I would be irresistible to women, both in and out of bed, and for those I sleep with, I would be by far the greatest lover they've ever had."

The demon smiled broadly and let out a throaty laugh that made the furniture shake.

"What's so funny?"

"Oh my," he said, his mighty sides still quivering with mirth. "That's wonderful. Such a human wish. Anything at all at your fingertips and you wish for women."

"Is that a problem?" Henry asked, a little annoyed at the beast's disrespect.

"Oh no. Piece of cake, as your kind says."

"So what's so funny?"

"You have no idea how many of you ask for that. It's become something of a joke in the underworld. But that is of no matter." He straightened to his full height, wiping the tears of laughter from his burning orange eyes. "You have named your task, and you have named your wish. I shall see you on Halloween as requested. I suggest you spend the time waiting to prepare your next task."

In a tiny puff of sulfur-tinged smoke, he was gone.

The smoke was wholly unnecessary, but Atchzneephchael rather liked the dramatic effect, and besides, no one ever summoned him. He wanted to make the most of his time topside.

On Halloween, a full hour before midnight, Henry went to the vacant parking lot whose coordinates he'd given the demon, and, with careful precision, proceeded to mark out a pentagram in thick chalk, using a line-maker borrowed from the local little-league baseball diamond. He was their top fundraiser, so there was little they could say but "of course" when he'd made the strange request to borrow it for the night.

Using a laser guide, he carefully lay down the shape of the pentagram, the one thing capable of containing a demon when summoned. He then took thick candles and lit them, placing them at the points of power as his many hours of study directed, ensuring that whatever materialized inside the ten-foot-wide space would most certainly be unable to walk the twenty paces north as required by the task.

Henry felt particularly clever as he waited for the stroke of midnight. He'd done his research, and he knew demons were tricky-clever in their twisting of words and meanings. Lucky for him, he spoke that language too, and after spending days focused on any loopholes the demon could possibly exploit, he had proposed his terms.

Reclining in a folding chair outside the pentagram, Henry sipped his cup of coffee and waited, merrily anticipating all the freaky monkey sex he'd soon be having with any woman of his choosing. And without fancy dinners, gifts, or prenups, no less.

His watch clicked over and showed midnight, but there was no sign of the demon. There were penalties for failing to show up. An automatic granting of the wish as well as forfeiture of any future claim to the wish-maker's soul.

Looks like I may have already won this one, Henry gloated.

The faint smell of sulfur wafted to his nostrils, and he turned to see Atchzneephchael leaning against the light pole behind him, an amused gleam in his devilish eyes.

"Done," he said calmly.

"Done?" Henry hissed. "How can you say done? I've been watching closely. You didn't perform your task. The wish is forfeit, it's mine!"

"Oh no, I most certainly did," the demon chuckled, "though I have to admit, that was a rather clever attempt. Far more than I would have previously given you credit for."

"But you didn't materialize there, on this soil, in this dimension, and walk twenty paces north."

"Ah, but I did," the demon replied. "You were well prepared, and perhaps a lesser demon might even have lost to your machinations," he mused. "But I am not a lesser demon."

"You still haven't made your case why this isn't a breach of our agreement."

"Simple. You specified so many parameters, yet as is typical of your kind, you still thought inside the box. Or pentagram, as the case may be. You see, I materialized exactly as you requested, on Halloween, at the stroke of midnight, and walked twenty paces north. But I did so last year."

Henry was silent.

It was rare he was bested in manipulation of rules and clever lawyer-speak, but his oversight was clear and he saw the writing on the wall. While tricky and not in the spirit of the task, what Atchzneephchael had done was *technically* legal.

The next task was far more difficult, an undertaking that required a rather sizable expenditure in the form of donations to a variety of churches and related charities.

Henry told the demon to meet him in two weeks time at his summer house, then promptly begun calling in favors and doling out checks. The priests and holy men came from far and wide, men of all denominations and ranks, each of them performing variations of the same task one after another until it was finally completed to Henry's satisfaction.

Finally, on the appointed day, Atchzneephchael appeared.

Henry sat comfortably on a raft floating in the large black-bottomed pool behind his estate. He looked at the demon, standing tall in the afternoon sun, and waved merrily.

"Hi there, glad you could come. There's some soda in the cooler if you like."

The demon looked at the cooler a moment, then cautiously opened the lid. While he could sense something was very wrong, at least the cool soda wasn't part of the mortal's little tricks.

"Thank you for the hospitality, human, though it will not make it any easier on you when you lose your soul to me," he said, opening the lid with his talon and downing the bottle with a gulp. "So, what would you have me do, and what is your price?"

Henry floated to the edge of the pool and climbed out, walking closer to the demon until he was just a few feet away. He was tempted to reach his dripping hand out and grab him, just to see what would happen, but that would spoil the surprise, and so, with great restraint, he named his challenge.

"At the bottom of this pool is a gold ring. My old wedding ring, actually, though I suppose that's not of importance. What I want you to do, *in this time,* on this day, in this location, in the physical form you are currently in, as well as in this dimension, physical reality, and any and all other variants thereof, including but not limited to interdimensional space, space-time, and any others not listed –" He was pretty certain that covered all the materialization issues. "– is to retrieve that ring by submerging entirely in that pool."

The demon studied the shimmering water a moment, his nostrils flaring at the smell.

"Very well," he answered. "And your price?"

"You may laugh, but I wish for never-ending wealth of the greatest magnitude ever seen on this planet." He was expecting the demon's snarky smile. "I know this seems trite, but have you considered the fact, demon, that the reason so many men have asked for it is because wealth and power is what so many of us spend our whole lives seeking? Just because others want it as well does not make it any less valuable. Hell, if you achieve it, you've won the game. And besides, with that kind of money, I'd still have my pick of women even without that wish."

"An interesting point well made," the demon replied. "Yet still a trivial wish. Regardless, should I fail, it shall be yours." The demon paused a moment at the edge of the pool, hesitant to jump in.

"I should also mention," the demon said with an unsettling smile, "you might want to start thinking about your third task."

He jumped high in the air, his body arcing above the swimming pool full of holy water, hovering for an instant, then plummeting down towards it. The surface began bubbling fiercely as his demonic mass neared it.

A millisecond before he hit, Henry thought he saw a flash of something, though he couldn't tell what it was. The water flew into the air, the spray of a demonic cannonball soaking him as Atchzneephchael submerged. The water boiled and churned, then slowly settled back to a level calm, only periodic bubbles from below disturbing the mirror surface.

A minute went by, then two. Finally the shape at the bottom swam to the surface and sprung to the deck of the pool, the massive demon's frame covered head to toe in a commercial-grade deep-sea drysuit.

Atchzneephchael pulled the custom diving helmet free, careful not to drip any holy water on himself, then reached his gloved hand into the pouch on his belt, producing Henry's gold ring.

"I believe this is what you requested," he said before grabbing another soda from the cooler.

Henry didn't even argue. Again the demon had played by the rules and bent them just enough. He didn't break them, though. It was technically legal.

"You know," Henry said, both annoyed and impressed, "you demons would make damn good lawyers."

The demon laughed heartily and fixed him with an amused smile.

"My dear fellow," he chuckled. "Who do you think invented them?"

The time had arrived for Henry's final task. Atchzneephchael expected the human to be at least a little nervous. It was, after all, his last chance before losing his soul to the underworld forever, but the man stood confidently before him, no fear in his eyes.

"What are you up to, mortal?" he asked.

"You know," Henry replied, "you keep calling me that. 'Mortal.'

"And?"

"Well, first, I'm going to tell you my wish." He gave the demon a long stare. "I wish for a lifetime judgeship atop the most powerful of courts, but I wish for that lifetime to be continuous."

"Oh no," the demon hissed. "You can't possibly want–"

Henry cut him off. "Yes. I wish to be immortal."

A rumble cut through the air, as if forces high and low heard this particular request, and neither of them was pleased with it.

"Are you certain this is your wish?" Atchzneephchael asked, his expression unreadable.

"Yes," was the reply. "And now for your task."

Henry paused for effect. *Oh, this is going to be good,* he thought. He wanted to stretch the moment out, to savor his victory against his surprisingly skilled opponent. Soon he'd be the most powerful judge in the land, and he'd never lose his soul, because he would never die. The perfect loophole.

"I want you," he began, gleefully playing the ace up his sleeve, "to enter Heaven and kiss an angel."

The demon stood stock-still, eyes locked on the tiny man before him. He remained that way for several seconds, then sighed, his massive shoulders sagging.

"Fuck it," Atchzneephchael said. "You win."

And with a puff of smoke, he was gone.

The Honorable Judge Henry Alexander Tyrell had been overseeing the court for well over a hundred years. His judgments were law, and the condemned faced fates worse than death.

Of course they were already dead, technically, making Henry's burned and tortured body the only living human in the burning chamber deep in the bowels of Hell.

He couldn't die, that having been granted to him as part of his wish, and he ruled the most powerful court in the land, as was also his wish. His body, while immortal, could, however, be damaged and burned, broken and torn, painfully regenerating between each torture session. His fate, within the guidelines of the agreement, was technically legal.

Judge Henry Alexander Tyrell's billowing black robes covered the horror that was his tormented body, hiding it from view as it slowly mended while he sentenced soul after soul to their eternal fate.

He slammed his gavel down with a mighty crash. "Next defendant!"

He only had 27,412 to go before his next torture session, his rare break from hearing case after case of whining men and women with their tired excuses.

It was the most powerful court, but every plea he heard was painfully trivial to his intellect. His mind ached from the boredom, and he often wished he could just kill himself rather than suffer through one more whining soul. More than once, he cursed his immortality.

The large demon tasked with the next few rounds of flaying stood by, an imposing bailiff of sorts, barbed whip in hand, waiting for court to adjourn and the mind-numbing pleadings to finally stop. Then the *real* torture would begin.

As another pathetic defendant was led before him and began to whine his case, Henry found himself almost looking forward to it.

Déjà Vu

I didn't know how long I'd been handcuffed to the sturdy metal cot in that bright, sterile examining room. With no clock on the wall and the lights totally out of my control, it could have been hours. Hell, it could have been days for all I knew.

That's the funny thing about sleep deprivation; it messes with your sense of time.

Wait, I'm getting ahead of myself. Or behind. Something like that. Sorry, time gets kind of mixed up like that these days.

So, which part was I at? Oh yeah, they were examining me. Yes, that's right. I'd been held there for several months at that point. But… wait, I did it again, didn't I? OK, right, let me start over, but from the beginning.

Not that long ago, I was just a simple production assistant, or PA as they call us, in the entertainment industry, constantly jumping from show to show as work came my way. When I'd started working in "The Biz" in my late twenties as a way to get a foot in the door, I thought I was embarking on an wonderful adventure in the glamorous world of film and TV.

I couldn't have been more wrong.

Glamorous? More like brutal, with hellishly long hours and low pay, at least for us non-union peons in the production department.

Rather quickly, I learned that being a PA was not only a thankless job, but an impossibly exhausting one as well.

"Darren, bring the background in and make sure hair and makeup know that we'll be doing last looks on talent in five," the assistant director would call out over the walkie-talkie. ADs loved their walkies, and they certainly excelled at speaking into them, though not always so much at listening.

"Darren, call last man at lunch, then print sides for the table read." "Darren, I need you to get a cappuccino with skim milk and agave to video village for the director." "Darren, make a vegan sandwich on gluten-free bread for the talent."

Yeah, it wasn't what I had planned when I left my master's program at UCLA, and as a thirty-two-year-old man, the menial nature of the job sometimes got to me. It's not that I didn't like the people I worked for, it's just I thought I'd be doing something more, you know?

And let's not forget the one major aspect of the business that the average person is painfully unaware of. The hours.

When I overhear some non-industry person complaining about working a ten-hour day, it takes every ounce of self-control I possess to not burst out laughing in their face. We *dream* of the day when we only have to work ten hours. The painful reality is that the production team, who are the first on set and the last to leave, regularly works sixteen-hour days, if not more, and we do so on minimal sleep more often than not.

That's how this all started. The lack of sleep. Well, that and a lot of coffee. But I'm getting ahead of myself – but only a little bit. At least I think so. Where was I?

Oh yeah, the show where it all started.

We were filming the first season of a new cable series. The budget was high, and the producers didn't flinch at spending millions per episode. They were ambitious, and that drive translated into increasingly long hours on one hell of a tough shoot.

By the third week, "Fraturday" became a normal occurrence. That's what we called it when a Friday shift went so long it was Saturday before we got home. Of course that killed your weekend, because you would get off work at sunrise Saturday and start work at sunrise on Monday. You can see how this would wear down even the hardiest of crew members.

Fortunately the gods brought forth the gift of Strong Coffee.

And it was good.

We'd get through work on four hours of sleep propped up by pot after pot of lava-hot jet fuel in a cup. Add a dozen packets of sugar and you'd stay alert for at least a half hour. Then refill and repeat.

The gig was brutal, to say the least, with the average day close to eighteen hours. I even started answering my walkie-talkie in my sleep. You could say I was a bit delirious. More than a bit, really.

It was at that point that the déjà vu started happening.

Now I had long posited a theory that the real cause of déjà vu was simply your mind being so exhausted that it began processing things you saw just a fraction slower than normal, resulting in your seeing something but having it register with your conscious brain a second after your subconscious had already digested it. It was just a theory, mind you, but it seemed to make sense. I couldn't think of a time that I'd experienced déjà vu when well-rested, but really, who keeps track of that sort of thing?

It's not like I keep a journal or anything.

Yeah. A journal. In retrospect, maybe those last several months of living hell might not have been so bad if I had. Then again, maybe they'd have been worse.

But I'm getting off topic again.

Five months. That's how long we'd been at it. Five months of eighty-plus-hour weeks back to back to back. That feeling of sand in your puffy eyes all day long, even when you're nowhere near a beach. The deep body ache and lethargic pace your every movement seems to decelerate into. Like walking in mud. Like pulling an invisible sled. Like your limbs had weights pulling them down.

I was a wreck.

I finally hit the point where I wouldn't even sleep some nights. At least not really. I'd lie down but be so tired I'd close my eyes and just daydream, unable to fall into proper REM slumber.

That was when the beginnings of "the pattern" fueling the whole thing finally arose.

I'd start the week with no sleep Monday, then roughly four hours Tuesday before finally being able to catch five hours on Wednesday. Thursday and Friday were back-to-back eighteen-hour days, which left me a jittery insomniac by the weekend, when I should have been out for days, recovering.

At that point, my body clock was wrecked.

I'd only get about four hours of sleep on Saturday after work, and since getting home after sunrise and going to bed just meant I was waking near dusk, I was unable to slip into a normal pattern. By the time Monday rolled around (far too quickly), that meant waking up at four to be at set by my five a.m. call time.

I have a belief, by the way. If you wake up at 3:59 a.m., you're waking up really, really late at night. If you wake at 4:00 a.m., you're waking really, really early. In either case, it sucks something fierce.

Coffee, as I think I mentioned, was my savior and curse. It kept me going but made any semblance of deep sleep even harder. A necessary evil, but I told myself it was just for a few more months until the show went into hiatus and I could take some time off to recover before the next one.

I think the excessive coffee consumption was the first trigger. If I had four cups before lunch, I would notice changes, and we're not talking upset stomach or pounding headache.

I saw things.

The déjà vu episodes became more frequent, sometimes as many as a dozen a day. That in and of itself was disconcerting, but what was really odd was their length.

I started having them for ten, twenty, even thirty seconds at a stretch. It was like living in a DVD that was skipping back and forth. All my actions during those spells were like watching a movie I'd already seen. I learned to roll with the odd sensation and do my job, but it made me wonder.

What if I was actually seeing into the future?

Yeah, crazy, I know, but when you're utterly exhausted, your mind will convince you of all sorts of things. Like the time I actually saw a pink elephant crossing the freeway heading home at 3 a.m. and swerved to avoid it. Yeah, I probably shouldn't have been driving.

Shit, I forgot what I was saying. My train of thought

derails more and more often these days.

Oh yeah, time travel.

So seeing the future. Right.

I thought it was pretty amazing, if only I could do something about it. Unfortunately the experience was like being in a dream, and I was just along for the ride. That's how it went for the next three weeks until the production trailer got its own espresso machine.

By the way, if you call it "expresso" I will hunt you down and beat you to death with your own appendage. You may think I'm kidding, and maybe I am, but is it worth the risk?

Anyway, espresso.

I may have overdone it a little when I brewed my jet-fuel strength quad-shot that morning, but I'd been without proper sleep for so long and was already on my seventy-first hour that week (and it was only Thursday), so it just somehow made sleep-deprived sense to me at the time.

The brew was strong enough to peel paint off a wall, and it hit my system like a sledgehammer, the caffeine forcing my body and mind to lurch into action when by all reasonable expectations they should both have been curled up fetal, snoring on the ground.

That was the first time it happened.

Even with my frequent déjà vu episodes, up until that moment, I had only been an observer of tiny snippets of my future. Along for the ride as long as the glimpse would last.

This time was different. This time was amazing. This time wasn't ten or even thirty seconds, but nearly a full minute, and rather than experiencing moments before it happened, I had the entire experience flash into my mind before it even started.

I walked in a daze, exhausted yet wired, and fully aware of every single thing that was about to happen.

Samantha is going to say hello, then step into the makeup trailer.

"Morning, Darren!"

Now Benny is going to slip on that cable and spill coffee on his shirt.

"God damn it! Anyone have a towel?"

Mark is going to ask me for a hot battery for his walkie-talkie.

"Hey Darren, do you have a…"

I handed him the battery.

"Thank you."

The blue ice chest is going to tip over while Sherri is filling it with water bottles.

I saw it begin to topple, as I knew it would, when without realizing what I was doing, I lunged forward and caught it before it fell to the ground.

"Whoa! Thanks Darren! That would have sucked!"

"No problem, glad to help," I replied.

That was when it hit me. The enormity of it.

My heart was pounding in my chest, and it wasn't from the caffeine. *Did I just do what I think I did?*

I'll go ahead and spoil the suspense. Yes, I did.

I changed the future.

"Red thirty-four," the croupier called out.

I had won again. Thirty-five to one odds and I'd been hitting them regularly across Vegas all week. I thought I was playing smart, only winning one big bet in each casino. I wish

I'd known then what I know now, namely that even though they are in competition with one another for patrons' money, the casinos all share a central tracking system of gamblers that come through their doors.

Maybe if I'd just stuck with playing horses and poker, I wouldn't have wound up in this mess, but what can I say? I was exhausted, wired on caffeine, and for the first time in my life, I actually had money.

A lot of it.

Did I skip ahead again? Shit, sorry. I should clarify.

I didn't start out as a high roller in the casinos of Las Vegas. Hell, I was still a broke-ass production assistant when I realized I had somehow stumbled upon something big.

At first I couldn't control it; the exact reasons and triggers that allowed me to catch glimpses of the future were still a mystery. Since that first incident, more often than not, I'd maybe be able to get a twenty-second flash, but nothing more. I managed to do fairly well playing poker with the Teamsters on set, but really there's not much you can do with twenty seconds. What I needed to re-create was that longer event, but I wasn't quite sure how.

Fortunately we are pretty anal about our paperwork in film production, and in my off hours I began charting out my sleep schedule on a spreadsheet.

I figured it had to be somehow tied in to my déjà vu theory, and that sleep deprivation was the trigger, or at least part of it. I was still having shorter flashes, but nothing I could really act on. Ironically, the excitement of discovering my sleep-deprived gift was being stymied by my increased insomnia as I labored into the wee hours to understand it.

Basically, I made myself too tired for it to work.

Two weeks after we wrapped the show, I began meticulously re-creating my sleep schedule from the weeks prior. Normally I would have been catching up on much-needed rest, but instead I was subjecting myself to increasingly brutal bouts of self-inflicted sleeplessness. It sucked, no doubt about it, but when the episodes slowly started to lengthen, it made it all worthwhile.

At two months I had figured out (only roughly at that point) a basic formula of sleeplessness to caffeine. I also found that it couldn't be the same every day. That was an unexpected but crucial discovery. Multiple days of no sleep followed by short periods of rest, then long stretches of miserable consciousness was what it took. Add to that the coffee intake and there was a baseline. The espresso jolt was what seemed to kick it into overdrive.

By the third month, it was dialed in. I had even stopped looking for shows to work on. I had no need of a menial job, I was making a very decent living playing cards or dice with street hustlers, winning just enough to seem like a fluke (and not get me stabbed in the back as I walked off with my winnings). Fortunately I was exhausted and looked like hell, so no one ever suspected I was anything more than a strung-out gambling addict who happened to get lucky. I desperately wanted to sleep, but the power, far more than the money, had me hooked, and I wasn't about to give it up.

Sure, it had taken a lot of fine-tuning and trial and error, as well as copious amounts of coffee, but I had finally cracked the secret. At the shortest, I was consistently seeing to the two-minute mark, while at times I could stretch as far as five. With that much time to work with, it wasn't long before I moved up from street hustlers to the racetracks, and from there it was only natural I'd try the lottery.

I really should have just hit the jackpot and walked away. All of this mess could have been avoided.

Unfortunately I mistakenly assumed that I was better off winning smaller amounts, the logic behind that being hitting it big would draw too much attention. So it came to pass that instead of the massive multimillion-dollar jackpot, I merely won a respectable five-figure sum to bankroll my future escapades. Naturally I couldn't come back and win a lottery again, it would make the news, and scrutiny was what I was avoiding.

That was when I got stupid and went to Vegas. That was when I got on the mob's radar.

Wait, did I already go over that? I was duct taped to a chair and– no, hang on, I started at the examination room, didn't I?

Right. I think I need more coffee.

So anyway.

Vegas.

Right.

Like I was saying, I kicked off my Las Vegas experience with some blackjack, poker, and craps. The games went long enough that I would win and lose over time, never raising too many red flags. Sure, I'd always come out ahead, but it wasn't anything excessive. I thought I was being so smart. Little did I know, they'd taken notice nonetheless.

Then I decided to try my hand at roulette. The odds were amazing – a thirty-five to one payout – and I, foolishly, couldn't resist. I started winning. A lot. Too fast, and too much.

The mob, needless to say, was not amused.

"I'm gonna ask you again, how did you beat the wheel at all five casinos?"

"I told you, I was just lucky. I picked a number and the ball landed on it. I mean it happens all the time, right?"

SMACK, another punch to the face. I strained my arms, but the duct tape binding me to the chair seemed to laugh at my feeble attempts.

"Maybe you're hard of hearing on account of all the blows to the head, so I'll ask again, really slowly. How. Did. You. Beat. The. Wheels?" The guy was a brute. Hired muscle who could likely pummel me into a meat paste without breaking a sweat. I knew it was silly to resist, I mean, what good would it do me? I wasn't keeping state secrets or anything. Besides, they almost certainly wouldn't believe me anyway.

That was what really scared me. What if they decided I was lying? What would happen to me then? If they thought I was just a waste of their time, I'd be in a shallow grave in the Nevada desert before morning.

SMACK.

Goddamn, that hurt! The guy had surprisingly sharp knuckles for such meaty hands. It was time to spill the beans before I was physically unable to do so. I turned my head and spat out the blood pooling in my mouth.

"It's a gift," I began. "Something I recently learned how to do." I wasn't speaking to the thug in front of me. It was his handler, the lithe man in the dark suit leaning against the wall like he hadn't a care in the world, who was really running things.

"Go on," the brute said, holding off on the beating, at least for a moment.

And so I laid it all out. The exhaustion, how it started as flashes, how it evolved, how I had more or less gotten it under control, but it took time and a lot of effort to get to that point.

"Show me," the handler said with a curious expression, like a cat humoring a mouse it could kill with one swipe of its paw.

"I can't."

He nodded to his associate.

SMACK!

"I can't right now! You've kept me up too long. I need to rest and get back to the proper state. It's not something I can just wish up when you snap your fingers."

I closed my eyes as the big man pulled back his arm for another blow.

"Wait."

A momentary respite.

"Time is something we have," the lean man said. "And though I'm not normally inclined to believe hoodoo voodoo garbage, I've seen the security tapes. We cross-referenced the database and found your face all over town in poker games, blackjack, craps, and you left a winner every time. Every. Single. Time. I wanna see if you can actually pull this off. Tell us what you need, and we'll try this again in a few days. But know this: If you are lying to me, they'll never find the pieces."

My cell could have been worse, I suppose. It was a relatively nice room on a lower floor of what must have been one of the older casinos on the strip. The doors and windows didn't open, obviously, and it didn't take a great leap of imagination to picture the armed goon hanging outside in the hallway.

At least it was clean, though I quickly found it incredibly hard to achieve my necessary state locked in one room. To stay awake for several days (after a short rest, of course) requires distraction. Sitting in a room just makes you want to sleep.

"I need a gym," I said. "Or somewhere to walk. Something to help me stay up."

Surprisingly, they agreed to my request. The roof of the building was made accessible to me, under guard, and the fresh air and blood pumping from moving around really did the trick. Five days later, I was in the zone.

"Black ten."

It was my fifth correct roll in a row. Lucky for me, because just as the ball dropped into the slot, the vision cut out.

"Utterly amazing," the lean man admitted. "You cheated us out of a good deal of money, you know, but I think we've just found a way for you to repay us."

I had been the mobster's pet psychic, or whatever you want to call it, for nearly two months, always staying on edge, always hovering between exhaustion and a caffeinated adrenaline rush. He said I was his guest, but we both knew better. Sure, I was kept in a luxurious penthouse suite, and sure I had 24/7 access to the rooftop should I want exercise or air. I even had a small gym in my quarters. But I was most certainly his possession.

He thought he treated me well, and I suppose, in his own twisted way, that was the case. Occasionally, if I'd scored him a particularly large win with one of the dozens of weekly bets he would have me try to get a fix on, he would offer me top-notch hookers as a reward. To help keep me "up," he would chuckle.

I took the girls into my room, but always declined their services.

Now if I was the type of man who didn't mind knowing a woman was just with me because she was paid to be, perhaps it would have been a good situation, but unfortunately that's just not my thing. Of course, I always told him we'd had a great time and the girls were amazing lovers. I wouldn't want them not to get paid (or worse) should he think they weren't up to snuff. Still, the whole thing left me feeling a bit skeevy.

By the time his brains were splattered on the floor in front of me, I'd estimate I must have won him over thirty-million dollars. He was far more sophisticated than I was when it came to the ins and outs of gambling. With his legion of lackeys to place bets all across town, he had a consistent churn coming from the competing establishments.

As for me, I had been sleep deprived for so long by that point, I was beginning to experience much longer stretches of foresight than my five-minute average.

I kept that little tidbit to myself.

One delirious morning it dawned on me that maybe it wasn't future memories that I was seeing, but possibly the key to time travel itself. Then I'd realize my body hadn't moved at all, so technically I wasn't a time traveler. Or maybe knowledge of the future really was slipping the bonds of time somehow. I guess, technically, it was still a sort of time travel, just not what anyone would have ever imagined.

Oh hang on, I mentioned my captor was killed.

Sorry, I should clarify.

He was visiting me in my suite after I had scored him a particularly hefty payday. Later, I thought it was actually sort of funny how if I'd just been in the zone at that moment, I could have warned him about the swarm of special operatives about to burst into the room and kill every single person who wasn't me.

They were quite efficient, I must say. The CIA trains them well, and they certainly got their money's worth. When the flash-bang grenades went off and they kicked the doors in, the entire floor was secured in under thirty seconds.

I was scared shitless, but when the smoke cleared, I saw the uniforms and realized my Mafia captivity was finally over.

"Thank God," I said, grateful for the rescue. "You don't know how long I've been here!"

A man in a black balaclava held up a photograph as he quietly studied my face.

"Target acquired."

"Um, excuse me? What do you mean, 'target'?" I asked. The stun gun in his hand quickly answered that question, and the last thing I saw was a black canvas sack being pulled over my head.

"Hello, Darren, I'm Dr. McNabb. I'll be running some tests on you these next few weeks," the man in the lab coat said when I finally woke in the sterile, windowless room.

"But you rescued me –"

"Yes, yes, but first we need to understand a few things about your condition. From what we've heard, you may be able to help us with a few of our more exotic problems."

"So I'm not free to go?"

"Not quite yet, but I assure you the government will take great care of you. You'll be a hero if you help us out."

I had thought I was being freed. No such luck.

Like the song says, "Meet the new boss. Same as the old boss." Only this one had a badge.

I was held in isolation for several weeks while they ran tests on me. Apparently my mob captors had kept copious notes on my condition and what they did to maintain my abilities, and the doctors were keen to test the limits of what I could do. My prior captors had made it very clear that I could only see as far as five minutes forward, so it was imperative to maintain a perimeter that would take longer than that for me to breach should I decide to make a run for it.

Gee, thanks guys.

Those notes led my government hosts to make quite certain their safeguards took that into account, and all patrols more than doubled it just to be safe.

The team of doctors drew blood more frequently than a goddamn vampire, though with the amount of high-octane coffee they were pumping into me I suspect they got more java than red stuff most of the time.

Being scientists, they controlled everything down to the amount of time I slept and when I ate. It was hell. I entirely lost track of time. The lights were totally out of my control, and with no clocks to be found, I never knew what time it was or how long I'd been awake.

"Don't worry about that," the staff would tell me. "We're monitoring the hours, and you're doing just fine."

Yeah, sure. As if they expected me to believe my best interests were their concern.

As for the tricks I had used to avoid sleep, my old rooftop prison seemed like heaven by comparison. In the painfully bland environment of their testing facility, they would use random noise generators to jolt me alert anytime I seemed to be nodding off. I asked if I could just go for a walk or at least get some fresh air, but that wasn't in their protocols.

After weeks of testing and re-testing we eventually got to the meat and potatoes of what they really wanted.

An army of me.

Not "me" me, but people like me. Oh those poor volunteers.

After three months of brutal experiments, the men and women who had stepped forward, hoping to become the country's next generation of super-soldiers, were nothing but a jibbering group of glazed-eyed floor warmers. All my regimen of sleep deprivation and caffeine had done was break them down, one by one.

It seemed, much to the doctors' chagrin, that I was unique.

I mentioned how much it sucked being handcuffed to a cot, right? I mean time just lost meaning after a while, though I knew the doctors watching me on the monitors had it measured and recorded down to the second.

For two months after the attempts to re-create my ability failed, they'd been using me in dirty ways. Things that made me feel ill. Things I wish I'd never seen.

The arms deals weren't a big issue, it was just making sure the coast was clear for their transaction. The stock trades, while totally unethical, were at least understandable. I mean, how could the CIA turn down the opportunity to quintuple their budget by a well-coordinated series of massive, covert flash trades over the course of several weeks? Insider trading might be illegal for the rest of the nation, but if you're in government, it seems to be perfectly acceptable, especially for the three-letter agencies.

No, it wasn't those that got to me. It was the drone strikes.

They started using me to confirm targets before sending missiles to blow them up, innocent bystanders or not. It was only a few months, but I'd already seen more death than I would ever have wanted. So naturally I am in hiding.

Wait, Did I get to the part where I escaped? Shit, my bad. I'm having more and more problems with time these days.

So, the escape.

It was fortunate I hadn't mentioned my extended sight when I was being held in Vegas. Had I said anything about it then, it would have wound up in those notes, and I'd have never stood a chance. As it was, it still took every bit of concentration I had to overcome the security measures and break out, and even then, it was only after weeks of planning, observing, and a big dose of luck.

Still, as you'd imagine, knowing when things are going to happen can prove really useful when you need to escape a maximum-security research lab. As far as they knew, given my limitations (on paper), a Rube-Goldberg-like thirteen-minute escape shouldn't have been possible.

But then neither should I, if you want to pick nits.

In any case, one day the stars aligned. I saw the farthest I'd ever seen, and the pieces, just barely, fit into place.

By the time they learned their prize lab rat was missing, I was long gone.

It's really not so bad out here. I mean, keeping off the grid and out of sight of any security cameras, traffic cameras, ATM cameras – well, it can be a bit tiring, but I'm getting the hang of it. The gift of foresight doesn't hurt either, though staying perpetually sleep-deprived and jacked on caffeine is certainly playing havoc on my body.

Smaller towns are the way to go, so I'm keeping on the move and laying low, winning a little money from street hustlers and paying for everything with cash. It sucks that I can't touch the hundreds of thousands in my bank accounts, but that's just not an option. Not with the CIA and their nameless affiliates looking for me. I know they're scanning everything. Searching. Trying to find me.

I just keep running.

The only problem is, it's getting harder and harder to keep a step ahead when I'm almost too tired to walk.

The Great Yoga Riot of Beverly Hills

Yogi Vinrasha Himdalay felt like a new man when he left the quaint little ashram in a remote corner of India. The mystic secrets imparted to him during his six-month intensive yoga retreat left his third eye open wide to the world, his chakras aligned, and his chi flowing in perfect harmony.

When Yogi Vinrasha Himdalay (formerly known as Burt Thompson) settled into his first-class seat, bound for his immensely popular yoga studio in Beverly Hills, he felt confident that he was bringing home with him not only a new series of asanas to share with his loyal followers, but also a new way of life. One his celebrity clientele would undoubtedly adopt with gusto.

Burt wasn't always a yoga guru to the slightly damaged rich and famous of Los Angeles. He'd sold frozen steaks (but was now a vegetarian of course), was a waiter at a chic beachfront restaurant on the Malibu coast, and had even spent time as a process server for a particularly nasty divorce attorney, thanks to a hookup from one of the tattooed Russian line cooks he worked with.

It was that last job, actually, that had led to his indoctrination into the ways of yoga.

Donny "The Beast" McNabb was a mid-level pro wrestling star with hair as long as his temper was short. Burt had been serving him with divorce papers all those years ago when his life was changed forever.

The huge man was outside the arena following one of his bouts, taking pictures and posing with fans. To say he hadn't taken kindly to the handsome, sandy-haired beach bum casually handing him a court summons under guise of asking for an autograph would be an understatement. The Beast's one saving grace was that there were no witnesses willing to make a statement against him. So it was that once Burt was released from the hospital with no lawsuit possible, he wound up in a workers' comp-mandated physical therapy program.

Once the casts were removed, of course.

It had been hard going, for a time. His joints were constantly sore, and his muscles were tight and stiff, but as fate would have it, one of the physical therapists (the surprisingly strong Filipino woman who performed the excruciating cross-fiber friction massage on his healing tendons) mentioned that yoga might be a low-impact and less-painful way for him to regain his strength and mobility.

Anything was better than her painful manhandling, so he gave it a try.

Fifteen years later, Burt Thompson was no more, replaced by Yogi Vinrasha Himdalay, guru to the stars, a man who had grown his humble workshops into the most popular yoga studio on the Westside.

For whatever reason, he was something of a magnet for the damaged people of Los Angeles, drawing scores of recovering addicts to his classes, right alongside the raw and vegan lifestyle models who liked his calm demeanor almost as much as his surfer good looks.

Actually it made perfect sense. Early on in his practice, he had applied what he knew of specialized marketing tactics (specifically targeting people needing a sense of belonging), and what better place to build a tight-knit yoga community full of people looking for a support network than at AA meetings?

He sat through discussions week after week, and slowly, over coffee and cookies, he gradually recruited a fiercely loyal following. It was their near-fanatical support in the beginning that had made him stand out and seem so attractive to newcomers in the years that followed. If his devotees were so loyal, people had reasoned, he had to be something amazing, right?

Of course Hollywood has never had a shortage of celebrities with addiction issues, and all it took was a few tabloid pics of them leaving his studio for his yoga practice to snowball.

Within only a year, he had to relocate to a much larger facility, bankrolled by his doting students.

When he took to the small podium upon his return from his six-month absence, the excitement in the packed room was electric as the crowd murmured with anticipation.

"Friends, it is so good to see you all again," he said, the crowd falling into silence. "I have many new things to share with you. Things that will change your lives forever. Your physical well-being will improve, and your strength and mental clarity will grow. In one month's time, I will begin a new program for those of you who wish to benefit from what I have learned in my time in the ashrams of India. The training will be intense, and your bodies will be pushed by the effort, but it will be worth it. I remain your servant, ever committed to helping you nourish your physical being as well as your spiritual one. For now I wish to simply say how glad I am to see you all again, and I look forward to your joining me when we begin this exciting and challenging new chapter in your self-improvement next month."

He scanned the crowd. All eyes were locked on him, waiting intently for his next words.

"In the meantime, I'll be teaching daily for those who wish to partake of my traditional offerings. I look forward to seeing you all soon. Namaste."

He spent an hour socializing with his students, most of whom had greatly missed him during his absence, then went to his private offices, slipped out of his robes and into some sweat pants, and hopped in his car, bound for Plummer Park, the old Russian chess battleground in West Hollywood.

He felt confident that most, if not all, of his followers would sign up for his new program, and that would help expand his reach beyond Los Angeles once it gained momentum. Now he just needed to make it happen. Fortunately he knew just the man for the job.

"Burt, is good to seeing you again," Yuri said, rising from the table where he was locked in an intense chess match with an elderly Russian man with tufts of hair sprouting from his ears.

Yuri was thickly muscled, heavily tattooed, and a few years older than his friend. He wore a red Adidas track suit and spotless matching Adidas shoes, the trio of lines running from his soles all the way to his broad shoulders. The big man gave his friend a crushing hug.

"Yuri, you know no one calls me that anymore," Yogi Vinrasha Himdalay laughed once the large man finally released him.

"Bah, you will always be Burt to Yuri," he grinned. "So tell me, why are you to coming here?"

"It has been far too many years, my friend. I knew I could find you in the park. Old habits die hard, eh?"

"Da, and much business is done over good game of chess."

"I remember. So listen, I was wondering, are you still connected in the food industry?"

"Foods? Da, I have connections in many things. Remember, it was Yuri who got you out of restaurant job. Sorry about what happen to you with wrestler, but if not for Yuri, you would still be waiter!" he laughed. "I like what you doing now. Many more beautiful women in yoga job, eh?"

"It's a better lifestyle, that is true."

"So what do you need, my friend?"

"I'm taking my clients to a higher level of fitness. They'll be stronger, sharper, more energized. I have a chef handling the organic meals, but I need someone to help me with the juicing aspect. Production as well as delivery."

"You need help for juicing? Yuri can get juice."

"It has to be top quality. Only the best."

"Don't worry," the big Russian said with a smile. "Leave to Yuri. I taking care of it for you."

When Yogi Vinrasha Himdalay introduced his new organic vegetarian meal plan and delivery service to his loyal followers the following month, the enthusiastic response was beyond what he had ever hoped for. Soon his meal prep staff as well as Yuri's juice delivery service both had to hire additional laborers to keep up with demand. The new health, energy, and vitality-boosting foods were a hit.

Meals, both hot and cold, were delivered daily, taking the stress of shopping out of the daily equation of so many people's lives. Then there were the juices. The novel combinations were fresh and delicious, and those who subscribed to the delivery program absolutely swore by them, claiming they'd never had never felt as good as when they downed a bottle of his special elixirs.

At the same time, Yogi Vinrasha Himdalay's new yoga classes were crowded to capacity, with him even having to add additional sessions to accommodate the dozens of overflow students who couldn't find mat space in the jam-packed sessions.

The new series of asanas challenged people, the combinations, rhythm, and intensity pushing them to new heights. That, combined with the top-notch nourishment they were now receiving, saw marked improvements in both their physical strength as well as definition of musculature.

His actor clients subsequently found themselves in higher demand as their sculpted physiques caught the eye of casting directors and obsessed fans alike, while his other clients who had been previously struggling with shedding extra weight saw the fat melt away, replaced by lean muscle.

Five months after his new regimen began, Yogi Vinrasha Himdalay's students' successes had spread by word of mouth faster than mono in a high school. New students would come from miles away to study with him, quickly jumping on board with his meal plans and juice regimen, replacing the toxic foods in their diets with his healthy ones.

Six months later, talk shows began interviewing the incredibly popular yogi, which only served to grow his reach further. The opportunities for expansion were lining up faster than they could be logged into the computerized future franchise system that had been set up when things began to snowball. He even had to hire another assistant.

Things couldn't have been going better, Yogi Vinrasha Himdalay thought to himself. He had effected an amazing change in people's lives with simple foods, juice, and yoga. Surely things would only improve further as time went on.

The first all-out brawl at the yoga studio started over the simple placement of a yoga mat.

The room was crowded, as always, and the air was hot. An intentional choice to optimize the cleansing and toning properties of the poses while helping the body purge unwanted toxins. Unfortunately those conditions also led the brawny man with thinning hair and spotty shoulder acne to lose his cool.

"Your mat is in my space," he had angrily grunted to the man set up beside him.

"Hey, it's all good, there's room for everyone. Chill out," the interloper had replied.

"What did you say?" His chest was puffed out, his eyes a bit wide with the adrenaline surge. "Did you tell me to chill out?"

"What's your problem man? It's a yoga class. You need to mellow out."

"Well you better namaste the fuck out of my way then," the angry man growled.

When an unfortunately timed loss of balance during a particularly difficult pose caused the man to bump into his pumped-up neighbor during class, the enraged fellow finally lost what was left of his cool.

By the time the police arrived, the brawl had sucked half a dozen other people into the fray.

The air of the studio was tinged with the pungent aroma of pepper spray long after the men were rounded up and carted off, and it took the better part of the evening to clean up the blood and granola scattered across the floor.

"What's going on?" Yogi Vinrasha Himdalay asked his facility manager when yet another confrontation occurred two days later, this time out in front of the building. Two spandex-clad yoga chicks had become involved in a vicious catfight over a parking space. "People are losing their minds. They're supposed to be centering, becoming one with the universe," the yogi lamented.

"I don't know what it is, boss, but tensions have really been flaring. A lot of people are just angry lately. And have you noticed, they aren't looking all that healthy anymore either."

He had noticed, actually. Skin, once glowing and clear, was pocked with acne. People's hair was no longer shiny, but dull, and their physiques looked unnaturally swollen.

"I wonder if maybe they're having food allergies or something," she posited.

The yogi pondered for a moment, then felt his gut twist as a thought flashed through his mind. He hoped he was wrong.

"Call Yuri and have him swing by after deliveries."

When the large Russian came by that evening, a feeling of increasing unease had settled into Yogi Vinrasha Himdalay's stomach.

"Hey Burt, is good seeing you."

"Yuri, good to see you as well," he replied, unsure how to broach the topic plaguing his churning mind. "So, have you heard?" he began. "Several of my students have gotten into fights at the studio."

"It happens sometimes," the Russian replied, untroubled by the news. "Is merely side effect. We see in Russia all the time. Totally normal. Not to worrying about it."

"Side effect?" The feeling of dread was spreading quickly. "What do you mean side effect? Side effect of what?"

"You know. Juicing," the Russian replied with a nudge and a wink.

"Wait, when I said I wanted you to get juice, you didn't think –"

"All good, boss. Yuri has taking care of it. Best quality, just like you ask. Your students all get big and strong, no?"

Yuri kept talking, but Burt couldn't seem to make out his words, the sheer horror of realization overwhelming his mind.

The writing was on the wall, and it was printed in ten-foot-high flaming block letters.

All he'd worked so hard for was gone in an instant.

Burt Thompson (Yogi Vinrasha Himdalay ceased to exist that day) was gone when his students arrived for class the following afternoon, headed for a non-extradition country far away on the other side of the world. His bank accounts were emptied, his phone was turned off, and no forwarding address was left behind.

All that remained were the several cases of juice in the refrigerated display and some monogrammed velour sweat pants.

When the angry and confused yoga chicks and yoga dudes realized their guru was gone, tensions flared.

Well, they more than flared. Then the formerly loving followers of Yogi Vinrasha Himdalay did what seemed like a good idea at the time. They torched the building.

And then they brawled.

Furious men and women fled the flames, spilling into the streets, fists flying, in a decidedly non-Zen free-for-all.

As texts and retweets of the yogi's disappearance flashed out across the city, his once-faithful followers collectively lost their cool. As the palm trees and electric cars went up in flames, so began the Great Yoga Riot of Beverly Hills.

The Gluten-Free Goddess of Bokano Maru

When they had first begun cataloguing the smaller islands of the remote patch of the Pacific, Professors Harrison and Marks had never once dreamed that the insanity of modern civilization would have somehow beaten them to the denizens of the tiny chunk of inhabitable land the rest of the world seemed to have forgotten.

They couldn't have been more wrong.

"Issa no goodayoo for eating," the tribesman said in halting pidgin English. "Issa no glootenfree."

"Oh dear," Harrison remarked.

"Oh dear indeed," Marks agreed.

The duo had only been on the little island of Bokano Maru for a few hours, arriving via seaplane, anchored nearby, then paddling to the white-sand shore. Having unloaded their gear from their raft, the duo were just starting to survey the gorgeous beaches and lush tropical interior of the almost mystical island, when an indigenous tribesman strode confidently toward them from the jungle canopy.

"Iorana!" Marks called out in what he hoped was the native greeting, "Pe'he koe?"

"Riva riva," the man replied, relaxing his posture a bit. "Yoo Marikens?" he asked.

"British," Harrison replied, astounded the man spoke a semblance of his native tongue. "I am Professor Harrison, and this is Professor Marks. We are here to learn about your island. Come, sit with us and share our meal."

Hospitality was a big thing for the island cultures, and if

an invitation was offered, the recipient was honor-bound to accept. So too was the tradition of providing shelter for those who washed up on their shores, a commonality the explorers had found amongst nearly all of the island-faring tribes, for in their varied cultures, they all knew full well that someday it might be they who washed up on someone else's shores.

Marks had begun uncrating some of their foodstuffs, specially sealed to survive the humidity of the region. The man –Ponoaru, they learned he was called – was one of the tribal leaders. Good fortune, it seemed, had smiled upon them, finding a figure of authority straightaway like that.

Seeing the strange white men spreading out food on a banana leaf, Ponoaru removed the pack from his shoulder and contributed some dried meat and a leaf-wrapped package of island yams to the meal.

"Excuse me," Hamilton said. "Is that a Louis Vuitton bag?"

"Looeeee!" Ponoaru exclaimed. "Dee goddess give me dis for to carry da foods."

"Dear Lord, that's a £1,500 bag. Where on Earth did he get that?" Marks asked, astounded.

"Patience, Marks, I'm sure we'll find out soon enough," his associate replied.

They popped open one of the mylar bags and passed around the contents: some tins of chicken, pouches of dried fruit, and, of course, some biscuits to go with their tea.

Without warning Ponoaru smacked the leavened snacks from their hands, crushing the biscuits into the sand with his foot until only crumbs remained.

"Issa no goodayoo for eating," he said, spitting on the

remnants of the biscuits. "Issa no glootenfree."

Ponoaru led the way as they navigated a narrow jungle path to his village. His attire, they noted as they followed close behind, was adorned with bits of metal, woven scraps of faded fabrics of several colors, and of course native thatching from the palm fronds so prevalent in the region.

The island was of moderate size, perhaps fifteen kilometers long and less than half that across. Fortunately for the visitors, their destination was but a simple hour's walk in the comforting shade of the tall trees swaying gently overhead.

Stepping out into a beachfront clearing on the far side of the island, Harrison and Marks were quite surprised to see a trio of weathered shipping containers, dents and gashes in their metal hides, positioned in a crude semi-circle, in the center of which was a highly decorated altar of wood, metal, and stones, shaded by the tattered remains of a once bright-orange emergency raft.

"Do you see that?" hissed Harrison. "A survival raft!"

"Indeed," replied Marks. "That must be how they learned English. But what of the survivor, then?"

The scarecrow idol behind the altar caught both men's attention. It was roughly five and a half feet high, human in shape, with a frizzy, and long-dried-out, blonde wig atop its head, which happened to be a very ornately painted coconut, complete with blush and lipstick.

"I say," Marks commented, stepping past a line of small white rocks as he approached the altar.

"Stop!" Harrison called to his friend. "I don't think they

want you in there, old fellow."

Villagers swarmed the site, crude spears in hand, shouting warnings as they waved their weapons.

"Ah, yes. So sorry chaps, my mistake," he said, backing out of the sacred space. "I meant no disrespect."

Ponoaru clasped him by his shoulders and fixed him with a stern gaze. "Ees no allow to goeeeng there," he said, making sure the strange white man understood. "Ees holy place," he added for emphasis. "Only elders go dere."

"We are sorry, Ponoaru. It will not happen again."

The man studied him for a moment, then, satisfied the message was understood, relaxed his grip, waved off the villagers, and took the men on a tour of the village.

The outer line of huts were of a somewhat more robust design, acting as wind blocks for the inner parts of the village as well as storage for various things that had washed up on their shores, lost overboard from ships caught in high seas. They were also used for housing the few animals in the village when the weather turned foul.

Closer in, the huts were of a smaller design, mostly providing shelter for families, but occasionally containing the few couples who were without children.

At the innermost were the tribal leaders, their accommodations a bit more plush, and all with entrances that faced the altar. It seemed that to lay eyes on the holiest of holies when you first awakened was considered a great blessing, and naturally the men of power were the ones to receive it. In this, their political structure was surprisingly akin to "civilized" cultures.

The explorers were given an unused hut in the middle of the village. Almost immediately the native children swarmed them, fascinated by their pale skin and unusual clothes.

"Yoo from hayven?" one child asked.

"Brighton, actually," Marks replied.

Disappointed, the child wandered back to his compatriots and headed out to frolic in the waves.

Come evening, the entire village joined for a communal meal of fish, plantains, and sea greens. The men were impressed with the culinary skills of the villagers, and when an opportunity arose, they pulled Ponoaru aside to ask about it.

"Your people are very skilled in food preparation," Harrison said. "Very different from other people in these islands."

The man smiled broadly. "Thassacause da goddess teach us. Wee da chosen peeple."

"You've mentioned your goddess before, is that her?" Marks asked, pointing to the idol under the canopied altar.

"Is her Loa, her speerit," was the reply. "She watchovering us now. Da goddess is in us all."

"We would like to learn about your goddess. Is it allowed to speak of her?"

"Of for certain we speaking of her! Da goddess save us from da eeevil!"

"Evil? What evil is that?" Both men leaned forward expectantly.

Ponoaru paused for effect. "Da eeevil of da glooten! You see. In da mornin you see." He laughed, then lumbered off to join the festivities. The curious professors would have to wait for the following day for any further answers, it seemed.

Come sunrise, Harrison and Marks were awoken by a low chanting.

"Is someone saying 'Om'?" Harrison asked, rubbing the grit of sleep (and perhaps a bit of sand as well) from his eyes.

Stepping out of their hut, the men marveled at what they saw. There before them, the entire village had rolled out individual woven grass mats before the altar. They weren't just chanting, it seemed. They were doing something else as well.

They were doing yoga.

"Is that downward dog?"

"It would appear so. But how? Why?" The men were flummoxed. A full hour, the yoga lasted, ending with the village shaman walking into the open cargo container, returning with a plastic-wrapped package in his hands.

"Are those Jammie Dodgers?" Marks asked, stunned to see his favorite biscuits in the hands of the indigenous.

"Must've been what the cargo ship lost when those washed overboard," mused Harrison. "I wonder what else they have. I could do with a spot of tea."

They watched as the shaman strode to the altar and ceremoniously placed the package upon it. The crowd was silent, watching intently as he scanned their anxious faces. With a sudden movement, he picked up a mallet that had been hidden from view and began smashing the cookies to dust while the crowd cheered.

"No mo dee Glooten!" he yelled, and the crowd went wild.

"What do they have against gluten?" mused Harrison. He spotted Ponoaru walking nearby when the ceremony ended and pulled him aside.

"Please," he began, "tell us more of this ritual."

The villager smiled at them and took them to a shady spot under a palm tree, sitting comfortably like a counselor at a campfire.

And so he told them the story of the Gluten-Free Goddess of Bokano Maru.

When she arrived, her skin was red from sun, but her hair was so golden, no one could deny she was a deity sent to them from heaven. Her sacred raft had washed upon their beaches, and the people of the island knew she was surely testing their hospitality when she failed to wake to their shouts. The village leaders knew what to do.

Gingerly they carried her, raft and all, to the center of the village, placing the goddess in front of the altar specially designed for sacrifices to appease the spirits of the seas. The holiest shipping containers protected her from the elements, and her sacred raft provided her shade as she rested on a bed of animal hides in their most holy space.

They laid out bowls of clean water and palm leaves of fruits, vegetables, and the magical cargo from the sacred containers. Crackers. Cookies. Even vacuum-sealed holiday cakes. They knew she would be glad to see they had her special foods (which, thanks to the miracle of sealed plastic, preservatives, and sturdy containers, had managed to stay fresh despite the tropical climate).

It was two days before the goddess woke. Her pale skin

had healed from the sun and had once more returned to its exotic whiteness, something unheard of in the islands. When she stepped out into the daylight, her hair shone like the sun.

The village leaders walked to her and kneeled, bearing gifts of food and drink. She picked one of the cookies from the wooden platter and sniffed it while the entire village watched in anticipation.

"Is this gluten-free?" their goddess asked.

In the weeks that followed, the villagers of Bokano Maru learned that their goddess had a fierce hatred of this thing called glooten. The goddess hated it so much and with such vehemence that they realized it must be an embodiment of evil, and so, with much celebration, they sacrificed their first packet of crackers in her honor.

She blessed them with knowledge of the heavens and more language of the gods. A missionary had once visited the island decades prior, so they did speak a smattering of English, but the goddess helped them learn even more.

Glooten, they discovered, wanted to kill them. It was a terrible thing that would hide in their foods and destroy them from the inside out. In haste, they started burning all of their foodstuffs before the goddess told them to stop, then explained the mythical ways of Paleo.

"Meat is good," she had said. "Fats, vegetables, fruits. NO gluten!"

The edict spread through the village in a single day, and from that moment forward, all things not Paleo were forbidden. The glooten in the holy containers was thereafter to be used to keep evil at bay via sacrifices carried out on the village altar.

Charlotte McAfee had been on a tropical adventure when her ship capsized in stormy seas. She took quite a beating, but managed to drag herself into an inflated survival raft that miraculously happened to float by just as she was about to lose hope.

When she woke, she found she was on a tiny but lush island, surrounded by a bunch of smelly little brown people. They had terrible dental hygiene and their hair looked like it had never seen a bottle of conditioner. Worse yet, they offered her wheat products to eat. What kind of savages would do that?

When they presented her with biscuits, she was very vocal about her dislike of gluten. She wasn't actually a celiac disease sufferer, but she was nevertheless certain she was gluten intolerant. Lactose too, but she didn't think there were any cows on the tropical island.

She could tell that the natives seemed to understand that she was smarter than they were, and that made perfect sense to her. After all, she'd finished nearly three years of university (majoring in art theory with an English lit minor) and had spent countless hours on the internet learning all about the evils of gluten. She was glad to share her knowledge with the ignorant savages. Besides, they brought her fish and vegetables from the island, so she figured she might as well teach them to cook properly while she was stranded there. So she showed them. Her way.

A few days after she had awoken, the tribal shaman gave her a small piece of jerky from the pouch around his neck.

"Ooh, meat!" she exclaimed, chewing it happily.

The old man seemed thrilled she was enjoying it so much. She figured there mustn't be much meat on the island, so they must save it for their special guests.

The villagers kept feeding her well, and her health improved by leaps and bounds. Soon, she felt good enough to start each morning with her regimen of yoga. It was only a matter of time before the curious locals began joining her, timidly at first, but eventually mastering the poses as she walked them through the different asanas.

The tribe readily took to the Paleo diet. It was, after all, pretty close to what they ate anyway, and having been presented with an abundance of foods of which she could now partake, Charlotte found herself beginning to put on weight. Not a lot, but she was certainly not in her peak yoga shape.

"What does it matter?" she mumbled to herself one day as she poked and prodded the soft layer on her abdomen. "It's not like there's anyone worth dating here anyway."

"Wee doo da holy yogaa fo da goddess," Ponoaru told the Englishmen with a proud smile. "We honor da goddess! She in all of us now!" He gestured to the villagers. "Her power wid us."

"But what happened to her?" Harrison asked. "Where did she go? Was she rescued?"

"Wassa meen rezcoo?" The man was puzzled.

"Let it go, Harrison, we can continue this later. At the moment I'm rather peckish."

Ponoaru led the men back to their hut, and as they

walked, he unrolled a small pouch from around his neck and offered each of the men a small piece of smoky jerky.

"Proteeen good. No glooten," he said.

"Thank you, good man, I'm famished!" Marks replied.

Chewing their treats, the men sat in the shade of the hut and discussed the unusual things they'd learned about the people of Bokano Maru and their unlikely deity.

Later that evening, there was a ceremony at the altar. The elder shaman led the event, the village leaders sitting before him in a small semicircle within the sacred area. After another cracker sacrifice, the shaman took a crude knife fashioned from a sharp piece of battered metal and sliced his arm open, his blood flowing onto the altar. The scholars were horrified, but that horror grew when the shaman moved to each village leader, dripping his blood into their eager mouths.

"Dear Lord, they're..." Marks, for once, found himself at a loss for words.

"Oh no," Harrison muttered. "It can't be. Oh please, no."

"What are you thinking?"

"Later. There's something we must see."

It was the dark of night, and everyone in the village was sleeping soundly when the two men crept toward the stone line marking the altar's border. Looking around, and finding no one watching, they stepped over the stones and approached the crude idol. As they got nearer, they noticed it was clad in an old bra and panties. Faint rust-colored spots could be seen in the dim light.

With great trepidation, Harrison lifted the dried-out wig from the coconut head and examined the inside of it. He dropped it to the ground and lurched to the side, vomiting a stream of hot bile.

"We have to go," he said, wiping the acidic muck from his lips. "Now."

Marks picked up the wig, and to his horror saw the scraps of meat, long dried but still dangling from the desiccated scalp.

When Ponoaru woke and completed the sacred asanas, he went to check on their guests. They'd been well fed during their visit. He had done his sacred duty admirably, as a village leader must.

Their hut was empty, their belongings gone as well.

He walked to the beach and found no trace of the two men or their small boat. In the distance, he heard what sounded like the sound of one of the sky-chariots, but he couldn't be sure. Perhaps the two white gods had gone back to heaven.

He reached into the small pouch around his neck and put a small piece of the goddess between his cheek and gums to best absorb her gift. He was running low on the meat and would need her power to explain where the two gods sent to replace it had gone under his watch. It would be all right, he knew. The sacred words would protect him.

"Paleo," he intoned reverently, bowing his head in reverence as he started the trek back to the village, chewing slowly as he walked.

Martin reacted quickly and ducked under the awning of a nearby office building. He moved fast, hiding his face as he did, hoping to dodge the prying eye of the small drone he'd seen hovering just above the department store across the street. If he was lucky, he had spotted it before it spotted him.

They were always watching, but he knew most of their tricks.

The helicopter circling the skies near the secluded spot he had eaten his lunch earlier that afternoon had tipped him off. They were monitoring him again, but he was used to it by now. In fact, he'd almost not know what to do with himself if They suddenly stopped.

When he exited his building that morning and scanned the skies high above, he breathed a little sigh of relief. At least there were no chemtrails that he could see.

A good sign.

The last time They sprayed the air, he had holed himself up in the relative safety of his HEPA-filtered apartment for a solid week, lest he inhale the toxins floating on the breeze outside. He was glad for the freedom to enjoy his wax paper-wrapped PB&J sandwich in the open air, and he hoped the renewed surveillance wouldn't put a damper on his outings. At least for today, he could enjoy his lunch and have a leisurely stroll downtown.

Or so he had thought.

Martin peered out from beneath the shelter of the awning. The buzzing little quadcopter drone he had spotted was nowhere to be seen. It didn't matter. He knew They were almost certainly monitoring his cell phone's GPS anyway (which reminded him, time to get a new burner phone). Nevertheless, he didn't want to make it any easier for Them.

It seemed most likely, given the renewed attention he was receiving, that one of his blogs or YouTube video exposés must've caught their attention again, though which one he had no idea. Could it have been the research article on the Bilderberg connection to famine and increased drought conditions in Africa? Maybe the one delving into the increase of chemtrails across the Western United States? That was an old one though, people were well familiar with the stories, and plenty of disinformation had been sown in the media in recent years. So if not that one, then which?

Perhaps his op-ed about the microscopic chips They were implanting underneath people's scalps as they slept, allowing Them to track their every move. It wasn't exactly news; people had been talking about brain implants for decades after all, but maybe the revelation that it was merely a sub-dermal chip with no invasive intracranial drilling that had caught their attention.

Or maybe it was the fracking piece, outlining the history of early investment and research into pumping chemicals into the water table, paid for by the Coca-Cola Company of all things.

He wondered, could it be the really fringe stories? Perhaps the sonic weapons testing out in the Mojave Desert? His photos were blurry at best, and no one had been willing to speak with him on the record. Or maybe the alien base on the dark side of the moon?

He decided it was time to do a bit of detective work when

he got back to his den and figure out what had piqued Their curiosity in him again.

Stepping cautiously back into the surging flow of post-lunch pedestrians, Martin made his way the remaining seven blocks to his apartment in the old, four-story mixed-use building. He trudged up three flights of stairs, veering left down the hall on the third floor, waving politely to his curious elderly neighbor (and building busybody) as he headed for his door.

The lone strand of hair taped across the doorjamb out of sight down at floor-level remained unbroken.

No unwanted visitors. Good.

He slid his key into the lock and stepped inside, securing the door behind him.

The apartment wasn't anything special. In fact it was about as average as possible, like something out of an Ikea catalogue, from the art on the walls to the furniture in every room. Actually, it looked that way for a reason. Ordering from Ikea was precisely what he had done, furnishing the whole place entirely from the Swedish catalogue's pages by mail.

Martin walked across the room, took his cell phone out of his pocket, and placed it on his kitchen counter. He then turned on the radio, cranking the volume as he walked out of the room.

The pantry looked normal enough, just a bunch of shelves roughly six-feet high, stocked with average food you'd expect in a bachelor pad.

That was exactly what he wanted people to think.

Reaching underneath the bottom shelf, he pushed the small hidden button, painted to match the wood grain of the cabinet's surface, then slid the entire shelf system from the wall on silent hinges.

The polished fireman's pole had a small platform on which he stood while closing the pantry's hidden door behind him. Once it had clicked shut, Martin hugged the cool brass and slid the several stories down through the narrow space he'd discovered, and subsequently modified, within the wet-wall of the building, all the way to the false storage closet he'd built in the basement.

After checking the tiny pinhole camera to ensure no one was present, he stepped into the dark, low-ceilinged space and began walking the twisted path through the labyrinth of pipes and conduits for nearly the entire length of the block, passing under shops and homes above, until he was underneath the large office building at the far end of the street.

No one had ever tried to open the locked utility door in the basement. They'd all just assumed it was something maintenance dealt with, and that disinterest had helped keep Martin's secret safe.

He turned the key in the heavy door and stepped inside, quickly locking it behind him before sliding his legs into the harness dangling from the darkness above. Flipping the switch powering the quiet winch two stories above, he began his slow ascent to his real home.

Copper wire crisscrossed every bit of the converted office space, a homemade Faraday cage effectively blocking all electronic signals from entering or exiting the space. Only the bathroom still lacked shielding. It had thick concrete walls, but he nevertheless intended to wire that room as well once he solved the corrosion problem from dampness.

Fortunately, aside from that one tiny issue, the den where his electronics resided was perfectly safe from prying signals and curious eyes.

His computer towers were hardwired into the fat pipe Tier-1 cable that serviced the legitimate offices surrounding his home. He was hiding in plain sight, that unexceptional office down the hall that no one ever looked twice at, though if ever asked, they would have to admit they never saw anyone come or go through its front door.

Martin fired up his machines and quickly scanned his emails. Immediately, a flashing message caught his eye.

Someone had contacted him through his unpublished email address. With trepidation he clicked on it. A terse message window popped up on his screen.

You have caught the wrong people's attention. They are watching you. Be careful. - A Friend.

An ominous warning to be received by anyone to be sure, but for a conspiracy theorist, those few words set off his warning bells with full force.

How did they get that email? Martin wondered. *What got their attention?*

He scanned the rest of his inbox and checked his RSS feeds but found nothing else of note. Just that one email, but that was enough.

Time to go public, he realized, his pulse racing. *Before something happens to me.*

"...and the results were surprising to the shopkeeper as well, the jackpot totaling over twenty-million dollars. Live from downtown, this is Bonnie Mulroon, KTBC News."

"We're clear," Bob called out when the live feed had been cut.

"Okay, I think we got what we needed. What's next on the list?"

"Kid saved by the family dog, or sinkhole snarls traffic in midtown."

"Jeez, slow news day."

"You're telling me."

"Well, load up the camera and let's roll to the feel-good piece. At least it'll beat sitting in traffic just to look at another sinkhole."

Bonnie noticed the slightly odd way the man walking rapidly toward her moved. He was tense, scanning the sky, eyes darting high and low as if he expected something to happen at any moment. His gray shirt and faded jeans were clean, and he looked well-fed and groomed, so she was pretty sure he wasn't homeless, but something felt off.

"Hey Bob, keep an eye on this one," she said, a bit unsettled as the man drew near.

"News lady!" Martin called out. "Hey, I have to talk to you right now!"

"Roll on this, who knows what we'll get," she hissed, as Bob quietly shouldered the camera, its little red light glowing as it took in the scene through its glass eye.

"Hello sir, I'm Bonnie Mulroon, KTBC News. What's going on?"

"They're on to me!" Martin replied in a hushed yet urgent voice. "Maybe it was the info I dug up on the Bilderbergs, I don't know, but I need to get my data into the hands of the media in case something happens to me."

"I'm sorry, who are you? You say you have information about the Bilderbergs? What can you tell me?"

It was then that Martin noticed the camera aimed at him.

"Is that live? Oh my God, turn it off!"

Bob lowered the camera.

"Don't worry, it's not broadcasting. Footage is just stored on our server for editing."

"We can't talk about it out here in the open, They're probably already watching. Come with me, there's a Starbucks down the street. It's a small, densely populated space. It's harder for them to watch us there."

She looked more closely at the strange man. He seemed harmless enough, though he was certainly agitated. Still, something interesting was going on, and that beat her other options.

"Alright, just give me a minute." She turned to her cameraman. "Hey Bob, I'm gonna talk with this guy, see what his story is. Who knows, might make an interesting human issues story. It'll be in a public place, so all's good. I don't think he'd be cool with a camera though, so meet back here in twenty?"

"Sounds good. I'll upload today's footage while you're doing your interview."

"Alright, I'll bring you a frappuccino."

"Vanilla."

"After all these years, you think I'd forget?"

The Starbucks was surprisingly empty for a mid-afternoon, and Martin grabbed an open table with a clear view of the entrance.

"I'm sorry if I startled you," he said, "but you have to understand They're watching." He pulled out a baseball cap and slid it across the table. "You need to put this on. Also put your phone in this," he said, placing a duct tape covered sack on the table. "It's a Faraday bag and will keep them from listening in."

"I can just turn it off."

"That won't stop them, believe me. I appreciate the offer though."

Bonnie reluctantly agreed and slid the phone into the bag, though she kept the portable recorder in her pocket running. Then she picked up the hat.

"Um, there's tin foil in this."

"Yes, I know. It helps block the signal from the chip."

"You think I have a chip in my brain?" she asked, thinking perhaps this wasn't such a good idea after all.

"What? No, don't be silly, They don't put chips in people's brains."

"Then why do you–"

"They put them under your scalp. Tiny ones. The wound heals in less than a day. The old brain chips were too easy to notice, so they switched. Thing is, the scanners need to be within twenty meters or so to pick up a precise location, so hopefully they haven't triangulated on us yet. Please, put it on. For me."

She hesitated, then reluctantly put the cap on with a crinkly tug.

"Okay. Happy?"

"I know you think I'm crazy, and I can live with that, but

this is for your safety as well as mine."

"Oh?"

"I received a warning on my email. My *unlisted* email. It said They were watching me. It said to be careful. It might have been the Bilderberg piece, or maybe the chemtrail story. The thing is, these are serious people with unlimited resources. There's no telling what they might do."

"But why you? I mean no offense, but you don't seem like much of a threat to massive multinational financiers."

"It's what I've figured out. I'm not sure which of my blog posts it was. Maybe the moon base, or the Bilderberg conspiracy. I don't know, but I've hit a nerve and it's got Them spooked."

"And you think they're tracking you? Because of a blog?"

"Earlier today there was a helicopter over the park, circling the whole time I ate lunch. Later a drone was hovering, watching me, just down the street, and last week I saw what looked like a snatch van idling in the alley, but once I ditched my burner cell, I shook them."

"Have you considered that there are a ton of helicopters over this city every day? Or that hobbyists fly drones all over the place? Hell, how many delivery vans park in alleys around here every day?"

"I know the difference. They were watching me."

"Okay, so let's say they were. Then why aren't you wearing a hat like this?" She gestured to the foil-lined cap on her head.

"I've subjected myself to repeated low-grade EMP bursts."

She waited for him to crack a smile, anything to show it was a joke, but nothing came.

"Perfectly safe," he continued, tapping his noggin. "Yes, perfectly safe, and guaranteed to short out any imbedded tech."

"Oooookay. Well, you know, this has been fascinating, but I have a story about a boy and a dog I really need to get to, so…" she rose to her feet.

"Please, you have to get this information out there. I need a credible media source to break this news!"

"Yeah, we're done. Good luck with your Bilderberg moon base story."

Bonnie tossed the cap on the table, scooped her phone from the metal-lined bag, and headed for the door.

That was one seriously strange guy, she thought as she walked the two blocks back to her news van. She texted Bob that she'd be there in a minute, then tossed her phone in her handbag.

Up ahead, the flashing lights caught her eye. A police line surrounded her news van. The officers on scene, she noted, weren't moving with any sense of urgency.

She rushed past the tape and nearly screamed when she saw blood in the back of the vehicle, Bob's camera equipment smashed to pieces, the memory card slot open and empty.

"Miss, this is a closed crime scene," the square-jawed officer said as he pulled her from the van.

"I'm Bonnie Mulroon, KTBC News. This is my van. What happened?"

"Looks like a mugging gone wrong. Witnesses say there was a scuffle, then the injured man was hauled off in the perp's vehicle. A white passenger van."

"But they didn't take anything, and why would they

kidnap him? None of this makes any sense."

The officer looked her over a moment. "Stay here, I'll get my supervisor." As he walked away, Bonnie noticed the cell phone laying on the step of the van. Her message to Bob would be on it. Had he even seen it?

Looking around to make sure no one was watching, she picked up his cell and slid it into her pocket, then stepped back outside the tape, scanning the men in blue to see where the officer she'd been speaking to had gone.

A man in a green Hulk hoodie grabbed her arm.

"Hey, take your hands off me!"

"I told you it was dangerous. What happened? God, I hope he didn't upload that footage. They monitor everything. We've got to get out of here." It was Martin, shielding his face from the investigators at the scene.

"But Bob, he was just my cameraman. He didn't do–wait, where did you get that hoodie? You weren't wearing it when I left you."

"I'm prepared," he said, gesturing to his impromptu disguise." You need to understand, They don't care if your friend was innocent, and the police work with Them. We have to go. Now."

As crazy as it seemed, Bonnie couldn't help but wonder, what if he was telling the truth, or at least a version of it? She made up her mind, and took the leap.

As soon as they'd rounded the corner, he made her open her purse, quickly digging out her cell phone and recorder and sealing them in his signal-blocking bag, then he handed her the ball cap.

"I'm not wearing this."

"Just humor me. A few minutes is all I ask."

She reluctantly slid the cap onto her head and followed him as he quickly wove through foot traffic.

"Are you going to tell me what's really going on?"

"Not here, not outside," he said, darting into the mixed-use building.

On the third floor, she noticed him checking a single strand of hair taped across the door at the bottom of the doorjamb before unlocking the deadbolt.

"Okay, now will you tell me–?"

He held up his hand. Not yet. Martin put the bag with her phone and recorder on the counter, then led her to his pantry, unlatching the secret door as she approached.

"What the hell?"

"Don't ask, just go. They could be coming any minute."

Bonnie hesitated, but Bob had been kidnapped, possibly dead, and for all she knew she could be next. Grabbing the slick pole, she slid to the basement, followed by Martin once he closed the hidden door behind him.

When they finally reached his hideaway (after a bit of convincing in regards to the harness and winch system), Bonnie found herself marveling at just how sophisticated his setup was.

Towers of computers with multiple monitors, all heavily encrypted and tapping into news feeds from around the world.

"How did you do this?" she asked. "I mean, where did you even get the money for it all?"

Martin's shoulders relaxed as he took off his hoodie, safe

in his shielded home.

"I worked for a government electronics contractor for a long time. Traveled the world installing secure systems, hacking insecure ones. It paid well, but I saw a lot of things I simply couldn't support. Now I try to bring the truth to the world. To pull back the lies and show what is real."

"Chemtrails? Bilderbergs? Secret bases?"

"I'm still working on getting high-resolution images of the dark side of the moon, so that's not a hundred percent proven yet. If it is true though, just imagine what the revelation would do to the world in a single instant. Suddenly we wouldn't be alone in the universe. Those in power would not want that to happen."

She picked up a folder. *Coca-Cola.*

"So what's this? The secret recipe? Look, my cameraman, my *friend* just got abducted over something, and I want to know what it was."

"I'm sorry about what happened. I truly am. If I'd known he would… It was a stupid oversight on my part and I wish I could fix it, but all I can do is say I'm sorry and hope he's alright. As for that file you're holding, it's my research into the Coca-Cola Company funding the original use of fracking decades before it was implemented by the oil industry. It's my belief that they were looking for ways to drive sales of bottled beverage products to increase stockholder payouts. What better incentive to buy a Coke when you're thirsty than having your local tap water catch on fire? Of course now they're in the bottled water game as well, so things have changed even more. I'm still compiling more research, but the stock market indicators show consistent surges in flash trading profits when negative water quality reports linked to fracked regions come out."

"You've got to be kidding me."

"Money over people. It's always been that way for the elites."

"This is just too much," she said, rubbing her temples. "I need the restroom."

Bonnie closed the door and sat on the toilet lid, her head heavy in her hands. Bob was abducted. Hell, he could even be dead. The tears flowed freely as the stress of the situation finally hit her.

"Fuck this," she said, wiping her eyes. "I'm going to find out what really happened."

Her phone lay on the counter back in the decoy apartment, but she still had Bob's cell taken from the crime scene secreted in her pocket. Bonnie scrolled through numbers until she found the network control room's direct line.

"Oh come on, give me a signal," she said, waving the phone in the cement room until by some amazing twist of fate, she actually got a single bar of service. She dialed, but the voice that picked up was not her producer.

"Miss Mulroon, we've been very worried about you. Please tell us your location and we'll send a squad car to escort you in."

She disconnected the call, staring at the device in her hand with horror. The same look was on her face when she walked back into the living room.

"What's the matter, you look like you saw a–" His eyes fell on the phone in her hand. "Oh shit! Where did you get that?

Did you…?" He looked at the open bathroom door and connected the dots. "Come on, we've got to go. Now!"

Martin reached under the counter and snatched his bug-out bag, sweeping his crucial files and external hard drives into a second messenger bag, then took off running for the front door.

"Wait, I thought you never used that door."

"No time! Run!" he yelled as he unbolted the thick door and shoved her into the hall. He was right behind her, running fast, when the windows exploded inward from the impact of multiple teargas grenades. Bonnie heard the crash and turned to look. Following the gas buzzed a quartet of armed drones, swooping in through the blown-out windows of his exposed hideout.

Martin slapped a large button on the wall next to the front door and yanked the door closed behind him just as the small drones unleashed a flurry of machine gun fire. The door slammed shut as the EMP wired into his walls discharged, completely frying every electrical device in the shielded space, including the attacking drones, while leaving the adjoining offices untouched.

"Come on," Martin gasped. "We have to get to the sub basement."

They ran for the elevator, where Martin produced a fireman's key, allowing him to override the normal controls. They piled in and the doors slid shut behind them. Martin turned his key and they descended non-stop to the building's lowest levels.

The blood leaking down his side startled Bonnie.

"Took a few when they opened up on us," he said through

gritted teeth. "Don't think I'm going to be making it much farther."

"What do you mean? You'll be fine, we'll get you to a doctor."

"You know as well as I do that as soon as I show up with a gunshot wound they'll lock down the building and cart me off. I'm not going to let that happen." He slid the bags from his shoulder and handed them to Bonnie as she exited the elevator.

"This has all of my research. You need to get it out there. You need to be the voice of mainstream media that gives it credibility. Do the research, back up your facts, then blow the lid off."

"I don't have the first idea how–"

"Here," he said, handing her an encrypted military-grade thumb drive. "This contains my coded bank details, a secure self-contained browser run through multiple proxies over piggybacked VPNs, and detailed files on how to access the vulnerabilities in the companies and organizations I've been digging into. The password is W@terf@ll1776. Memorize it. More than three wrong tries and the drive will brick and become unusable. The bank accounts have a few million left, that should suffice, but you'll need to stay off mainstream radar. I have details how in the blue folder. I wish I could tell you more, but there just isn't time."

"What are you going to do?" she asked.

"Something satisfying," he replied as the elevator door started to shut. "Follow the red painted line through the service shafts to the parking garage. The black Mercedes' keys are in the bag."

The door shut. Bonnie was safe.

Martin took a deep breath and began the ride back upstairs, leaving her to complete what he had started. His mission would continue, even if he wouldn't.

The elevator opened and a dozen gas-masked men pointed guns at him as the smoke cleared.

"Hands up! Don't move!"

Martin held his hands up and smiled. It took the masked men a second to recognize the grenade pins looped on his fingers, but by then it was too late.

Sitting in a thick cement basement, copper wires lining the walls, shielding her from prying eyes, Bonnie Mulroon aimed the digital camera at herself, checking her image on the laptop screen and adjusting the foil-lined hat she wore atop her head before going live to the world.

I really need to see about hitting myself with an EMP, she thought as she tweaked the cap, then pushed the enter key and went live.

"Hello, this is Bonnie Mulroon, KTBC News, coming to you live from a secure location. What I am about to tell you may sound fantastical, but I promise you, every bit is true."

The board members of the secret committee at Coca-Cola were almost ready to adjourn their meeting. The recent water crisis in Michigan had helped boost profits even more than they'd previously hoped for, and they were on track to exceed quarterly revenue projections by several points.

"So, the last order of business," the gray-bearded man said. "This reporter. She's off grid and causing problems. Our teams can't seem to track her."

"What about her chip? The Bilderberg network should be able to triangulate a position."

"No, there's nothing. Whatever she'd doing, she isn't showing up on our scans."

"Not to worry, sir," the dark-suited man quietly standing at his side said. "We're calling in a favor from our *special friends* to track her down."

Far above the Earth on the dark side of the moon, the alien craft powered up its cloaking shields for a covert search-and-destroy mission to the blue planet below. It was a good relationship they had with the humans, and the favor they had asked seemed reasonable. Besides, it had been getting rather boring up on the moon. It would be nice to get out for a little excitement.

Water, Water Everywhere

Dominique licked her cracked lips with an uncomfortably dry tongue. Her thirst had been growing by the hour as the heat of the day slowly ratcheted up in sync with the lazy arc of the sun. Degree by miserable degree, the metal shell surrounding her acted like a conductor for the radiant discomfort.

She found her misery becoming especially pronounced as she struggled to pry open the ancient, weather-sealed hatch to access the old fishing vessel's bilge. If she could just get to that brackish water, perhaps she could skim off the oil and whatever else had filtered down to the compartment and maybe, just maybe, produce something remotely drinkable.

Her water reserves had grown dangerously low, and though she desperately wanted to take a swig from the near-empty plastic bottle slung over her shoulder with a piece of cordage, she knew she had to make it last.

"Oh come on, you bastard!" she cursed at the rust-coated lever stubbornly resisting her efforts.

When she had first tried to open it, the crusty metal actually shifted a tiny fraction of an inch, enough to give her hope that at least this one thing would go her way, but a fraction of an inch was all it had moved, and she'd since spent the better part of an hour making no progress in anything but increasing her thirst and causing further grief to her already sore hands.

The lever, she had found, was actually a rather comfortable size for her delicate hands to grip. She simply lacked the strength to force it open.

“This is crazy,” she muttered to herself, exasperated. “I’m using too much energy.”

Dominique walked through the semi-dark belly of the old boat, feeling her way along the rough walls until she reached the ladder leading topside. The flashlight she’d found had been slowly fading the last few days, and the decision to conserve the batteries had been a simple one. Fortunately, with the hatch open, the sun’s rays provided enough light for her to make her way around, albeit carefully.

Grasping the time-worn rungs, she slowly made her way up through the opening and into the hot, but fresh, sea air.

Walking in the shady spots when she could to save her bare feet from the sharp bite of the hot metal of the old boat’s deck, she made her way the length of the seventy-foot craft until she reached the cabin, slipping into its welcome shade.

The loose-fitting fisherman’s clothes she had found provided at least some protection from the elements, but the one pair of comically-oversized galoshes she had come across were such a trip hazard on her small feet that she felt it was safer to walk without them. It was uncomfortable, but better to scrape a toe here than trip over the side and into the vast expanse of the open sea.

The boat was adrift, deserted. There was no one to jump in and rescue her, and all the life vests were gone, likely taken by the crew when they had escaped the disabled boat on one of the two small zodiacs that had been strapped to the deck. How chivalrous of them to not leave a vest for her.

The remaining zodiac seemed sound, its inflated rubber hull, intact, but there was only enough gas aboard for a few hours of travel tops, and with no land in sight, heading off at random would be suicide.

With an exhausted sigh, she took a sip from the near-empty bottle slung across her torso and closed her eyes.

In the weeks she had been adrift, alone somewhere on the high seas in the rusting hulk of the fish-stinking craft she found herself forced to call home, her immense thirst had quickly burned through all the fresh water on board.

At first, the several cases of water stowed in the galley had seemed like such a plentiful amount for a single person, but it soon became clear it would be woefully inadequate for a stay of any lengthy duration. In fact, all of the supplies were sadly lacking. The fresh produce had lasted but a few days, the canned foods just a few longer.

Apparently, whoever had drugged her and snatched her up hadn't planned on a long voyage, their preparations were nowhere near enough for an extended trip. She wondered if the old boat was even seaworthy enough for the open seas.

Adrift with the engines dead and no land to be seen, it seemed she had little choice but to find out.

Dominique conducted a thorough search from aft to stern, but while she managed to discover a secreted bottle of whiskey under a ragged bunk, there hadn't been any more fresh water anywhere to be found. After her first cursory pass, it had taken her a few days to more thoroughly dig through all of the compartments. That is except for the forward hold, the stubborn door to which was firmly stuck shut.

Down in the belly of the vessel, the wooden crate in which she had awoken, naked and disoriented, still sat fastened to the floor by sturdy straps. She had peered in the open lid, but like the rest of the abandoned ship, it contained nothing of use, no signs of other captured girls, not even her missing clothing. She wondered what their plans for her had been. Her recent memories were a blur, but given her circumstances, she wasn't so sure that was a bad thing.

She hadn't been raped, that much she could tell, but given the nature of her surroundings and heavy-duty drugs she'd been dosed with, she didn't really want to know her captors' ultimate intentions. All she could recall was a brief flash of fading awareness as the crate was being hammered shut, sealing her in the dark before she slipped into a drug-induced sleep's smothering embrace.

After she opened the lockers lining the bulkhead beside the crate, she tried the door to the forward stowage hold but found it was shut tight. Dried fish blood caked the floor and walls, a testament to the unseen brutality of the fishing trade.

The lever simply would not open. She couldn't budge it, no matter how hard she pulled. She nevertheless tried to loosen the stuck hatch every few days, hopeful there might be something of use besides gutted fish, perhaps even a barrel of fresh water stowed inside.

She shuddered at the thought of any other kidnapped girls trapped in there, though she felt that rather unlikely when her pounding on the thick metal door went unanswered. Regardless, her weakened frame was no match for the rust-caked obstacle.

Fortune did smile upon her, or at least flashed her a little grin, in the form of some old fishing gear that helped provide her with a semi-regular source of protein. Those trips fishing with her father as a young girl, though a tiresome task at the time, had proven to be a life-saving lesson.

She thought back on those camping outings and dredged up the fragments of a few dusty memories that could possibly serve her well, if she could just focus and recall them in detail.

That was the difficult part. Remembering.

Whatever they had drugged her with was strong, and it had muddled her brain, leaving her in a near-fugue state, wide swathes of memory dangling tantalizingly just out of reach, the images and memories blurred and unreadable.

Then there was the dehydration problem.

As the water supply dwindled to but a few bottles, she started to panic. She'd die of thirst, she mused, surrounded by a billion gallons of cool, blue water. At night Dominique found herself dreaming of fresh, clear pools, and during the day the thought of a bath to rinse the salt from her skin sounded far more desirable than any fortune or treasure.

When the first storm hit, she tried to capture water in the pots from the galley, but all she managed to gather was a pathetic trickle. She watched in frustration as the water ran across the deck but was unable to do anything about it. For some reason, the flowing water triggered a flash of memory, something about the rushing water, but as quickly as the glimmer had appeared, it was lost.

By the time the second storm came around, she had discovered a couple of dirty old tarps deep in the belly of the ship and strung them up with cord from the hold, then placed the empty water bottles at intervals along the tarps, small weights at the edges forming creases to divert the meager rainfall into the awaiting containers.

It seemed, so long as she was fortunate enough to encounter periodic rain, she might survive long enough for rescue.

Dominique's sides hurt from forcefully emptying the meager contents of her stomach onto the deck of the boat. She wasn't worried about the mess, the crashing waves washed it away before she could give it a second thought.

For two days the rough sea had tossed the boat with little reprieve, up and down, side to side, and all manner of gut-wrenching combinations thereof. All she could do was close the hatches as best she could and hole up in the cabin to ride out the storm in misery.

The morning the storm finally passed, she woke with a pounding headache, her lips cracked and mouth dry, her body aching from the seemingly endless onslaught she'd endured. She greedily swallowed the last of her water, savoring the cool liquid as it refreshed her bile-stung throat.

Slowly, she rose to her feet and gingerly stepped out to collect her now-full bottles and reset her rain collection setup.

The tarps were gone.

She saw the tattered edges where they had been ripped free during the night, the high winds carrying away her one source of fresh water. In a panic, she searched the deck for the bottles she'd strung up beneath them. All but a few had been blown out to sea, the remaining bottles strewn across the deck lay tipped over, mostly empty.

The contents she was able to save amounted to only four full bottles. Worse, the storm had contaminated them with seawater, though Dominique felt the quantity was likely small enough that it wouldn't cause her any harm. The real problem was she'd run out of water entirely, soon enough. The only plastic remaining on the vessel was the thin cling-wrap in the galley, but that wasn't remotely sufficient to catch much rainwater.

Watching the sun warm the deck as she ruminated, Dominique found herself entranced by the trails of steam wafting skyward as the remaining pools evaporated away into the air.

"Of course!" she blurted. "Solar stills!"

It was an old technology, a precursor to distillation, something she'd actually been trying to achieve by boiling sea water and collecting the evaporated mist with a jury-rigged system of old copper piping before she ran out of propane for the small galley stove. Solar stills didn't produce a lot of water, but as long as the sun was out, they'd give her enough to survive for a short while.

Barely.

She set out to build as many of the evaporative collectors as possible with what was at hand. Her brain was still fuzzy, the days of rough seas hadn't helped that any, but she could recall the basics from the YouTube video she'd seen one night when she fell down the rabbit hole of internet links.

Somehow, one sleepless night, she had stayed up watching bushcraft videos of outback survivalists. It seemed totally random at the time, but now, in the most unlikely of places, those skills she'd learned from the comfort of her couch would come in handy far out in the middle of the ocean.

She would fill larger containers with anything moist.

Water if it were available (and that, there was plenty of), or even damp sand. A smaller container would then be placed in the middle to catch the evaporated condensation from the cling-wrap stretched above. The trick to the solar stills was to keep the center container from becoming contaminated by the outer liquid, something that could prove a bit of a challenge should the seas grow choppy again.

Dominique utilized any empty vessels she could find, scavenging the hold for containers, and soon, she had over a dozen in place. All she could do now was wait.

One full bottle. A single liter of water. That was all her efforts had produced. It would help, but it wouldn't be enough. She'd need to boil and distill seawater again. Unfortunately the galley stove was out of gas.

The outboard on the remaining zodiac contained barely any fuel, not even enough for an adequate fire to boil the water to distill something to drink. Nevertheless, she considered it.

No, she reprimanded herself for even entertaining the thought. *If you get close to land, that's your only way off this boat.* She thought hard for several minutes. *You'll just have to find another way.*

She had a dislike of going into the hold. It stank of fish and old blood, but the crate, *her* crate, was down there.

Dominique unfastened the sturdy straps that held it in place and started prying boards free one by one with a rusty hammer. It took her exhausted arms the better part of the afternoon, but come nightfall, she had wood to burn. She only hoped it would distill enough water to keep her alive a bit longer.

In two days, Dominique had produced just over a dozen liters of fresh water. Unfortunately she had used the last of her flammable materials. Her supply of wood was gone, and while there might be a few other tiny things that would burn onboard, nothing would do the trick like her old crate.

All that was left was a pile of char, which she carefully gathered up and saved. She still had one more trick up her sleeve. She just hoped she could make it work.

The bucket was heavy, but Dominique persevered and pulled with all her might, hand over hand until it finally landed on the deck of the boat, like a stubborn fish at the end of a lengthy battle.

A bucket full of sand.

She had taken a gamble when she dropped it overboard on a long line, hoping she'd hit bottom at some point in the day. Luck had been on her side, and her grainy reward brought a satisfied smile to her face.

She stuffed bits of cloth into the necks of a few bottles she'd cut the bottom off of. On top of that, each bottle received a layer of charcoal from her fire, which she crushed thoroughly with weary hands before firmly tamping it in. Then the final step, adding a layer of sand until the upside-down bottle was nearly full.

A primitive version of what she had in her kitchen back home, but the principle was the same.

A water filter.

With anything but sea water (its salinity was simply too high), it would work well enough, at least if she gave the output a few extra runs through the filters, and she had an idea where she could find some brackish but usable water.

The bilge hatch had been uncooperative. Every day she had gone below, hammering at the lever with a large mallet found in the maintenance supplies, and every day the lever moved just a fraction of an inch despite her hours of labor.

Days later, she was nearing the end of her rope when the latch finally broke free, the seal releasing with a loud hiss.

The stench of the bilge should have been stronger, reeking of runoff from the decks, blood from the fish, even oil from the engines. To her chagrin, the predominant smell was salt.

She felt the air rushing up to her face and shone her near-dead flashlight into the space.

The water was rising.

Dominique slammed the hatch and frantically hammered at the lever until it sealed shut. It closed far easier than it opened.

Now she knew why it had been so difficult to release. The force of the water flowing in through the large break in the hull had created a pressure differential over however many weeks or months it had been building up, the strain put on the hatch effectively wedging it shut.

She couldn't help but let it out, the stress of the weeks adrift cumulating in a good old-fashioned tears-streaming-down-the-face belly laugh.

"Oh that's just perfect," she chuckled to herself when the laughing fit died down. "Of all the boats to be Shanghai'd on. This thing would be better off as a sunken reef." She considered the condition of the boat. "It's probably not too far off actually."

With no source of salt-free water, her elaborately constructed filtration setup would be of no use, and the solar stills remaining would only keep her going for what, two, maybe three weeks at the most? There was one last pipe-dream of a hope. Her imaginary pot of gold, her pirate's booty, if she could just manage to reach it.

The long pipe took most of her strength to place on the forward hold's door lever, its round opening just wide enough to slip over the end of the handle. She chided herself for not thinking of it earlier. A lever. She knew she couldn't simply force it open, so she endeavored to be patient, slowly hanging chains and other heavy things from the distant end of the pipe, the force exerted increasing every time she did so.

By mid-afternoon there had to be near two hundred pounds of miscellany dangling above the metal floor.

"Come on already," she muttered. "Just open."

The door did not obey her command.

Exhausted and frustrated, her energy sapped, Dominique climbed back to the fresh air of the deck and curled up for a nap. It was simply too hot to keep working.

As she drifted to sleep in the warm breeze, her thoughts flashed to nights in a cool forest, the moon overhead bright and full, illuminating the ground as she ran through the trees.

The sharp clang of metal on metal jolted her from her slumber.

She was fuzzy-headed, still half in her dream for a good minute before reality refocused around her. Some noise had interrupted her rest.

Metal? she mused. *Shit! Metal!*

With adrenaline-renewed energy, Dominique scurried down the ladder into the hold and raced to the front. The pipe and dangling metal bits had slammed into the ground as the latch finally released its death grip on the door frame.

"Finally! Please let there be water, maybe even a working radio or something to eat," she said as she slid the pipe from the lever and gave it a final tug.

The door opened and the stench of month-old death spilled out of the darkened space, nearly knocking her off her feet.

A flash of memory.

There had been a commotion. Yelling.

Steeling her nerves, Dominique opened the door wide and shone the flashlight inside.

The dismembered crew were in a horrible state. Faces torn off, limbs ripped from their bodies, huge bites taken out of their flesh. Their life vests hadn't protected them from the tearing of the massive claws.

Though she didn't want to, Dominique remembered.

It had been nearly a month since they'd captured her, keeping her drugged and locked in a cage until the boat had been secured.

That night, they shot her with a powerful tranquilizer, enough to put out a tiger, before loading her into a crate and transferring her to the fishing boat. She'd heard them talking, as the drugs took hold. It would be an eight-hour ride, hugging the shore until they met with the larger vessel that would take her the thousands of miles to the man who had paid handsomely for her.

The tranquilizer should have kept her down, and if they hadn't mistimed their trip, perhaps it would have. Unfortunately, they misread their lunar calendar, and the full moon shone brightly into the hold through the open hatch.

A storm was coming, but the change came long before it arrived.

The crew didn't stand a chance.

The men in the hold were dead before they knew what hit them, their bodies piled in the forward space, a larder holding her kills to be eaten later. One of them must've still been alive, able to lock the door in a desperate attempt to avoid the beast. Whichever man it was, he'd bled out long before she had come back.

Up on deck, she raged. Her massive claws tore the escaping zodiac to shreds as the men tried to lower it into the sea, her jaws snapping necks and limbs like twigs. Blood flowed across the deck as the rain started to fall, washing it all away.

"Oh God," she gasped, vomiting up what little was in her belly, tears streaming down her face as the memories became clear.

Dominique spent the next day in a daze, slowly digesting the revelation of what she was. What she had done.

The moon would be full in another few hours, and there was plenty of meat for the taking. She forced down the bile rising in her throat at the thought. In a few hours she would have no such squeamishness, and she would feast. She swallowed hard and slowly walked to the boat's galley.

Dominique took her time slicing the rubber zodiac to shreds with the large knife from the kitchen before heading into the hold. The change was coming, she could feel it.

With her last human thoughts fighting the animal within, she swung the heavy wrench, the bilge hatch flying open from the pressure it contained, then climbed the ladder and sat quietly on the deck in the darkening eve, watching her last moonrise while the hold quickly filled with the rising sea.

For the Love of Art

The affair had been going steady for a week, David realized as he lay in his lover's arms. It felt like so much longer.

It was a Sunday when they met. He had just finished for the evening and was unwinding with a little snack and some hot tea at the little corner café he so often frequented when she walked in.

It was the highlight of his day.

Vibrant. That's how he'd describe her if he was forced to use only one word. A difficult task, choosing the one that summed her up best, but now, as she lay in his arms, head nuzzled deep in his neck, her dazzlingly bright clothes in a soft pile on his floor, he thought no other word could encapsulate her spirit, her energy, and her poise, better than that.

The briefest surge of guilt hit him. Just for a second, though. He was quickly becoming comfortable with the situation.

Adjusting.

Moving on.

Letting the guilt tickling the back of his conscience melt away. Sure, they had been separated for nearly eight months, so technically it wasn't an affair, per se, but still, he hadn't been with another woman since he and Jacqueline were married twelve years ago.

Twelve years. A marriage older than some scotch, though many would argue the accumulation of years alone was not what made a bottle great. It was that special *something* that just clicked. A magical alignment of all those little factors and ingredients that blossomed in unison and steadily improved the flavor over time, until one day, you realize you couldn't possibly want to drink anything else.

Their marriage had most certainly not been of that vintage. While the early years were flush with potential, the bloom wore off the rose, and their union revealed itself to be more like a decent bottle that served to get you pleasantly buzzed, at first, but then left you with a nasty hangover the next morning.

He was just out of grad school when he first encountered his future ex-wife. Having landed a solid gig managing a medium-sized hedge fund, he felt on top of the world when he met Jacqueline, and his poise shined like a high-polished suit of the brightest armor. It was attractive, that confidence, an almost pheromonal magnet powered by his high spirits.

He had been invited to a weekend get together thrown by one of his fellow MBA grads up at his family's house in the Hamptons, the playground of the ultra-wealthy. David was amazed, despite existing at the fringe of that world, just how different the life of easy-living and old money was. It was one that whispered of few concerns, and it was welcoming him with open arms.

Over those remarkable days, he made many acquaintances, several of which would become incredibly profitable business relationships, but the most important person he met was Jacqueline.

It started simply enough. A glance across the crowd. An introduction from a mutual friend. By the end of the weekend they were sharing a bed, and within two travel-filled months, they had decided to move in together.

They settled on New York. It was convenient for both of their work schedules. While David was jumping between cities (and occasionally a tax haven island or two) in his management of the funds of millionaires and billionaires, Jacqueline's commercial real estate career saw her jet-setting wherever a prized boutique hotel or five-star resort was quietly being sold.

They were a young power couple in love, and it seemed things were only getting better.

After five years of high finance, David started to feel the drain of existing in that world. What had once been exciting and fun, no longer stirred his adrenaline.

Hundred-million dollar transactions had become an unexciting part of his daily life, and while he and his wife were amassing quite a nest egg, he nevertheless found himself profoundly dissatisfied. It wasn't the relationship. Not entirely, anyway. He still loved his wife, or at least the idea of her, but it was himself he was growing weary of. His life needed *something*, and so he began his year of deep introspection.

At first, Jacqueline hadn't been all that concerned. People have ups and downs, and in any relationship you have to accept that sometimes your partner just needs to work through something. She was there for him, supportive and understanding, while he struggled with whatever seemed to be gnawing at his psyche.

"I want to be an artist," he blurted out over coffee one

morning.

"I'm sorry, you what?" she asked, eyebrow raised high, askew as she looked up from her crossword puzzle.

He took a deep breath. "I said I want to be an artist. I want to create beauty, not just shuffle money from one pile to another, making nothing of real worth."

She eyed him quietly for a moment.

"So take some classes," she finally said. "I'm sure you can find some time on weekends to indulge your whim."

"It's not a whim," he replied. "It's what I want to do. Who I want to be." He struggled to put the thoughts and troubles of the past year into words. "My job, it's robbing me of my humanity. I'm starting to see everything in terms of profit and cost basis. I wasn't always this way. When we met, I wasn't this way, remember? I just need to do this, to make the conscious choice to get back to being the kind of man I want to be."

Now all her attention was on him. She locked her gaze on his as she folded her hands in front of her.

"What are you saying, David?"

"I'm saying I'm going to quit," he answered.

She could see he was dead-serious.

"Let's think this through a minute. You're a partner at the fund. You handle billions of dollars every year. You do a lot of good, David, and you're talented at what you do. Let's not throw that away."

"It's not throwing it away," he said with a pained look in his eye. "I don't know how better to explain it than I have. I need to create beauty. We're well off. We don't need the money. Please," he pleaded. "I need to do this."

The discussion stretched into the weekend, and when all was said and done, they had come to an agreement. David would take a sabbatical for a year to pursue his artistic dream. After that, if he had fulfilled his desire, he would come back to work and perhaps continue to paint, sketch, or whatever it was he enjoyed, but on the weekends.

If only it were so simple.

The strain between them was quite tangible by his third year of art studies. The easy laughter that had always flowed so easily between them was a rare occurrence, and while David was elated to discuss painting techniques and the works of contemporary artists, he seemed disinterested in the world of finance and real estate altogether.

Jacqueline would go to their friends' gatherings in the Hamptons alone while David would stay home, working on projects in his studio until the wee hours of the night.

Soon thereafter, he became fascinated with what he felt was living art. Art that changed and flowed with the world around it. Art that was transitory in nature, but all the more beautiful for it. He would spend hours watching people perform in public, more often than not, creating for an audience that cared more about their text conversation on their phone more than the work of art being birthed before them.

But sometimes, on those most wondrous of occasions, a pedestrian would look up from their glowing screen and find themselves confronted with a thing of such beauty, they'd stop in their tracks and stare. David loved the days he happened to witness this, and hoped beyond hope that one day he'd wield such artistic power himself.

He started coming home covered in a rainbow of colors.

Pastels and vibrant hues rubbed deep into the woven mesh of his clothing, dazzling smudges streaked haphazardly across his cheek or brow.

The chalk dust quickly became an issue. No matter how well he washed, traces always managed to appear somewhere around the house. On a light switch. On the counter. On a pillowcase.

It was more than she could take, and the rift between them grew.

Eventually they stopped sleeping together. Sure, the warning signs were there well beforehand, but when the physical intimacy finally trickled into nothing, they had become, for all intents and purposes, two very different people, both fond of one another, but most certainly not in love.

It was winter when David moved out. A separation she had called it. Some time to think. They both knew what it really was.

A first step toward the final one.

And so David moved into a spacious two bedroom above a café in the arts district. It afforded him his own space to sleep, but more importantly, a space to create.

Money wasn't an issue, he'd amassed a small fortune during his decade in finance, and thus he was able to immerse himself in his art. He'd claim sections of the pavement for his own, creating entire worlds in chalk without worry of having to please a crowd to eke out a living.

Perhaps that was how it started.

Because he was unfettered and free of worry, able to tap into something that only the rarest of artists could touch.

His hands became a conduit, laying out dazzling imagery on the ground as if pulled directly from his soul. Some days he'd work straight through, forgetting to eat entirely, so engrossed was he in his work.

The interesting thing about his process, his utter lack of caring about other people's opinions as he poured his heart into his work, was the profound impact his imagery had on people.

More and more often, as he honed his skills over the following months, people would find themselves forgetting they were texting when they spied his work. Amusingly, with his artistic goal finally achieved, he was too engrossed to even notice.

Crowds would gather, people would take pictures, small piles of cash would amass despite his not even putting out a hat or collection tin. Most impressively, his work would go unmolested.

People would go to lengths to step around the delicate chalk designs, leaving them preserved until the weather would finally erase them to the distant realm of memory.

That was how they had bonded, his lover and he.

Art.

He had just completed what he somehow knew was his best work yet in the plaza out front of a nearby office building. It had flowed from him like a torrent unleashed from his core, the scene of a beautiful village with a serene river meandering lazily through its environs.

It was populated with warm villagers, the faces so lifelike, as if speaking to him from just behind a thin muslin veil, asking his skilled hands to draw it back and reveal them to the world. It was a large piece, the quaint café in the foreground drawn nearly to scale, its wooden door so lifelike, the grain of the wood seemed real and not mere chalk. The road leading through the town somehow seamlessly shifted perspective as it stretched out into the distance.

Some passersby subconsciously stepped back as they neared it for fear they might fall in and plummet toward that horizon.

He was exhausted from the effort. It had taken so much out of him that when the wild-haired woman sauntered in to the café late that night, he hadn't even noticed her until she pulled up the seat beside him, her piercing gaze locking on his with an intensity of feeling he couldn't explain.

She stared quietly at him, and for some reason as he stared back into her crystalline eyes, the world felt right.

Small talk was unnecessary, he found. From the first words they shared, a common language was spoken between them. Art. Beauty. Love. In just a few short hours' time, they found themselves upstairs in his bed, limbs entwined in a passionate embrace that crescendoed with an intensity that brought tears to both their eyes.

In the morning, she was gone.

The following night, well past dark, she found him again, joining him in the empty café. Her name was Desiree, he had learned upon their first meeting, and she spoke with the slightest of accents, though from where it originated, he couldn't quite deduce. He briefly considered asking her, but the delectable question dangling in the air was something to savor. He could get the answer easily enough, but for now he enjoyed the unknown.

Every night was the same that glorious week. She'd join him after dark when the streets were quiet and they would talk and talk until late, then retire to his apartment and each other's arms. Every morning when he woke, she was gone.

The aching spot in his heart left from his years of slow withdrawal from his former life was flooded with warmth and love such as he'd never known, and for the first time in his life, David knew true happiness.

A storm was brewing. You could smell it in the air, and Desiree seemed worried and distracted when she stepped into the café. She hurried to David and took his face in her hands, kissing him deeply and with such force he felt dizzy.

"I have to go now," she said. "I wish we had more time–" A distant thunderclap made her jump. "You are my everything. Thank you."

She kissed him one last time, then hurried out the door into the increasingly windy night.

David sat dumbstruck, at a loss for words, a visceral pain tugging his core as she dashed from the café.

He slumped in his seat, defeated and depressed when another thunderclap jolted him to action.

"No," he said, determined. "It's not going to end like this."

He threw a wad of cash on the table and bolted out the door. As he scanned the street, he could just make out her brightly clothed figure as she turned the corner down the block.

He took off at a jog after her, but when he rounded the building, he was shocked by what he saw, just as he felt a drop of water fall upon his cheek.

The dark skies would open up any moment.

In a panic, he ran to the plaza just as Desiree, illuminated by the light from inside, stepped down into the chalk painting, closing the wooden café door behind her.

Another drop hit his cheek. Then his neck.

Now or never burned in his mind, and without another thought, he ran to his creation and bent forward, reaching *into* its depths. He felt the warm iron handle fill his hand as he closed his fingers. He tugged and pulled, but it stubbornly resisted his efforts.

Come on! Damn you, open up!

Finally, with an audible *click* the latch relented, and the door swung open, the smell of good food and the sound of good friends flooding out to meet him, engulfing him in a warm light.

Without looking back, David stepped down into the doorway and into his lover's arms, closing the heavy wooden door behind him.

The latch clicked shut, and moments later, a cleansing deluge poured from the sky above, flowing across the ground in a purifying rush, leaving nothing but pristine pavement in its wake.

A clean slate.

"Enough of your tomfoolery!" the long-bearded man in the faded, golden coat and comical tri-cornered hat bellowed as he stepped between the two young combatants, his sizable mass physically blocking them from inflicting further harm on one another.

"These shenanigans of yours are unbecoming of denizens of my fine community. You will cease this hostility at once!"

The two men stepped back from the normally jovial man standing between them, arms outstretched like a referee at a heavyweight bout. Though they were bloodied and bruised, clothes askew from their tussle, and each bearing long red scratches on their sun-worn skin, they both knew better than to cross the Honorable Mayor of Palisades Park.

All eyes were on them, their fellow vagrants and homeless watching to see how the excitement would play out with eager anticipation as the drama unfolded.

The two men were well aware what would happen to them if either laid a finger on the Mayor.

The retaliation would be swift, it would be thorough, and it would come from all sides.

The Mayor had helped them all, at some point, and nearly everyone on the streets owed him in one way or another. Even the local gang-bangers that frequented the dangerous underbelly of the neighboring pier treated the old man with respect. Not the kind given because you're told to, but the kind that has been earned.

Their fists slowly lowered, the fight at an end.

"Now, I want you two gentlemen to shake hands and

leave whatever issues you had with one another behind."

"But–" the lean, sandy-blonde man started to say

"If you feel the need to discuss transgressions, I will be glad to sit down with you like civilized men and address any impropriety, but for the moment…" the Mayor fixed his gaze on the man.

Reluctantly, the man held out his hand, knuckles scraped and raw from both the rough pavement and his opponent's stubbly jaw.

The other man, a newer resident of the lengthy ocean-front park, accepted the offered hand and shook, and the amazing thing about it was both men realized they actually *did* feel better. Sure, they might not go out and buy each other rounds of drinks like the rough-and-tumble brawlers of Glasgow or Boston might after a good scrum, but whatever bad blood there may have been with them seemed to have melted away.

That was one of the Mayor's skills, among his many unofficial, yet self-imposed duties. Conflict resolution. And it was something he had an uncanny knack for.

"Now, gentlemen, if you won't be needing my assistance any further, I must attend to my other tasks and bid you both *adieu*."

With a tip of his ratty, old, colonial-style hat, the Honorable Mayor of Palisades Park strode off down the beachfront promenade.

No one knew exactly when the Mayor had first shown up, or where he had come from for that matter. For most of the homeless camped out in the outskirts of Palisades Park, he'd been there as long as they had been on the streets, a jovial touchstone of compassion and stability in an otherwise tumultuous and uncaring world.

Need a coat in the relatively mild coastal winter? The Mayor would reach out to the Salvation Army or city shelter management and procure one free of charge.

Have a chronic foot infection, as was quite common among the homeless population? The Mayor arranged for free medical clinics from local physicians as well as frequent outreach, for school credit no less, from medical students from the nearby teaching hospital.

The dignified man with the silly hat, gray-streaked beard, and patched golden overcoat, was the unlikely guardian of the community. Not necessarily the representative the local government wanted, but most certainly the one they needed.

From time to time, the Mayor would disappear.

"Off on an adventure," he'd say upon his return.

Some would rumor he had been locked up in jail, which seemed unlikely given his demeanor, while still others posited that more likely, perhaps he had been away in a psychiatric ward, a theory only reinforced by the Mayor's outlandish tales.

"My ion-drive engine design will revolutionize space travel," the Mayor humbly boasted, if there were such a thing as a humble boast, that is. "We'll be able to fly to Mars in a matter of months rather than years. And my zero-G hydroponics systems will provide a plentiful food source during the voyage. No freeze-dried astronaut food for me!" He laughed and patted his ample belly.

"Of course with my robust physique, there were some issues obtaining the necessary approvals to be on the inaugural flight. Fortunately I'm personal friends with the president, so he pulled some strings. We met back when I was researching cold fusion at JPL. Mind you, that was many years after I had ceased giving lectures at MIT." He looked around cautiously.

"But don't say that too loud. The Cal Tech boys have listening devices all throughout the city and might hear," he whispered. "You know how that rivalry can be."

Frequent were the Mayor's wild tales, merrily told to those who cared to listen, which was surprisingly more than most would expect. Something about his dignified nature and calm manner of speech seemed to put people at ease around him, and his stories, if at times bordering on fantastical, at least never failed to amuse.

"If you just follow Ocean Avenue until it becomes Pacific, you'll see the fork in the road," he told the Australian couple on a global walkabout for the year. "You'll want to stay to the right, which will put you along the shoreline. You know, a funny thing. Back in nineteen-seventy when I was researching musical theory with Janis and Jimi, we would often sit at the beach right along that very stretch. It was really quite fortuitous that this was also during my overlapping government-funded research into the mind-enhancing properties of lysergic acid diethylamide."

"Wait a minute mate," the Aussie said incredulously. "You're telling me you were singing songs and dropping acid at the beach with Jimi Hendrix and Janis Joplin?"

"Well, my good man, I wouldn't call it 'dropping acid.' It was highly specialized research, quite cutting edge at the time."

The visiting couple laughed at the wild tale. If nothing else, the crazy Yank had given them a great story to tell when they got home.

"Just over two weeks," the Mayor said, a shadow of sadness cast over his normally smiling face.

"What's that, mate?"

"Sixteen days," he replied. "I lost them both that year, barely two weeks apart." He wiped his teary eyes. "Terrible loss. Terrible. Such bright souls they were." The Mayor fell silent for a moment, reflecting on days long past, then came to his senses, noticing the tourists as they watched him mourn.

"But that was a long time ago, eh?" he said, quickly brightening back to his usual self. "Now where was I? Oh yes, so you travel down the right fork and there's a curve before an alley. You know, it was right down that alleyway that Arnold and I built cinderblock walls for the construction company he ran with Franco Colombu. I was something of a fitness buff back then, you see."

"Arnold? *The* Arnold?"

"Go on, pull the other one," the woman chuckled.

"Yes, Arnold. Though for a time we called him Mr. Governor. But that was years ago as well. So, as I was saying, you follow that quaint little roadway toward the drum circle. You'll love that, most visitors to our fine region do…"

A small mountain of food sat on tables in Palisades Park.

"Stack the larger cans like so," the Mayor said, brushing his beard with a regal sweep before demonstrating, rearranging the pile of canned foods. "This creates a stable base that distributes the load more evenly across a greater span, thus allowing for a more sturdy, as well as visually pleasing, formation prior to disbursement."

"Thank you, Mr. Mayor, but you do realize it's just canned food, right? I mean, we're handing it all out soon anyway, so what does it matter?"

"Presentation is as important as structure, my dear fellow. Aesthetics matter. There is beauty in everything, if you but stop to look for it."

They young man was one of the two dozen volunteers who had assembled in Palisades Park for the weekly distribution of food donations given out by local shelters, as well as the occasional open-air hot meal provided by the nearby soup kitchen.

A great many of the homeless population didn't like being indoors, the volunteers had been informed in no uncertain terms, so it was determined that an outdoor setting would help ensure they would still receive proper nourishment while reducing anxiety and social stress.

Of course this had all been the Mayor's doing.

He himself preferred the outdoors, though he didn't mind coming inside from time to time, and had long made it a habit to sleep in the fresh air of the park.

In times of inclement weather, the Mayor could often still be found within the verdant confines of his hand-crafted, ocean-front home, a surprisingly stable and water-tight arrangement of palm leaves sheltering his makeshift abode.

"You know, the tribes of Polynesia weave the palm fronds in such a way as to direct any rainfall or morning dew from the apex of the domicile, guiding it downwards toward a receptacle from which they would reap the reward of collected water," he said as he removed a small flask from his pocket and took a swig.

"I learned that from the tribal chief during my time charting islands for the Navy. We don't get much rain here, but the condensed ocean air has certain bio-electrical properties that are most pleasing to one's system. Would you like to try some?" he asked the young man.

"Um, no thank you sir, I have a Diet Coke. I do appreciate the offer though."

"Bah, Coke. You realize it was originally designed to help remove calcium from corpses, don't you? Makes the bones more pliant and bendable for easier burial. How that ever caught on as a refreshment is beyond me."

"My mom told me it was a cola root extract for upset stomach. They just added soda water to make it go down easier."

The Mayor fixed his gaze on the boy.

"Your mother is a wise woman, and she's obviously raising a very wise boy. You know, I'd very much like to make her acquaintance one day. Should she ever wish for a personal tour of my city, I'd be happy to oblige."

"Thanks, Mr. Mayor, I'll be sure to tell her."

The boy, the Mayor of Palisades Park noted with a smile, had begun stacking the cans in the new manner.

"Very well, then. Carry on. I shall return shortly."

The Mayor picked up his small pack and bid him adieu, walking to his favorite quiet spot to write in his journals. Invariably, he'd only get a little work done before being interrupted by one person or another, but such was the busy life of the overseer of this domain.

"What'cha workin' on today, Mr. Mayor?" the blue-uniformed officer asked with a grin, peering over his shoulder at the scribbles covering the page like the chicken scratch of an over-caffeinated bird with epilepsy.

"Officer Denkins, a pleasure seeing you this fine day, sir! I am glad to see you are in good form today. Looking very sharp indeed!"

"Thanks, my wife cut my hair. You don't think it's too short?"

"Preposterous, she did a commendable job! You shall give her my regards and appreciation of her fine work."

"Will do, Mayor. So what's the project today?"

"Oh, just finalizing some calculations for my flight to Mars. You know how touchy those NASA boys can be if everything is not in perfect order. I most certainly wouldn't want to disappoint them."

"Mars, huh? Long way from the beach isn't it?"

"Yes, I will miss this place, but sometimes a higher calling must be answered. Why, did you know that in a mere twenty years there could be enough viable terra-formed farming permaculture built into the Martian terrain to support a sizable human population? I would think we could have full-scale colonization efforts underway within a hundred years."

"Too bad we won't be around that long."

"Preposterous! We've had cryogenic preservation systems for decades, they just keep them hush-hush, you know. Not everyone approves of life-prolongation techniques. In any case, I will enter one such cryogenic chamber after we've sufficiently set up the planetary base and worked out any kinks that may arise in my ion-drive system. Of course there won't be any. I've quadruple checked the redundancies, and it will run perfectly. I only hope that by the time they thaw me out in a few hundred years, the technology required to prove my time travel theories will have finally been developed. It's quite exciting, really."

"Sounds like you've got it all lined up, Mayor."

"As best I can, my dear fellow, as best I can. Still, there's always work to be done, so if you'll excuse me, I must get back to my calculations."

"Sure thing. You take it easy."

"You as well, Officer Denkins, and please do send my regards to your lovely wife."

By mid-June the weather had reached what could best be described as coastal perfection, the sun shining brightly every day, and that dreaded June-Gloom nowhere to be found.

The homeless crowded around the long tables as volunteers dished out plate after plate of barbecue meals to the hungry throngs. The Mayor of Palisades Park stood at the head of the line, personally greeting every one of the grateful, and hungry people, shaking their hands warmly, hugging those with whom he had a bond of friendship, which quite frankly was most of them.

The local police department had taken some convincing, but the Mayor could be quite persuasive, and when he produced pledges for matching donations from both the local fire department as well as the two large grocery chains in the neighborhood, a permit was procured for the largest free beach-front cookout in city history.

"Now, now, don't be shy. Please, stop and have a taste of

this delicious food, won't you?" the jolly, bearded man would entreat passersby. Soon the line filled with a healthy mix of tax-paying citizens and homeless alike, all standing side by side in good-natured conversation, one and all inspired by the Mayor's example.

Most of the line had gone through when a pair of large, black SUVs pulled to a stop in the nearby red zone, two men climbing out into the afternoon sun.

"Hi there, fellas. I'm sorry, but you're going to have to move your vehicles," the veteran traffic cop said to the dark-suited men with a friendly smile.

The Team Leader stepped forward and flashed his credentials while the exceptionally fit young man accompanying him surveyed the crowd.

"Sorry to disturb you. We'll be out of your hair shortly," he said, his eyes unreadable behind the mirrored sunglasses.

The officer did a double take then handed back the leather wallet.

"Yes, of course, whatever we can do to help. I'll get my captain–"

"That won't be necessary. Like I said, we'll be out of your hair shortly."

The Mayor saw the men, his gaze pausing on the young, well-muscled fellow in the sharp suit. The man flashed a warm grin and winked, then gave a little wave before stepping back into the rearmost SUV.

The lead agent observed the exchange and stood by, patiently awaiting the Mayor, who gestured that he'd be just a minute longer. The agent nodded and spoke quietly into his hand

"What's going on, Mr. Mayor?" asked a young man, relatively new to the streets, and whom he had only recently taken under his wing.

"Nothing to worry about, Toby. It just looks like I'll be leaving a bit sooner than I had anticipated." He waved over Officer Denkins, who had been observing the official-looking visitors from afar while happily chatting with a small group who lived in the park.

Community policing the way it's supposed to be, the Mayor noted with an approving grin.

"What's up, Mayor?" the man in blue asked as he walked over to the patron of wayward youth.

"Officer Denkins, I'd like to introduce you to Toby. He's new to the area and a good lad. I would be ever so appreciative if you would keep an eye on him for me."

"You going somewhere?" Denkins asked, eyeing the blacked-out SUVs.

"Yes, I'm afraid I must at last take my leave, wonderful as this charming hamlet has been to me."

"Don't you worry about it, Mayor. I'll look after him until you get back."

The Mayor's cheerful smile didn't fade, but rather shifted to a different kind of smile.

"I'm afraid I won't be coming back. At least not for quite a long time. It's been a pleasure knowing you, Thomas, a true pleasure. I wish you and your wife a wonderful life."

Thomas? He had never told the Mayor his first name, yet somehow the man had that knowledge tucked away in that constantly churning mind of his. Strangely, he wasn't bothered by it, though perhaps a little confused.

The Mayor made a brief round of his dear friends, imploring them to live lives worthy of being proud of, and to set a good example for those yet to arrive on the streets and benches of the city.

And then the he was gone.

Whisked away in a shiny black motorcade, the bearded man never to be seen again in Palisades Park.

Two months later, Thomas Denkins sat in his kitchen enjoying a quiet morning with his wife, sipping a cup of coffee as they playfully worked on the daily crossword puzzle together.

"Honey?" she said. "Isn't that the Mayor?"

He glanced at the television set.

"No, it's just the president giving a speech about something. I doubt they'd invite the Mayor to something like that."

"No, not the mayor. *The Mayor*."

He looked at the television again, turning the volume up as he scrutinized the scene.

"And so it is with great pride that I send this first manned exploration to Mars on their journey. God speed, and good luck."

He turned and walked down the row of astronauts, all decked out in their trim flight suits. One man looked quite out of place among the top physical specimens in that line. He was clean-shaven, his hair neatly trimmed, but his body was, shall we say, more *robust* than your normal astronaut.

The Honorable Mayor of Palisades Park had lost some weight in the months since Tom Denkins had seen him last, his beard and silly hat were gone as well, but as the camera passed over him, standing at the head of the line, ready to command his crew of the best and brightest, that familiar gleam in his eye and jovial grin were unmistakable.

The camera panned, showing the faces of the politicians and scientists lining the pre-launch facility. He nearly did a double-take when former Governor Schwarzenegger's face filled the screen, his unmistakable gap-toothed grin wide and bright as he waved to his departing friend.

The Mayor, trying to maintain decorum as best he could, nevertheless smiled broadly and gave a little wave back.

The president walked the line, wishing them all the best of luck, but when he reached the Mayor and grasped his hand, he stopped. Unlike the other astronauts, he pulled him in for a big hug. The two men whispered a few hushed words of friendship before the Mayor set off to colonize a new world.

I wonder if I'll ever see him again, Tom wondered, as he turned off the TV and kissed his wife's forehead, knowing that after the Mayor's task was complete, it would be decades, if not more, before his friend was thawed out to bring his wisdom to another generation.

A knock at the door that evening roused Tom from the warm comfort of the couch where he and his wife sat intertwined, enjoying a football game and a cold beer.

"I'll get it, babe," he said. "Coming," he called out, rising to his feet.

Officer Tom Denkins opened the door to the sight of a young, muscular man in an impeccable suit beaming at him. The same man he had noticed at the cookout in the park.

"Hello, Thomas," The man said. "It's so very good to see you again."

"Um, do I know you?"

"Ah, yes, of course. I sometimes forget. Cellular rejuvenation and reconstruction, cutting-edge in age-reversal, you know. Really, it's amazing, the things modern technology can do these days. Well not *these* days. Good heavens, nothing like that exists in *this* century."

Tom's mouth hung ajar. He knew only one man who spoke like that.

"No, it can't be–"

"Honey, who is it?" his wife called from the other room.

The man smiled at him, and waited for it to sink in.

"Mayor? Is that you?"

"Indeed, my good fellow and I'm afraid I require your assistance. We've had a bit of a kerfuffle on the Mars colony, you see. The Interplanetary Congress requested an unbiased and fresh policing perspective to help with a bit of social unrest. As my personal favorite law enforcement professional, I naturally thought of you. Might you be free to assist for a few months?"

"I…" Tom was speechless. "How is this even possible? And why me?"

"Ah, well, I was not exactly alone in recommending you. The decision was agreed to, much to her amusement, I might add, by our chief colony law enforcement official. Your great, great, great, great, great, great… Well you get the idea. Your granddaughter."

"My granddaughter?"

"Indeed."

"But we don't even have any kids."

The Mayor smiled broadly.

"Yes, about that," he reached into his jacket and presented Tom with a cigar. The stunned man turned it in his hand, slowly reading the blue band encircling it with a message proclaiming *It's a boy!*

"Congratulations, my dear fellow! Now, don't worry, I'll be sure you're back well in-time for your son's birth. Of that you can rest assured. Time travel and all that, you know. Your family's story really is quite amazing, and from what I understand, you are going to have quite an adventure. Your granddaughter showed me many of your old family pictures and told me all about it."

Thomas Denkins swallowed. Hard.

I'm going to be a father?

"Come now," The Mayor said. "No time to dilly-dally. Let's gather your things, shall we? You've got a date with Mars."

Sine Qua Non

A pony.

Ever since Evelyn was but a child, she was certain the one thing in the world she could absolutely, positively, under no circumstances ever do without was a pony. Not just any pony mind you, but *her* pony.

Harrison, the four-year-old show horse her mother had purchased for her seventh birthday, was her pride and joy, and her every spare moment was spent grooming him, talking to him, tying bows in his hair, and, of course, riding him.

Dressage, that rather bizarre sport of prancing horses and socially oblivious patrons, was one of her earliest childhood memories. She and Harrison had wowed the crowds with their performances, which fed into the young girl's growing ego. Evelyn and Harrison were a hit, though she would really have liked her pony to have been called Peaches or Sparkle Pony. But, her mother had named him upon purchase, and that was the name that stuck.

Once, Evelyn had asked her mother why the horse was named Harrison. She got a faraway look in her eye and blushed, then made some excuse about an old fling from her days as a young actress.

That was before she'd married Bernard Waterman Hartley III, and long before Evelyn was conceived.

The couple had caused quite a stir in Hollywood, a young up-and-coming starlet romantically linked with a much older and unlikely beau, though his being an investment fund billionaire might have played some part in the attraction.

Rule Number One of dating models and actresses: Be

Attractive.

Rule Number Two of dating models and actresses: Don't be Unattractive.

Rule Number Three of dating models and actresses: Money can overcome Rules One and Two.

At age twelve, Evelyn developed a fixation on Sons of New Romance, the hottest teen boy band on the planet.

Harrison? Who was Harrison?

While she was still fond of her old friend, she was now more certain than ever, that she could never, ever, survive without the Sons of New Romance. They were the Yin to her teen-angst Yang. The whipped cream to her sundae. The… well, you get the idea.

And so, with single-minded drive, Evelyn set about her quest to be their biggest fan. She started a blog, but who didn't have a blog? So she convinced her father (who was well and truly wrapped around his daughter's finger) to hire the top PR firm in the country to publicize her writings.

They weren't bad, per se, but far more deserving of accolades were the writings of a good several dozen other likewise-smitten teenage girls. Unfortunately for them, despite a plethora of talent, they lacked that one key ingredient that Evelyn possessed.

A billionaire father.

Oh, he loved his little girl, and so, for her thirteenth birthday, who should happen to play a surprise show just for her and her three hundred closest friends?

Sons of New Romance.

It was the best time of her life, and she was absolutely

certain she'd never top it.

By the time Jonathan, the single greatest person in her life, had broken up with her shortly after her nineteenth birthday, Evelyn was already discovering a new world. One which she might have loved even more than boys (and besides, she didn't really need him anyway. He was a jerkface, and she totally didn't mean it when she swore she'd die without him). The breakup just helped push her there a little faster. To her destiny.

Fashion.

High fashion, to be exact. The type of clothing you'd never actually see on a real person outside a runway or private show.

Hobo Chic, Post-Modern Pirate, whatever the trend, you'd likely be mugged and stripped of both your possessions and your dignity (what little of it remained after venturing out in such an outfit) in no time flat if you went out in public like that.

All of that mattered little to Evelyn. She knew now that these marvelous designs and uses of unlikely fabrics and accoutrements were her calling. Never, ever, could she do without fashion.

Though not even twenty, and barely out of high school, being the daughter of Bernard Waterman Hartley III did not lack its benefits, and soon she had landed an internship at one of the top designers in New York. Like novice samurai and sushi chefs, she was given the proverbial "wash the rice" tasks that popped up, her superiors intending for their young charge to learn the ropes by first observing and absorbing, gaining responsibilities over time.

No.

This was her destiny! No snooty designer, no matter who she was, would keep Evelyn from the thing she needed most in the world. A carefully placed phone call from Daddy quickly set things in order, and so it came to pass that at the tender age of twenty, Evelyn Hartley had the thing she couldn't do without. The thing that made her life complete.

Her very own line of clothing under the flag of one of the world's top designers.

It was a train wreck, of course, but by the time the scathing reviews hit the trades, Evelyn had already moved on, positive that her *true* calling, the thing she absolutely could not live without, was acting.

Not one to let those old men in Hollywood tell her what to do, and with the backing of her father's considerable pull and finances, she soon starred in a series of surprisingly not-entirely-horrible films.

The writers she had hired with her massive bankroll were some of the finest in the industry, and the supporting cast was happy to cash their fat paychecks to work alongside the neophyte actress. The one universal thing spanning the productions that kept those movies from true success, were the inevitably wooden performances of one Ms. Evelyn Hartley.

Of course she didn't believe the critics. After all, this was her calling. Besides, she couldn't possibly do without the Hollywood lifestyle, it was what made her life complete, and in order to live up to the expectations of her (imagined) fans, she decided she needed to focus on looking the part.

Rather than spending her time on dearly needed acting lessons, Evelyn spent her father's money on a racy new Bugatti, an enormous mansion in the Hollywood hills, and a private jet.

When she saw the lustful stares of every man she passed on the highway, she knew the beast of a vehicle was the single greatest thing she'd ever owned. And the power it gave her over any man? She knew she couldn't possibly do without that amazing car in her life. She was a terrible driver, but that made no difference. Everyone she offered to give a ride in the ultra-rare machine leapt at the chance.

That car actually landed her a husband, a man she knew in the depths of her soul she would be her forever, a man without whom she would surely wither and fade away.

He was one of the most desired actors on the planet, and Evelyn had him cast opposite her in a truly dreadful romance just so she could have a love scene with him. (It would be worth mentioning that the writers were pressured to add not one but two additional scenes of that nature just so she could sink her hooks a little deeper.)

Not surprisingly, as happens with actors who spend months on end pretending to be in love, the two were spotted publicly as a couple shortly after wrap, and to Evelyn's delight, they were wed not long thereafter.

The wedding was obscene in its opulence.

Royalty should have such a wedding. Princesses and presidents didn't have events like hers. Yet despite the cost, her father simply smiled as he footed the bill. Nothing was too good for his little girl.

Taking a hiatus from the movie world, the couple flew off in the incredible privacy and comfort of their private jet on a glamorous three-month honeymoon around the globe. Evelyn reveled in the sheer pleasure and freedom to go anywhere in the world at the drop of a hat that her jet gave her.

"I couldn't imagine life without my private jet," she had told her beau, who smiled broadly as he agreed with her. Yes, it was most definitely a perk of being the daughter of a billionaire.

Little did she know that the insanely popular actor on whose arm she hung had recently been on the verge of bankruptcy, which their union conveniently put an end to straight away. Two years later, when he filed for divorce and a hefty palimony, she consoled herself with the knowledge that she still had her jet, her car, her production company, and even a pony.

When Bernard Waterman Hartley III was sent to Federal Prison for defrauding investors, his sentence, had he been able to live long enough to carry it out, would have made him the longest-serving prisoner in white-collar history. One disgusted juror posited that perhaps he could be cryogenically frozen, his popsicle body put on display for the full three-hundred-seventy years of his sentence.

As it stood, he served only six months before suffering a fatal heart attack while playing golf on the prison's nine-hole course. Ironically, he actually *would* have been frozen, but his long-standing deposit for storage in a cryogenics chamber upon his death had already been forfeited to the court to pay attorneys' fees.

Of course all of his other assets were seized as well, including any and all that could be clawed back from his now-destitute wife and daughter, leaving them to fend for themselves for the first time in decades.

Her mother fared well. She played the victim card to the hilt, and quickly landed a husband in the form of one of her ex's former colleagues who had always had a thing for her. Soon she was living in lesser, but still comfortable luxury.

Evelyn, on the other hand, did not adjust so well.

Her constant backer, her daddy-shaped safety net, the bottomless piggy bank she could always count on, was gone.

After a lifetime having everything she felt she needed handed to her on a silver tray, the loss of her entire way of life was a catastrophe she had never imagined possible for someone of her pedigree.

Her friends, once thought so indispensable and true? Gone.

Her advisers and lawyers, men and women made rich by her hand? Gone.

Her beautiful car? Gone

Her private jet and holiday house in Cannes? Gone.

The list went on, and Evelyn, unsurprisingly, found herself deeply depressed. Unfortunately her therapist wouldn't take her calls anymore now that her checks were no longer any good.

And so it came to pass that in a very uncharacteristic move, Evelyn pawned her old wedding ring and travelled to Alaska, hoping time in the wilderness would perhaps help her gain new perspective and reinvigorate her soul.

Six months she spent there, living in a sparsely furnished

cabin just outside of Juno.

She didn't make friends. She didn't socialize.

For the first two months, she didn't even venture into town, rather having supplies delivered to her door. It wasn't until the third month that she began plotting her comeback.

She realized she didn't *need* all those people. She could do it all again, but this time without her daddy's help. She'd done it once already, and he hadn't helped all that much, had he? How hard could it be?

Upon landing in New York after her half-year absence, Evelyn was about to set her plan in motion, when she learned her father's attorney had been trying to reach her for some time. Something about a gift left for her in his will. Something he had invested in many years prior that was miraculously shielded from his other ventures and clean of the taint from his expansive wrongdoing.

She opened the envelope and read what was inside.

A smile blossomed. It was going to be alright. Daddy had come through for his little girl yet again, even from beyond the grave.

She was going to be famous again.

Sitting in the comfortable, deep-cushioned chair, gazing out the window at the twinkling stars, Evelyn was uncharacteristically quiet and reflective. As she rode in silence, she thought back on her life, the things she'd said and done, the people she'd taken for granted.

What really mattered in the world.

She could do without a pony.

Good lord, who actually *needs* a pony anyway?

A man?

Nice, but optional.

A fast car and a private jet?

Things she'd happily do without, now that she had some perspective.

After she'd deactivated the alarms, the slow hiss was an almost soothing white-noise in the background as she soared above the continents, flying far, far up in the sky.

Her father, a visionary in many ways, had invested early and had left her the most amazing gift he could think of for his then-infant daughter. It would be decades, but it would be worth it.

The inaugural flight no less.

Evelyn would be famous. She would go down in history.

He was right, and as Evelyn Hartley, the first civilian to ever orbit the globe in a private spacecraft, felt her head grow lighter as the pressure continued to drop, she had just one thought ringing in her mind. One that stood out, clear as crystal.

There was only one thing she *truly* couldn't live without.

Air.

Snow White's Walk of Shame

What a night, the raven-haired beauty reflected as she picked her way through the forest in the wee hours of the morning.

Snow White's lipstick was a thing of distant memory, her mascara little more than a faint blur. A sweaty remnant, leaving her somewhat resembling an exhausted raccoon. She wove through the trees in silence, the hood of her silken cloak sheltering her as best it could from the prying eyes of her woodland friends.

What would they think if they saw the tangled bird's nest her hair had become?

It's going to take hours to get those knots out, she lamented that morning at first light as she quietly dressed and snuck out of the dwarves' camp.

Oh yes, things had gotten more than a little out of hand.

It had all begun several weeks prior when poor Snow White had burst from the thickets into the dwarves' encampment. The sight of a tall, pale woman crashing through the woods and into their camp had been most unexpected. The seven small but rugged men, hardened from years of mining, were nevertheless startled by the sudden appearance of such a beautiful and unexpected guest.

"Oi! What's this ruckus all about?" Grumpy groused as the tall woman stumbled into their midst.

The dwarves, picks and shovels in hand, ready to defend their treasure, slowly lowered their weapons when they saw the source of the commotion.

"Please, can you help me?" the girl asked as she tried to catch her breath.

"What's the problem, young lady?" Doc inquired as he sized up the lithe woman towering over them.

"The evil queen is trying to kill me!" the girl blurted out, her eyes welling up with tears.

"Why on Earth would she want to do that?" Happy asked. "You seem like a nice girl."

"How the hell would you know that?" Grumpy barked. "You don't even know the wench. For all you know, she could be a thief, just like the rest."

The seven dwarves reassessed their unexpected guest, fourteen eyes ogling her from head to toe (and lingering in between).

"Nah, she seems harmless enough. But what's this of an evil queen?" Doc asked.

"Yeah," Dopey interjected. "I don't know any evil queen around here. Hey guys, is there an evil queen around here? Why didn't anyone tell me about the evil queen?

"Oh, for fuck's sake, will you shut up about the evil queen?" Grumpy spat.

"Wait, there's an evil queen?" Dopey asked, eyes wide with fear.

"Dopey, would you please go fetch something to drink for our guest?" Doc interrupted.

"Oh, sure, Doc," he said, then merrily trotted off toward the large communal hut.

"Sorry about that," Doc said. "He's a nice fella, but a bit slow, if you know what I mean."

"Always has beee– achooo!"

Doc handed the watery-eyed dwarf a handkerchief.

"Thanks, Doc," said Sneezy. "These allergies are killing me."

"Speaking of killing," Doc continued, "now what's this you say about someone coming after you?"

"The queen," Snow White managed, between sobs. "She is jealous of my beauty and wants me dead. She said no one but she can be the fairest in the land. She has sent the woodsman to find me. To kill me and bring her my heart! Oh, it's not my fault, I can't compete with her for the affections of a prince or king, nor would I ever want to. I'm just a poor farmgirl from her realm, and besides, I'm saving myself for marriage. I'm no threat to her at all. I didn't ask to be born looking like this! I didn't want to cause any trouble! And look at me now, on the run for my life. My clothes are filthy, my skin's a mess, and I've not eaten for days!" The overwhelmed girl began crying once more, her shoulders shuddering with every gasping sob.

"A virgin, eh?" Bashful said quietly. "There, there, we'll take care of you." He put his arm around her waist. Well, more like her upper thighs, given the height disparity. "You're welcome to stay with us. We have some robes inside that may fit you, and Happy is a whiz with laundry. I'm sure he'll get those stains out in no time."

The girl slowly stopped sobbing and looked at the group of wee men. They seemed nice, even if they were perhaps a bit rough around the edges. Dwarves were legendary for their mining skills, so it was only natural they'd be built so sturdily, muscles thick on their short frames from years of hard work underground.

"Well," she began, "if you think I'll be safe here, then–"

"Of course you're safe here!" Grumpy rumbled. "We've fought off bandits and robbers and thieves and monsters, though nobles do pass through fairly often as well."

"Nobles?" she said, her sobbing finally trailing off to a stop.

"You know, princes and the like. We trade with them from time to time. Point is, I doubt one little woodsman will cause us any trouble."

"What about this evil queen, now?" Doc queried. "I'm still curious about that bit. We've never heard of her."

"You wouldn't have," Snow White replied, dabbing her eyes with the hem of her dress. "I've been running and have come a very long way to escape her. I only hope she won't follow me so far from her lands."

The dwarves looked among themselves, a silent discussion passing between them. They nodded in unison.

"Very well then," Doc said. "You shall stay here under our protection. So long as we draw breath, no harm shall come to you."

The distraught girl's face lit up with such a glow it made the little men's hearts race and their cheeks flush.

"Oh, thank you! Thank you so much! I promise I'll earn my keep. I'll do whatever you need. I can cook, and I can clean. Oh, you're such wonderful men!" She then proceeded to bend forward and hug each of them, burying their faces in her ample bosom.

"Um, well…" Grumpy was for once at a loss for words.

"Come on," Bashful said. "Let's get you out of those filthy clothes and into a hot bath." Snow White jumped in surprise as his surprisingly nimble fingers started undoing her dress.

"Bashful!" Doc barked. "I'm sure our guest can do that herself. Go find her a robe, won't you?

"Oh. Yes. So sorry. I'm not used to having company."

"It's all right," she said, regaining her composure. "I know you didn't mean anything inappropriate by it."

The dwarf smiled at her and headed off to find some suitable post-bath attire.

"Thank you all. You've saved me from a terrible fate."

"Happy to help!" Happy said. "I'm Happy!"

"I can tell."

"No, that's my name! Happy!"

"Oh, I see. Well, it's a pleasure to meet you, Happy. A pleasure to meet all of you. My name is Snow White."

In the week that followed, Snow White worked diligently to repay her hosts for their hospitality. She cleaned their huts, laundered their clothes, which were well-soiled after daily mining expeditions, and cooked them wonderful meals. As an added bonus, the men learned she had an almost childlike innocence to her, a purity so great that even the birds and woodland creatures would approach her without fear. Soon enough, all seven of the men were quite smitten.

One day, Snow White was hanging laundry just outside the common room when the dwarves returned from their day's work.

"Hello, my friends! I'll have dinner ready just as soon as I finish hanging the wash."

"Thanks, Snow White," Sleepy said, then trudged off for his pre-dinner nap. The other dwarves marched into the common room and shut the door. Curious, Snow White peered through the parted shutters to see what they were up to.

At the far end of the room, Doc reached inside his shirt and removed a heavy key from a chain around his neck. He then moved aside a tapestry on the wall to reveal a chest tucked away in a nook and unlocked its heavy lid. Bashful approached him with a small pouch, from which he removed a single, shimmering ruby. Doc opened the lid, briefly revealing a large mound of jewels to which he added the new addition. He then quickly locked the chest and pulled the tapestry back into place.

"No wonder they're so cautious around strangers," she mused.

By the following week, Snow White had become a comfortable and integral part of the seven dwarves' tight-knit community. While the lads were off mining or gathering supplies, Snow White would do chores, cook, and clean. When they returned, they'd all gather for meals and share tales of their adventures in the mines.

For her part, Snow White didn't have much to contribute to the storytelling, having lived such a pure and sheltered life, but she laughed loudly at the little men's tales. Though they knew each other's exploits by heart, the dwarves nonetheless took great pleasure in regaling her with stories they had each told (and heard) dozens of times.

Late one afternoon, Snow White was off walking in the woods, leaving the men alone to sharpen their tools, when a leather-clad huntsman strode into the clearing, a small axe hanging from his side.

The seven dwarves lunged to their feet and quickly surrounded the man.

"Whoa, whoa, what's the problem, fellas?" the man asked the pickaxe-wielding dwarves.

"You're the huntsman," Grumpy growled.

"I'm *a* huntsman, yes," the huntsman replied.

"Well, you'll not be having her. You'll have to come through us first, and believe me, we're harder men than you'll ever hope to be."

"Wait, what?"

"You heard him," Happy replied, an uncharacteristically angry look in his eye.

"I think you fellas must have me confused with someone–"

"We know who you are, lad, and we'll not have your wickedness here," Doc said as he strode up to the man. The huntsman towered several feet over him, but it wasn't the dwarf who was afraid.

"Look, I don't want any trouble, I was just out chasing game."

"Oh, I bet you were, boy. Let me give you a bit of advice. Take yourself far from these woods while you still can," Doc said as he stared up at the man.

"I can totally do that. No problem. I just can't go back empty-handed, is all. I'll have hell to pay if I do. You see–"

"Ah yes, the evil one," Grumpy mused.

The huntsman looked confused. "You know of her?"

"Aye, that we do, and while we're fierce to protect our own, we also recognize your plight. Wait here a moment." Doc walked into the common room, returning a minute later with a small wooden box. He handed it to the huntsman, who opened it up, confused by what he saw.

"Um, what's this for?"

"That, lad, is a stag's heart. It's big, and it's fresh. Take that to your queen that she may be satisfied you've done your duty." He paused, then held out a tiny leather pouch. "And this is for your trouble."

The huntsman tilted the contents of the into his palm. His eyes went wide when he realized what it was. A small, but flawless, diamond.

"I…" He was at a loss for words.

"Now go, and never come back here again."

The huntsman tucked the stone back in its pouch, looked at the motley gang of dwarves in disbelief, then quickly turned-tail and fled, rushing back through the woods at top speed.

"Well, that ought to take care of that, eh?" Doc mused.

"I'd think so," Grumpy agreed. "Though we still could have just buried him in the ravine."

"No, this way the queen will think she is dead. Now our Snow White is truly safe here with us."

The men spun, weapons held high, as a twig snapped across the clearing.

"What's going on?" Snow White asked as she stepped from the woods.

"Um… nothing. We're just, uh, doing some stretches is all."

"With your pickaxes?"

"Of course! What of it? All the better to limber up, we always say."

"I've never heard you say that."

"Well, that's because you've only been here a few weeks. We say it all the time, right, fellas?"

They all chimed in. "Yeah," said Dopey.

"Uh huh," added Happy.

"Sure we daaaachooo!" Sneezy agreed.

Snow White flashed her heartwarming smile at her odd little friends.

"Well, then, you finish your exercises. I'm going to start dinner. Don't forget to wash up!"

With that, she headed inside, safe, at least for the time being.

Hours later, the huntsman exited the thick woods, making a beeline directly to his humble cottage.

"Where the hell have you been?" his wife yelled the moment he stepped through his door. "You were supposed to be out catching our supper."

He held out the small wooden box to her.

"And what's this, then?" She snatched it from his hand and opened it. "Oh, fer chrissakes, is this a fucking joke? I send you to kill a stag, and all you bring me is a heart. I swear, I don't know why I ever married you. You're a shit huntsman, do you know that? All the other women's husbands bring them plump rabbits and juicy deer, but what do I get? A bleeding heart, that's what!"

Cheeks flushed, he gingerly held out the small pouch.

"And what's this, now? A tiny pouch? What did you do, gather up a single acorn for dinner?"

Her eyes went wide as she dumped the diamond onto the

table.

"Do you like it?" he asked timidly.

His wife's face was flushed as she moved closer.

"Oh, you wonderful man," she said, grabbing him lustfully. "Come here!"

She was very pleased, and that meant so was he.

"Yes, my queen," he managed to blurt, before his wife threw him to the bed and had her merry way with him.

The weekend arrived, and as the weather was fine for it, the dwarves planned a party. They'd worked hard in the mines and were in need of blowing off some steam, so festivities were in order. Snow White was more than happy to help with the arrangements.

The men watched as she twirled and danced between their huts, hanging wreaths of garlands and flowers as bluebirds chirped merrily above her head. Come evening, they feasted, laughed, danced, and sang.

Eventually, they settled down by the fire to share enormous goblets, filled from their finest bottles of wine. Sleepy succumbed quickly, falling asleep with his head in Snow White's lap. He was jostled awake, briefly, when Snow White jumped as Bashful's wandering hands found their way to her chest.

"Oh, I'm sorry! I lost my balance there. Must've had a little too much to drink," he said with a merry laugh. "Here, have some more wine."

She took another sip, the wine making her cough.

"Are you alright?" Doc asked, concerned.

"Just a cough, is all," she replied before succumbing to

another bout of coughs.

"Better let me take a look," Doc said, his nose and cheeks flushed red with wine.

"I'm sure it's nothing."

"Nonsense. I'm a professional. Now, pardon my stethoscope, it may be a bit cold."

He stepped behind her and slid the device down onto her back beneath her top.

"Now take a deep breath," he instructed.

She did as he asked.

"Good. Now… ah, this is getting in the way. I'm just going to loosen this a bit." His fingers deftly unlaced the back of her dress in an instant, the fabric threatening to fall forward if she leaned the wrong way.

"Yes, that's better," the drunken dwarf mumbled. He ran his hand down her back, then along her flank, brushing the side of her breast.

Snow White jumped to her feet, clutching her dress to herself.

"Ah, yes. Well, thank you for your concern. I think I'd better be off to sleep now."

She quickly shuffled off to her bed, leaving the dwarves to their own devices.

"Ow, my head," Sleepy muttered, before passing out again on the warm ground.

The following afternoon, the men were all nursing hangovers as they trudged back to work. Snow White, after clearing the dishes, stood at the laundry lines, hanging a batch of small pants and britches to dry in the warm afternoon sun.

Sleepy, miserably hungover, was still napping, but the others simply left him, knowing he'd rouse himself eventually to come finish the day in the mines.

A loud rustling from the woods caught Snow White's attention, and even Sleepy opened his eyes to see the tall, withered hag as she made her way into their camp. The woman had strawlike salt-and-pepper hair and sagging skin, and she wore a ragged, old hooded shawl. Sleepy's eyes fell lower to the basket of shiny, red apples she was carrying.

"Oh my, those apples are lovely!" Snow White exclaimed.

"Yes, my dearie, the finest apples in all the land. Crisp, juicy, and sweet like nectar."

"I have no money, I'm afraid, but if you come back later, I'm sure the men who live here will be glad to buy some from you."

The old woman sized her up a moment, then looked down at Sleepy as he struggled to stay awake.

"Are they all like this one?"

"He's just hungover, is all."

"Ah, I see. Well then, I will return later. But you are such a beautiful young woman. I want to give you one of my apples free of charge."

"But I couldn't possibly accept!" Snow White blushed.

"Consider it a sample. I'll return to sell the rest later."

She pondered the offer.

"Well... okay. Thank you for your generosity."

"It's my pleasure. You are indeed the fairest of them all."

"You're too kind."

"And what of your friend?" the old woman asked.

The women both looked at Sleepy.

"Just ten more minutes, then I'll get back to work," he mumbled, then closed his eyes and fell back asleep.

When the six dwarves returned several hours later, they found Sleepy napping in the same place they'd left him. Snow White, on the other hand, was sprawled out on the ground, a shiny apple next to her with a single bite taken out.

"Sleepy! What happened?" Doc shouted as he ran to Snow White's immobile form.

"Huh?" the napping dwarf replied. "What're you on about?"

"What happened to her, Sleepy?"

The tired dwarf focused his eyes and felt a rush of panic in his body.

"She was just buying apples."

"From who?" Grumpy asked, a cloud of anger forming over his head.

"Just some old woman. She said she'd be back later but gave Snow White one for free. A sample for the fairest of them all, she said."

Doc sniffed the apple. "Faint hint of… what is that? Poison? I'll have to run some tests."

Sneezy, in the meantime, was trying desperately to rouse the sleeping girl.

"Wake up! Please wake– achooooo!" He sneezed so forcefully, a mist sprayed across Snow White's face.

She didn't budge.

"Let me try," Bashful said, moving closer. "Snow White, can you hear me?" he asked, gently shaking her shoulders.

"Doesn't seem to be working. Let me try something else."

He placed his hands on her waist and shook again. "Snow White, wake up!"

Again, nothing.

"Well, this calls for drastic measures." He grabbed her breasts in his hands and squeezed. "Snow White, tell me if you want me to stop."

"Stop it," Doc ordered. "Not cool, Bashful. Not cool."

The dwarf removed his hands and stepped back.

"Sorry, Doc."

"Happy, do we still have that glass from the greenhouse project?"

"Yeah."

"Then get it. I have an idea. One that should keep her safe, but also lets us keep an eye on her in case she wakes."

The men hustled into action, and a short time later a Snow White-sized glass coffin was masterfully constructed. While the dwarves may have specialized in mining, after all those years on their own, they'd become proficient in all sorts of crafts and trades.

"All right," Doc said to his fellow dwarves. "We keep her safe in this until either she wakes up on her own, or we find a way to do it ourselves. Now help me move her to the common room."

Snow White lay unconscious, resting in her glass home for nearly a week. During that time, the dwarves would try to rouse her every morning before heading to the mines, as well as every evening before going to bed, but the beautiful young girl didn't wake.

It wasn't until nearly a full week later that the dwarves

heard a horse trotting to their door as they ate their dinner.

"Grumpy, go see who that is, would ya?" Doc asked.

"Why do I always have to do it?"

"Because you've got the best demeanor for it," Doc replied.

He grudgingly crossed the room and opened the door, whereupon a tall man, dressed in regal finery, ducked his head and stepped inside.

"Gentlemen, I hear you are the finest gemstone miners in all the lands. I have ridden from my kingdom to acquire a ruby of exquisite clarity for the pommel of my sword."

He unsheathed his weapon, showing the ornate blade to the dwarves.

"So, you a king or something?" Grumpy asked.

"No, I am a prince," the man replied.

"Prince, king, your money spends as good as the next man's. So, how large a stone were you thinking?" Doc asked.

The prince showed the dwarves the space reserved on his sword.

"Yeah, we've got just the thing. Come with us."

Doc led the way to the common room, then ushered the prince to the far end.

"Wait here, I'll get it for you."

It was then that the prince noticed the young woman in the glass coffin. She was by far the most beautiful creature he'd ever seen, and he fell immediately in love with her at first sight.

"My God!" he gasped. "Who is that girl?"

"That's Snow White," Happy answered somberly.

"How did she come to perish? It's such a waste, a lovely

thing such as her devoid of life."

"Oh, she's not dead," Happy informed him. "She was fed a cursed apple. We thought it was poison, but Doc checked it out and said it was like no poison he'd ever seen before. Well, Doc's wicked smart, so naturally that left only one alternative."

"A curse?"

"Yup, a curse."

The prince was leaning over the glass, staring at the girl, when Doc returned, tucking the key back into his shirt.

"Hey now, what are you doing?" he asked.

"Marveling at this young woman. She is the most divine thing I've ever laid eyes on."

"Well, she's not for sale."

"I didn't mean..."

"Uh huh," he answered skeptically. "Anyway, here's your ruby." He tossed an almond-sized stone to the prince, who held it to the light, examining it, but really wanting to further examine the girl in the glass box.

"Perfect. I'll take it. How much?"

"Twenty gold pieces."

"Twenty? A bit steep, don't you think? That's a small fortune."

"You're welcome to try and find a higher quality stone elsewhere if you wish," Doc replied, crossing his arms.

"Very well," the prince grudgingly answered. "But I want one more thing."

"Oh?"

"I want a kiss."

Doc shifted uncomfortably in his boots.

"Hey, I appreciate the offer, but you're really not my–"

"Not you, fool. Her."

Doc looked over at the sleeping beauty in the room.

"Nope. Thank you for your time, but–"

"I'll throw in another five."

Doc stared a moment.

"Five? For just one kiss?" He pondered a moment. "Well... okay, but no funny stuff."

Carefully they removed the lid from the glass coffin. The prince reached in and touched Snow White's cheek.

"She's warm."

"Like we said, she's not dead, just cursed."

"Such a pity," the prince mused. "Were she whole, I'd make her my princess in a heartbeat."

With that, he leaned in and planted a tender kiss. It lasted a bit longer than Doc would have liked, but when Snow White parted her lips and kissed the prince back, well, what was he to do?

"What happened?" she asked, sitting up in the coffin. "Why am I in a glass box? And who is this handsome man?"

"You bit into a cursed apple, Snow White. You fell into a deep sleep, and the prince's kiss finally woke you from it."

"A prince?" she asked, blushing, as the man helped her from the glass coffin.

"Yes, I am my father's heir. Snow White, come with me to my kingdom and be my princess. You will want for nothing and live in my castle, high above the commoners, protected and safe."

"I..." She paused, looking at her dwarf friends.

"Go ahead. You deserve to be happy," Grumpy sighed.

Snow White paused. The prince smiled warmly at her, and she knew her path.

"I'll never forget you, my friends. Never!"

She followed the prince outside, mounted his steed behind him, and rode off to her new life.

Happy shed a tear as she shrank from sight in the distance.

It had been several days, and the mood in the dwarves' camp was grim. They didn't mind cooking and cleaning for themselves. Hell, they'd been doing that all along anyway. What they really missed was the beautiful girl they'd all become so fond of.

As evening approached, the sound of rapidly approaching footsteps could be heard crunching in the forest.

"Oi, who's that, then?" Grumpy challenged.

The hooded figure in the woods put down a large bag and walked into the clearing. It wasn't until she dropped her hood that they realized who it was.

"Snow White!"

A huge smile on her face, Snow White hugged all seven of her friends, tears of joy on all their faces.

"But you rode off with the prince," Dopey said, confused.

"It was terrible. I missed you all so much. I couldn't stop crying," she began. "Once I saw the way he lived, all closed off from the world, behind high walls, well, I knew I had to come back to you all. I gathered all the supplies I could carry and snuck out in the middle of the night. And here I am!"

"This calls for a party!" Happy said, jumping to his feet. "I'll get the wine!"

"Make it the good stuff," Grumpy called after him. "And lots of it. We've got some serious celebrating to do!"

The feast that night was magnificent, and the wine flowed liberally. The small men had quite an appetite, and their capacity seemed endless. They drank, and then they drank some more. Within a few hours, the sturdy little men had downed enough wine to stun a horse.

"I missed you guys so much," Snow White sighed, resting her head on Bashful's shoulder.

"We missed you too, Snow White," he replied.

There was a weighty pause as he slipped his hand up her body and cupped her breast. The others watched with great interest.

"We missed you *a lot*," he added, giving her erect nipple a little squeeze.

This time, she didn't push him away.

It was an odd sight, a half-dozen tiny, naked men engaged in an all-out brawl. There had actually been seven of them, but as one would expect, Sleepy had no sooner gotten his rocks off than he passed out, sound asleep. Would that the others had done the same.

Instead, wine had flowed, and sarcastic taunts about size and prowess were carelessly tossed. The combination was a volatile one, because, as everyone knows, dwarves are known to get a little bit fighty when drunk. Even more so when you add a bit of jealousy to the mix.

Doc, inebriated as he was, was tasked with cleaning up the scrapes and bruises, as Sneezy's allergies rendered him pretty much useless as an extra set of hands. His broken nose didn't help things; the red mist he'd periodically trumpet forth left him desperately clutching a towel to his face.

Of course Happy would cheerfully clean it up come morning. Good old Happy, nothing kept him down for long.

In more ways than one, Snow White had learned.

Bashful, too, would be glad to lend a hand. The exhausted girl had found his name somewhat incongruous, deciding that "Handsy" would've been a far better moniker.

Fortunately, Dopey, while quite focused and talented in certain areas, much to Snow White's delight, couldn't really hold a grudge.

As for Grumpy, well, he eventually put on his pants and drunkenly sulked off to pass out alone.

Eventually, they all drifted off into a deep, sound sleep. Sweaty, satisfied, and more than a little sore.

She had been walking for miles through the woods, and despite the ample padding, the large bag slung across her shoulders was beginning to wear on her.

Not much further now, Snow White comforted herself.

Less than a half-hour later, she came upon a small clearing on a rise just above a freshwater stream. The door to the large tent erected there stood open, the flap affixed to a wooden peg.

"Snowie, is that you?" a woman's voice called out from inside at the sound of footsteps.

"Yeah, Rose, it's me."

"Well, you certainly were out late."

Snow White dropped the heavy bag to the ground with a metallic clunk.

"What can I say? Things happen."

"And?" Snow White's sister asked with a devious little grin paired with a highly arched eyebrow.

"And that prince was far too impressed with himself for his own good. Typical narcissist royal. Like I should be in awe of how handsome he is. 'Ooh, look at my washboard abs. Look at my perfect hair.' The guy actually expected me to do *all* the work, and even then, he was busy looking at his own reflection the whole time."

"Eww, creepy."

"Right? And then when he finished, he just rolled over and went to sleep."

"What a selfish prick!"

"I know! I couldn't get out of there soon enough!"

"Well, judging by the size of your haul, at least it looks like it was worth it. So how'd we do?"

Snow White dug into the bag and produced a beautiful crown of gold, along with an assortment of golden chalices, jewelry, and a gold-framed mirror. Rose stepped out of the tent and looked at the haul.

"Nice, sis," she said. "But why the mirror? Seems too heavy to be worth the hassle."

"Nah," she replied while unknotting her hair. "It's magic. It talks."

"Really?"

"Yeah."

"Talk to me, mirror," her sister commanded.

Silence.

"It's not working."

"You need to hang it up first, then say, 'Mirror, mirror on

the wall.' That's what wakes it up."

"We don't have walls, doofus. We live in a tent, in case you forgot. Now come on, we've gotta pack up and hit the road before that prince comes looking for you."

"Not just him," her exhausted sister added.

Snowie marveled at her big sister's beauty. It really was impressive what a little makeup and a carefully worded charm could do. Rose was beautiful, and looked nothing at all like the old hag she'd become to deliver the cursed apple.

Man, the look on those stupid dwarves' faces, she chuckled at the memory.

"I was thinking," she began. "What about heading far away? Maybe south, somewhere warm year-round. We could buy a villa and live a life of luxury."

"Would that we could, little sis, but you know once we fence this stuff, the cash won't last us too long. It never does. Eventually we'll have to find another realm with a lonely royal and run the hustle again."

Snow White looked at her sister a long moment before pulling a small satchel free from under her cloak. She opened it and dumped the contents to the ground before her.

Huge diamonds, emeralds, and rubies, each one worth a small fortune, sparkled in a small pile at her feet.

"Holy shit!" her sibling gasped. "How the hell did you get those away from the dwarves?"

"I have my ways. You don't think I went through all of this for shits and giggles, do you? Though it was actually pretty fun, all told. I've gotta say, those little buggers can hold their liquor, that's for sure, and they've got stamina aplenty. But after a hard day in the mines, and a harder one in bed, they all finally slept like babies when I was through with them. It was a cinch after that. I just snagged the key from around Doc's sleeping neck and took as much as I could carry."

"But damn, Snowie, all seven of them?"

"Yeah." A wistful look and a happy little smile briefly warmed Snow White's face. "And let me tell ya, sis. Don't believe the rumors. The only thing small about them is their height."

The dwarves slept in late that morning. They'd certainly earned it and needed the rest, but eventually they roused themselves, stretching in the cool air.

Snow White was gone, naturally.

They had kind of hoped she'd stick around, but who were they kidding? The likes of her staying with the likes of them? They knew the good times would be brief.

Doc filled a goblet of water and slowly walked over to their treasure chest, left open in her hasty flight.

"Looks like she took about a satchel's worth," he said, calmly sipping his water.

"Better refill it then," Grumpy sighed.

The dwarf walked across the room and pulled a large, plain-looking basket from a cupboard. He opened it and scooped out a few kilos of precious stones, walking them to the open chest.

"That should about do it," he said, pouring them into the box.

"Yep," Doc agreed. "I just hope it won't be too long before the next hustler comes along. That was a hell of a party."

The dwarves all nodded in agreement.

With a vapid grin on his face, Dopey stood and stretched, his impressive morning wood waving in the wind. He yawned, then turned to his friends.

"I hope we get a blonde next time."

Blood Money

Drop by crimson drop, Amanda Holmes watched her life essence slowly drain from her body. She sat there, looking on casually, fascinated how every beat of her heart was forcing more of the red stuff from her veins. Fascinating thing, the human body.

Of course she had planned it this way.

When the Have-A-Heart blood drive bloodwagon had come to Albuquerque, she, along with several dozen others, had been eager to help out. It warmed her heart, knowing her donation would help save the life of some poor soul in need.

And there were free cookies and orange juice.

One mustn't forget that.

"Next!" the slender, brown-haired man in gloves and a lab coat called from the shade of the wagon's interior. The group of donors was patiently waiting in the shade of the nearby pop-up canopy. "Come on in out of the heat, and let's get you started."

The donor in the chair closest to the door rose and stepped inside.

"Welcome, and thanks again for participating. Do you have your paperwork filled out?"

The man handed him a clipboard.

"Excellent. Thank you, uh–" He scanned the form. "–Mr. Johanson. We appreciate you coming. Your donation is helping save lives."

The man took a seat in the empty chair and relaxed while the pale blonde girl in gloves and scrubs wiped his arm with an alcohol pad.

There was space enough for three donors at once, and two chairs were already occupied, blood bags slowly filling from the IV lines protruding from the arms of their occupants. To the back of the vehicle was an air-conditioned recovery space, capable of seating six at a time as they sipped on orange juice, getting their blood sugar up before stepping back out into the bright daylight.

"How many more out there?" the girl asked her associate.

"Five," he replied, closing the door against the late-afternoon heat.

"All right, these two are nearly done, so I'll get this one started while you get the others set up in the recovery area. We should be done by sundown.

It was day two of a three-day holiday weekend blood drive. The duo had started across town a few weeks prior, having traveled south from Santa Fe. They had been slowly moving through the city each weekend, taking donations from the thoughtful men and women ready and willing to do their part to help save a stranger's life.

Across the road, about a block away, Crowley and Veller sat in their late-model sedan.

Watching.

"Jesus, Dom, why couldn't we get a car with better A/C?" Crowley grumbled, sweat staining the armpits of his button-down shirt.

"Don't blaspheme. And quit whining, John. It works, you just want to keep running the engine all day."

"Yeah, that's generally how one keeps the goddamn thing working."

"Hey, language. And that's how you destroy the ozone layer. Come on, man, don't you care about the environment?" He had long since unbuttoned his shirt, exposing his small, gold crucifix dangling over his damp tank top.

Detective John Crowley shot him a look.

"Seriously? Dude, every cop keeps his engine running. You know that."

His partner, Detective Dominic Veller, was having none of that.

"And if we were in a marked car running computers that needed continuous power, I'd agree, but on a stakeout, we not only do *not* have a squad car needing continuous power, but we also have to be at least a little inconspicuous. Idling here all day? Someone might take notice."

"Hell, if they get a whiff of us, they'll sure as shit take notice. I'm sweating like a pig!"

"Was that a cop joke?"

"Ha ha, very funny. And speaking of stakeouts, did you remember the stakes this time?"

His partner's muscled jaw cracked a little smile.

"In the trunk."

"Good. Hey, the door's opening. Gimme the binoculars."

Down the street, Tommy Hicks stepped out of the cool confines of the bloodmobile and called in another donor.

"This guy's been in and out of there all day. Full sunlight, no less," Crowley noted. "You sure we've got the right one?"

"Our source is solid," Veller replied. "Has the girl come out yet?"

"No, she's been inside all day."

"Alright. If we don't get some sort of positive

confirmation today, we'll have no choice but to go undercover tomorrow. You up for it?"

"Hey, don't look at me. It's your turn. Remember what happened last time?" Crowley massaged the still-fresh scar under the collar of his shirt.

Veller looked grim. Oh yeah, he remembered.

"Fine," he grumbled. "I'll do it. But that means you've gotta refill the good stuff tonight."

"Consider it done."

"Cool. I just hope things don't get out of hand again," Veller mused, a slight worry crease forming on his brow.

"Fuckin' A," his partner replied.

"Language!"

Night fell, and with it, the final donor exited the vehicle as Tommy began gathering the folding chairs set up outside.

"Hey, Vanessa, would you mind grabbing the pop-up tent?"

"Alright," she replied, stepping out into the rapidly cooling darkness, peeling the gloves from her hands. "You okay to drive tonight? I'm wiped out."

"Yeah, no worries. You should eat, we don't want you having any problems."

"Yes, dad," she chuckled.

Ten minutes later, they fired up the engine and pulled out.

Crowley and Veller followed from a safe distance.

"Same blonde who stays inside during the day, but the male is driving," Veller noted.

"Yeah, I saw. I ran the pics we took yesterday, but neither of them has turned up a positive yet. We'd be better off with prints."

"These ones are good. Gloved up at all times. It won't be easy."

"Yeah, but this ain't your first rodeo, Dom."

"Great. My tombstone can read, 'Here lies Dominic Veller, killed on his second rodeo.'"

Crowley laughed. "But it's far more than your second."

"True, that," Veller replied, the smile fading from his face.

They drove the rest of the way in silence, both men thinking about the horrors they'd seen since they took on their special assignment. By the time they pulled into the hospital parking lot, any levity had evaporated, like so much moisture in the desert air.

"We've got a fresh delivery of whole blood," Vanessa told the nurse at the night desk as they walked into the hospital.

"You're not one of our contracted firms, are you? Do you have the donor files and–"

"We're new to the area. Just started providing last week. The details and paperwork are all right here, uh…" Tommy interjected as he scanned her nametag, "…uh, Nurse Dorner." He handed her a thick manilla envelope. Beside him was a wheeled cooler, biohazard stickers firmly affixed to all sides.

The nurse reviewed the documents for a few moments before looking back at the pair with a much friendlier smile.

"Oh, a new operation, I see. Well, everything looks good. So very glad to have you with us," she grinned, then called to a nearby orderly. "Andy, would you please show these folks to lab 4-B?"

"Sure thing, Barb. Y'all follow me," the stocky man

replied.

When the duo had wheeled the cooler far down the hall, Crowley and Veller stepped out of the night and into the bright fluorescence of the hospital.

"Hey detectives, how are you this evening?" Nurse Dorner asked with a warm smile as she eyed Crowley.

"Doing great, thanks," he replied, flashing his pearly-whites right back at her. "We're just doing some basic background checks on a few out-of-town vehicles. Saw you had a new bloodmobile out in the parking lot and–"

"Detective Crowley!"

The two policemen turned. Dr. Tyler strode in from the ER. A tall man in his early forties with a smattering of salt and pepper at the temples of his otherwise dark hair, he had been the head of emergency medicine at Kastleman Hospital for nearly a decade, his team treating dozens of officers injured in the line of duty over that span.

Including one of the men standing before him.

"Hey Doc," the pair chimed, their moods lifted by the friendly face.

"So, tell me, John, are you still having mobility issues with that shoulder? That was one hell of a nasty bite that crack dealer's dog gave you."

"It's getting better every week, Doc, but you know how it can be with rehab. Shit takes time, ya know?"

"Language!"

"Oh, I don't mind, Dominic," Dr. Tyler laughed. "You know I've heard far worse in the emergency room. Daily, in fact."

"Say, Doc, do you know this new outfit, Have-A-Heart?

They're from out of town, but lately they've been doing blood drives in Albuquerque," Crowley queried.

"Can't say that I do. I did, however, meet the lovely young people bringing in donations earlier this week. It's been a busy month, and they couldn't have come at a better time. Our resources have been stretched a bit thin lately. Why, have they done something wrong?"

"No, nothing like that. We're just keeping track of new commercial vehicles in the city, and since this one transports biohazard materials, we just wanted to make sure things were up to snuff. So no issues with them?"

"None."

"Great. That's really great to hear," Veller said with a forced laugh. "Makes our job easier. Come on, John, let's get on to our next follow-up."

"What?" Crowley replied. "Oh, yeah, that. Thanks again Doc. And Barbara, lovely to see you again, as always."

"Don't be a stranger!" she called back as the pair exited the hospital.

Sliding back into their sedan, Veller quietly stared at his partner.

"What?" Crowley asked, defensively.

Veller waited a moment for effect.

"Why don't you just ask her out already? You two have been doing this dance for months. She's been nothing but interested ever since you rolled in that night."

"Yeah, but maybe it's just what nurses do. You know, I was hurt, she was staff…"

"As your friend, I'm telling you she's interested."

"Well, maybe, but–"

"No. No but. Tomorrow, if that pair leads us back there again, you're asking her out. And I don't want any excuses or arguments, okay? You've gotta enjoy life more. Sure, you're still dealing with that night. Who wouldn't be? But you've got to let that go. You were taken by surprise in the dark, it can happen to anyone. The important thing is the bite didn't kill you, and you survived, *intact*. Take it as a sign. A sign that you need to start living."

Crowley listened quietly, for once, absorbing his partner's words.

"You know what?" he finally said. "You're right. Barbara and me? Yeah, that's gonna happen."

"Now that's more like it," Veller said with a big grin. "Alright, it's going to be an early morning and we've still got supplies to pick up. Let's go, partner."

The men drove off into the night.

Twenty minutes later, Tommy and Vanessa rolled their cooler back to their vehicle and headed out. Tomorrow would be a busy day. There were just so many people, anxious and willing to give them their blood.

The plain sedan parked up the road from the Have-A-Heart blood drive early the following morning. The large bloodmobile had just parked and set up its seating area, and the first few donors were trickling in.

"I look ridiculous," Veller whined.

"Oh quit the bitching, you look great," Crowley laughed. "Besides, you're too beefy to pull off hippie garb. Better to go as a gym rat, you'll look more natural."

"Ugh. Fine. Is the mic transmitting?"

Crowley checked his receiver, using the earpiece to avoid feedback.

"Yep, hear ya loud and clear."

The big man took a deep breath. He was nervous, like he always was, but it had to be done.

"Okay, I'm ready," he said. "Might as well get this over with. Wish me luck."

"Luck has nothing to do with it," his friend replied. "But as they say in theater, break a leg. Though if you do, just make sure it's someone else's."

The sedan door opened, and Veller stepped out, wearing a tight tank top, spandex gym shorts, and, most emasculating of all, a fanny pack.

"Call it a 'Manny Pack' if that makes ya feel any better," Crowley had said.

With friends like these… Dom grumbled. He took a deep breath, tucked his crucifix inside his shirt, and began walking down the road.

"Hi! Thanks for coming to donate today," Tommy greeted him as he approached the waiting area. "Please fill out this form and take a seat. I'll come get you shortly."

Dominic Veller made up a name and filled in the blanks, then sat nervously on the wobbly folding chair as he awaited his turn.

His wait wasn't long.

"Okay, Mr. Smith?"

Veller rose to his feet.

"Please follow me," Tommy said pleasantly as he opened the door with his gloved hand. "If you'll just have a seat over there in the empty spot, Vanessa will be right with you."

In the other seats, two college kids relaxed as their essence flowed out into the bags next to them. Dom felt a little ill.

After all these years, how can I still react to the sight of blood?

"Hi there!"

The young woman's silent appearance at his side startled him.

"So, first time giving blood?" she asked as she wiped his arm with an alcohol pad.

"No," he replied. "A friend of mine needed some not too long ago. We have the same type."

"Wow, you're a good friend!" she smiled. "Not everyone would do that. Well then, you know how this goes. I'm going to insert the catheter into your vein, then, slowly, we're going to let gravity do its work and fill this bag. Afterwards you may feel a little woozy, so you can sit in the recovery area as long as you need. We have cookies and orange juice to help get your blood sugar up. Any questions?"

"Nope, we're good to go," he replied.

"My, my," the pale girl said, fixing him with her crystalline eyes. "Your pulse is racing. Do I frighten you?"

Something about her smile made him feel very uneasy.

"No," he lied. "Not at all. I'm just a little wary of needles, is all."

She sized him up a few moments longer, silently staring at him as though she could see into his very soul. Then, as quickly as it began, her look snapped to a cheerful grin.

"Don't worry yourself, big guy, your veins are great. You'll be an easy stick. I doubt you'll feel a thing."

"Yeah, maybe, but–"

"Hey," She leaned in closer. He got a slight whiff of

something. Something not quite right. "Can I tell you a secret?" she asked.

His heart pounded. *I know she can hear it,* he thought.

"Uh, sure," he replied as coolly as he could.

"Well," she began, "I kinda tricked you."

"You what?"

Vanessa leaned back and looked at his arm.

"I already stuck you," she said with pride. "See, I told ya you wouldn't feel a thing." She rose and patted him on the shoulder. "Okay, I'll be back to check on you in a few minutes. Just sit still and relax."

She peeled off her gloves, tossed them in the bin, then grabbed a fresh pair from the box on the wall and went to see how the donors in the recovery area were doing.

Detective Veller quietly got to his feet and stepped to the trash bin.

"Hey dude, you should be sitting down," one of the college kids said.

"I know, but I feel a little queasy." He leaned over the open bin, blocking it with his body as he reached in and carefully balled up several disposed gloves before standing up straight and stepping back to his seat.

"Oh, thank God, the nausea is passing. I think I'll be okay. Thanks for your concern," he said, casually slipping the wad of gloves into his fanny pack as he reclined back into his chair.

Both chairs next to him rotated new donors before it was finally time to unhook him. Veller didn't mind, it gave him more time to note the interior of the vehicle. Everything was spotless, and not a single item seemed out of place. Additionally, both suspects wore gloves at all times, only changing them between patients.

"Okay, now put pressure here," the pale girl had said as she drew the catheter from his arm, pushing a folded gauze pad over the exit point before securing it with a piece of tape. "Hold that for a couple of minutes to help prevent bruising. While you do that, come with me to the recovery area and get some sugar into your system."

He rose to his feet, a bit wobbly at first.

"Careful now, don't rush."

Moments later he was sipping juice, his head a bit light from a surprisingly small amount of blood loss. Five minutes later, he felt well enough to leave.

Tommy and Vanessa were blocking his path.

"Are you sure you feel well enough to walk?" Tommy asked.

"We wouldn't want anything to happen to you," Vanessa added.

"Um, yeah, I'm fine. A friend's going to give me a ride, I just have to call him."

The pair stared at him for a moment longer, blocking his path, then parted, Vanessa heading deep into the vehicle while Tommy opened the door for him as he stepped out into the morning sun.

"Thank you for your donation, Detective. You have a good day," he said before closing the door.

"You're welcome," Veller said, still a bit fuzzy as he walked to his waiting ride.

Come evening, the detectives had already made a run to the station, dropping the gloves with forensics to see if they could pull any prints off the insides. It was a difficult, but not entirely impossible, task. They then picked up some Subway sandwiches and returned to their stakeout, Veller dressed in a far less humiliating outfit.

"I don't know," Crowley teased. "The spandex was a pretty good look for ya!"

"Shut up, John."

"The tank top really showed off your pecs."

"Shut up, John."

"And that manny pack? Priceless!"

"Dude, shut up already!"

"So you don't want copies of the pics, I take it?"

"Oh, you did not–"

"Don't worry, don't worry," he chuckled. "I mean I only sent them to Carter, Burke, Wilson, Hiller…"

"One of these days..."

"Yeah, yeah, you and your threats. Eat your sandwich, that low blood sugar is making you cranky."

They chewed their meals silently, Crowley checking his phone periodically between bites.

"There was something earlier. Something off. I just can't quite put my finger on it," Veller mused, a worried look on his face.

"Did they do anything suspicious?"

"No, I think they said something. I was still a bit out of it." His brow furrowed. "Well, it'll come to me eventually. Always does."

Crowley checked his phone again.

"Anything yet?" Veller asked.

"No, still nothing. They got a couple of partial prints, but the database hasn't found a match yet."

"That's a lot of years to parse through. Let's hope they get a hit before it's too late."

Darkness finally fell, and Tommy and Vanessa once again packed up and drove off. Once again, Crowley and Veller followed.

As the unusual pair had done the night before, the bloodmobile pulled up to Kastleman Hospital. After a few minutes, the pair stepped out and rolled their cooler into the building.

This time, however, the detectives waited until the young pair had made their delivery before stepping inside. Tommy and Vanessa were rolling their cooler and about to exit the building when the detectives confronted them.

Both men wore long overcoats, despite the warm temperatures. Crowley was also carrying a large styrofoam cup in his hand.

"Hello again, Detective," Vanessa chirped pleasantly when she saw them.

That was it, Veller suddenly realized. *Sloppy, Dom. Very sloppy.*

"So, you know who we are," he replied with the lightest smile he could manage.

"Of course. We're always thrilled to have law enforcement participate in our blood drives. You know, our services have helped save the lives of several of your colleagues in the past." She spoke pleasantly, but a tension was still in the air despite the kind words.

"Hey, everything okay over there?" Nurse Dorner asked, a

concerned look in her eye.

"Everything's fine, Barbara, thanks," Crowley replied. "Just chatting with our friends here."

"So, what's in the box?" Veller asked.

"What, are you Brad Pitt?" Tommy laughed.

He was the only one.

"Jeez, I was just making a joke," He squirmed under the detectives' not-amused glares.

"My partner asked you a question."

"Just our dinner," Vanessa answered, a sly look in her eye.

"Show us."

Reluctantly, Tommy opened the cooler and took out a large plastic bag. Inside were a half-dozen foot-long cylinders, wrapped in paper.

"And what are these?" Veller asked, beginning to unwrap the topmost package.

"Those are sandwiches, gentlemen. Is there some sort of problem going on here?" Dr. Tyler asked from across the room as he stepped through the ER doors.

"Just following up on a tip," Veller replied.

"Well, by all means, follow up on your tips, detectives, but while I don't approve of using a biohazard cooler to carry food, those were a gift from the hospital. We had quite a few left over, so I offered these lovely youngsters as many as they wanted to take with them. I know how hungry you can get working those long hours."

Veller unwrapped the package in his hand.

Bread. Bread with lettuce, tomatoes, and mustard leaking onto the paper.

"Just sandwiches, John," he called to his friend,

rewrapping it and putting it back in the bag. "Here," he said, handing it to Tommy. "Sorry for the mix-up."

"No worries, it happens," he replied.

"Yeah, I'm sorry too," Crowley said. "No hard feelings?"

He moved towards them, hand extended in peace, but stumbled, though there was nothing to stumble on. The contents of the cup in his hand splashed out onto Vanessa and Tommy as he tripped forward.

"Oh, I'm so sorry!" he blurted.

His eyes, however, remained alert, and his hands seemed ready to reach under his coat at a moment's notice.

"Christ, we're soaked!" Vanessa lamented. "What the fuck!"

"Language!" Veller grumbled as he studied the damp pair's reactions.

No flailing. No screaming. No bursting into flames. Nothing.

"Hey, that was really clumsy of me. Good thing it was just water. Let me get you a towel or something," Crowley apologized.

"Ugh, forget it. I've got dry clothes in my bag. Come on, Tommy, let's get out of here." Vanessa glared at Crowley as she passed, Tommy right behind her, pulling the cooler.

Dr. Tyler grabbed a large bottle of disinfectant from a custodial cart and poured it all over the area of the spill.

"Hey doc, it's alright. It's just water."

"No, it's not alright. If you have a cold, that is now all over this floor. If there was a tiny pocket of germs on the tile, it is now spread. That's why we always disinfect everything. Our patients' health is too important!"

"Sorry Doc, I didn't mean to–"

"It's not your fault, it was an honest mistake," he said, calming down. "We simply have to maintain a clean environment. I'd have done the same thing if it were soda or vomit," he said soothingly. "Barb, would you please have custodial clean this up? We wouldn't want anyone to slip."

"Of course Doctor."

"Gentlemen, I have patients I should attend to," Dr. Tyler said. "You both be safe out there."

"Will do, Doc. Sorry again," Crowley sheepishly replied before heading for the door.

"So, dead end, eh?" Veller sighed.

"Looks that way."

"Well, there's still one thing left for you to do."

"But–"

"Nope. Do it," his partner replied with a little smile backstopped with a forceful stare.

Crowley took a deep breath and crossed the room to the nurses' desk.

"Hey, Barbara, I was wondering, um…"

"Yes?" she asked, expectantly.

"Well, if you're not busy this weekend, could I take you out to lunch?"

She beamed at him. "Make it dinner and you're on."

"Uh, great! Give me your number and I'll call you," he said, handing her his phone.

She quickly entered her digits and handed it back with a smile.

"You know, I wondered if you'd ever finally ask me out."

Crowley smiled like a happy idiot as he walked out to his

partner, floating on air.

"So?" Veller asked as he unlocked the trunk of the car. "What did she say?"

Crowley said nothing, but a huge grin spread across his face.

"Awww yeah, nice going!" Veller smiled. "I told ya she'd say yes."

"We're gonna get dinner this weekend. At least one thing went right tonight."

Veller opened the trunk, and both men began removing their long coats, as well as the numerous implements hidden within.

Stakes. Mallets. Long, silver blades and small UV lights.

"How much holy water do we have left?" Crowley asked.

"We still have at least a liter," Veller replied. "Man, I was so expecting the girl to start smoking. She fit all the signs. I just *knew* there was something off about her. Weird. Never been wrong like that before."

"Bound to happen eventually. At least we can get back to our normal caseload."

"Yeah, until the captain gets another call from The Order."

"Hey, enjoy the downtime while you can, partner."

Their vampire-fighting gear stowed, the men climbed into their sedan and headed off into the night.

"Speaking of dinner. Italian?" Veller asked.

"Dude, I am so sick of fucking garlic!"

"Language!"

In the locked break room of Kastleman Hospital, Dr. Tyler sighed in bliss as he sipped his drink. It had been a long day, and he really needed to take the edge off.

A single knock rang out through the solid wood door. Then three. Then one.

He rose to his feet and let Nurse Barbara in. She locked the door behind her.

"Oh my," he began. "Wasn't that interesting?"

"Could have been worse, though. I think the kids handled themselves quite admirably."

"They've had decades to practice, I'd certainly hope so," he replied, then reached into a small cooler and tossed her a bag.

Nurse Barbara opened the seal and sipped the fresh blood, an orgasmic rush flushing her cheeks as the coppery liquid hit her tongue. It was so delicious, her fangs almost sprang forth on their own.

With a shudder, she licked her lips.

"So, what about your little detective friend?" Dr. Tyler asked. "Are you finally going to finish what you started?"

"I don't know," she replied. "I'm actually rather fond of him."

"You shouldn't grow attached to your food. I don't know why you didn't finish the job when you bit him."

"His partner nearly saw me, I had no choice but to run." She hesitated. "But you know, I really do like him." She paused again, uncertain. "There was something I wanted to run by you."

He looked at her, eyebrow raised, knowing exactly what she had in mind.

"Well, I suppose having a detective as part of the family couldn't hurt."

Later that night, Crowley's cell phone pinged as he sat on his couch drinking a whiskey, watching a recorded football game. He glanced at the text. His heart raced as he did a double-take, then frantically dialed his partner.

"Dom!" he blurted into the phone.

"What's up, John?"

"The prints came back," he gulped. "We got a hit."

"Yeah? So what was it, some stupid petty theft or something?"

"You won't believe it. The prints belong to a couple dead over sixty years."

"But… but they passed the test. They aren't vamps," Veller gasped through the phone.

"No," Crowley replied, baffled. "They're something else."

Driving north, already hundreds of miles out of Albuquerque, Tommy and Vanessa greedily wolfed down their sandwiches, looking more and more invigorated with every bite.

"Good call, heading out of New Mexico," Tommy said through his stuffed mouth. "That was a little too close."

"Agreed. Let's keep heading north. Shorter days should make it easier to deal with our contacts up there."

"Agreed," he replied. "You know, that was a pretty clever idea the doc had, paying us like this. I'm kinda glad he noticed those cops sniffing around. I've gotten so used to eating brains plain, I hadn't even thought to make sandwiches out of them."

"Yeah, the pickles and mustard really do go well with

them. Let's pick up some bread and condiments when we hit Colorado."

"Sounds good. Shouldn't be hard to find the Network contact up there. We still have a good amount of the fresh stuff to trade with."

Sated and safe, the two zombies wiped their mouths and drove further into the night.

Random Acts of Violence

Funny, the way a body will drop when the invisible strings guiding it are suddenly cut. Legs at odd angles, arms akimbo. Sometimes looking completely at rest, while at other times painting a portrait of a sudden and violent end.

Detective Abigail Knowles circled the dimly lit crime scene, taking in information that would be lost on most passersby. The way the young man's leg draped over the curb. The direction his torso had impacted the gutter. The quantity and direction of blood flow in the street. From just these three items – on her mental list of far more – even before the medical examiner arrived, she could tell he had met a near-instant demise.

Take the blood, for instance. The pool was small, despite the numerous gunshot wounds to the man's body. While he had been struck repeatedly, the initial injuries were kill-shots. So far as she could tell, at least one had pierced the heart, stopping it from pumping blood out of the dozen other holes that followed.

Then there was the way the body fell. Midstride, by the look of things, the young Chinese graduate student had taken a chest full of lead completely unexpectedly. No struggle. No sign of panic or flight. After all these years on the job, it still disturbed her, the way life could simply end like that. No fanfare, or meaningful last words, like in a movie, just here one second, then gone the next.

He'd been texting when he was killed, she surmised by the bloody phone in his hand. They'd have technicians check who he had been messaging later, but for now they'd have uniforms canvass the neighborhood while she and her partner interviewed friends and roommates.

"Tommy, you see this?" she asked Detective Thomas Stockton, the stocky man squatting next to the body. She pointed to the phone clutched in the dead man's hand.

"Yeah," her partner grunted. "Poor kid was so preoccupied he didn't even see it coming. Someone should have given him a heads up when he landed."

"How many is this now? Five foreign grad students in the last two years? I don't know how safe the streets are in China, but with all the gangs still active around here, it's just too damn easy to get caught in a crossfire."

"I'd wager that nobody told them USC is right in the heart of gang territory."

"Yeah, but it's a top-notch school. If you weren't from L.A., why would you ever think it was a war zone just off campus?"

"True that," he replied. "Hey, looks like Martinez might have something."

Dana Martinez, the senior lead officer for the LAPD's Southwest Division, had been speaking with neighbors directly after the incident. She'd worked the area nearly as long as the two detectives, and her history and familiarity with the locals afforded her a level of respect from the community that often led to a bit more information than a rookie beat cop could obtain.

"Stockard, Knowles, good to see you guys," she called out as she approached. "Neighbors said they heard probably two dozen shots fired, all semi-automatic, then an engine revving and tires peeling out. Nobody got a look at the perps, but one did say they're pretty sure it was an older car."

"Make? Model? Color?"

"She thought it was blue, but it's hard to tell at night. Said it looked like a late-'80s sedan of some sort. Domestic."

"Gee, that narrows it down to just about every car in the area," Detective Stockard lamented. "Thanks Martinez, let us know if your guys turn up anything else."

"You got it. Poor kid. Awful way to go. Goddamn gang-bangers. This shit's just senseless," she replied as she turned and headed back to see what, if anything, her officers had learned so far.

Tommy continued to survey the area with a steady gaze.

"Abby, no one reported any other peds or vehicles at the scene. I don't think this kid was simply caught up in a drive-by on someone else."

"Yeah," she replied, "I noticed. There's a good chance this was a gang initiation and he was just in the wrong place at the wrong time."

Stockard's jaw flexed.

"Some days I really hate this town," he growled.

"I hear ya. Come on, let's see if we can find anything out at his apartment. Maybe we'll catch a break and be able to give this kid some justice."

The pair climbed into their unmarked Crown Vic and drove off to the address pulled from the victim's ID.

"Xian Li?" the young stoner said, shifting uncomfortably in his seat. He was obviously baked, and having two detectives in his apartment was most certainly harshing his mellow. "Yeah, he's my roommate. Why? What did he do?" he asked.

The female detective leaned closer and held his bloodshot gaze. "I'm sorry to have to tell you this, Mr. Berger, but Mr. Li was killed earlier this evening." She watched him for a reaction. His look of surprise seemed genuine.

"Do you know if he had any problems with anyone? Local gangs, perhaps? Gambling debts?" She glanced at the pipe on the table. "Drug dealers he might have owed money."

Stoned or not, Johnny Berger was most definitely not relaxed. Nervously, he wrung his hands as he looked between the two detectives.

"Hey, uh, that's not mine. A friend was over and must've forgotten it."

"Uh huh," Detective Stockard grumbled. "Sure, kid."

"No, really, I never touch the stuff."

His red eyes told a very different story.

"Mr. Berger," Detective Stockard interrupted. "Pot's legal in Los Angeles, and I'm sure you have a medical marijuana card, and to be honest, I couldn't give a shit what you smoke in your own home. What I am concerned about is why your roommate was killed. Did he have any friends here? Family? Any enemies? Have you heard about anything at all that might have made him a target?"

"No, man. He was a really quiet guy. Just went to school, kept his head down, and studied all the time. We didn't really hang out, ya know? He was just kind of a weird guy."

"Then why did you move in together?" Stockard asked.

"His folks paid the majority of the rent on this place, and I was just happy to get a good deal on a room close to campus."

"So you two didn't interact much?" Knowles inquired.

"Nah. I mean, he offered to share food with me sometimes, but he ate some pretty strange shit, ya know? I usually just fend for myself most of the time. I mean, I hear they eat dogs in China. That shit's not cool, man."

"Any visitors? A girlfriend maybe?"

"He didn't really have friends to speak of. His uncle would swing by maybe every three or four months with a care package, but that was about it. Just magazines and more of his weird food from home."

"Do you have his uncle's number?" Stockard asked.

"Nah, he kept everything on his phone or laptop. Secretive guy, but I guess coming from where he did, that's pretty normal, with all the dissidents being snatched up and jailed and all. Hell, everyone locks down their devices these days."

Knowles looked at Stockard, their silent communication honed to a fine edge after many years together.

"Alright, that's all for now," she said. "Here's my card. If you think of anything at all that might be of use, please don't hesitate to call."

"Okay, Officer–"

"Detective."

"Sorry. Detective. If I think of anything at all, I'll let you know."

Knowles and Stockard walked from his building and slid once more into their sedan.

"You know the kid's never gonna call us," Stockard said.

"Nope," Knowles agreed. "Didn't seem to know anything anyway. As for the uncle, he might not even be related. Family friends are often called auntie or uncle in China. Our best bet for contacting the family will be through the admissions office."

"They're going to want to call the consulate themselves."

"Good. One less thing we have to deal with. I hate notifying parents."

Detectives Knowles and Stockard drove off, surveying the neighborhood, periodically stopping to question the many street people who were often privy to information that would otherwise be impossible to obtain. That was one of the few benefits of living on the periphery of society: being nearly invisible even when in plain sight.

"Might have been Trey's crew, from what I hear," the raggedy man said from his cardboard castle. "But the MS13 boys have been raising a ruckus lately, so it coulda been them too."

"Thanks, Willie," Tommy Stockard said, handing the man a crisp twenty and a bag of In-N-Out. "You take care of yourself."

"Always do, Detective," the old man replied. "And you do the same."

Stockard nodded, then climbed back into his car.

"Got a couple of possibilities, but it's late, and I don't want to be heading deep into the hood at this hour. Whaddya say we call it a night and pick up in the morning?" he asked his partner.

"Sounds like a plan," Knowles replied.

"Cool. I doubt we'll get any straight answers out of 'em, but at least it's something to go on."

Trey Cooper was a thickly muscled, heavily tattooed shot-caller for the nearby County Crips gang. They dealt mainly in crack and prostitution and mostly kept to themselves. So long as other gangs didn't cross into their turf, that is. Unfortunately, such transgressions were fairly common, and like an indiscriminate wildfire jumping from hotspot to hotspot, the violence that resulted spread and touched all corners of the neighborhood. Some streets were untouched, while others suffered its full wrath.

Knowles and Stockard pulled up in front of the weathered California Craftsman bungalow to find him sitting on the porch, sipping a 40 of malt liquor with Big G, one of his faithful underlings, lounging beside him.

"Morning, detectives," he called out. "What'chall want with me this fine mornin'? I ain't done nothin', ain't that right, G?"

"Uh huh." Big G nodded his confirmation.

"We're just seeing if anyone knows about a shooting on Hoover last night. Chinese grad student was killed, and word on the street is maybe one of the local crews was jumping in some new blood. You wouldn't know anything about that, would you?" Stockard asked.

"Nah, man. Why you doin' me like that? You know we ain't doin' none of that 'round here," Trey lamented. "Can't a brotha sit in peace and enjoy hisself a nice day without being accused of some bullshit?"

"What about you, G?" Knowles chimed in. "You hear anything on the street?"

"Nah, man. Like Trey said, we ain't done shit."

"You hear anything going on with the MS13 fellas?"

"Yo, fuck them punks. Those mothafuckas be all up in our business. Y'all need to keep them in check. They riling shit up, ya hear?"

"So are you two in a shooting war again? I thought there was a truce."

"Nah, nothing like that, man. They just crossin' lines. Shit's gonna get serious if they keep at it. So what the po-lice gonna do about it?"

"We'll be sure to let SLO Martinez know. If there's something going on, she'll keep an eye on it."

"Martinez is all right. She from around here, knows how things be. Anything else you need, Detective?"

Knowles and Stockard glanced around. While not hostile, several of the gangbangers' compatriots were gathering on the street. The detectives shared a look and began walking back to their vehicle.

"Alright. Thanks for you time. If you hear anything, you be sure to let us know."

"A'ight, detectives, we can do that."

As they drove away in their unmarked vehicle, the tension eased as they breathed a bit easier.

"You think Trey was a little on edge?" Stockard asked.

"Yeah, but isn't he always? Didn't seem more so than usual, really. But the MS13 thing really got him riled up. There's probably something going on there beneath the surface. We should give the gang unit a heads up when we get back to the station," his partner replied.

"What do you say we swing by Chopper's pad before we do?" Knowles asked.

"You serious?"

"We'll call for a couple of black-and-whites to come with, obviously," she said with a laugh. It wasn't a happy laugh, however. It was a tense one. "They won't try anything if we have numbers."

Stockard thought hard, then looked at her with a grim smile. "You really have a way of ruining a guy's day, ya know that?"

"So I've been told," she chuckled. "Keep driving, I'll call for support."

The East L.A. home belonging to Eduardo Velazquez, aka "Chopper," was situated on a small hill near a swarm of power lines and industrial warehouses. The kennel out back housed his massive pit bulls, as well as what was certainly a small grow house. Though the gangbanger had a license –who didn't these days?– they were pretty sure a thorough search would turn up some rather illicit activity.

The dozens of MS13 gangsters perpetually hanging out at the home served to discourage any such search, and the narcotics unit long ago decided they would only ever move on that particular property if they had rock-solid evidence of something worth the risk to their team. The MS13 did not mess around, and they were not afraid of the police.

Three squad cars parked along the street as Detectives Knowles and Stockard pulled up to the curb.

"You ready, Tommy?"

"As ready as I'm going to be. Let's get this over with."

They stepped out of the car, senses on high alert as more than a dozen men in tanktops and chinos watched them with interest. They knew full-well that there were other, hidden eyes fixed on them as well. The detectives steeled their nerves and walked toward the house.

"We're looking for Chopper. Is he home?" Knowles called out.

"Who's asking, esse?" a flannel-wearing tough with a shaved head asked from his seat blocking the stairs.

"Tell him the LAPD just wants to ask a couple of questions," Stockard replied, meeting the man's icy stare.

They stayed like that for a moment, neither breaking eye contact, when a voice came from within the house.

"It's okay, Downer, I know these two."

"Hey, Chopper," Stockard greeted the wiry gangster as he stepped out into the sunny day. "Good to see you again."

The man laughed. "Yeah, sure thing, *cuilio*."

"Es *detectivo*, Chopper," he replied, fixing the man with a solid gaze. Weakness was not an option. Not when dealing with Salvadoran killers living in LA.

Chopper did a little double-take, then laughed. "Okay, *Detective*. Whatchoo want?"

"Just a little information is all. You hear about the Chinese kid shot on Hoover?"

"Yeah. A real shame," he said, not at all meaning it.

"We've heard conflicting rumors. Some say one of your boys may have done it. Maybe someone new getting jumped in. People say there was a security camera on one of the buildings and they might have a video of the shooter. Now, we don't want any trouble, Chopper, we just want to know if you know who did it."

The Salvadoran sized up the detective, his gaze flicking to the patrol cars spread along his street. Ever so subtly, he gestured at his men to stand down. From a dozen hiding places, dangerous-looking men stepped into view, then filed into the back yard.

"Go ahead and look at your video. We had nothing to do with any Chinese," he said. "Have a nice day, *Detective*." Not waiting for a reply, he turned his back and walked into the house.

Stockard nodded to Knowles and headed back to the car. They rode in silence until they were blocks away.

"Jesus, Tommy, what the hell was that about video cameras? They were already on a hair-trigger."

"Chill, Abby. Chopper may be dangerous, but he knows it's more trouble than it's worth to start a gun battle with the LAPD on video. Part of the reason I was glad for the black-and-whites. Standard-issue body cams on uniforms, and Chopper knows it. If it were just you and me, I doubt we'd have walked out of there without an incident."

"Let's not bluff when I'm not in class-3 Kevlar, alright?" Knowles said, punching him in the shoulder.

"Fine. But it was your idea, don't you forget it," he teased. "You notice, though, that when I said it was about shooting a student, he relaxed? All the shit he has his fingers in, that was one thing that didn't concern him in the least."

"So it wasn't MS13 either. Something tells me this may be turning into a dead-end case."

"But we owe it to the kid to keep trying," Stockard replied. "Let's see who he was talking to that night. They should at least know their friend is dead. Then we'll have the school notify his family."

"Wiped," the technician said.

"What, like there's nothing on it?" Detective Knowles

asked.

"No, nothing like that," the LAPD forensic tech replied. "This phone *had* information on it, but when I tried to bypass the fingerprint reader and secondary lock-screen code, it bricked."

"In English, please," Detective Stockard asked.

The young computer expert sighed. "What it means is the phone had some pretty serious data-theft-prevention technology on it. Whoever this kid was, his devices were protected excessively for your run-of-the-mill student."

"So his laptop was a no-go too?" Knowles asked.

"Oh, that one locked me out, then ran a DoD 5220.22-M data wipe. Twice."

"Again– English, please."

"In layman's terms, his laptop was rigged to run a Department of Defense-level data wipe if anyone tried to log in. It completely erased the hard drive. Whatever he had on there, it's long gone now. Pretty curious for a student, if you ask me."

"His roommate said something about how dangerous it was in China. How they secured their devices so they wouldn't be in jeopardy from government detention. His paranoia seems to have carried over when he came to the U.S.," she mused. "Well, thanks for trying. I suppose all we can do now is notify his parents and cross our fingers that something turns up, though my hopes aren't high at this point."

"Sorry I couldn't be of more help."

The detectives trudged out of his lab and back to their car, ready to make the drive to the university. At least they could make sure the family was notified. It was one thing, no matter how small, they could do for the dead man.

"Ah, this is terrible!" the woman sobbed into the phone. "How did this happen? My only son!"

The administrator on the other end of the line fumbled for words.

"I'm so terribly sorry about your loss. It appears to have been a random incident. There are gangs in the area, and sometimes they target students."

The woman pulled herself together.

"I wish to see the police report."

"I'm sorry, you what?" the administrator asked.

"The report. I want to read how my son died."

"Um, I don't know if I can do–"

"My son was killed at your school! You have a duty of honor to help me find peace!"

There was silence. Her request was unusual, but not impossible.

"I'll see what I can do. It might be some time, I must warn you. The LAPD is very hesitant to release reports to the public, but I'll do my best."

"Thank you! Oh, thank you so much!" she sobbed. "I must go now. I must inform his father."

"I understand. Again, my deepest condolences."

The line went dead.

The distraught woman rolled her shoulders and straightened her uniform as she rose to her feet, then walked across the industrial-gray room to the general's large wooden desk.

"General Tsai," she said, standing at attention. "It has been confirmed; Agent Li is terminated."

The general looked up from his large stack of papers, a frustrated frown on his face.

"Do we know who did this?"

"No, General, not yet. It appears to have been a random attack. As you know, the capitalist pigs live in dangerous cities overflowing with unsavory criminals. I am, however, attempting to obtain a copy of their incompetent police department's report for further review."

He gave a satisfied nod to the woman. "Major Zhi, you have done well. While this is a regrettable setback, we will overcome. Are the agent trainees on schedule to complete their insertion preparation?"

"Yes, General, we are already generating cover identities and financial statements and applying them to the most strategically desirable universities."

"Excellent," the general smiled. "We shall continue to infiltrate, and there is nothing the ignorant Americans can do about it."

Major Zhi returned to her desk to set more wheels in motion, while General Tsai relaxed in his comfy leather chair and went back to looking at the vintage American *Playboy* magazine tucked in his files.

Months had passed, and the next quarter was beginning at the university. With it, an influx of new students flooded through the neighborhood, oblivious to the dangers around them as they snatched up any housing they could find.

Sitting on his porch, Trey and Big G relaxed on another

perfect Southern California day. The beer was cold, the air was warm, and the women in the hood were most certainly hot.

"Ain't this the life?" Trey asked with a contented sigh.

"Shit, dawg. You know it." his friend replied.

"Word."

The men clinked beer bottles and drank in unison.

"Ya know," Big G said after a moment. "Them MS13 punks is steppin' in again. We gonna have to do somethin' about that."

"True dat," Trey replied. "Still, it's been quiet for a while. I'm thankin' it can stay that way a little longer."

"Whatever you say, boss."

A bleep-bloop chirping pierced the air. Not too loud a ringtone, but a very distinct one.

"Aww, shit," Trey grumbled, digging through the duffel bag next to him. From underneath the Uzi machine gun, assorted pistols, and boxes of ammunition, he pulled out a highly encrypted satellite phone, entered his seven-digit access key, and pressed it to his ear.

"Ident: Mojave Rattler. Pass-Key: Two-Sierra-Whiskey-Niner-Niner-Zulu-Foxtrot. Go."

He paused, listening.

"Copy. Backstop 5x5."

Another pause, then a beep as a file transferred to his phone. He glanced at the screen, noting the details, then placed it back to his ear.

"Received. Wheels up in thirty."

Trey rolled his shoulders and cracked his neck as he placed the sat-phone back into the bag.

"I know that look," Big G grumbled. "Aww man, and I

was just beginning to enjoy a nice, relaxing afternoon. You do realize I have a date with Yvette tonight, right?"

Trey laughed. "Sorry to salt your game, captain. I'll try to get you back in time for your festivities." He stood, shouldering the bag of weapons. "Intel fellas say it looks like the Chinese are trying to infiltrate another agent. Round up the boys, we goin' on a drive-by."

Road Rage

Sometimes shit just happens. Shit like being flung forcibly to the ground in front of oncoming traffic.

Darryl Hartson had been adjusting the surprisingly uncomfortable seat in his brand-new Perpetua sedan when the stubborn electric-assist lever malfunctioned, ejecting him with great force through the windshield and onto the roadway in front of his vehicle.

Had he not been stopped at a red light, fiddling with the annoyingly uncomfortable seat, his injuries would have been far more severe, if not fatal. Even so, being launched through a quarter-inch of safety glass, then run over by his own idling car, had left him in an understandable state of discomfiture.

Billionaire visionary Tyler Price, Ph.D., had come to visit him in the hospital personally.

The handsome, mid-thirties CEO and chief technologist of Perpetua Motors brought a gaggle of press with him, along with a check for any and all medical bills, a rather busty personal assistant-slash-physical therapist for Mr. Hartson's rehabilitation, and set of keys to a top-of-the-line, next-generation Perpetua luxury sedan with all the bells and whistles money could buy.

Of course it would be months before his fractured femur would allow the poor man to drive again, but the buxom Swedish aide would shuttle him around, and take care of his every need until he regained full use of his leg.

And yes, his *every* need.

Tyler Price hadn't reached his position by doing things half-assed, and this was no different.

He had researched Mr. Hartson in depth well before visiting the fifty-year-old bachelor in the hospital, meticulously determining the best way to avoid a costly lawsuit. Judging by the injured man's "confidential" internet browsing history, he had a fondness for blondes.

At a mere $20,000 per week, the beautiful young "therapist" was a far better investment than scores of lawyers to defend a multimillion-dollar lawsuit, and when Darryl Hartson was finally ready to sign off on completion of his rehabilitation in a few short months, the tiny clause in small print would ensure there would be no future legal trouble.

Naturally, his buxom therapist was guaranteed a more-than-modest bonus to ensure Mr. Hartson's ample distraction, and compliance, when it came time to sign.

Nevertheless, the incident had caused potential buyers as well as the media to focus on the somewhat uncomfortable seat design, and that needed to be dealt with promptly.

"Fiona," Tyler said into his wireless. "We're going to need a new user-interface technician. Someone whose hiring would make a great press release in relation to the Hartson incident." Tyler thought a moment, the plan already forming in his ever-churning mind. "

"Line up candidates for early next week."

"Of course, sir," his longtime aide replied as he disconnected the line.

The thing about Perpetua Motors wasn't just that it was founded and run by a young, charismatic, self-made billionaire, but that it truly did offer something groundbreaking. Game-changing, in fact. A *disruptive* technology that actually deserved that moniker.

Perpetua cars never needed gasoline.

Tyler Price had been a standout student at Cal Tech, focusing on harnessing different sources of power. He was also fascinated by the many novel materials being invented, the creative applications of which could then be used to store that bountiful energy.

By age twenty-three, he had made his first million in the lithium-ion battery world, increasing capacity tenfold before he'd even graduated.

By twenty-six, he had expanded his reach into the field of implanted, bioelectric-powered pulseox and blood-glucose monitors for insulin-dependent diabetics. A simple wireless notification to a user's device of choice alerted them of their current blood-sugar status twenty-four hours a day with no need for external batteries. They could even push that data to their doctors in real time, a feature which would shortly thereafter be utilized in numerous medical studies around the world.

From there, Tyler had segued into the solar arena, ever fascinated with invisible waves of power that floated in the air around us. Even at night, there were invisible fields of energy bouncing at us from the moon's asteroid-pocket visage, and Tyler Price figured out how to harness it.

Sure, it wasn't nearly as efficient as daylight solar energy storage, but it allowed trickle-charging of devices overnight, and could be utilized on a miniaturized scale. This was something of a boon for the hiking and travel community, as their phones and wireless speakers could charge as they slept, providing them a full day of enjoyment upon their waking.

Then, at age thirty-one, he saw a new need.

A need that, if he could fill it, could lead to not only greater freedom of travel for men and women worldwide, but also a reduction in carbon, even a possible *reversal* of the carbon emissions that were poisoning our atmosphere and altering the planet's very temperature.

Global warming, he believed, could be rolled back with his invention, and with that lofty target in mind to save the planet, he embarked on his greatest endeavor.

Combustion-free vehicles.

After several false starts while undertaking that ambitious quest, it finally seemed that he had actually done it, and all while managing to keep his proprietary, and self-funded, technology a well-protected secret.

In the past year, Perpetua Motors had finally perfected its vehicles, rolling them out to the general public at a price on par with that of conventional cars. They were incredibly popular, unbelievably affordable, and were helping save the planet with every mile driven.

The company seemed untouchable.

That is, until a young scientist from Boston sent them a disturbing email.

"Mr. Price, the head of tech development and customer relations has flagged an email for your personal review," his assistant informed him as he sipped his morning latte.

"A customer email? For me? Can't Barry handle it? It's his department, what do I pay him for?" he laughed good-naturedly.

"Ah, yes, sir, but he forwarded it. The message is marked

your eyes only, top priority."

Tyler's face blanched ever so slightly.

"Get him on the line," he asked quietly, the even tone of his voice concealing a lurking dread. Moments later, his right-hand man's voice filled the air.

"Ty, did you see the email?"

"Not yet, Fiona just forwarded it to me. What's this all about?"

"You've got to see what it says. The author – this guy says it's urgent that as the ultimate developer of the technology, you, and only you, review it. He's out in Boston and claims he's reverse-engineered the Perpetua's rooftop solar."

"Shit, how could a random actually do that? Is he trying to steal the technology for other uses? What's this guy's angle?" Tyler asked, increasingly perturbed.

"He claims it can't possibly power the car," Barry replied. "In fact, he says, so far as he can tell, the only thing the entire array powers is the stereo system."

"Shit."

"Yeah, I know. He said he would like to offer you a chance to comment before he goes to the media."

Tyler sank in his chair, a grim look on his face.

"No one was supposed to be able to do what he did."

"I know, but he did it."

"Actually quite impressive, when you think about it."

"I know. And he did it all without any of our resources."

"Has he cracked our power storage?"

"No. That's rock solid. The failsafes are untouchable, and if the casing is opened outside our facilities, the auto-destruct fries the whole thing. But Ty, this is serious. We need to address this. Given this guy's background–"

"Wait, hang on. What is his background?" the genius billionaire asked, suddenly quite curious.

"MIT, applied sciences. Triple major. Specializes in a bunch of things, including solar radiation, room-temperature superconductors, sub-micro processors, as well as advanced electrical engineering. A real jack-of-all-trades kind of guy."

The tension in the air cleared a fraction as Tyler allowed himself to take a deep breath.

"Have him brought in. On our dime, of course. Top-notch hotel, limo, the works. Tell him I'd like to meet with him personally."

"Mr. Price, Dr. Furley is here to see you for your eleven o'clock interview," Fiona informed him through the wireless intercom on his desk.

"Excellent, send him in."

Matthew Furley, Ph.D., stepped into the comfortable office, looking a bit out of place with his slightly disheveled attire and dated attaché case. Not all scientists looked the cliché part, but Dr. Furley came close.

"Ah, Dr. Furley," Tyler called as he entered. "So glad you could make it. I'm Tyler Price. Please, won't you have a seat?"

"Thank you, Dr. Price," he replied.

"Please, I never use that title, it's so stuffy. Just call me Ty. May I call you Matt?"

"Um, okay," he agreed, a tad off-guard. "Ty."

For all his quirks, of which there were many, Matt Furley was a rather handsome man; thirty-two years old, tall, with sandy hair and an athlete's build, which was something of an anomaly in the applied ergonomics and power consumption sciences crowd.

Matt, it turned out, thought better when he worked out, often solving his most troublesome problems when he was finally able to turn off his constantly buzzing mind and just *be*. At the end of his workouts, more often than not, the solutions were there, ready for him.

Exercising helped him brain.

In his youth, Matt would go for long walks (often leaving his parents searching the neighborhood for their genius son as he worked through some problem or other). By the time he was a young adult at MIT, he had progressed, both socially and athletically, playing rugby and lacrosse, as well as running trail races nationwide. What people didn't see, as they watched him sweating on the pitch, were the equations running through his mind simultaneously.

"Matt. May I call you Matt?" Tyler queried with a warm smile.

"Of course."

"Excellent. I'm glad we're on friendly terms, Matt." Tyler Price smiled at his potential new recruit.

"So, Matt, I read your email, and I have to say, I was rather impressed at your level of understanding of our vehicles, especially for someone with no schematics available to them. Would you mind telling me, what do you know about the Perpetua designs?"

"Well, for starters, the early line was entirely covered in molded solar panels, from bumper to bumper. This provided fair power yield, but also led to issues with minor damage interfering with proper energy collection, not to mention cost-overruns for replacement materials. Mileage was decent, but not amazing, and speeds never quite reached highway-acceptable levels."

He looked at the billionaire seated across from him, pausing for his input or comments. None forthcoming, he continued.

"Then three years ago, you had a breakthrough in power regulation, conversion, and storage, and the current Perpetua design was born, utilizing a single modified solar array on the roof and a reactive polymer body on the rest of the car, creating highly effective self-repairing crumple zones. As for the solar collection system, the exact technology is a trade secret," he said, eyeing the man behind the machines.

"And by the way," he added, "those self-destructing, sealed power-conversion packs you've employed are truly groundbreaking IP protection, if I do say so myself. Though also a bit frustrating for us tinkerers."

Tyler allowed himself a little smile.

"Thank you. Protecting our intellectual property and underlying technology has been the top priority of Perpetua. But please, continue. I would like to hear what you discovered in your own words."

"Well, the rooftop solar you invented does produce a significant improvement over prior outputs from available technology, but the numbers still don't seem feasible. There's the rub. The real magic in your vehicles is that conversion and storage mechanism. You've somehow done what has been said to be impossible. At least so it seems. You've created a vehicle that never needs to stop for fuel, and the numbers just don't pencil out."

Tyler beamed like a proud father.

"It's been a challenge, but yes, we've finally cracked the holy grail of energy production. No plugging into a wall, and no filling up a tank. It's a fully contained energy supply system, and we're making it available to the whole world."

"Aside from it being unexplainable in terms of energy consumption to production ratios, there are other issues, of course," Matt chimed in.

The smile faltered on Tyler's face.

"Do go on."

"For starters, the thermostat system does seem to have sporadic shifts. Sometimes drastic ones, leading to rapid heating or cooling of the passenger compartment."

"True, but we're working on that. What else?"

"Multiple complaints about the factory-installed entertainment cluster. The stereo turning on and off at random. The wireless phone connection quietly draining drivers' devices without warning. Then there's the inaccurate GPS system and sticking power locks. I mean, these all seem easy enough to overcome, but for some reason they plague the Perpetua."

"Yes, I realize there are some bugs in the system, but to save the environment and not ever pay for gas again, I think people are willing to forgive us as we iron out the kinks."

Matt thought about it, then continued down his list.

"What about safety issues such as the tendency for the powertrain to engage at inconvenient speeds during acceleration and deceleration? The lurching stops and starts, while not exactly whiplash-inducing, have led to numerous complaints about the overall ride of the vehicle."

"But our safety record?"

"I must concede, it is impeccable. The car is fantastic when faced with an accident scenario. In fact, I believe it is by far the safest car on the road today, though complaints remain."

"So you still have doubts?"

"Why, if you can design such an incredibly groundbreaking powertrain, have you not been able to upgrade the passenger compartment?"

Tyler sighed, then leaned back in his chair.

"Let me ask you a question," he began. "If you never had to pay for gas again. Never. Would you tolerate a few minor glitches and inconveniences?"

"I suppose I would."

"And if that same vehicle was also the safest thing on the road? Would you be inclined to overlook certain *issues*?"

"Again, I suppose I would."

The brilliant mind behind the most groundbreaking vehicle ever invented evaluated the man before him, and recognizing not only a genius, but a genius who would keep digging no matter what, he made a decision.

"You have a gift, Matt," he began. "You see things others miss, and you have a knack for putting information together in novel ways that elucidate certain issues."

"Thank you."

"You're welcome. Now I want to ask you a very important question. What if I offered you a position at Perpetua?" He eyed the man's reaction before continuing.

"And what if that position was heading your own department, working with our top scientists to further develop the user experience? Would that be of interest to you?"

Tyler had already seen the file on the man seated across from him. His job was heavy science, sure, but it wasn't exciting, and what better way to tempt a mind of this caliber than that?

"I… uh…" Matt paused. "I'd have to think about it."

"I see," Tyler replied. "Perhaps I can make this a bit easier for you." He reached into a deep drawer on his desk and produced a single sheet of paper. Printed on it was a job description a scientist would give his right arm for.

Below that was a salary that could damn near pay to have a new one grown and reattached, bionics included.

Matt Furley had a decision to make, and unlike so many he had made in his life, this one didn't require a thirty-mile run.

"How can I turn this down?" he asked, astonished.

"I doubt you can," Tyler replied. "I just need you to sign this little NDA covering our technology and proprietary company secrets, and then I'll hand you off to my assistant, Fiona, to get your ID badge and an office. I assume a corner one will suffice?"

"Uh…"

"Excellent."

Matt nevertheless read the entire twenty-page NDA, and though sections seemed a bit Draconian in their severity of repercussions, given the nature of the technology at hand, they also seemed reasonable.

Ultimately, he signed, and the next week, he started at Perpetua Motors.

Three months had passed, and Matt was growing frustrated with the pushback he was receiving on design modifications to make the passenger compartment more user-friendly.

He would get standard, boilerplate answers about timelines and production cycles, when all he wanted was to see his brain-children implemented in the real world. To make a difference. To become tangible.

Sorting through the complaints that had piled up, a pattern began to emerge as he parsed the huge amounts of data. People were irritated, he noted, and some were absolutely furious, but none of them were willing to give up their Perpetuas, despite the issues.

On top of that, none of the problems were severe enough to draw the attention of federal regulators or safety inspectors.

This just isn't normal, he thought as he ran through the reports. *I'm missing something, I know it.*

That thought was churning in his head for weeks as he worked in and around the various models either in production or slated for future release. For his never-resting mind, the conundrum of the seemingly weak solar roof system was a constant source of confusion, but the few scientists truly in the know would not deign to share with him.

So Matt did what he always did.

He went for a run.

Late into the evening, his feet plotted a course through the streets and neighborhoods surrounding the Perpetua Motors facilities, until, sweaty and red-faced, he finally stepped back into the lot.

His run had eventually looped to a far part of the property, and rather than run all the way around once more, Matt chose to simply enter by the nearest gate. A gate he was previously unfamiliar with. The guard, surprised to see a disheveled and sweaty man strolling up to him, stepped in front of the stranger, hand held up.

"Stop, this is a restricted facility," he barked.

"Um, I work here," the scientist replied.

The guard scanned his badge, nearly snapping to attention when he realized the level of clearance the sweaty man had.

"So sorry, sir. My mistake."

"No worries, I know I must look a bit out of place like this." He gestured to his sweats.

"Took me by surprise, that's for sure," the guard laughed, then waved him through.

A massive crash echoed nearby, causing Matt to jump, nearly knocking the guard to the ground as he did.

"What the hell was that?" he blurted in alarm.

The guard laughed again.

"Just the crash tests, doc. Ain't ya ever seen one before? You should check 'em out. Gotta be a pretty cool job, wrecking cars for a living."

Matt's pulse lowered, but his curiosity was piqued.

"You know, I've been meaning to observe one. Can you point me in the right direction?"

"Yeah, just go through those double doors, hang a left down the hall for about, I don't know, fifty yards or so, then hit the doors on the right. Can't miss it. Big warehouse space full of wrecked cars."

The curious scientist thanked the man, then headed off to

investigate the strange facility.

"You here to help strip the car?" the man in the control booth asked as Matt stepped into the test area. "You've gotta wear your hard hat. I swear, we keep telling people, but they never listen."

"Um, I'm here for–"

"Either help out or get out," the man barked brusquely. "We've gotta get those power units back to storage, or Doc Price'll have a cow."

"Oh, I see. Um, yes, let me just put a hard hat on," Matt replied, grabbing a bright yellow head cover from the rack. "Let's get to it, then!"

His casual attire and shiny helmet gave Matt the free run of the floor. Looking like a grunt afforded him the ability to dig deep into the guts of the wrecked vehicles in ways he'd never been able to access in his sterile work environment.

He pulled the wires running from the rooftop solar panel, tracing them to the power conversion and storage module. The casing had been cracked slightly from the impact, and the inner workings, though mostly obscured, could be seen through the gap.

The failsafe didn't go off, he noted. *They didn't expect the flat surface to be torn. The safeguards didn't trigger.*

He took a small penlight from a workbench and peered into the tiny gap in the metal. The circuitry designed to utterly fry everything inside in case of breach appeared set to go, it was only the smallest of fractions of millimeters in the damage that had prevented their discharge.

This can't be right… this looks like… Matt's jaw dropped in shock.

But… He moved to the driver's seat, prying the cover free as he dismantled the tubular aluminum frame. As he pulled it from the wrecked car, he saw it. A fine wire running through the entire frame. Grabbing a pair of heavy-duty pliers, Matt pulled the frame open wider, exposing the interior of the metal.

To a layman, it would look like nothing. A metal seam, maybe. Some rivets. But to Matt, it was a sight that made his heart race. Every few inches, the small, divoted bits were spaced within the seat, the hidden wiring running to join the power controls, which then plugged into a small connector on the floorboards. It was so subtle, no one would ever notice it. Not even a mechanic.

But Matt wasn't a mechanic.

"Sir, you can't just barge in–" Fiona blurted, but the sweaty scientist cut her off, shoving Tyler Price's thick wood doors open with a bang.

"What have you done?" Matt blurted.

Tyler looked up from his desk and noted the piece of bent metal in his employee's hands. With the utmost effort, he maintained his visage of calm.

"Fiona, would you please give us a moment. And hold my calls."

His assistant closed the doors behind her.

"How could you do this?" Matt asked, waving the metal frame. "You're siphoning energy from passengers! I mean, with your background in biopowered medical devices, I suppose it shouldn't surprise me, but stealing life force to power the Perpetuas? Is nothing sacred? You're killing people to sell cars!"

"Listen, Matt, it's not what you think it is," Tyler began.

"No, I saw part of the power conversion unit. Now it's all clear," the angry scientist replied. "Your career, this whole company, it's all over. I'm taking this public, and when the press is through with you, when they know what you–"

"What you saw was only a part of a carefully designed system!" Tyler shot back. "Don't overreact until you understand the sum of the parts. Don't you *dare* lecture me when you aren't operating with all the facts! I assume you wish to know how it all ties together, don't you?"

Matt paused.

Tyler knew he would. What scientist could possibly resist a dangling carrot of that magnitude, after all?

"We are not siphoning life force, Matt. While your remarkable intellect allowed you to recognize part of the design, you're misunderstanding what our apparatus does."

"The solar panel. I'm right, aren't I? It can't possibly power the vehicle."

Tyler sized him up, then made a decision. Speaking with carefully chosen words, he continued.

"You are correct. Your initial assessment of the power output of the solar array was spot on. We cannot possibly run the cars off something so minor. What we can run them on is a limitless energy supply, and one that drivers bring with them every time they get in the car. All we do is help nudge them along a little further."

"Nudge them?" Matt asked, confused, yet curious. "What do you mean, nudge them?"

"I'm glad you asked," Tyler continued. "You see that piece

of seat frame in your hands? Well you noticed what ninety-nine out of one hundred people would fail to see. The collection array. But what you missed was the source of the energy. We don't gather life force, that would be immoral. Rather, we collect something far more abundant. Something renewable. Our marketing materials do not lie. We are, in fact, all about renewable energy, just not solar or life force. Instead, we power our vehicles on something drivers have in abundance. We harness their rage."

"Rage?" Matt was angry, but intrigued. His scientific mind couldn't help but be. "You mean spikes in human bioelectricity due to anger fluctuations are pulled from the passengers by the arrays hidden in the seating. Then following that logic, the power converting…" He trailed off as the numbers churned in his mind.

It really could be done, he realized, and the power collection didn't actually harm the passengers– the human batteries, if you will– one bit. All it took was a little annoyance. A bit of aggravation. A smidge of anger.

"All those design flaws," he gasped in shock. "They were intentional."

"Now you get it," Tyler said with pride. "The uncomfortable seats, the faulty entertainment system, the GPS giving wrong turns. All of that helps provide a continuous, low-grade annoyance that my system taps into and harnesses. We're saving the world, Matt, and all it takes is a little anger."

Matt turned ready to storm right out the door, but he paused. The gears were turning so rapidly in his mind, you'd wonder if smoke might pour out at any moment.

"I can't let this go on. It's not right."

"I understand," Tyler replied. "Not many could possibly comprehend the system as you have, and even fewer could improve upon it. I had hoped perhaps we might have found that one-in-a-million mind with you, but I guess I was mistaken. Go ahead. Do what you need to do."

"I…" Matt's hand trembled as he held the doorknob, yet the door remained closed. Doing the right thing was in his nature, but so too was science, and he just couldn't shut that off. Not when there was a fascinating new problem to solve.

"I… I think," he continued. "I think if you introduced a dual-purpose cup holder with an unstable base, the tipping action could cause a rise in energy production, while adding a secondary collection unit in the floor of the vehicle could further compound power transfer." His eyes lit up as he worked the math in his head.

"In fact, I would estimate that when the fluids complete the circuit between the passenger and the new floor receptors, you'd be looking, at minimum, at a threefold increase in power capture. As an additional bonus, there'd likely be a residual power spike lingering on top of that, which could be trickle charged to an overflow storage system."

"That's genius!" Tyler gushed, a knowing gleam in his eye. "Can you draw me a basic flow on my whiteboard?"

Matt Furley turned and grabbed a marker and quickly began sketching out his design, his mind a raging machine of creation and excitement. This was new. This was cutting edge. Technically it might be in a morally gray area, but it was for the greater good after all. Sure, a layman wouldn't understand, but they were saving the planet, and if a little irritation was all it took, Matt decided it was worth it.

Behind his large desk, Tyler Price gently took his fingers off the trigger of the silenced pistol in his lap and quietly placed it back in its drawer.

He was glad the clever scientist had made the right choice. Science rules, he always said, and a true believer would agree.

The last one hadn't been quite so committed, he thought as he looked at that fateful spot on his carpet, perfectly clean, and not a trace of blood remaining.

Tyler stood and walked to his associate, marveling at what he'd already sketched out.

"This is amazing, Matt. You're a genius!"

The scientist beamed at the praise.

"I'll have R&D get on this right away," Tyler said, a friendly hand on Matt's shoulder. "Welcome to the family."

Thank You Dear Reader!

Word of mouth is an independent author's lifeblood. Your ratings and reviews really help indie authors reach new readers, so if you enjoyed this little collection of odd stories and have a spare moment, if you would leave a rating or review, or perhaps share with a friend or two, it would be greatly appreciated.

Thank you!

~ Scott ~

Also by Scott Baron:

Living the Good Death

About the Author

A native Californian, Scott Baron was born in Hollywood, which he claims may be the reason for his off-kilter sense of humor.

Before taking up residence in Venice Beach, Scott first spent a few years studying abroad in Florence, Italy before returning home to Los Angeles and settling into the film and television industry, where in addition to writing, he has worked as an on-set medic off and on for many years.

Aside from penning books and screenplays, Scott is also involved in indie film and theater scene both in the U.S. and abroad.

www.ingramcontent.com/pod-product-compliance
Lightning Source LLC
Chambersburg PA
CBHW050602170726
48283CB00001B/70

* 9 7 8 1 9 4 5 9 9 6 1 7 7 *